Praise for the novels of Leonard Goldberg

Lethal Measures

"Fast-moving. Goldberg enlivens [*Lethal Measures*] with his formidable knowledge of forensic investigations, creating a graphic but believable foundation for his tale." —*Publishers Weekly*

"Acutely observant . . . Goldberg grips the gold again in a believable thriller with one humdinger of a tension-filled finale." —*Booklist*

"Exciting and intellectually interesting . . . an absorbing tale." —*Library Journal*

"Anyone who enjoyed a Patricia Cornwell tale will gain much pleasure from *Lethal Measures* . . . fast-paced." —Harriet Klausner

Deadly Exposure

"Goldberg mines his considerable knowledge to create a story that will terrify his audience. This is the stuff of nightmares." —*Library Journal*

"Rushes along at a brisk clip." —*Chicago Tribune*

"Goldberg has created another exciting story." —*Booklist*

"A lethal microbe, a brutal murder, and a sentient iceberg menace coolly competent forensic pathologist Joanna Blalock . . . salty . . . zingy." —*Kirkus Reviews*

"Compelling." —*Publishers Weekly*

"A riveting biological thriller . . . a nonstop thrill ride of medical suspense." —*Lincoln Journal Star* (NE)

continued . . .

Deadly Harvest

"Diabolical . . . a first-rate medical thriller."
—The Virginian-Pilot

"Excellent . . . a tangled web of a case . . . Goldberg has the anatomy of ingenious murders down pat."
—Kirkus Reviews

"A page-turner with ample plot twists, medical realism, believable dialogue, and characters who command our sympathies."
—Charleston Post and Courier

Deadly Care
A *USA Today* bestseller and *People* magazine "Page-Turner of the Week"

"[Goldberg] has clearly hit his stride in this brainy nail-biter. . . . *Deadly Care* offers not only fascinating forensics and insider insights into the health care system, but plenty of intriguing characters and a devilish plot—the perfect Rx for curing those reading blahs."
—People

"A fascinating, fast-moving, thought-provoking thriller."
—Booklist

"A scalpel-edged page-turner . . . cool cuttings by a sure hand."
—Kirkus Reviews

"*Deadly Care* is fast-paced, gripping, and informative. . . . A wonderful forensic detective . . . A book everyone should read." —Michael Collins

"*Deadly Care* is a first-class medical thriller, loaded with suspense and believable characters."
—T. Jefferson Parker

"Illuminating, entertaining, grips readers with its realism . . . This is state-of-the-art forensic medicine and sharp social commentary."
—*Liberty Journal* (FL)

A Deadly Practice

"Goldberg keeps Dr. Blalock in jeopardy and the culprit is well-concealed. . . . The sense of events happening in a real institution matches the work of other, longer-established doctors who write. The sights, sounds, smells, and routines of a great hospital become a character in the story."
—*Los Angeles Times Book Review*

"Terrific! Guarantees medical authenticity, non-stop enjoyment . . . Joanna Blalock is a great character. . . . This is truly a gripping mystery, well-written and altogether an extremely satisfying read."
—*Affaire de Coeur*

Deadly Medicine

"A shuddery venture, worthy of Robin Cook or Michael Crichton, into the cold gray corridors of a hospital that confirms our very worst fears."
—Donald Stanwood

"A terrific thriller, with unflagging pace, a driving sense of urgency that keeps the reader turning the pages, great characters (Joanna Blalock is especially good), and the kind of medical authenticity that really rings true."
—Francis Roe

ALSO BY LEONARD GOLDBERG

FATAL CARE

Leonard Goldberg

A SIGNET BOOK

SIGNET
Published by New American Library, a division of
Penguin Putnam Inc., 375 Hudson Street,
New York, New York 10014, U.S.A.
Penguin Books Ltd, 80 Strand,
London WC2R ORL, England
Penguin Books Australia Ltd, Ringwood,
Victoria, Australia
Penguin Books Canada Ltd, 10 Alcorn Avenue,
Toronto, Ontario, Canada M4V 3B2
Penguin Books (N.Z.) Ltd, 182–190 Wairau Road,
Auckland 10, New Zealand

Penguin Books Ltd, Registered Offices:
Harmondsworth, Middlesex, England

First published by Signet, an imprint of New American Library,
a division of Penguin Putnam Inc.

First Printing, November 2001
10 9 8 7 6 5 4 3 2 1

 REGISTERED TRADEMARK—MARCA REGISTRADA

Printed in the United States of America

PUBLISHER'S NOTE
This is a work of fiction. Names, characters, places, and incidents either
are the product of the author's imagination or are used fictitiously,
and any resemblance to actual persons, living or dead, business
establishments, events, or locales is entirely coincidental.

In memory of B. K. G.
Always in my heart
Forever on my mind

Above all, first do no harm.
—Hippocratic oath

1

The men in the bar suddenly went silent. Nobody moved or shifted about. They just stared at the woman who had walked in.

She was tall and blond and attractive and in her early thirties at the most. Her clothes were expensive—faded jeans, blue blazer with a white turtleneck sweater beneath it. She looked like real money. The men followed her with their eyes, all wondering who she was and what she was doing in a seedy bar on the south side of Santa Monica.

Was she a hooker? Naw, most of the men decided. No one in Sully's could afford her type.

A boozer? Probably not. At least she didn't have the appearance of one.

A housewife cheating on her husband, waiting for the guy she was screwing on the side? Maybe.

The men were talking in low voices, but they kept their ears turned to the bar, listening for the woman's order.

"A glass of white wine," she said softly.

The men nodded and smiled to each other. She was passing time while she waited for someone. The customers went back to their loud conversation and to their shots of whiskey with beer chasers.

Sara Ann Moore sipped the cheap wine and studied herself in the mirror behind the bar. Her blond wig was a really good one. It looked so natural, particularly with the loose strands that fell across her forehead. She brushed at the strands with her fingers and gave the impression to anyone still watching her that she was primping. But her eyes were slowly scanning the room, measuring each of the customers. Most were middle-aged construction workers, still wearing their hard hats. There were a sprinkling of deliverymen in their uniforms and a few overweight postal workers. At the end of the bar were two old men hunched over their drinks, and next to them an old woman with caked-on makeup trying to hide her wrinkles.

And standing next to the old woman was a tall, muscular man with jet-black hair that was beginning to show some gray. On his forearm there was a prominent tattoo of an ornate cross.

Sara wetted her lips and, picking up her wineglass, moved down the bar and approached the man. "Can I buy you a drink?" she asked.

The man stared at her for a moment as he tried to size her up. "Sure. Why not?"

"What are you drinking?"

"Vodka," he said, his Russian accent obvious.

Sara signaled to the bartender for another round, pointing to the man's shot glass.

The men in the bar lowered their voices once more as they watched the woman make her move. They all realized they had misjudged her. She wasn't waiting for a man, she was looking for one. She wanted to get laid and had picked the Russian. The crazy goddamn Russian.

"He's drinking doubles, lady," the bartender announced.

"Then pour doubles," Sara said.

The Russian gulped down the vodka like it was water. He wiped his mouth with the back of his hand.

"What's your name?" Sara asked.

"Vladimir," Vladimir Belov said, and then stuck his tongue inside the shot glass to lick out the last few drops of vodka. "What do you want?"

"Some company."

The old woman wearing too much makeup cackled loudly. "Are you two going to be lovebirds?"

"Shut up!" Vladimir snapped.

The old woman cackled again and reached for the shoe box on the bar stool beside the Russian. "Why don't you give her a little present? I bet she'd like that. Give her the shoes you're always carrying around." She picked up the lid of the box, but had to drop it when Vladimir grabbed her wrist and squeezed it.

"Owww!"

"You touch my box again and I'll break your goddamn hand," Vladimir growled.

"I was only fooling around," the old woman complained, rubbing the soreness from her wrist.

"Fool around with somebody else," Vladimir said stonily, and turned back to Sara. "You said you wanted some company."

Sara licked her lips. "You're kind of rough, aren't you?"

Vladimir shrugged, then signaled to the bartender for another vodka.

"I like it rough," Sara said, her voice low and husky.

"It's going to cost you a hundred dollars," Vladimir said matter-of-factly.

Sara recoiled. "I'm not accustomed to paying for it. I won't do that."

"Then find somebody else."

Sara reconsidered, tapping her finger nervously on the bar. "All I've got is seventy-five in cash."

"All right," Vladimir agreed. "But it'll be a hundred and twenty-five next time."

"What makes you so sure there'll be a next time?"

"When you do it with a man, how many times you come?"

Sara hesitated, blushing. "Only once."

Vladimir smiled crookedly. "There'll be a next time."

The bartender put down the double vodka and glanced at Sara's nearly full wineglass before walking away.

Vladimir sipped his vodka slowly, calculating numbers in his head. He was making five hundred dollars a week with his burial work, and he would soon be taking in another hundred a week screwing the blond woman. He had ten thousand in the bank and needed to reach the twelve-thousand mark. That's how much it would cost to bring his mother and brother from Siberia to America and get them their green cards. Just two thousand dollars more, and he would have them away from that Siberian shithole, where the electricity could be turned off for days on end, where people still chopped down trees for wood to cook with and give them heat, where the roads were unpaved because there were no cars, where people who died in the winter had to wait until spring to be buried because the ground was frozen stiff. Two thousand dollars more, and his family would be together again.

He quickly downed the vodka. "Let's go."

"Wait a minute," Sara said hastily, keeping her voice down. "I don't want people in here to know I picked you up."

Vladimir groaned to himself. Americans and their goddamn morals. "I think they already know."

Sara ignored the remark. "Why don't you leave first?"

Vladimir nodded. "Good. I have to make a delivery a few blocks away, anyhow."

"When you come back I'll be in my car across the street."

"What kind of car?"

"A Mercedes coupe."

Shit! Vladimir cursed himself, now regretting he hadn't asked for $250 to screw her. Maybe he could raise the price later. He pushed himself away from the bar and picked up his shoe box, then said loudly, "I have had enough. Good night to everyone." For effect, he feigned a stagger as he walked to the door.

"Where's the phone?" Sara asked the bartender, already knowing it was next to the door by the window that looked out onto Lincoln Boulevard.

The bartender pointed. "By the front door."

Sara hurried to the pay phone, where she inserted

coins and punched in numbers, all the while watching Vladimir through the window. He crossed the street and headed north.

The recorded message on the phone instructed Sara to deposit more money for her call. She pretended to have a brief conversation and then hung up, making believe she was angry. Sara gave the bartender a twenty-dollar bill and left.

She spotted the Russian a half block ahead on the opposite side of the boulevard. Traffic was light at 9:30 P.M., and there was no one strolling the sidewalks. The Russian was moving faster now, and she picked up her pace, not wanting to lose sight of him. At the corner was a large, all-night mini mart service station. The Russian went inside.

Sara stopped abruptly and stayed in the shadows and waited. And waited. Whatever the hell the Russian was doing in the mini mart, he was taking his time. Sara didn't like the position she found herself in. The neighborhood was tough, with Mexican gang markings everywhere. And the side streets were known for drive-by drug deals. The last thing she wanted was to be confronted by some wise-ass punk or by a strung-out addict looking to make an easy score. A car went by with its sound system so loud it caused the sidewalk to vibrate. Its occupants had shaved heads and tattoos and looked like gangbangers. Sara moved back deeper into the shadows.

The Russian came out of the mini mart munching on a candy bar. The shoe box was still under his arm. He glanced around and then hurried down the side street that bordered the service station.

Sara crossed the boulevard and quickly moved into the side street. She closed the distance between herself and the Russian, but still stayed twenty yards back. The lighting on the side street was dim and growing dimmer. She could barely see the Russian. Then she heard a loud noise that sounded like wood cracking and splintering. Then the cracking sound came again. Cautiously Sara moved in for a closer look.

The Russian was kicking through a wooden fence that surrounded a huge construction site. He gave it one final kick and opened a hole in the fence large enough for a man to walk through. "There!" he said, satisfied.

The Russian placed the shoe box on the ground and quickly cleared away the splintered wood. Then he bent down for the shoe box.

Sara reached into her oversize Gucci bag and took out a semiautomatic pistol. Quickly she attached a silencer.

"Just leave it there," she said evenly.

Vladimir jerked his head up, seeing the blonde from the bar. "What the hell are you doing here?"

"A job," she said calmly.

Sara assumed the firing position, knees bent, arms straight out, both hands on the pistol. She squeezed off two shots. Both went into Vladimir's forehead, blowing the top of his skull off. He fell sideways into the gaping hole in the fence. Only his legs could be seen.

Sara hurriedly removed his watch and emptied his pockets, taking cash, change, and wallet. Then she pushed the Russian's legs through the fence. Vladimir Belov's body tumbled down into the six-story excavation site.

Carefully Sara picked up the shoe box and opened it. She removed a clear glass bottle filled with fluid. Floating in it was a very small but well-developed human fetus.

Sara inspected the bottle, making sure it was intact. Then she placed it in her Gucci bag and walked away.

2

The pain started halfway through dessert. It was a burning pain located high up in Oliver Rhodes's chest. He thought it was indigestion caused by the rich food he'd just eaten at Fiori's. *Must be the fried calamari in tomato sauce,* he thought. *That plus the red wine.* He reached for a glass of San Pellegrino water and took a sip. The pain eased.

A waiter came over to refill the coffee cups. Rhodes and his longtime friend and confidant, Sid Appleman, waved the waiter away.

Appleman waited until the waiter was out of earshot and then leaned across the table. He kept his voice low. "I hear the lieutenant governor has prostate cancer."

Rhodes's eyes narrowed. He, too, leaned forward. "Is that rumor or fact?"

"Fact. And according to my sources, he has metastatic disease. It's really widespread."

"Will he be able to serve out his term in office?"

"Maybe. But his name will never appear on a Democratic ticket again. That's a guarantee."

The men nodded to each other. Both understood that a perfect political stage was being set for Oliver Rhodes. The current governor of California was a Democrat in his second term with two years left in office. His popular lieutenant governor was almost certain to be the next governor. But prostate cancer had changed all that. Now the race for the governorship would be wide open.

Appleman broke the silence. "The Rhodes name is

still magic in California. They know your father; they remember your brother."

"But I've been out of office for almost two years," Rhodes said.

Appleman made a scoffing sound. "In politics, that's like the blink of an eye."

Rhodes leaned back and sipped his sparkling water, thinking about the possible contenders for the governorship and who would be the most difficult to beat. "People will remember that I was ill when I left office."

"And we'll make damn sure they know you're now healthy."

The burning pain in Rhodes's chest came back and radiated up to his throat. He drank more water. And again the pain subsided. He wondered if his ulcers were returning.

"Well?" Appleman prodded.

"I'll have to think about it," Rhodes said, and pushed his chair back.

"Don't take too long, Oliver."

Rhodes walked through the restaurant, waving back absently to those waving to him. He tried not to smile, but couldn't help it. A golden opportunity had fallen right in his lap. He'd be a fool not to grab it. But before any decision could be made, he would have to talk with his father, who still controlled the Rhodes family fortune. His father would meet with the other power brokers, and together they would decide whether Oliver should run. And, of course, their answer would be yes.

He stepped outside into the bright sunlight and handed his parking ticket to the attendant, who said, "Just a moment, Mr. Attorney General."

A well-dressed man standing nearby waved. "Hello, Mr. Attorney General."

"Hello to you," Oliver said, nodding to the man, a lawyer he'd met once at a fund-raiser. He couldn't remember the name.

"Word has it that you're going to be running for governor."

"That word hasn't reached me yet."

The lawyer smiled. "A lot of people would vote for you. And I mean a lot."

"I'll keep that in mind."

A Mercedes sedan pulled up to the curb outside the pricey restaurant, frequented by the rich and powerful of Los Angeles. The attendant hopped out and handed the keys to the lawyer.

As he tipped the attendant, the lawyer turned once more to Oliver Rhodes. "Mr. Attorney General, California always does better when there is a Rhodes running things."

Oliver Rhodes nodded, basking in the public eye he loved so much. He had been away from it for too long. Two years back, he'd been riding a wave of popularity, already asked to run for lieutenant governor, almost certain to win. Then the chest pains started and the big heart attack occurred. He hadn't really recovered. He was always weak and tired, waiting like a condemned man for the final attack that would end his life. Bypass surgery had been considered, but it was too risky. There were too many blockages. In all likelihood he would never have gotten off the operating table. He managed to serve out the last few months of his term in office, leaving all the work to others. His political career was over.

Then the miracle came. A new technique developed at Memorial Hospital was said to almost magically clear out coronary arteries. They used a laser device to break up the obstructing clots and plaques, then added a detergent-like enzyme to remove any remaining fatty deposits. Yet it was experimental and risky, and no one knew what the long-term outcome would be. Oliver Rhodes had the procedure done one year ago. The results were unbelievable. He was now jogging two miles a day and playing tennis three times a week. And it would soon be announced that he would be running for governor of California.

Rhodes looked up at the crystal-clear blue sky. It had rained heavily in Los Angeles during the early morning hours, clearing the air and removing any trace of smog. The air even smelled good. He inhaled deeply, feeling wonderful. Life did not get any better than this, Oliver Rhodes thought contentedly.

His six-year-old Jaguar pulled up in front of the restaurant. Climbing into his car, Rhodes gave a generous tip to the attendant, who thanked him and again addressed him as Mr. Attorney General.

"Oh, by the way," the attendant said, holding up an opened pack of Marlboro cigarettes, "I found these under the front seat."

Rhodes was about to say they weren't his because he hadn't smoked since his heart attack two years ago. But then he remembered that his secretary had taken the car earlier to have a slow leak fixed in one of the tires. The cigarettes were hers. "Thanks," Rhodes said, and placed the cigarettes on the passenger seat beside him.

He drove away, keeping the window down and letting the fresh air blow across his face. Too bad it didn't rain in Los Angeles every day, Rhodes thought. Then the air would be clear and respiratory illnesses drastically reduced. But the rains would also bring mud slides and washed-out roads and backed-up sewer lines. Rhodes smiled to himself. Now he was thinking like a politician. Always respond to problems with at least two answers to make sure you've covered all the bases.

He came to a stoplight and waited. To his right was a convertible with a young couple smoking cigarettes. They were talking and laughing and enjoying themselves. Rhodes's gaze went to the opened pack of Marlboros on the seat next to him. He wondered how a cigarette would taste after a two-year abstinence.

The light changed and Rhodes drove on, but he kept glancing at the cigarettes. Just one, he thought. How much damage could one cigarette do?

Rhodes reached for a Marlboro and lit it with the dashboard lighter. It tasted awful and great at the same time. The smoke burned his throat and bronchial tubes, but the nicotine in his blood quickly reached his brain receptors. Suddenly he felt a high, his senses becoming sharper and more focused. He took another drag and inhaled deeply. His high heightened, his pulse racing but still nice and even. Of course, he reminded himself, your coronary arteries are as clean as a baby's bottom. One more drag and then—

Abruptly his heart skipped a beat, then another. And with the skipped beats came a burning pain high up in his chest. Rhodes hurriedly flipped the cigarette out the window and held on to the steering wheel tightly, praying the pain wasn't what he thought it was. The pain grew less intense, but it still frightened him. He brought his hand up to his carotid artery and felt for a pulse. It seemed even and regular. But why didn't the burning pain go away?

Rhodes came to another red light and stopped. He took deep, slow breaths and tried to calm himself. The pain had subsided almost totally. Rhodes breathed a sigh of relief. Probably a false alarm caused by the damn cigarette. But better have it checked out, anyhow. Memorial Hospital was only six blocks away.

As the light turned green, the chest pain returned. But this time it was a crushing pain in the middle of his sternum, radiating into his left shoulder and arm. He sensed his heart flip-flopping and beating erratically. *Oh, God!* he screamed to himself, feeling the terror of impending death.

Rhodes sped down Wilshire Boulevard, blowing his horn loudly and continuously. He was having trouble breathing, and the cars and people he was passing seemed out of focus. He came to another red light and ignored it.

Rhodes made a sudden left turn into oncoming traffic. Drivers slammed on their brakes, trying to avoid a collision. Tires screeched and cars spun out of control, but Rhodes got through unscathed. His weakness had become so overwhelming that it took all of his effort just to steer the car. And the pain seemed even worse as it spread to his entire chest. Rhodes heard himself gasping for air.

Up ahead he saw the imposing buildings of the Memorial Medical Center. *Just two more blocks!*

He sideswiped a parked car and swerved to the middle of the street, narrowly missing an oncoming truck. Horns were blaring at him, but they sounded like he was in an echo chamber. The pain seemed to lessen for a moment; then it came back with a vengeance. His vision blurred more and he could barely make out the large sign that read EMERGENCY ROOM with a large red arrow pointing to the left.

He turned left, straining to follow the signs. The road curved and curved again. Rhodes's right hand went numb, and he had to steer the car with one hand. Just ahead he saw the ramp leading up to the ER.

He tried to drive up the ramp, but all the strength had left his body, and his hand slipped off the steering wheel. The car careened off a cement pillar and crashed into the wall of the hospital.

By the time the medical personnel reached Oliver Rhodes, his lifeless eyes were staring up at the clear blue California sky.

3

A photograph of Oliver Rhodes made the front page of the *Los Angeles Times*.

Simon Murdock, the dean at the Memorial Medical Center, stared down at the newspaper on his desk and wondered how many more nightmares would befall the Rhodes family. They were like the Kennedys. Both families were wealthy and powerful and cursed by one tragedy after another. And theirs was the worst of all tragedies. The children were dying before the parents.

Murdock's mind drifted back twenty years to the death of his only son from a drug overdose. He still felt the pain and emptiness that didn't seem to abate with time. He could only imagine the heartache that Mortimer Rhodes was experiencing. Mortimer Rhodes, the patriarch of the family, had now lost all three sons. The eldest, Alexander, had been governor of California before being elected to the United States Senate. He died in a plane crash at age fifty-two. Jonathan, the middle son, had the business mind and controlled the family's oil and real estate fortune. He, too, had died in his fifties in a motorcycle accident outside Munich. And now the last of the sons, Oliver, was dead.

The intercom on Murdock's desk buzzed loudly. "Dr. Murdock, you have a call from a Mr. Lawrence Hockstader on your private line. He's Mortimer Rhodes's attorney."

Murdock picked up the phone and pressed a lighted button. "Simon Murdock here."

"Dr. Murdock, I hope I'm not calling at an inconvenient time," Hockstader said.

"Not at all."

"Good," Hockstader said, his voice all business. "I represent Mortimer Rhodes, and I'm calling on his behalf. If you wish to verify this, you can—"

"That won't be necessary," Murdock interrupted. "I know who you are."

"Good," Hockstader said again. "Let me begin by telling you how much Mr. Rhodes appreciates the flowers and card you sent."

"We were all saddened by Oliver's death," Murdock said, wondering what the lawyer really wanted. One didn't have a four-hundred-dollar-an-hour attorney just to say thank you. "If there is anything we can do for the family, please let me know."

"There are several things Mortimer would like done as soon as possible."

Murdock quickly reached for a pen and legal pad.

"First," Hockstader went on, "Mr. Rhodes wants to know the cause of Oliver's sudden death. He would like an autopsy done today, and he wants it to be performed by Dr. Joanna Blalock."

"Blalock," Murdock mumbled as he wrote.

"Is there a problem with that?" Hockstader asked.

"None whatsoever."

"The autopsy is to be done in a private setting, and the results are to be kept strictly confidential. No one—I repeat, no one—is to know the results until Mortimer Rhodes is informed. At that time he will give you further instructions."

"Mortimer can rest assured that—"

"And if by chance there is any evidence of foul play," Hockstader continued, "Mortimer Rhodes is still to be the first person to be informed."

"Oh, I don't think we need to be concerned about that."

"One never knows," Hockstader said darkly. "Powerful people with political ambitions always seem to have enemies, don't they?"

Murdock hadn't thought of that. Like most people, he believed Oliver Rhodes had died of a myocardial infarction, given the man's past medical history. "He will be carefully examined for that possibility."

"Finally," Hockstader concluded, "if it is determined that Oliver died from heart problems, Mr. Rhodes is prepared to donate ten million dollars to establish a cardiac institute at Memorial in his son's memory."

The sum took Murdock's breath away. Ten million dollars on a silver platter. Unbelievable! Murdock quickly gathered himself. "Please thank Mortimer for all of us at Memorial."

"Mr. Rhodes will expect to hear from you later today."

Murdock put the phone down and hurriedly reached for the button on the intercom. "Find out where Dr. Blalock is."

Murdock moved away from his desk and paced the floor, rubbing his hands together. A new cardiac institute was exactly what Memorial needed. It would be a perfect fit, the crowning achievement of Murdock's tenure as dean at the medical center. *Ten million dollars*, Murdock thought again. Astounding! And with that ten million in hand, he could go to his friends in Washington and obtain another ten million in matching funds. Twenty million would construct an incredible institute.

Murdock went over to the window overlooking the huge medical complex. Before him he could see the high-rise redbrick institutes that had been built during his twenty-year stay at Memorial. There was the Cancer Institute and the Neuromuscular Institute and the Biogenetics Institute, all lined up with their windows sparkling in the morning sun. It had been Murdock's vision to build new, impressive institutes that he was certain would attract America's best and brightest physicians and researchers. With the exception of Mortimer Rhodes, the board of trustees did not agree and were firmly against the large expenditures. But

Murdock prevailed—with Mortimer Rhodes's assistance—and time had proved him to be right. Memorial was now considered to be the finest medical center west of the Mississippi and was consistently ranked among the top five hospitals in America.

The intercom on his desk buzzed. "Dr. Blalock is in the autopsy room. She's about to start a case."

Murdock grabbed the legal pad off his desk and hurried out of his office. Passing his secretary, he said, "Tell Dr. Blalock not to start the case. I'm on my way down."

Murdock took the elevator to the B level and walked quickly down a wide corridor, thinking about the instructions he'd received from Mortimer Rhodes's lawyer. The family wanted privacy and confidentiality, the two most difficult things to deliver in any hospital, even when a patient was dead and in an autopsy room. Doctors and residents and medical students were always roaming around in the pathology department, as well as technicians and assistants and orderlies. And when the patient was famous, everybody wanted a look at the patient or his chart. Plus, the autopsy report would have to be dictated and then typed by a secretary who would read it and talk about it with her friends over lunch. Then there was the press, which would do anything to get a picture or a story. The body of Oliver Rhodes would have to be isolated, Murdock decided, maybe even guarded.

Murdock went through a set of double doors with a sign that read POSITIVELY NO ADMITTANCE EXCEPT FOR AUTHORIZED PERSONNEL. Then he pushed through another set of swinging doors and entered the autopsy room. He scanned the area with its eight stainless steel tables lined up in rows of two. There were bodies on all the tables with doctors hunched over them. Standing on his tiptoes, he saw Joanna Blalock at the rear of the room.

Murdock walked around the periphery, passing corpses in various stages of dissection. As usual, they seemed so unreal to Murdock. They looked more like plastic models than dead humans. He wondered for the hundredth time what it was that attracted doctors to become pathologists and be constantly surrounded by death.

Joanna Blalock saw Murdock approaching and held up a finger, indicating she'd be with him in a moment. Then she turned back to the X rays on the view box and pointed out a finding to a young assistant professor, Lori McKay.

Murdock stepped in for a closer look. The films showed multiple views of a human skull. Someone had drawn an arrow in red crayon to highlight something in the posterior parietal bone. Murdock saw nothing abnormal.

He moved back, his gaze wandering to the refrigerated wall units where the corpses were kept. Oliver Rhodes was in one of them. In his mind Murdock began laying the groundwork for the Oliver Rhodes Institute of Cardiology. From drawing board to completion would probably take two years. With a little luck they could have the institute's grand opening on Murdock's seventieth birthday.

Seventy years, Murdock groaned to himself. Where had all the years gone? When he had first come to Memorial, the staff physicians all seemed to be his age. Now most of them looked young enough to be his children. He looked at Joanna Blalock, who still seemed too young and pretty to be so bright. She was strikingly attractive with patrician features and sandy blond hair that was pulled back severely, held in place by a simple barrette. Although she was close to forty, most people thought she was five years younger. The only signs of aging were small crow's-feet at the corners of her eyes when she smiled.

Murdock's gaze turned to Lori McKay, who appeared young enough to be a medical student. She was thin and petite with long auburn hair and scattered freckles across her nose. She could have passed for Murdock's granddaughter. Murdock sighed deeply, knowing that a sure sign of getting old was when everybody else seemed so young.

Joanna broke into his thoughts. "Sorry to keep you waiting, but these skull films are really tough to read."

Murdock gestured with a hand toward the view box. "Well, somebody must have seen something and drawn arrows to point to it."

"Those arrows are mine," Joanna said, turning back to the view box. She used a magnifying glass to review the skull once more. "I think I see a small linear fracture, but I'm not sure. And it just might be the single most important clue I've got. It could tell me everything."

"Such as?"

Joanna pointed at the autopsy table with her magnifying glass. "Such as how and why this man died."

Murdock stared down at the grotesque corpse on the stainless steel table. The face and body were badly bloated, and the skin had a peculiar green color. In scattered, localized areas on the man's legs, the flesh was torn open. Murdock backed away, detecting the stench of rotten eggs. "What caused all this?"

"Drowning, presumably," Joanna told him. "When a body has been submerged for a week or more, as this one has, it begins to putrefy and form gases. That's what causes the bloating, and that's what causes the body to float to the surface."

And the gases cause the stench, Murdock thought, and took another step back. "And the open wounds on his legs were caused by decomposition, as well. Right?"

Joanna shook her head. "I don't think so. Most likely some sea creatures were feeding on him."

"I see," Murdock said, feeling a twinge of nausea. He looked down at the corpse once more, now wondering why a drowning victim would require an autopsy by a forensic pathologist at a leading medical center. "Is there a reason why this case is being done here?"

"An insurance company asked for my help," Joanna told him. "It seems this man took out a two-million-dollar life insurance policy last year."

"I see," Murdock said again, trying to hide his displeasure with Joanna Blalock doing private cases at Memorial Hospital. But he had allowed her to do consultations for a fee five years ago when she threatened to resign because of Murdock's insistence that she limit her work solely to patients seen at Memorial. At first he'd given real thought to firing her, but then decided he couldn't let her go. She had become too valuable to Memorial. Her reputation was outstanding, and it grew every time she handled a high-profile case for the LAPD. So Murdock had grudgingly allowed her to spend a third of her time doing private consultations. He had heard she charged five thousand dollars a case. Murdock's jaw tightened noticeably, once again feeling that Joanna had taken advantage of Memorial to further her own goals and enrich herself.

Joanna could sense the tension growing between them and knew exactly what Murdock was thinking. Her private consultations were a source of constant irritation to Murdock, and given the chance, he would happily replace her. But that was easier said than done. He knew it. She knew it. Joanna shrugged. She wasn't going to worry about it. She wasn't going to change her professional life to suit Simon Murdock.

The awkward silence continued.

Lori McKay cleared her throat and turned to Joanna. "Do you want me to have these skull films reviewed by a radiologist?"

Joanna nodded. "I want to know if that's a fracture, and if it is, I need to know its exact location."

Lori thought for a moment, tapping a finger against her chin. "He may want more films with different views. Maybe even an MRI."

"Whatever. Just pinpoint the fracture if it's there."

"You know, Joanna, even if he does have a skull fracture," Lori thought aloud, "it doesn't mean somebody conked him on the head. Remember, he fell off a yacht. He could have hit the boat on his way into the water."

"Or it could' have happened postmortem," Joanna added. "His head could have bashed up against some rocks while he was submerged on the bottom of the sea."

"Then why spend so much time studying the fracture? It could have happened before or after he died, and we can't tell the difference."

"Sure we can."

"How?"

"Think about it."

Lori wrinkled her forehead, concentrating. Maybe the brain tissue beneath the fracture would show some reaction and that would only occur if he was alive when the fracture occurred. But they'd have to examine his brain to find out, and by now it had probably turned into jelly.

"From a vascular standpoint, tell me one thing live people do that dead people don't," Joanna clued her.

Lori's eyes brightened. "Bleed! Live people bleed; dead people don't. If there's blood in that fracture line, his skull was fractured while he was alive."

"Exactly."

"But," Lori countered, "he still could have hit his head on the side of the yacht as he fell into the sea. So, finding blood in the fracture doesn't necessarily mean our guy got bashed on the head and thrown into the sea."

Joanna grinned and gave Lori a big wink. "But it would surely open up that possibility, now, wouldn't it?"

Lori grinned back. "Oh, yeah."

"Ask the radiologist to read those films for us today."

Lori quickly took down the X rays and placed them in a large manila envelope. She glanced over at Murdock, wondering what he wanted from Joanna. It had to be something big. Otherwise Murdock wouldn't have come down here. "Dr. Murdock, do you want me to hang around for a while?"

"That won't be necessary," Murdock said, and gestured dismissively with his hand.

Screw you, you pompous ass, Lori wanted to say. But she held her tongue and looked over at Joanna. "I'll be down in radiology if you need me."

Joanna waited until Lori was out of earshot. Then she turned to Murdock. "What can I do for you, Simon?"

"You've heard about Oliver Rhodes?"

"Of course."

"The Rhodes family wants an autopsy done now, by you, and in the most private setting possible. Do you have any problem with that?"

"None whatsoever," Joanna said at once.

"Where will you do it?"

Joanna thought briefly. "In the room we use for contaminated cases. It's separate and isolated and has no windows."

"Good." Murdock nodded his approval. "Now we'll want as few people as possible involved in the autopsy."

"Lori McKay will assist me. She'll be the only other person in the room."

Murdock sucked air through his teeth. "She's so young, and she'll talk."

"No, she won't. She's more mature than you think, and she knows how to keep her mouth shut."

Murdock hesitated. "If she talks about any aspect of this case, she's gone from Memorial. Let her know that."

"What else do you need?"

Murdock quickly checked the list on his legal pad. Private setting, as few people as possible, no press release. The autopsy report. "You will dictate your findings. Correct?"

"Yes."

"Tell me how the dictation is done and typed."

"I dictate into an overhead microphone while I'm

doing the autopsy. The dictation goes to a tape in the steno room, and then it's typed."

"Will it be on a separate tape?"

"Yes," Joanna said. "There'll be no other dictation on it."

"I'll want that tape before it's typed."

Joanna gave Murdock a long look. "I won't allow that tape to be altered, regardless of what I find."

"Understood. I just don't want it typed until I've discussed the results with Mortimer Rhodes."

"Agreed," Joanna said, now thinking about Mortimer Rhodes, the nice old man who had built the Karen Rhodes Forensic Laboratory at Memorial in memory of his granddaughter, a nursing student who had been murdered by a psychotic doctor. Karen had been the apple of his eye, and those closest to Mortimer Rhodes said he never got over her death. And now he had lost the last of his three sons. That would almost certainly kill the old man.

Murdock lowered his voice. "And the family wants you to look for any evidence of foul play."

Joanna's eyelids narrowed into slits. "Had he received any threats?"

"I don't know," Murdock stammered.

"We have to find out."

"I can't call this grieving family and ask that kind of question," Murdock said. "Not now."

"I know it seems cold and cruel to bother them," Joanna said. "But the information could be very important, particularly if there's no obvious cause of death."

Murdock sighed wearily. He would place a call to Lawrence Hockstader and let the lawyer earn his four hundred an hour. "I'll take care of it."

"And please have his medical records at Memorial sent down to me in a sealed envelope."

"Done." Murdock reached for a pen and wrote a brief note on his legal pad. "Anything else?"

"We have to contact the emergency room and make

sure all his clothes and personal effects were sent along with the body."

"My office will see to that," Murdock said, and scribbled down a reminder.

A petite receptionist wearing a scrub suit hurried over to the table and looked up at Joanna. "Dr. Blalock, there's a police detective outside who says he has to see you. He wants to come in."

"This is a restricted area," Murdock said tersely.

"He said it's official business," the receptionist said.

Joanna nodded. "Send him in."

Murdock frowned disapprovingly. "Really, Joanna, we can't have unauthorized people just strolling in and out of here."

The receptionist glanced back and forth between the two doctors, uncertain what she should do.

"Go." Joanna motioned to the receptionist and watched her leave, then turned to Murdock. "Two of the cases down here belong to the LAPD."

"So?"

"So let me take care of their business. Then I can concentrate on Oliver Rhodes."

Murdock stared at her, regretting even more his decision that allowed Joanna Blalock to do private consultations. He wished someone would turn the clock back twenty years to a time when faculty did what they were told. "Just get the autopsy done promptly."

"That's my plan."

Joanna moved away from the autopsy table and leaned against the tiled wall, feeling its coolness through her scrub suit. Her gaze went over to the bloated corpse, and she wondered what new information Detective Lt. Jake Sinclair had in the case.

It was Jake Sinclair who persuaded the insurance company to let Joanna do the autopsy on the supposed drowning victim. Something didn't fit, Jake had said. A sixty-year-old entrepreneur-multimillionaire who had spent half his life on the sea doesn't just suddenly fall off the back of his yacht while his young, pretty wife and a dozen other party goers are enjoying themselves. The sea had been calm, the yacht barely moving that night, yet no one heard screams or cries for help. It just didn't make sense, Jake had commented, except maybe to the widow who would inherit twenty million dollars. Plus two million from a life insurance policy.

Joanna smiled as a picture of the handsome homicide detective came into her mind. For over ten years he had been her lover and partner and confidant and best friend. Oh, they had had their ups and downs, but the last six months had been perfect. Jake was still tough as nails, but with Joanna he was becoming warmer and closer and more intimate than ever. He was even doing the little things that women love so much. Like giving her small gifts for no reason and sending flowers when she least expected them. And there were the subtle winks and touches when they were out in public. She adored that.

The door to the autopsy room opened, and Detective Sgt. Lou Farelli entered. The receptionist pointed the way for him.

Joanna stared at the swinging doors, waiting for Jake Sinclair to come through. The doors remained motionless. Farelli walked slowly toward her, a somber expression on his face.

"Hello, Doc," Farelli said flatly.

"Hello, Sergeant," Joanna said. "Where's Jake?"

"At a crime scene," Farelli answered. "He sent me to get you. We need your help."

"I'm afraid she's unavailable," Murdock said at once.

Farelli stared at Murdock as if he were a potted plant and then turned back to Joanna. "It's a real tough case, and it's going to be high-profile."

Joanna shook her head. "I'd like to help, but I'm really tied up here."

"Let me tell you what we're up against," Farelli said.

Murdock stepped forward. "Dr. Blalock has told

you she's unavailable. That should end the conversation."

Farelli gave Murdock an icy stare. "I'm trying to talk to the doc here, so you put a lid on it until I'm finished. Understood?"

Murdock hesitated and then backed off, mumbling under his breath.

Farelli looked back to Joanna. "Some guy gets whacked in Santa Monica last night during a robbery. They dump his body into an excavation site where a high-rise is going up."

Joanna exhaled wearily. "Can it wait until tomorrow?"

"No," Farelli said. "We've only got a few hours of daylight left, and it's supposed to rain. Jake wants you to see the crime scene before anything gets washed away."

"What's so important about a murder victim at the bottom of an excavation site?"

"It's not the guy that's important. It's what we found buried around him."

"And what was that?"

"Babies," Farelli said gravely. "Premature little babies."

"Jesus! How many?"

"A whole bunch," Farelli told her. "Jake says it's a cemetery of human fetuses."

Joanna stripped off her gloves and discarded them. "I'll follow you over in my car."

4

"It doesn't fit," Jake Sinclair said. "The pieces don't fit together here."

He was standing near the fence at the top of the excavation site in Santa Monica. Below him, medical examiners were sifting through sand and debris at the bottom of the pit.

"We've got a big hole in the fence and an empty shoe box next to it," Jake went on. "And at the bottom of this dig we've got a guy with half his head blown off. He's got no watch, no wallet, not even loose change in his pockets."

"Did he have anything at all in his pockets?" Joanna asked.

"A receipt for a candy bar bought last night at the mini mart on the corner."

"Does the receipt say what time the buy was made?"

"Nine-o-five."

Joanna looked slowly around the crime scene, her gaze going from the hole in the fence to the empty shoe box to the candy wrapper next to it. "Have you ID'd the victim?"

"Not yet."

Joanna went over to the gaping hole in the fence and peered down through it. The slope was steep, going down at least sixty feet. Just inside the fence, the ground and large pieces of scrap lumber were soaked with blood. In some areas the blood had coagulated and formed mounds of clots.

She backed away from the fence, inspecting the

ground around the shoe box and candy wrapper. No blood. But a yard farther away was a half-dollar-size piece of bloodied scalp still attached to bone.

"This is how I put it together," Jake said. "The guy wanders into a tough neighborhood where drug deals go down all the time. Some crackhead sees an easy score and whacks the guy. Then the picture gets fuzzy. Why does the perp kick a hole in the fence to dump the body? Why make all that noise?" Jake shook his head. "That doesn't make any sense. The perp has got the money. He's not going to stick around and attract attention. He's going to run like hell."

"The hole was in the fence before he was shot," Joanna said matter-of-factly.

"How do you figure that?"

"Just inside the fence is a pool of clotted blood," Joanna told him, and then pointed at the shoe box. "And just beyond the box is a piece of the victim's scalp and skull. He was shot about where I'm standing with the bullet taking part of his head straight back. Then he fell sideways through the hole in the fence and stayed there long enough to bleed a fair amount."

"How did he get to the bottom of the pit?"

"Two possibilities. Either he tumbled down, or somebody gave him a push."

Jake smiled at her, thinking she was better at deduction than most of the cops he knew. "You're getting pretty good at this."

"It comes with practice." Joanna smiled back. Jake was a big man with broad shoulders and rugged good looks. His thick brown hair, now graying noticeably, was swept back, accentuating his high-set cheekbones. On his chin was a small jagged scar that women couldn't help but look at and wonder how he got it.

"Does your crystal ball tell you who made the hole in the fence and why?" Jake asked, getting back to business.

"No, it doesn't. And it doesn't tell me if all this is connected to those dead fetuses, either."

"A damn cemetery of dead babies," Jake said, shak-

ing his head in disgust. "You've got to see it to believe it."

Joanna glanced around the crime scene once more,
focusing in on the shoe box. "Do we know if the shoe
box belonged to the victim?"

Jake shrugged. "We can't be sure. But it was found
next to the candy wrapper, and its lid was off. We
think the perp took whatever was in it. With a little
luck, the box will have the victim's fingerprints on it."

"And maybe the perp's, too."

"Yeah," Jake said pessimistically, "along with his
address and home phone number."

Joanna slipped on a pair of latex gloves and picked
up the shoe box. It was empty, with no store logo or
other markings on it. She brought the box up to her
nose and sniffed carefully. It had a faint, disagreeable
odor that Joanna couldn't identify. Yet there was
something familiar about it. She lifted the box up to
Jake. "Take a whiff and tell me what you think."

Jake smelled the box. He, too, detected the faint,
unpleasant odor but couldn't place it. "At first I
thought it was methyl alcohol. But it's not."

"No, it's not that," Joanna agreed. "Maybe we can
extract it and identify it using a chromatograph."

"We've got a lot of maybes here," Jake said unhappily. "Maybe this, maybe that. All we've really got is
a guy with half his head blown off and a bunch of
dead babies."

"Which may or may not be interconnected."

"Another maybe," Jake growled, taking her arm.
"Come on. Let's go look at dead babies."

They walked along the periphery of the excavation
site. The sidewalk was uneven with cracked cement
slabs that jutted up. Joanna stepped cautiously, inspecting the ground and surrounding area. The fence
next to her was made of plywood and painted green.
There were Mexican gang markings sprayed on it and
a scattering of posters announcing a rock concert.
Across the street were small, run-down apartment

buildings with faded stucco surfaces. The cars on the street were at least five years old.

They passed by trees and tall bushes that blocked their view of the street. On the ground were broken pieces of glass and a discarded milk carton. Joanna's heel caught in a crack of the sidewalk, and she stumbled badly. Quickly she grabbed Jake's arm and steadied herself.

"Christ," Joanna grumbled. "You'd think they'd fix these sidewalks."

"Not in this neighborhood," Jake said. "The people who live around here don't have much pull at city hall."

"I'll bet these sidewalks are fixed promptly when this multimillion-dollar project is completed."

"Oh, yeah," Jake agreed. "Money always talks."

Jake grinned at her, studying her profile. She was so damn pretty and sexy, and she seemed to get prettier and sexier with time. Everything about her turned him on. He glanced over his shoulder and, seeing no one, he reached for her waist. "How do you manage to look so good at the end of a long work day?"

"I primp," she said softly. "I always primp for you."

Jake pulled her closer and gave her a quick hug, smelling the shampoo-fresh aroma of her hair.

Joanna brushed her cheek against his and then playfully pushed him away. "Control yourself."

Jake smiled mischievously. "Aw, you're no fun at all."

"That's not what you said last night."

They chuckled at one another and walked on, their arms touching ever so slightly. Ahead of them, the street curved and began to slope downward.

Jake asked, "Do you want to go out for dinner later?"

"Sure. I should be finished at Memorial sometime after midnight."

"You're that backed up, huh?"

"I don't even want to talk about it."

They came to an opened chain-link gate. Ducking under yellow police tape, they entered the excavation site. Directly in front of them was a steep dirt ramp that went down six stories. At the bottom of the huge pit, a team of medical examiners and their assistants were turning up the earth with small shovels. Joanna could see miniature red flags on sticks that were stuck in the ground.

"The red flags mark the places where the bodies were found. Right?" Joanna asked.

"Right."

Joanna counted seven flags.

Lou Farelli trudged up the incline, huffing and puffing loudly. At the top he paused to catch his breath. "Goddamn it! We need an escalator here."

"You got anything?" Jake asked.

"Nothing. Nada. Zilch." Farelli coughed hard and then cleared his throat. "Nobody saw anything. The construction gang gets here at seven a.m. and leaves at four p.m. sharp. They saw nothing unusual. Nobody was hanging around or casing the place."

Jake pointed over his shoulder with his thumb. "What about the people in the apartment units across the street?"

"Mainly blue-collar workers who lock their doors real tight and turn television sets way up so they can't hear the drug deals and fights that go on all night."

"So nobody heard anybody kicking in a fence last night, huh?"

"If they did, they ain't talking about it."

"What about addicts?"

"They congregate in a park three blocks from here. I've got a black-and-white over there now, rounding them up." Farelli slowly twisted his shoulders and stretched his sore back. "This isn't going to be a good day. It started out crummy and it's staying that way."

Jake nodded. "Have you heard anything more about Billy Cunningham?"

"He's not going to make it," Farelli said morosely. "They got him on life support."

"Shit," Jake hissed.

"Yeah." Farelli took a deep breath and exhaled loudly. "Anyway, I'm going to that park to see if I can find an addict with a wallet and credit cards that don't belong to him."

Joanna and Jake started down the steep dirt ramp. Joanna held on tightly to Jake's arm and took slow, cautious steps. Her heels dug into the soft ground.

"Walk in the tire tracks," Jake advised. "The earth is firmer there."

Joanna kept her head down, watching her step and putting most of her weight on her toes. "Who is Billy Cunningham?"

"A homicide dick I know."

"A friend?"

"An old drinking buddy," Jake told her. "We hung out together when I first joined the force. Then his wife got cancer and died, and Billy became a loner. He crawled into a bottle and stayed boozed up most of the time. It almost cost him his career. Then he met and married Cynthia, and she straightened him out. He's been sober for over three years, doing real good until this morning. He walked into a convenience store for a cup of coffee, not knowing a robbery was in progress. The perp had a semiautomatic and unloaded three into Billy. Two went into his chest, one into his head."

"Oh, Lord!" Joanna moaned softly.

"It happens," Jake said matter-of-factly.

Joanna glanced over at him, knowing that his tone of voice didn't match his true feelings. It hit cops hard when a fellow policeman went down. And it was the same, she thought, when doctors learn that a colleague is dying. Then death is no longer impersonal. Now it's right up on your doorstep, reminding you of your own vulnerability and mortality. And that it might be your turn to go next.

Joanna pushed the grim thoughts from her mind, remembering something she wanted to discuss. "Jake, the next time you need me for a case, it might be best to call rather than send Farelli for me. He caused a little bit of a stir in the autopsy room."

"Yeah? What happened?"

"Farelli strolled into the autopsy room when Simon Murdock was there," Joanna told him. "And Murdock became upset because it's a restricted area."

Jake rolled his eyes skyward. "As if Farelli had never seen a stiff, for chrissakes!"

"That's not the end of it," Joanna went on. "Murdock and Farelli got into a word battle, and finally Farelli gave him an icy look and told Murdock to put a lid on it."

Jake smiled thinly. "I'll bet Murdock shut up real quick."

"And how."

Most people misjudged Farelli on first glance, Jake was thinking. Farelli was short and stocky with a round face and tired eyes. Everyone thought he looked like a waiter in a neighborhood Italian restaurant. But he was really tough as a brick and took crap from no one. Anybody who crossed him did it only once. "Farelli is not a man you want to piss off."

"I think Simon Murdock found that out," Joanna said.

They reached the bottom of the ramp and stepped over a narrow trench. Then they walked around a giant earth mover. The ground was softer there, and they were sinking in deeper. Ahead was another trench, wider than the last one. Jake took Joanna's arm and helped her across.

They came to the corpse.

Joanna slowly circled the body, getting an overall picture. The man was big—at least six feet tall—with broad shoulders and muscular forearms. He wore dungarees, a faded plaid shirt, and heavy-duty work shoes. His hands were callused, his fingernails cracked and dirty. He did manual labor, Joanna thought, with a fair amount of lifting. Her gaze went back to his shoes. The right one had a deep green discoloration on its toe. Quickly Joanna looked over at the corpse's forearms. They were covered with loose dirt, but she could tell the right forearm was larger than the left. And it had a tattoo of a cross on it.

Joanna moved to the man's head with its lifeless blue eyes. His mouth was half-open, and something inside was glistening in the afternoon light. Joanna reached for a tongue blade and raised the upper lip. The man's front teeth were made of a silvery metal.

Joanna stepped back and examined the body once more. It was dusted with soil from his slide down the slope, but there was no dirt on his face. "Did someone clean his face?"

"Yeah," Jake answered. "We wanted to take Polaroids and show them around to see if anybody could ID him."

Joanna reached down with her tongue blade and scraped off loose dirt from the tattooed area on the forearm. There was no writing or names associated with the large cross. "I'm surprised the rain last night didn't cake mud all over him."

"We got lucky there," Jake said. "It only drizzled in Santa Monica last night."

Joanna nodded to herself. That explained why the blood and blood clots near the plywood fence hadn't washed away. It also explained why the empty shoe box was dry and hadn't lost its faint, disagreeable odor. What was that smell?

Jake broke into her thoughts. "Well, what do you think?"

"There are a few things of interest," Joanna said, going back to the corpse's shoes to make certain there was no green paint on the soles.

"Ah-huh," Jake said, taking out a ballpoint pen and notepad. He wondered why the corpse's shoes were so interesting to Joanna.

"To begin with, he's not an addict. He's not emaciated, did a fair amount of heavy labor, and has his shirtsleeves rolled up, which tells us he wasn't trying to hide any track marks."

Jake glanced down at the man's hands and the calluses and split nails. "What kind of work you figure he did?"

Joanna shrugged. "Carpenter, plumber, handyman, construction worker. Any one of a dozen occupations."

"Is there any way to narrow it down?"

"Not out here," Joanna said, thinking about the tests that needed to be done in a forensic laboratory. For starters, analysis of the calluses might yield some material that pointed to a particular occupation. Components of fertilizer, for example, would indicate that the man was a gardener or perhaps worked in a factory that made fertilizer.

"Can you tell if he's from around here?" Jake asked.

"No," Joanna replied. "But I can tell you he wasn't born or raised here."

Jake squinted an eye. "How do you know that?"

"His teeth." Joanna leaned over and pried up the corpse's top lip with a tongue blade. "Using metal to replace teeth is kind of archaic, but it's how dentistry is practiced in Russia and in some parts of Eastern Europe. That's where this fellow is from."

Jake nodded. "That fits with his tattoo."

Joanna's gaze went to the tattoo. It was a large, dark blue cross with orange borders. "You think that tattoo is Russian?"

"I think the cross is Russian Orthodox, and that's a religion practiced mainly in Russia and the countries around it." Jake pointed at the ornate details of the cross with his pen. "See the fancy whirls and swirls, particularly at the ends of the cross?"

"Pretty fair artwork," Joanna commented.

Jake tilted his hand back and forth. "So-so. The color is uneven and the symmetry is not all that good."

Joanna smiled over at him. Jake was an expert on tattoos. He loved them. They were the perfect identification mark. Perpetrators never bothered to hide them, and victims always remembered them.

"So," Jake concluded, straightening back up, "we've

got a Russian or Eastern European immigrant who does heavy labor. He walks down this street—for what, only God knows—and gets his head blown off."

"He came down this street to kick a hole in the fence, Jake."

"What!"

"Look at the toes of his shoes, particularly the one on the right."

Jake saw the green discoloration on the toe of the right shoe. On closer inspection he detected small green splinters stuck between the sole and the upper part of the toe.

"And he's right-handed," Joanna continued. "That's why we see green paint only on the toe of the right shoe. That's the foot he would use to kick through the green plywood fence."

"Jesus," Jake muttered, more puzzled than ever. "Why the hell did he want to kick a hole in the fence?"

"To get inside," Joanna said simply.

Jake shook his head. "That doesn't work. Why kick in a fence and make all that noise? That's only going to attract people. All he had to do was walk down another forty yards and he could hop over a gate."

Joanna nodded in agreement. The victim could easily have climbed over the gate. The chain link in the gate would have given him an excellent toehold.

Jake looked up the dirt ramp to the street, picturing in his mind the apartment units across from the gate. "The streetlight," he said to himself.

"What about it?" Joanna asked.

"There's a streetlight in front of the apartments across from the gate," Jake explained. "He didn't want to jump over the gate because the area was lighted and he thought somebody might see him. That's why he kicked a hole in the fence."

"But why'd he do it?"

"Like you said, to get in."

"For what?"

Jake shrugged his shoulders. "That, I don't know."

They turned as Girish Gupta, a senior medical examiner for the County of Los Angeles, came over. He was holding a medium-size bottle in his hands. "Dr. Blalock! What a pleasure to see you again."

"It's nice to see you as well," Joanna said, liking the man and his genial yet formal manners. "Lieutenant Sinclair tells me we have some nasty business here."

"Indeed, indeed," Gupta said in a clipped British accent. He was a short pudgy man who was born in New Delhi but raised and trained in London. "We have dead fetuses strewn about everywhere."

"How many so far?"

"This is number eight." Gupta held up a capped, fluid-filled bottle. A small human fetus was floating inside it. "This has to be the work of a crazy person. Who else would preserve fetuses in bottles, then bury them in the ground?"

Joanna's brow went up. "Are all the fetuses in bottles?"

"Every one so far," Gupta replied. "And all are perfectly preserved. Here, see for yourself."

Joanna took the bottle and held it up to the light. In it was a small human fetus with well-formed arms and legs. The mouth, nose, and eyes were easily discernible. It was at the three- to four-month stage of development. Joanna tilted the bottle and the fetus floated around, facing her. Its chest and abdomen had been cut open. "Are all of them cut like this?"

"Every one of them," Gupta answered. "It looks as if somebody has been performing abortions, doesn't it?"

"I guess."

Joanna continued to examine the floating fetus, wondering why the incisions were so straight and the arms and legs untouched. That usually didn't happen when the abortion was done by a D and C. She handed the bottle back. "You've got a tough case on your hands."

"I was hoping you might help us," Gupta said with an ingratiating smile.

"I wish I could," Joanna told him. "But my work at Memorial is really stacked up."

Jake stepped in. "We could really use your assistance here, Joanna," he urged. "I can guarantee you that this is going to be a high-profile case. The story about a cemetery of dead babies is already out, and the press will play it for all it's worth. You'd be doing us a big favor to take this one over."

"But it's Dr. Gupta's case," Joanna protested. "And he—"

"No, no!" Gupta interrupted quickly. "We are so far behind at the county morgue that this case would sit on the shelf for weeks. And I don't think we want that, do we?"

"No," Joanna had to agree. The Los Angeles medical examiner's office received over two hundred cases a day. They were always backed up, usually for weeks, sometimes longer. But her own workload at Memorial was also heavily backed up and getting worse. And there were still Oliver Rhodes and the drowning victim to do.

"All right," Joanna said reluctantly. "I'll take the case."

"Excellent!" Gupta breathed a sigh of relief. Fetal pathology and embryology were not his strong points. "Of course, I would like to assist you."

"We'll arrange the autopsy schedule so you can be there," Joanna said. "I'll have my secretary call yours to set up the times."

"Excellent," Gupta said again, and turned to leave. He stepped in a small hole and tripped. As he tried to regain his balance, the bottle slipped from his hands. It hit a piece of wood on the ground and then bounced up and hit the wood once more. Gupta retrieved the bottle and held it up to the light. "There's a crack at the bottom, and it's leaking."

Joanna detected a strong, disagreeable aroma. She waved at the air to disperse the sharp odor. "Is that formaldehyde?"

"Yes," Gupta replied. "And that explains why the fetuses are so well preserved."

"The shoe box," Joanna muttered under her breath.

"What?" Gupta asked, ears pricked.

"Nothing."

"Well, then, let me transfer this fetus to another container," Gupta said, and walked away, this time watching his step.

Jake moved in closer to Joanna. "What about the shoe box?"

"I think that faint smell we detected in it was formaldehyde or something closely related to it."

"Are you sure?"

"I'd bet on it."

"Jesus," Jake grumbled, pacing around the corpse with his hands clasped together behind his back. "This case gets stranger by the minute. Now we've got a Russian immigrant carrying around a dead baby in a shoe box, and he kicks down a fence so he can dispose of the baby and plant it with the others. And while he's doing all this, he ends up with two bullets in his melon. Now, how in the hell do you figure all this out?"

"Well, for starters, this wasn't a matter of simple disposal," Joanna said thoughtfully. "The fetus in that bottle was about four inches long. If you just wanted to dispose of it, you could have just flushed it down the john."

"Or put it in the garbage disposal," Jake added.

"Right," Joanna said, sickened briefly by the thought. "And if they were only interested in disposal, they wouldn't have put the fetuses in formaldehyde."

"So they wanted the damn things preserved."

"That would be my guess."

"But why?"

"I don't have the faintest idea."

Jake shook his head, even more confused now. "So our guy wanted to bury preserved babies and, at the same time, make sure they were never found."

Joanna looked at Jake quizzically. "How do you know he meant for the babies to never be found?"

Jake pointed across the excavation site to two large cement trucks. "The digging part of this project is over. Today they were supposed to finish leveling off the ground and start laying down cement."

Joanna thought for a moment and then slowly nodded. "And while those earth movers were leveling the ground, they probably unearthed the bottles with the babies. Is that what you're thinking?"

Jake nodded back. "That's how I put it together. The guy who buried those babies figured they'd be under a foot of cement by now."

"But why go to the trouble of preserving babies, only to hide them in a place where they can never be found?"

Jake shrugged. "Who the hell knows?"

"This case gets crazier with each new clue."

"Tell me about it."

The overcast sky suddenly darkened, and large raindrops began to fall.

Joanna signaled over to Gupta and made a vertical zipping-up motion. She wanted the corpse placed in a body bag. Gupta shouted instructions to an assistant.

"Come on," Jake said, taking Joanna's arm. "Let's get out of here before this place turns into a pool of mud."

They hurried to the ramp, glancing over at the junior medical examiner, who had found another buried fetus. He planted a red flag in the ground to mark the spot.

"That makes nine fetuses and one adult I have to examine," Joanna said, exhaling wearily. "And that's going to take some time."

Jake watched the medical examiner hold the newly found bottle up to the light. Nine babies so far, he thought, and probably more to come. "When you're doing those autopsies, I want you to keep asking yourself one question. It's the big question. And the answer may well hold the key to everything."

Joanna's eyes narrowed. "What's the question?"

Jake gazed out at the miniature red flags fluttering in the breeze. "Where did all these babies come from?"

5

Sara Ann Moore was reading Shakespeare's *Julius Caesar* when the phone rang. She continued to concentrate on her favorite passage and read it once again.

> There is a tide in the affairs of men
> Which, taken at the flood, leads on to fortune;
> Omitted, all the voyage of their life
> Is bound in shallows and in miseries.

Damn right, Sara thought. *You either seize the moment, or you end up being a big nothing all your life.* And there were no second chances.

The phone rang a fifth time before the answering machine clicked on.

"Sam, let's meet for drinks around five," a man said, and then made a sniffing sound. He hung up without identifying himself.

But Sara knew the voice. It belonged to the man who arranged the hits and collected the fees and handed her the money—minus his 20 percent commission. The message "Let's meet for drinks" meant he had a job for her. And the sniffing sound he made told her that everything was all right. He wasn't being forced to make the call. She wasn't being set up.

She played the message back, making certain the sniff was there. Assassins had enemies, too. It paid to be careful.

Sara walked over to the sliding glass doors of the tenth-floor condominium, which she rented for two thousand dollars a month from a Hollywood producer who spent most of his time in Europe. Outside, the sky was cloudy and gray, a light rain falling. She glanced around the living room and wondered if the writer had an umbrella hidden away someplace. She grimaced at the tasteless furniture, hating every piece of it. The furniture had a heavy Mediterranean style, the sofa and chairs covered with a deep red velvet material. The furnishings looked like they belonged in a bordello.

Sara decided just to wear her Stanford warm-up outfit. The jacket had a hood attached and that would be good enough to keep the light rain off her. She erased the phone message; then she left the apartment and took an empty elevator to the first floor. The lobby was well appointed with a marble floor and oil paintings on the walls.

The uniformed doorman tipped his hat. "Good day, Miss Moore. How's the computer business?"

"Not bad," Sara lied easily. She had told him she worked as a computer programmer out of her apartment. In fact, she used the computer only to buy and sell stocks and to keep track of her portfolio. Sara had made a bundle investing in Internet and high-tech companies. Recently she had sold those stocks and placed the money in blue-chip corporations, like IBM, GE, Ford, and Du Pont. Her portfolio was now worth over half a million.

Artie, the doorman, was saying something to Sara as he opened the door. She hadn't been listening.

"Sorry," Sara said. "What was that?"

"I said the weather is getting real bad," Artie repeated. "Watch your step out there."

"Oh, I will," Sara assured him, and walked out into a very light rain.

She couldn't understand the people who lived in Los Angeles. All it took was a little rain, and they scampered for cover. And the television news programs, with their stupid anchors, went on storm alert. For a drizzle.

Sara sighed, wishing she were back in New York, where she owned her own apartment and had all her things. New York was so electric and exciting, with everything on the move twenty-four hours a day. Sara missed that. But she had to be in Los Angeles because most of her work was now here. She had to know the city and the lay of the land. Often she had to follow her targets for days and sometimes weeks, learning what they did and where and when they did it. And most important, what were the target's habits and vices and foibles? Only after she had all this information and thought about it at length could she decide how to kill the person. Although she occasionally did straightforward hits, most of her work involved her specialty—making death look accidental.

Sara came to the intersection and waited for the red light to change. She glanced over at the front window of a bookstore and saw her reflection in the glass. Her brown hair was cut too short, she thought, and the blond streaks were too obvious. But it did make her seem younger. She moved in closer to the window and studied her angular face and thin lips and doelike brown eyes. There were no lines, but there weren't supposed to be any at the age of thirty-two. *Thirty-two. Interesting*, Sara thought. That was the number of people she'd killed so far.

The light changed, and she crossed the boulevard, then turned down a smaller street. Up ahead she saw a bar named Club West. Most people believed it was named after the bartender and presumed owner, David Westmoreland. But in fact, the club was owned by the Westies, a powerful New York–based gang that had recently expanded into the Los Angeles area. David Westmoreland was a midechelon lieutenant in the organization. Among other things, he provided a hit service that could have anyone killed—for a price. Straightforward hits cost ten thousand dollars. Difficult high-profile hits could run as high as twenty-five thousand. Minus the Westies' 20 percent commission, Sara thought sourly.

But she had to admit, they were worth it. David always set everything up in a smooth, efficient fashion. Although their relationship was strictly business, she felt a strange loyalty to David, who had gotten her started as a hitter. But when he announced he was moving to Los Angeles, she balked at the idea of following him. She wasn't convinced there would be a great demand for her talents in Los Angeles. She was wrong. Business was booming. She was averaging two hits a month.

Sara entered Club West and walked to a booth in the far corner. She sat facing the door.

"Be with you in a minute," David Westmoreland called out from behind the bar.

"No rush," Sara said.

She reached for her cigarettes and then remembered California's law against smoking in public places. She groaned, again wishing she were back in New York. Her gaze went to the well-dressed men sitting at the bar. They were laughing at something David was saying. Probably a joke. She wondered how hard the men would be laughing if they knew the number of people David had arranged to have murdered.

David carefully poured a martini from a shaker into a glass. That's what he was doing when she first saw him in New York, Sara recalled. He was tending bar. At the time she was getting a master's degree in English literature at Columbia. Her friends had dared her to go into Westies, a bar not far from her apartment. It was known to be a hangout for toughs and wiseguys. Sara had hesitated, but eventually she worked up enough courage to go inside. She found the bar exciting and fun and filled with interesting people who had wonderful stories to tell. And they treated her so well, particularly when they learned she was a college student at Columbia. At times they made her feel as if she were one of them.

David befriended her and looked out for her at Westies. It was he who introduced Sara to Richie

Malfitano, a handsome tough guy who tried to sweep her off her feet with gifts and flowers and trips to Atlantic City and Las Vegas. She really liked him and slept with him a few times a week, but she knew the relationship wasn't going anywhere. Richie was a hood. He was also married, with three kids. But, Lord, how exciting he was! Everything about him was a thrill, even his job. He told her he was in the disposal business. She knew what that meant. And with his last name, she thought he was connected. But he wasn't. Richie was a freelance hit man. She learned about that one night when he was taking a shower. He had left his .38 caliber Smith & Wesson in its holster on the bed. She picked up the weapon and was inspecting it when Richie came out of the bathroom.

"Hey!" he shouted. "Put that down before you hurt yourself."

"Don't worry," Sara said, and expertly emptied the rounds from the revolver. She held the weapon up to the light and peered into the barrel. "You'd better clean this or you're going to get your hand blown off."

"How do you know so much about guns?"

"My father taught me." Sara told him about the suburb she'd grown up in just outside Pittsburgh. It was a good neighborhood, but break-ins and robberies were happening there like everywhere else. Her father spent a lot of time traveling as a senior sales representative for a major steel manufacturer, and he thought it best to teach his wife and daughter about firearms so they could defend themselves.

"But can you shoot?" Richie had asked.

"There's one way to find out."

They went to an all-night firing range where she hit so many bull's-eyes she qualified as an expert marksman. She was so good the owner of the range offered her a job as an instructor at fifteen dollars per hour. She politely declined.

Later that night they went to Westies, where Richie bragged to David about Sara's incredible marksmanship. David listened while he made their drinks. He appeared to be uninterested, but Sara could sense he was storing information away. Lord! David and Richie and Westies in New York. It all seemed so long ago now, Sara reminisced.

David broke into her thoughts. "Here you go, Sam, a vodka martini with a lemon twist."

"Thanks," Sara said. He was the only person in the world who called her Sam. It was a nickname he made up from the initials of her full name, Sara Ann Moore. "Do you mind if I light up in here?"

"Can't. It's against the law." David grinned, but his green eyes stayed ice cold. He was a big, barrel-chested man with thinning red hair and a ruddy complexion. "You can take your drink out back and have your cigarette there. I'll join you in a few minutes when Eddie gets back."

Sara studied his face briefly. Something about his voice bothered her. "Have we got trouble?" she asked in a low voice.

"I'll see you out back," David said, and walked away.

Sara took her drink and went out the back door of Club West. She stepped into the narrow alleyway and lit a cigarette, wondering what the trouble was. Her last two hits had gone really well. The schnook last night had half his head blown off. He was surely dead as hell. And so was the millionaire she tapped on the head and pushed over the side of his yacht. There was no way the old man was still alive, unless he could swim ten miles while unconscious. No. It wasn't that. Maybe, she thought, the customers weren't paying their bills. She shook her head at the idea. If you owed the Westies, you paid or you ended up with broken legs. And if you still didn't pay, you ended up dead. She wondered if she had made a mistake, if someone had seen her. Deep down she had the feeling that was it. And in her line of work, a mistake was very bad for business. It could also get you killed.

She remembered back to the night Richie Malfitano had bought it. He had a contract to ice Two-Ton Tony

Giamarro. Two-Ton Tony was stealing from his family big time and was also trying to muscle in on another family's bookmaking business. He was causing trouble and ignoring repeated warnings. He needed to be killed, but he was connected and he was the don's nephew, so nobody in the family wanted to do it. They contracted out for the hit.

Richie botched it. Sara watched the whole thing from the front seat of Richie's Cadillac, which was parked in a lot next to the health club. Two-Ton Tony came out the side door, and Richie jumped out from behind a Dumpster and opened fire. His first shot missed. His second jammed in the chamber. An associate of Two-Ton Tony's suddenly burst through the door, gun drawn, and put a slug right through Richie's handsome face.

Sara quickly slid down in the front seat, praying they hadn't seen her, because if they had, she was dead. She sweated blood as she waited, but they never came. *Stupid Richie!* she kept thinking. He thought he had all the bases covered, that he had done his homework.

Two-Ton Tony, Richie had explained to her, was a creature of habit. He did the same things at the same time every day. A steam bath and massage at the health club at 6:30 P.M. was part of his daily routine. Richie planned to clip Two-Ton as he left the club and walked to his car. But Richie didn't get there early enough to see Two-Ton Tony enter the club—with one of his soldiers at his side. He didn't know there'd be two of them. And he didn't look after his weapon, either. Richie Malfitano hadn't done all of his homework. And that cost him his life.

Sara went to Westies that same night to tell David what had happened. For the first time she saw David Westmoreland become angry. He took a glass of beer and smashed it against the wall in his office, breaking it into a thousand pieces. Richie had screwed up royally. Not only had he missed the target, he had alerted Two-Ton Tony that someone had a contract out on him. Tony and his boys would search high and low to find out who set up the hit. And the Westies were out two thousand dollars, which would have been their commission for a successful kill.

"Shit!" David growled. "Two-Ton will look under every rock between here and Staten Island to find out who set him up. And he'll come up with an answer, too."

"Not if he's dead," Sara said matter-of-factly.

"And how is he going to get dead?"

"I'm going to do it for you."

"Forget it," David said, waving off the offer. "Even the best hit men won't touch this now. Two-Ton Tony is really going to be on guard, and he'll have two goons with him wherever he goes. Nobody is going to get near him."

"You let me worry about that."

David gave her a hard stare. "Just because you can fire a gun doesn't mean you can shoot a man."

"Who said anything about shooting?"

"Then how are you going to do it?"

"This is my offer," Sara said, ignoring the question. "I can arrange for Two-Ton Tony to die within the next two weeks. For my work I want to be paid ten thousand dollars. And I guarantee you his death will look accidental."

"Why is accidental so important here?"

"Because if he's murdered now, the people close to Tony will come after whoever did it with a vengeance," Sara explained. "Two-Ton Tony may be an asshole, but he's connected."

"Right."

"If he dies accidentally, everybody will shrug and walk away. It'll be like water under the bridge."

"Makes sense."

"Ten thousand dollars."

David hesitated. "Let me talk with—"

Sara shook her head. "You make the decision now. Yes or no."

David hesitated again before saying, "Don't get yourself killed, Sam."

"I wouldn't dream of it."

For six straight days Sara trailed Two-Ton Tony Giamarro. He was a creature of habit, all right, but a very closely guarded creature of habit with two goons constantly at his side. There seemed to be no detectable flaws in his schedule. Then, on the seventh day, Sara saw a possible opening. It was one she never expected.

On Tuesday afternoon, Two-Ton Tony visited his girlfriend. While his two bodyguards waited outside, Tony climbed the stairs of the old two-story apartment building. Moments later, Tony and a frizzy-haired blonde stuck their heads out a window. Tony yelled down for a pack of cigarettes. One of the goons threw a pack up to him. An hour later, Tony hurried out of the building, tucking in his shirt as he got into his car.

Sara carefully cased the building. There was a fire escape in the alleyway on the side of the apartment house. The front door had a buzz-in security system, but it wasn't working, so Sara could just walk in. Leading up to the second floor was a steep staircase at least twenty-five feet long. And at the top of it was a large utility closet. At the bottom of the stairs was a rock-hard tiled floor. Sara had her plan.

The following Tuesday morning, Sara arrived at the apartment house at noon and waited in the utility closet for Two-Ton Tony's arrival. He entered his girlfriend's apartment at two o'clock sharp. Quickly, Sara strung a wire across the top step and went back into the closet, hoping no one else would use the staircase. No one did. Thirty minutes later, Two-Ton Tony hurried out of the apartment, tucking his shirt in over a grossly protuberant gut. He never saw the wire. Two-Ton Tony took a header straight down twenty-five feet. His head bashed into the tiled floor at the bottom of the staircase, with three hundred pounds of fat driving it in. Two-Ton Tony Giamarro was DOL—dead on landing. Sara hurriedly retrieved the wire and went back into the closet until the coast was clear. The next day she collected her ten thousand dollars.

Sara's thoughts came back to the present. She again

wondered about the concern in David's voice. Something was bothering him. It had to be the hit before last, the old guy she'd conked on the head before pushing him into the ocean. No one had seen her—she was sure of that. But then again, how sure could one be? And if someone had seen her, the man's death went from accidental drowning to murder. And that would be bad, very bad. She would have a dissatisfied client who might demand some sort of refund on the $15,000 fee. Sara would hate that. She had already invested the money.

The back door opened. David Westmoreland stepped out and looked up at the gray sky and light drizzle. "It's more mist than rain," he commented.

"It's supposed to get heavy later on," Sara said.

"The plants could use it."

"Yeah."

David lit a cigarette and glanced around the alley, making certain they were alone. "How did it go last night?" he asked, keeping his voice low.

"It was straightforward," Sara told him. "He went down a dark street in a bad neighborhood where they deal a lot of drugs. They'll think an addict killed him for his money."

"You empty his pockets?"

Sara nodded. "I didn't even leave small change."

David handed her a thick manila envelope. "There may be a problem with the guy you iced on that yacht."

Sara's heart skipped a beat, but she kept her expression even. "Like what?"

"Like they're going to do an autopsy on the guy."

Sara shrugged. "They do that routinely in suspected drowning cases."

"Is it routine to have the autopsy done by a renowned forensic pathologist at Memorial Hospital?"

"No," she had to admit. "But that won't change the diagnosis. The guy was holding his head as he went overboard. That meant he had plenty of time to suck seawater into his lungs before he died."

"And that's all they need to prove he drowned?"

Sara nodded again. "That's what the pathology text-book I studied says."

"Well, I hope you're right," David said evenly, but his eyes stayed cold as ice. "Because we don't like screwups, do we?"

"No, we don't."

"I've got another job for you." David pointed to the manila envelope. "The information is in there. It's a doctor. A high-profile hit."

"How high?"

"Big time," David answered. "And it's got to look like an accident. They'll pay twenty grand, but they want it done within a week."

Sara shook her head. "Accidents take time to happen. I'll need a minimum of two weeks."

"There's a five-thousand-dollar bonus if it's done within seven days."

"Do you want it done right or not?"

David thought for a moment and then reached for Sara's empty glass. "Okay. Take your time. But remember: it's high-profile, and the cops will be all over it."

Sara walked away, thinking about the next hit. A doctor. High-profile. *Do your homework*, she reminded herself. *Do it very carefully*.

6

Lori McKay looked down at the face of Oliver Rhodes and studied it. Even in death he appeared aristocratic, with his chiseled features and aquiline nose. And he had so much wealth and power to go along with it. But that was all gone. Oliver Rhodes was just another lifeless body now. He had died slumped over a steering wheel, like her own father had twenty years ago. Lori could barely remember her daddy's voice and touch. It all seemed so long ago.

"Oh-oh!" Joanna said, holding up the lungs she had just resected from Oliver Rhodes's chest. "Was he a smoker?"

"An ex-smoker," Lori said, and moved in for a closer look. There was a white nodule on the superior aspect of the left lower lobe. It was firm and fixed with scattered hemorrhages on the periphery.

"What do you think?" Joanna asked.

"I'll bet it's malignant."

"And he was an ex-smoker, huh?"

"That's what his records say."

Joanna reexamined the nodule. It was almost certainly a tumor, but there were other possibilities such as a walled-off abscess or foreign body. "Briefly review his medical history for me, would you?"

Lori walked over to a side table and picked up a large file card. "Mr. Rhodes was in perfect health until he had a myocardial infarction two years ago. His angiogram showed so many blocked vessels that bypass surgery was not possible. He suffered from chronic, progressive angina and had trouble walking across the room. A year ago he underwent an experimental coronary artery-cleansing procedure. Do you want details on that?"

"Please," Joanna said, examining the other lobes of the lungs and the pleural membrane that covered them. There were no additional lesions.

Lori went to a second index card. "The cleansing procedure is done by running a catheter from the femoral artery up to the left main coronary. The big blockages are removed by a tiny laser that acts like a Roto-Rooter. Any debris is sucked out with a vacuum. Then they squirt in a lipolytic enzyme that cleans fatty deposits off the walls of the arteries. The results were spectacular. Within a few months he could jog and play tennis on a daily basis."

"Did he have any fever or infections from these procedures?" Joanna asked. "Did he have anything that resembled pneumonia?"

"Nope."

"Were there any episodes of loss of consciousness when he could have aspirated a foreign object?"

Lori shook her head.

"And he never worked around asbestos or anything else that would enhance an ex-smoker's chances of developing lung cancer?"

"There's nothing like that in his records."

Joanna exhaled wearily, trying to think and put the pathologic clues together. But she'd been on her feet for over fourteen hours, and the effect of it was starting to show. "See if you can find somebody to do a frozen section on this pulmonary nodule."

"You want it done *now*?"

"Now."

Lori walked over to a wall phone and began punching in numbers.

Joanna moved around on her feet and tried to get the circulation going. Her fatigue seemed to be increasing by the minute. She had to resist the urge to go directly to the heart, where all the answers lay.

With effort she forced herself to examine the lungs once more.

The door to the special autopsy room opened, and Simon Murdock hurried in.

"Have we got anything yet?" he asked.

"He probably has lung cancer," Joanna said.

"But that didn't kill him, did it?" Murdock asked quickly.

"No. Lung cancer doesn't kill suddenly unless it erodes into a major blood vessel."

Murdock nodded, breathing a sigh of relief. He was sorry that Oliver Rhodes was dead, but he'd be sorrier yet if Rhodes died of anything other than heart disease. It had to be heart disease that caused Oliver's death. That was the condition that needed to be met for the Rhodes family to donate ten million dollars for a new cardiac institute at Memorial. "Have you looked at his heart yet?"

"Not yet," Joanna replied, spreading the lobes of the lungs apart so she could examine the central area where the lymph nodes were located. They weren't enlarged. The cancer probably hadn't spread beyond the nodule.

Murdock glanced up at the wall clock. It was 10:40 P.M. "How much longer?"

"As long as it takes," Joanna said, focusing all of her attention on an area of thickened pleura. It looked like a scar, not a tumor.

"Do I need to remind you that the Rhodes family is waiting?"

"They're going to have to wait a little longer."

Murdock's face tightened. "There would be no delay at all had you not used up the afternoon on police work."

Joanna exhaled heavily. "That was a very important case, Simon."

"Nothing—I repeat—nothing is more important at Memorial than the Rhodes family," Murdock snapped. "Do you understand that?"

Joanna dropped the mass of lung tissue onto the stainless steel table. It landed with a loud thud. She moved in closer to Murdock. "I understand that the Rhodes family has suffered a tragic loss. And I understand that they want the autopsy results as soon as possible. But you and I arguing down here won't get the work done any faster."

"That may be so," Murdock countered. "But I still think your order of priorities is inappropriate. Your police cases should *always* come after your patients from Memorial."

"Not always," Joanna said firmly. "Every now and then there are cases in which the search for evidence can't wait. In some instances the evidence can change or even disappear with time."

"Those must be very rare exceptions."

"Well, a rare exception happened today."

Murdock gave her a long, hard look. "Maybe we should discuss this before the entire department of pathology."

"You just let me know when." Joanna fixed her eyes on Murdock, disliking him even more than usual.

They glared at each other, the tension rising close to the breaking point. Neither blinked or backed down.

Lori McKay watched the confrontation, despising Murdock almost as much as she liked Joanna. He was a bully who seemed to enjoy manipulating people and keeping them under his thumb. And he did it to just about everybody at Memorial except Joanna. She never tolerated his abusive behavior and never backed down.

The wall phone rang. Lori picked it up and spoke briefly; then she called over to Joanna, "It's the pathologist on call. He wants to know if the frozen section can wait until morning."

Murdock asked, "What's this all about?"

"I want a frozen section study done on the pulmonary nodule we found," Joanna explained, regaining her composure. "That way we'll know tonight if Oliver Rhodes had lung cancer."

Murdock looked over to Lori. "You tell that pathologist he'd better get in fast if he values his job."

Lori relayed the message and then returned to the stainless steel autopsy table. She distanced herself from Murdock, fearing the man as much as she disliked him.

"All right," Joanna said, getting back to business, "let's examine the heart."

Murdock put on reading glasses and moved in closer to the autopsy table.

Joanna picked up the heart and carefully studied its size and consistency. It was smaller than she expected and had a healthy red color. There was no evidence of ventricular enlargement or scarring. The anterior surface of the heart glistened in the light. It weighed four hundred grams.

"The heart is usually bigger in someone his age," Joanna commented. "Particularly when there's a history of cardiac disease."

"Don't forget he had his coronary arteries cleaned out," Lori said. "They're like new."

"But this is the heart of an athlete," Joanna went on. "You said he was a jogger. Right?"

Lori nodded. "He ran a couple of miles on an almost daily basis, and he was an avid tennis player, too."

Joanna cut into the wall of the left ventricle and studied the cardiac musculature. "This heart looks like it belongs to someone twenty-five years old."

"A new set of coronary arteries can do wonders," Lori said.

"Maybe," Joanna said, unconvinced. She had done autopsies on patients who had had coronary bypass surgery and died of other causes. Their grafts were still open and had provided excellent coronary blood flow. But their hearts never looked this good.

"Is there any evidence of myocardial infarction?" Murdock asked worriedly.

"Not so far." Joanna sliced open a major coronary artery and studied its interior. There were no fatty deposits or occlusions. "The left main coronary looks very clean."

Murdock groaned to himself. No heart attack, no new institute. "Perhaps one of the other coronaries is blocked."

"Perhaps," Joanna said. But the other coronary arteries appeared to be wide open with not even a hint of blockage. There was no evidence for a myocardial infarction. Joanna began thinking about noncardiac causes of sudden death in a middle-aged man. An acute cerebral hemorrhage topped the list. "Simon, we may have to examine Oliver Rhodes's brain."

"The Rhodes family wants to avoid that," Murdock said. "At the funeral service his body will be viewed."

Joanna shrugged. "We may have no choice but to open his skull."

She went back to the heart and split it apart, exposing the interventricular septum and the endocardial wall. There were postmortem blood clots blocking her view, so she swept them away.

Then she saw it. A large pinkish red mass growing out of the septum. She looked over at Simon Murdock. "Oliver Rhodes did not have a myocardial infarction. But he did have a cardiac-related death."

Murdock's eyes brightened. "Are you *sure*?"

"Take a look at the superior aspect of the interventricular septum."

Joanna spread the heart open again and pointed at the large mass that involved the upper septum and extended down into the endocardial wall. "It's a tumor."

Murdock stared at her quizzically. "Of the *heart*?"

Joanna nodded. "It's rare, but it happens."

Murdock snapped on a pair of latex gloves and felt the firm, fixed mass. "How rare is it?"

"I've been here over ten years, and I've seen only one case."

Lori leaned in for a closer view. "How do you know it's not a metastatic lesion? Maybe it's a metastasis from that pulmonary nodule."

"That's a possibility," Joanna conceded. "But I think it's unlikely for several reasons. First, metastatic lesions to the endocardium are rare, even rarer than primary cardiac malignancies. Secondly, metastases from the lung to the heart are usually the result of direct extension and almost always involve the outer pericardium, not the endocardium. That having been said, the only way to really tell if it's a primary tumor of the heart is by examining it under a microscope."

Lori nodded to herself, thinking aloud. "If it's a primary heart tumor, it'll be a sarcoma. If it's a metastasis from the lung, it'll be a carcinoma."

"Right."

Murdock asked, "Can you tell the difference between the two on frozen section?"

"I would think so," Joanna answered.

Murdock glanced up impatiently at the wall clock. It was eleven. "Where the hell is the on-call pathologist?"

"He should be here in a minute," Lori said. "He lives close by."

Murdock gazed down at the opened chest of Oliver Rhodes. One man's death was another man's gain, he thought. That's the way it always was. Oliver's death would give Memorial a new heart institute—if his death was cardiac related. And it was, according to Joanna Blalock. Murdock wondered how a heart tumor caused someone to die suddenly. Mortimer Rhodes would want to know that, too. "Joanna, how does a tumor like this induce sudden death?"

"By inducing an arrhythmia," Joanna told him. "This tumor has invaded deeply into the interventricular septum where the heart's conduction system is located. All electrical impulses travel from the atria to the ventricles via the septum. If the septum is diseased, such as by an infiltrating tumor, the conduction system goes haywire and you end up with severe cardiac arrhythmias."

Murdock gave the explanation thought as he peeled off his gloves. "Can that be proved here?"

"No," Joanna said. "But it's the most likely sequence of events."

"So there's no doubt in your mind that Oliver's death was cardiac in nature?"

"No doubt at all."

The ventilation system clicked on, and Murdock felt the air stir in the special autopsy room where contaminated cases were done. He leaned against the wall and organized his thoughts. Once the frozen sections confirmed the diagnosis, he would call Mortimer Rhodes. After that, Oliver's body would be meticulously sewn together and sent to the funeral home in the early morning hours. Then a carefully worded statement would be released to the press. There would be no need for Murdock to mention the new institute to Mortimer Rhodes. The old man would bring up the subject himself.

The door opened, and a portly, balding middle-aged man entered. He was wearing a long white laboratory coat over a green scrub suit. His name tag read DENNIS GREEN, M.D.—ASSOCIATE PROFESSOR OF PATHOLOGY.

"Thanks for coming in, Dennis," Joanna said.

"No problem." Green nodded to Joanna and then to Murdock, who didn't bother to nod back. "What have you got?"

"We're doing an autopsy on Oliver Rhodes," Joanna replied. Then she sneezed and reached for a tissue.

Green glanced over at the body, thinking that Oliver Rhodes looked a lot larger in life than in death. He turned his attention back to Joanna. "And?"

"And," Joanna continued, wiping her nose, "he has a pulmonary lesion and a heart lesion that appear to be malignant. We want that confirmed on a frozen section."

Green looked at Joanna strangely. "You called me in to do a frozen section on a dead man who has carcinoma of the lung that metastasized to the heart?"

"It's not so straightforward," Joanna explained. "I think he's got a primary malignancy of the heart."

"Well, well," Green said, becoming interested. "Do you think it's a rhabdomyosarcoma?"

"That would be my guess," Joanna said. "And it may be metastatic to the lung."

"Or the lung may just be a run-of-the-mill carcinoma," Green thought aloud. "He may have two separate cancers."

"Exactly."

Joanna picked up two small bottles containing small fragments of tissue. One was labeled A, the other B. "*A* is the lung; *B* is the heart."

Green took the specimens from her. "I'll be back in a flash."

Murdock waited for Green to leave and then asked Joanna, "Is he as good at this as people say he is?"

"He's the best," Joanna assured him. "The oncology surgeons always ask for him to do their cases."

Murdock stretched his neck, trying to relieve some of the tightness. "Was there a reason you found it necessary to mention the name of Oliver Rhodes to Dr. Green?"

"I wanted him to know why I was dragging him out in the middle of the night to do frozen sections on a corpse."

The cell phone inside Murdock's coat chirped. With a weary sigh, he reached for it. Mortimer Rhodes was on the other end. "Yes, Mortimer. . . . We're almost done, and it seems that Oliver's death was cardiac in nature. . . . Yes, yes. But we are confirming it with microscopic studies at this very moment. . . ."

Joanna gestured to Murdock and softly whispered for him to ask Rhodes if there was any family history of unusual cancers.

"And Mortimer," Murdock continued, "there was one other disturbing finding. It seems that Oliver had a somewhat unusual lung cancer, as well. Is there any history of uncommon cancers in your family? . . . No. I see. Well, we should complete all the studies within the hour. Should I call you back then? . . . As soon as I have the results."

Murdock put the cell phone down and then wavered on his feet for a moment. He steadied himself with a hand on the wall. Slowly he eased himself down onto a metal stool.

Joanna saw the peaked look on his face and hurried over. "Are you all right, Simon?"

"Just a little tired," Murdock said. "It's been a long day."

"For all of us."

Murdock tilted his head back against the cool wall, thinking about the death of his own son and the autopsy they did on the boy. "It's very difficult to talk to a father about the death of his son."

"I know," Joanna said, studying Murdock's heavily lined face. He was in his late sixties but seemed older with his snow-white hair and stooped posture. And like Joanna, he, too, had put in a long fifteen-hour day. Too long, Joanna thought, now wondering why she always seemed to take on more work than she could handle. Three cases at once—Oliver Rhodes, the drowning victim, and the Russian with the dead fetuses—were too much, way too much. She'd be lucky to get home before midnight.

The door swung open, and Dennis Green returned.

"It's straightforward," he announced. "There are two different cancers in Mr. Rhodes. The lung is an adenocarcinoma; the heart, a sarcoma."

Joanna asked, "Was it a rhabdomyosarcoma?"

"Probably," Green replied. "I'll know for sure when we do the routine stains."

Murdock pushed himself up from the stool. "And you believe that caused his death?"

"Oh, yeah," Green said with certainty. "It was a nasty-looking malignancy that extended way into the septum. He died a cardiac death beyond any question."

Joanna shook her head sadly. "And his heart looked so good from the outside, like the heart of an athlete. And his coronary arteries were wide open."

"It's kind of ironic," Lori said, more to herself than

to the others. "He undergoes a risky procedure to clean out his coronary arteries so he'll have a heart that will last for another fifty years. Instead, the organ that was supposed to prolong his life ends up killing him."

Green's eyebrows went up. "He underwent that experimental artery-cleansing procedure? The one where they use the enzyme?"

Joanna nodded. "He had it done a year ago. So what?"

"So he represents the second case of cancer I've seen in this group. That's what."

"Are you telling us that you've seen two sarcomas of the heart in patients who've undergone this procedure?" Joanna asked carefully.

Green thought back and then shook his head. "The first patient had her cerebral arteries cleaned out and later developed an astroblastoma."

"A what?" Murdock asked.

"An astroblastoma," Green answered. "It's a very rare form of brain cancer."

The group went silent, each person lost in his or her own thoughts. The ventilation system overhead clicked off. The air became still.

"We've got trouble here," Joanna said gravely.

"Not necessarily," Murdock said at once. "We have only two cases of cancer occurring in this group."

"Two cases of very rare cancer occurring in a very *small* group," Joanna corrected him. "That's not happenstance, Simon."

"But it doesn't prove cause and effect," Murdock argued.

Joanna ignored him, trying to put the pieces of the puzzle together. Two rare cancers pop up in patients whose only common denominator is that they both had their arteries cleaned. But how could that cause a malignancy? "How many people have had this procedure?"

"The NIH allowed us to do ten patients initially," Murdock replied. "The results were so encouraging, they granted permission for us to include another twenty patients in the study."

Joanna quickly calculated numbers in her head. Of the thirty patients in the artery-cleansing study, two had developed malignancies. A cancer rate of one in fifteen—an astronomical incidence. "You'll have to report this to the NIH, Simon."

"Oh, I will," Murdock said, his mind racing ahead. The NIH would insist that the artery-cleansing study be discontinued until the matter was thoroughly investigated by a scientific committee at Memorial. And the news was certain to be leaked to the press, who would have a field day throwing mud at Memorial. Then there would be the multimillion-dollar lawsuits that were sure to follow. And, until all questions were answered, there would be no new cardiac institute in memory of Oliver Rhodes. The consequences of an adverse finding by the committee would be staggering.

Murdock felt his world crumbling around him. Quickly he gathered himself. The first thing to do was to keep the investigation quiet and in-house.

"The NIH will almost surely ask you to form a committee to investigate," Joanna said, as if she were reading his mind.

"I'm certain they will," Murdock said, now seeing his opening. "And I would like you to head that committee."

"Whoa!" Joanna blurted out. "This is not my area of expertise."

"But you're a very good scientist," Murdock countered, and meant it. Joanna had headed similar committees for Murdock in the past. She was bright and incisive and, most important, she knew how to be discreet. "You'll chair the committee. And you can include Dr. Green here, since you say he's such a fine oncology pathologist."

Dennis Green groaned to himself. The last thing he needed was to sit on another committee, particularly one that would be so time consuming. But he had no choice other than to gracefully accept, if he wanted to stay on Murdock's good side. "I'd be glad to help."

"Do you know anything about the method they use to clean out the arteries?" Joanna asked Green.

He shrugged. "Damn little. But I think they remove the blockage with a laser, then add an enzyme to clean the fatty deposits of the artery walls."

"What type of enzyme?"

Green shrugged again. "I think it's a lipolytic enzyme which is produced by gene splicing."

Joanna sighed deeply. She had no laboratory experience with gene splicing. None. It was a subject she'd only read about. From what she could recall, the technique consisted of isolating a segment of a human chromosome that contained the gene responsible for the production of a given protein. The chromosome segment was then inserted into *E. coli* bacteria and became incorporated into the microorganism's DNA. The bacteria would then begin producing the human protein in quantity. Human insulin was now being made this way and was commercially available.

Joanna sighed again, unhappy with the position she'd been placed in. Her knowledge of gene splicing was little more than rudimentary. "I'm really not qualified to head this committee, Simon."

"Yes, you are," Murdock insisted. "And I know you'll do a fine job for us. Now, I want you to pick your people carefully and keep the committee small. I want everything kept under wraps until the findings are in."

Joanna sighed once more and gave in. "I'll need an expert in tumor induction and another in biogenetics."

"Fine," Murdock said agreeably. "But I want them to be from Memorial, and I want to talk with both before you give them any details."

"You won't be able to keep this quiet, Simon," Joanna told him. "Sooner or later the news will surely leak out."

"We'll see," Murdock said, and hurried for the door.

7

Jake and Lou Farelli entered the mini mart in south Santa Monica. The store was empty except for the cashier behind the counter. Jake opened his notepad and studied it. The cashier's name was Freddie Foster. He had been on duty the night the Russian was murdered.

Farelli leaned over to Jake and said in a low voice, "The cashier looks like death warmed over."

"The flu will do that to you," Jake commented.

"Let's hope it didn't affect his brain."

They walked over to the counter and flashed their badges. Up close, Freddie Foster looked even sicker. His face was pale, and he was sweating through the front of his Santa Monica College T-shirt.

"Do you want to sit down?" Jake asked the young cashier.

"I'll be okay," Freddie said. "But I'd sure like to get rid of this virus."

"Bad, huh?"

Freddie coughed and swallowed back phlegm. "I couldn't even walk across the bedroom. I swear to God, it was like a truck hit me."

Jake began flipping through pages in his notepad. "Freddie, we've been trying to reach you for the past couple of days, but you weren't at your apartment. Most sick people stay home."

"I did," Freddie said at once. "I went to my mom's house in the Valley."

Jake nodded and briefly studied the young cashier. The kid was thin, in his early twenties, with long brown hair and silver earrings. "You work here every night?"

Freddie nodded back. "From four to eleven."

"And you were here Monday?"

"Right."

Jake showed the cashier a Polaroid photograph of the dead man found at the bottom of the excavation site. "Do you recognize him?"

Freddie peered at the photograph. "The top of his head looks funny."

"That happens when somebody puts two slugs into it."

Freddie continued to stare at the picture. "His face is kind of familiar, but I can't place it."

The front door swung open, and two Hispanic gang-bangers walked in. They were heavily muscled and wore tight-fitting white T-shirts. Their arms and necks were covered with tattoos. "Hey," the older one yelled out. "Where's your beer?"

Lou Farelli turned to the pair. "He's busy. You're going to have to wait."

"Yeah? For how long?"

Farelli gave the pair an icy stare. "It might be best for you two assholes to come back later."

It took the gangbangers a moment to realize they were facing a cop. "Yeah, yeah," the older one muttered. "We'll be back later."

Farelli watched the pair leave and then turned back to the cashier. "You get that kind in here a lot?"

"All the time," Freddie said.

"Do they pay in cash or credit cards?"

"Always in cash," Freddie answered. "They don't buy that much. Usually beer and chips and stuff like that."

"If they start using credit cards, particularly ones that have funny-sounding European names, you let us know."

Jake grinned to himself. He hadn't thought of that. The Hispanic gangbangers were probably stupid enough to use a credit card with a Russian-sounding name on it. He looked back at the cashier. "So you can't place this guy?"

Freddie studied the photograph again. "I think I served him in here, but I can't be sure."

"What if I told you he had metal teeth and a tattoo of a cross on his forearm?"

Freddie quickly tapped the photograph with his index finger. "Yeah. That's him. I served him in here."

"When?"

"At least three or four times."

"Do you remember the last time?"

"Monday night," Freddie said promptly. "It was late, like after eight."

"What'd he buy?"

Freddie wrinkled his brow, concentrating. "I don't remember."

Farelli asked, "Was he carrying anything?"

"A shoe box," Freddie recalled. "He always had a damn shoe box under his arm."

"Did you get a look inside the box?"

"Nah. It had a lid on it."

"Did he ever take the lid off?"

Freddie thought back. "Once, that I can remember. But he did it by the door. And then he did something real strange."

"What?" Farelli and Jake asked almost simultaneously.

"He sprayed some breath freshener into the box," Freddie told them. "I don't know what that was all about."

I do, Jake was thinking. The guy wanted to cover up the smell of formaldehyde that had leaked out into the shoe box. That's why Joanna couldn't detect the formaldehyde right away. It was an odor she would ordinarily have picked up instantly. But it was covered over with some sort of breath spray. "Did the guy always pay in cash?"

"As far as I remember."

"Did he ever use a credit card?"

Freddie shook his head. "He wasn't the credit card type."

"Was he a loner?"

"He always came in here alone."

"Did he ever mention his name?"

"Not to me."

"Shit," Jake growled softly. They still didn't have a name for the victim, and without a name they'd never identify him. His fingerprints had turned up nothing, and no one had inquired about him at Missing Persons. "Did he ever have other packages under his arm? You know, like things he might have bought in the neighborhood?"

"I never saw him with anything like that."

Jake rubbed at the stubble on his chin, trying to get a handle on the man's identity. Outside the store, a car was pulling up. An elderly lady was driving. Jake turned back to the cashier. "Did this guy have a car?"

"I don't think so," Freddie said, and then added, "I sure as hell hope he wasn't driving."

"Why?"

"Because he was always loaded when he came in here."

Jake leaned forward. "Was he fall-down drunk?"

"No. But he was pretty boozed up. You know, enough to slur his words and stagger some."

"How many bars are in this neighborhood?" Jake asked at once.

Freddie considered the question at length. "There's at least a half-dozen. Just about all of them are south of here."

"What's the closest?"

"A bar called Sully's."

Jake and Farelli left the mini mart. It was seven-thirty, and the night was already pitch-black. Traffic on Lincoln Boulevard was heavy.

"Do you want to take the car?" Farelli asked.

"No," Jake said. "Let's walk it, the same way the victim did."

They headed south, passing a quick-oil-change facility and a used-furniture store. Both were closed. Next
they came to a doughnut shop with its door open. A
sweet, mouthwatering aroma drifted out to the sidewalk. Inside, customers were lined up. The detectives
walked on, coming to a restaurant called Morocco.
They peered in the window. The restaurant was small,
with all of its cloth-covered tables occupied. Off to
the side was an empty bar.

"What do you think?" Farelli asked.

Jake shook his head. "A real boozer is not going
to come in here. The drinks would be expensive."

"Yeah," Farelli agreed. "But let me check it out,
anyway."

Jake lit a cigarette and waited outside while Farelli
went inside to question the bartender. He blew smoke
into the night air, again trying to fit the pieces of this
strange puzzle together. *A drunk carries around dead
babies in bottles so he can bury them. And then he gets
his head blown off and his body is dumped into a pit
next to the babies. Go figure.* It just didn't make sense.

Farelli came out of the restaurant. "No luck."

Jake and Farelli crossed the street in traffic, ignoring
the horns and angry shouts of the passing motorists.
They strolled down a half block and came to Sully's.
Its neon sign was blinking intermittently. One of the
*L*s was dead.

They entered the bar and quickly scanned the clien-
tele before nodding to each other. This was the sort
of bar they were looking for. The customers were all
blue-collar workers, most of them standing with drinks
in their hands and talking too loud. At the bar were
the heavy-drinking regulars.

Jake led the way over to the bartender and flashed
his shield. "We need some information."

"About what?" the bartender asked as he continued
to dry a glass with a dirty towel.

Jake showed him the Polaroid snapshot. "You know
this guy?"

The bartender glanced at the photo briefly. "Sure. That's the Russian."

"Did he come in often?"

The bartender nodded. "Maybe two or three times a week."

"Was he a longtime customer?"

"Nope. He just started coming in about a month ago."

Jake did some rapid calculations in his head. Two to three visits a week for a month came to a total of eight to twelve visits. That averaged out to ten visits and that's how many dead fetuses were found so far. "You know the guy's name?"

The bartender shook his head. "He never mentioned it."

Jake could sense the eyes of the customers on him. He looked over at them. They quickly looked away. Jake came back to the bartender. "Did he ever drink with the guys?"

"No," the bartender said definitely. "He was always at the bar."

"Along with his goddamn shoe box," croaked an old woman with too much makeup on her face.

Jake turned to the woman. "Did you ever look in the shoe box?"

"I tried once, but he grabbed my wrist so hard he damn near broke it. I dropped the lid back on the box real quick."

"Did you smell it?"

The woman looked at Jake oddly. "Did I *what*?"

Jake rephrased the question. "Did you ever detect a funny smell coming from the box?"

"No."

"I did once," an old man next to the woman said. "It kind of smelled like bad vinegar."

"Did he ever tell you his name?"

"I never asked," the old man said, and went back to his drink.

The old woman said, "I called him Doubles."

"Why?" Jake asked.

"Because that's what he drank."

The old man looked up from his bourbon once again. "You know, once I think he called himself Blahdie. He was getting ready to leave one night, and he said something like, 'That's enough for old Blahdie.'"

"Spell it for me," Jake requested.

The old man shrugged. "Shit! I can hardly say it."

Jake made a mental note to return to the bar at an earlier time in the evening when the old man wouldn't be boozed up. Maybe he'd remember more about the Russian's name. *Blah-dee*, Jake thought phonetically, wondering if it was a nickname.

Jake turned back to the bartender. "When was the last time you saw the Russian?"

The bartender thought for a moment. "Monday night, I guess."

"What time?"

"His usual time. He came in about seven-thirty and left around nine."

"Did you notice anything unusual?"

"Nope."

"So he just drank and kept pretty much to himself, huh?"

"Right."

"Don't forget the blonde," the old woman chimed in.

Jake quickly looked back and forth between the old woman and the bartender. "What blonde?"

"Oh, yeah," the bartender said, nodding, now remembering. "This broad comes in about eight-thirty. Blonde. High class. Looks like money. She sits at the bar and orders a white wine, which she doesn't drink. Then she makes a play for the Russian. She buys him a couple of rounds. They talk real low, but everybody knows what's happening." The bartender picked up an olive from a tray and chewed on it. "She was looking for some action."

Jake leaned in closer. "Was she a hooker?"

"I don't think so," the bartender said at once. "She

was more like the Beverly Hills type. And besides, hookers don't buy their johns drinks."

"So," Jake concluded, "you figure she was out looking for some excitement. Maybe a quick bang; then she goes home to her husband."

"That's how I figured it."

"Can you describe her?"

The bartender stared up at the ceiling, thinking back. "Long blond hair. Thin. Attractive, but nothing special."

"Anything unusual about her facial features?"

"Naw. Of course, I was real busy so I didn't get that good of a look."

"Had she ever been in here before?"

"No."

Jake tapped his finger on the bar, digesting and assimilating the new information. "Did the Russian and the blonde leave together?"

"Yes and no."

"What the hell does that mean?" Jake snapped.

"It means he left first," the bartender explained. "A minute later she went to the phone and made a call, all the while peeping out the window. Then she hurries back to the bar, plunks down a twenty for a twelve-dollar tab, and hauls her little ass out of here."

Jake nodded. "You think he was waiting for her outside?"

"That's what I figure."

"And they left separately for appearance's sake?"

"I guess."

"But you don't know?"

"Sure, I do," the bartender said, and smiled thinly. "I heard them set the price. A hundred and twenty-five bucks."

"But you told me she wasn't a hooker."

"She wasn't," the bartender said. "She was going to pay *him*."

"The whole world is fucked up," the old woman complained. "Now girls are paying guys for it. Jesus Christ!" She held up her glass. "Hit me again."

Jake watched the bartender pour and asked, "Which way did they go when they left?"

"I don't know."

"Maybe they went to the doughnut shop across the street," the old man suggested. "I seen the Russian in there a lot."

Jake handed the bartender his card. "If that blonde comes back in, you call me pronto."

Outside, the night was becoming misty and colder. Traffic was less heavy on the boulevard. Jake lit a cigarette and tried to fit the pieces of information together. "Assuming the two met after they left, why did the Russian go to the mini mart to buy a candy bar? Remember, he left the bar around nine and bought the candy bar at nine-o-five. A man who's about to get laid and get paid a hundred and twenty-five dollars for it doesn't go to buy a candy bar first, does he? And if by chance he does, where the hell is the blonde?"

"Maybe they were going to meet at the store," Farelli theorized.

"Are you saying he first strolled down a dark street, nibbling on a candy bar and heading for an excavation site where he's going to bury a baby?" Jake asked, shaking his head. "Uh-uh. That doesn't work. He'd bang her first, get his money, then take care of his other business. Keep in mind, he's not in any hurry to bury the baby."

"And she's not going to follow him down a dark street like that, either," Farelli said. "Even if she was in her car."

"And he wouldn't want her to," Jake picked up the scenario. "He doesn't want her to see him kick a hole in the fence and go down into the excavation site." He shook his head in disgust. "None of this shit fits."

"Maybe the blonde chickened out and decided to go home after she left the bar."

"That's a possibility," Jake said, but he didn't think so. She'd gone to too much trouble to set it up, and she'd handled it like someone who had done it before.

"Let's check the doughnut shop before we call it a night."

They crossed the street and entered the small, empty doughnut shop. A middle-aged Asian American woman bowed to them politely. "May I help you?"

Jake showed the woman his shield and then the photograph of the Russian. "Do you know this man?"

"Oh, yes," the woman said at once. "He comes in often for chocolate doughnuts."

"And I'll bet he comes in two or three times a week."

"Exactly."

"For the past month or so. Right?"

"Oh, no," the woman told him. "He has been a valued customer for over a year."

Bingo! Jake nodded to himself. The man lived or worked in the neighborhood. "Do you remember his name?"

"He never told me."

"Do you have any idea where he lives?"

The woman thought for a moment before saying, "Not too far away, I think. On several occasions I have seen him carrying a large bag of groceries."

"At night?"

"Usually," the woman replied. "But sometimes in the afternoon."

"When was the last time you saw him?"

"It's been almost a week now, which is very unusual for him."

"Thanks for your help."

Walking back to their car, Jake told Farelli, "He lived in the neighborhood. That's for damn sure."

"Yeah," Farelli agreed. "With him carrying a big bag of groceries home, I'd bet he didn't live more than five or six blocks away."

"Could be as much as eight blocks," Jake said thoughtfully. "He was a big, strong guy."

Farelli jotted down a reminder in his notepad to check out every house and apartment within an eight-block radius. And if nobody could ID the victim, they'd have to extend the radius to ten blocks. A shit-load of work that would take weeks to complete.

"Don't forget to check the grocery stores and any other places he might have used a credit card."

"Right," Farelli said, still writing.

"And we've got to look into all the bars to see if the blonde made any pickups elsewhere," Jake went on. "And we have to talk to all the motel managers in the area, too."

Farelli looked up. "You figure the blonde is important here?"

Jake nodded slowly. "If our thinking is correct, she may have been the last person to have seen the Russian alive."

"And she might know his name."

"That, too."

8

"Are you certain about the histology of these tumors?" asked Wallace Hoddings, the director of the Biogenetics Institute at Memorial.

"There's no doubt," Joanna told him. "One is a rhabdomyosarcoma of the heart, the other an astroblastoma of the brain."

"Such rare and different forms of cancer," Hoddings pondered. "It seems so unlikely that they could somehow be associated with one another."

"But malignancy is malignancy," Joanna argued, "no matter what name you give to it. And we have two malignancies occurring in a very small group of patients."

"And their only common denominator is that both patients underwent the artery-cleansing procedure. Correct?"

"Correct," Joanna said. "And for obvious reasons we need to establish whether there is cause and effect here. Can you help us?"

"I can try."

With an effort Hoddings pushed himself up from his swivel chair. He was a big, heavyset man with jowly features and disheveled gray hair. His most prominent feature, however, was his large head which had a bulging frontal area, as if his brain were too big for his skull. And that may well have been the case, because Wallace Hoddings bordered on genius. He was a pioneer in gene splicing and was said to have narrowly missed winning the Nobel Prize for his work in that area. But the prize might come to him yet.

Hoddings was also an expert in environmentally induced tumors, particularly those in which some agent caused chromosomal mutations that led to cancer. He fit perfectly into Joanna's committee. Hoddings not only knew all about gene splicing, he was also a renowned authority on tumor induction.

Hoddings walked over to a computer in the corner of his office and began punching buttons on the keyboard. "Come on over and take a look, Joanna."

Joanna sat beside him as he pushed the ENTER button. The computer screen lit up instantly and began listing agents associated with various malignancies. It was like someone flipping through the pages of a large book. The computer flashed from one list to the next. The columns of agents seemed endless.

"What we're looking at now," Hoddings said, absently reaching for his pipe, "are all the definite and probable carcinogenic agents known to man."

"Lord!" Joanna said softly. "The list must be in the thousands."

"Perhaps we can narrow it down."

Hoddings punched in another set of instructions. "Let's see if there are any environmental enzymes that are known to induce cancer."

The computer screen blinked and flashed up numbers and names almost too rapidly for the eye to follow. The screen went blank and then spelled out its message.

NO ASSOCIATION FOUND

Hoddings leaned back in his chair. "That's what I was afraid of. There are no enzymes that have ever been shown to induce cancer."

"But this is a new enzyme," Joanna countered.

"Not really," Hoddings said. "From what I understand, the enzyme used to clean arteries is a form of lipase, which is as old as mankind itself."

Joanna tried to think through the problem, wondering if the enzyme wasn't the culprit at all. "Could there be some contaminant in the enzyme preparation used in the procedure?"

"I can't answer that," Hoddings said. "But I know someone who can."

"Who's that?"

"Eric Brennerman."

Joanna squinted an eye. "I thought he left Memorial to start his own biotech company."

"He did start his own biotech company, and it's done wonderfully well. But he never really left Memorial."

Joanna stared at Hoddings, surprised at what she'd just heard. There was supposedly an ironclad rule at Memorial that forbade any faculty member from owning a for-profit medical research corporation. "And how did Brennerman manage to pull that off?"

"He and Simon Murdock worked out an arrangement that benefited both Eric and Memorial." Hoddings reached for the phone. "Let's see if he is in his laboratory."

Joanna leaned back in her chair, nodding to herself. That was just like Simon Murdock. He'd sell out to anyone and break his own rules if there was enough money in it for Memorial. She wondered what the payoff was. It had to be in the millions if Brennerman's Bio-Med Corporation was as profitable as everyone thought it was.

Hoddings placed the phone down. "He'll be with us shortly."

"May I ask about the arrangement Eric has with Memorial?"

Hodding's face closed. "I really don't know that much about the details."

Oh, but I'll bet you do, Joanna wanted to say. You know every detail, including the dollar amount that came from Bio-Med to Memorial and how much of that ended up in the coffers of the Biogenetics Institute. "Let me tell you why I'm interested," she said. "As you may know, I do a lot of consulting work outside of Memorial."

"I'm aware of that," Hoddings said, carefully lighting his pipe.

"And I've been giving a lot of thought to opening a private office," Joanna went on. "But I was always under the impression I'd have to leave Memorial to do it. Now it seems as if that may not be so." She quickly held up her hand. "I hope you'll keep what I'm telling you in confidence."

"Of course," Hoddings said earnestly.

Bullshit, Joanna thought. Hoddings and Murdock were close, and within the hour they would be talking on the phone. Which was fine with Joanna. It would make Murdock think twice before he imposed any more unreasonable demands on her. "So anything you could tell me about Eric's arrangement might be very helpful."

Hoddings shrugged. "I don't know all the details of their arrangement, but I could give you a broad outline, if you'd like."

"That would be great," Joanna said appreciatively.

"Let me start from the beginning. That way you'll understand why the arrangement was made."

Hoddings puffed on his pipe as he told the story. Eric Brennerman began his career at Memorial ten years ago as a postdoctoral research fellow in Hoddings's laboratory. He was a genius right out of the gate, with a unique insight into gene splicing. It seemed as if he made an important discovery every month, and his work was published by the very best scientific journals. Brennerman was given a faculty position after only one year at Memorial. His star shone brighter and brighter. He became a world expert in transspecies gene splicing and was one of the first to show that the vitamin A–producing gene in a daffodil could be inserted into a rice plant with the end result being a type of rice with very high levels of vitamin A. Brennerman's research led to over a dozen patents involving genetically modified foods, and both he and Memorial received handsome royalties from agricultural conglomerates eager to buy their patents.

But Brennerman's main interest was atherosclerosis, the deadly process that lays down plaques in arteries, occluding them and leading to heart attacks and strokes. And his intense interest in this disease process wasn't just a case of scientific curiosity. He was trying to save his own life. His father and brother had died of heart attacks in their mid-forties. His mother dropped dead of a stroke on her forty-sixth birthday. In his family, atherosclerosis was rampant. Very few people lived beyond the age of fifty. Brennerman was already forty-five.

It was as if Brennerman were racing with the clock.

"So that's how he came up with the lipolytic enzyme to cleanse arteries," Joanna interjected.

"That's almost another story in itself," Hoddings went on. "But a damn interesting one."

"I'd love to hear it."

Hoddings relighted his pipe before continuing.

Brennerman had found a family living in Santa Barbara that had extremely high levels of cholesterol, yet never suffered heart attacks or strokes. He surmised that the family must have some genetic factor—perhaps an enzyme—that prevented plaque formation and protected the family members. So he began studying the genes in that family, looking for the magical factor. He worked in his lab seven days a week, sometimes even sleeping on a cot in his office. He skipped lectures and meetings so he could spend every sparc moment looking for this factor. Finally he requested that he be relieved of all teaching and administrative duties so he could concentrate solely on his research.

Simon Murdock refused, not wanting to set a precedent. Brennerman was furious and promptly went out and searched for a venture capitalist who would fund the start-up of a new biotechnology company. He found one and resigned the next day. Murdock quickly backtracked and offered to give Brennerman whatever he wanted. But it was too late.

"So they reached an agreement," Hoddings concluded. "Brennerman was made an adjunct professor of genetics at Memorial and allowed to keep his laboratory, and this permitted him to continue to receive NIH grants. He was also given permission to run his new Bio-Med Corporation, in which he holds a substantial interest. As I understand it, the majority interest belongs to the venture capitalist who put up the initial funding."

"And what does Memorial get out of this?" Joanna asked.

"Royalties on everything that comes out of his lab at Memorial," Hoddings told her. "So far, there are four patents on genetically modified foods which are owned by Bio-Med, but from which we receive royalties."

Joanna nodded, noting the word *we*. Contrary to his earlier statement, Hoddings knew exactly how much money changed hands between Bio-Med and Memorial.

"So," Joanna thought aloud, "for some handsome royalties, Memorial allows Eric Brennerman to use its name and laboratories, and of course he can also do his clinical trials here—as he did with the arterial cleansing procedure."

"Precisely," Hoddings said. "In these days of tight money for medical research, Memorial is like all the other medical centers. We have to scratch and claw for every nickel."

"Scratch and claw," Joanna repeated agreeably. But she was thinking that Murdock and Hoddings had sold out for a price.

"Did Brennerman discover his magic enzyme here or at Bio-Med?"

"At Bio-Med," Hoddings replied. "But it's not quite as magical as people make it out to be."

Joanna leaned forward. "What do you mean?"

The intercom on Hoddings's desk buzzed. It was his secretary informing him that Brennerman would be tied up with an experiment for another twenty minutes.

Hoddings pushed his chair back. "Twenty minutes to Eric can turn out to be two hours. We'd better go see him."

They walked out of Hoddings's office and down a long corridor that was lined with laboratories. Most of the doors were closed and unmarked, although some had warning signs indicating the presence of biohazardous materials. Over the entrance to one laboratory was a flashing red light and a sign that read:

EXPERIMENT IN PROGRESS
DO NOT ENTER

Joanna turned to Hoddings and picked up the conversation where they'd left off. "You mentioned that the arterial cleansing agent wasn't quite as wonderful as people had thought. Is there something amiss with it?"

"No," Hoddings said at once. "It's just not as potent as we'd like. Unfortunately, it doesn't work on old, hardened plaques. That's why they use a laser to clean out the hard material first."

"Do you think there'll ever be an agent which will clean out the walls of all arteries, regardless of the types of deposits?"

"We're working on it."

"So, with one injection, your arteries would be clean as a whistle." Joanna marveled at the thought. It would make myocardial infarction a disease of the past. "Do you think one shot would do it?"

"Who said anything about a shot?"

Joanna's eyes widened. "Are you talking about a pill?"

"We're working on that, too."

They came to a closed set of double doors at the end of the corridor. On one door was a sign reading LABORATORY FOR BIOGENETIC RESEARCH, on the other the name ERIC BRENNERMAN, M.D., PH.D.

Hoddings led the way inside. It was a huge laboratory, measuring five thousand square feet, with walk-in, glass-enclosed cubicles lining the walls. In the center of the room were workbenches with sophisticated equipment atop them. A skylight overhead let in natural light.

Hoddings took Joanna's arm and guided her past a glass cubicle where a technician was tending to a grossly deformed rat. Joanna paused to study the animal more closely. There was a rounded object protruding out from under the skin on the rat's back. It took her a moment to realize what it was. "Is that a human ear growing out of that rat?"

"Yes," Hoddings said, watching the animal jump around. It seemed oblivious to the growth on its back. "And it's coming along rather well, don't you think?"

"Why doesn't the rat reject the human ear?" Joanna asked.

"Because the inner part of the ear is a flexible form of plastic," Hoddings explained. "It's covered, however, with skin cells from a human."

Joanna scratched her neck, still not understanding. "But why doesn't the rat reject the human skin cells?"

"Because the rat has been genetically altered so that its immune system believes that those human skin cells are its own."

"I take it that those skin cells belong to a patient?"

Hoddings nodded. "To a young girl whose ear was chewed off by a pit bull."

Joanna grimaced as she envisioned the young girl's mangled ear and the heartache and pain it must have caused. She pointed to the animal inside the cubicle. "And the ear growing there will be removed from the rat and then surgically attached onto the young girl?"

"That's our plan."

They moved on to the next cubicle. It was climate controlled and contained patches of growing plants and vegetables. The tomatoes were large and juicy and bright red. Stalks of corn were eight feet tall and glistened in the natural light coming from above.

"And here we have problems to be solved," Hoddings said.

"But everything looks so fresh and delicious," Joanna commented.

"Looks can be deceiving." Hoddings pointed to the ripe tomatoes. "Those tomatoes have been genetically modified so they contain thirty percent more flesh and thirty percent less fiber. And they can last on the shelves in food stores for days longer than ordinary tomatoes."

"So what's the problem?"

"They've lost their taste and we have to find out why."

Hoddings peered over at the corn, his head moving up and down as if he were measuring the stalks. "And the corn presents an even greater problem. These plants were genetically altered by a Midwestern university so they would resist various pests. In essence, a piece of DNA was inserted into them and this instructs the plant to make its own pesticide. That way farmers would no longer have to spray. And it worked fine. But unfortunately the corn's inborn pesticide killed more than pests. It killed butterflies and caterpillars and other lower forms of life."

Hoddings took a deep breath and exhaled loudly. "And what kills them can eventually affect us."

"Has this genetically modified corn already been commercially planted? I mean, is it in widespread use?"

"You don't want to know the answer to that."

They approached the back of the laboratory where Eric Brennerman was conducting an experiment. Blood was being pumped through a long, slender glass tube and then through coils before emptying into a large flask. The blood flowed into the flask and sat there a moment; then it was pumped out again into another glass tube that curved around and connected to the front tube, forming a closed circuit system. Brennerman watched the blood moving in a smooth, even fashion. He seemed pleased.

Hoddings cleared his throat audibly.

Brennerman looked over and waved. "I'll be with you in a second."

Abruptly, Brennerman turned off the pump in his

experiment. The flow stopped. The blood remained stationary in the tubes. Brennerman watched the clock on the wall. Thirty seconds passed. Then a minute. Then two minutes. He started the pump again and the blood moved smoothly. No clots had been formed.

Brennerman gave some instructions to a nearby technician and then walked over. He was a well-built, handsome man with a strong jawline and dark hair that was slicked back and held in place by some sort of gel.

"Hey, Joanna," Brennerman said genially. "What brings you to Fantasyland?"

Hoddings's face tightened at the word *Fantasyland*.

"Business," Joanna said. "I need some information from you."

"You got it."

Joanna motioned over to the experiment Brennerman had just completed. "Is that blood in those glass tubes?"

"Yes."

"Then why didn't it clot when you stopped the pump?"

"Because it contains an anticoagulant," he explained.

"Is there anything unusual about the anticoagulant?"

"It might be heparin."

Joanna's eyes widened. "Have you discovered the gene that produces heparin?"

"Could be," Brennerman said vaguely, not wanting to give out too much information.

Joanna glanced back at the blood in the glass tubing. Heparin was an excellent, widely used anticoagulant whose chemical formula was so complex it had never been synthesized. All heparin now used in patients was extracted from porcine intestines. If Brennerman had discovered the gene that coded out for heparin, it was worth billions of dollars. She wondered when his company would go public.

"Tell me about this information you need," Brennerman broke into her thoughts.

"Perhaps we'd better talk in your office."

They walked across the spacious laboratory and entered a small, cluttered office. Shelves on the wall were packed with books and journals and scientific manuscripts. On the floor were stacks of computer printouts.

Brennerman plopped down in a swivel chair behind his desk and gestured to two director's chairs across from him. He waited for Joanna and Hoddings to be seated. "What can I do for you?"

"I need information on your artery-cleansing agent," Joanna said.

"Anything in particular?" Brennerman asked.

"I need to know what's in the solution that's injected into patients."

"The purified enzyme and a preservative," Brennerman said carefully. "Why?"

"I'll get to that in a moment," Joanna told him. "What's the preservative?"

"Benzyl alcohol." Brennerman looked back and forth between Joanna and Hoddings. "What is this all about?"

"Two of the patients who underwent the artery-cleansing procedure have developed cancer," Joanna said straightforwardly.

Brennerman's jaw dropped. "What!"

"Two of the thirty subjects in the study have come down with malignancies," Joanna went on. "One patient had a rhabdomyosarcoma, the other an astroblastoma."

Brennerman rocked back in his swivel chair, stunned by the news. "But these cancers are so rare and so different from one another." He rubbed his temples and tried to concentrate. "It's hard for me to envision one enzyme or any other single agent inducing two such diverse cancers."

"We don't know if that's the case here," Joanna said. "But we have to investigate that possibility."

"Of course. Of course," Brennerman said quickly. "I'll help in any way I can."

Joanna reached into the pocket of her white lab coat for a stack of file cards. "Let's begin with the composition of the artery-cleansing solution. Are you certain it contained only the lipolytic enzyme and a preservative?"

"Absolutely," Brennerman answered firmly. "We checked each batch a dozen ways for purity. There were no contaminants present."

"Do you have samples from all the batches which have been used in patients?"

"We do."

"And you'd have no objection to our retesting those batches for purity?"

"None whatsoever."

Joanna went to the next card. "Are the batches of the purified enzyme all made here at Memorial?"

"No. They're produced at our plant outside Lancaster."

Joanna looked up from her card. "In the desert?"

Brennerman nodded. "The land was cheap and security was easy to maintain. But now we're in the process of building a plant in Thousand Oaks."

"Doesn't Amgen have a plant out there?" Joanna was referring to Amgen, Inc., one of the world's largest and most profitable biotechnology companies.

Brennerman smiled without humor. "Yeah. We want them to see us coming."

Joanna glanced down at her file card and asked, "Once the solutions of enzymes are shown to be pure, what happens next?"

"They're frozen away until used."

"How are they transported from Lancaster to Memorial?"

"By helicopter," Brennerman replied. "It's brought into Memorial by either me or my associate, and it's always hand-carried. The frozen solutions are thawed just prior to being injected into patients."

"Who is this associate you mentioned?"

"Dr. Alex Mirren. He's a senior research scientist at Bio-Med."

"He's also an adjunct professor of genetics at Memorial," Hoddings added.

Joanna jotted down the information. "Is he also involved in the production of the lipolytic enzyme?"

Brennerman nodded. "Absolutely."

"So," Joanna said, mentally tracking the lipolytic enzyme from production to injection into the patient. "The solution arrives at Memorial and is hand-carried to the facility where the artery-cleansing procedure is done?"

Brennerman nodded again.

"Who does the actual procedure?"

"Either a cardiologist or radiologist, depending on which arteries we're injecting."

"Are you or your associate there for the entire procedure?"

"Every second of it."

Joanna went to her final file card. "Before the enzyme was used in humans, I take it that it was extensively tested in experimental animals?"

"Man, oh, man!" Brennerman said, sighing heavily. "We tested it in God knows how many dogs and rats and rabbits. We even used monkeys, which cost us a fortune. We never saw one adverse effect."

"Were their hearts and brains studied?"

Brennerman hesitated. "I think representative studies were done."

"But you don't know how many hearts and brains from those animals were viewed under the microscope?"

"I'd have to check the lab data books."

Joanna pushed her chair back. "I'm going to have to visit your plant out in Lancaster."

"Any time."

"Tomorrow is Friday," Joanna said, thinking about her full schedule for the next day and the day after that. "We'd better make it Monday morning."

"Is there anything in particular you'll want to see?"

"I want to look at all the microscopic slides on the experimental animals that received injections of the lipolytic enzyme."

"You're talking about thousands and thousands of slides," Brennerman said. "You might want to limit yourself to slides of the animals' brains and hearts."

"I want all the slides," Joanna told him. "And I want to see all the data books that go with them."

"I'll have everything set out for you Monday morning."

Joanna pushed her chair back and stood. "And, of course, there will be no further clinical trials on the lipolytic enzyme until this matter is settled."

"Of course," Brennerman and Hoddings said at the same time.

"Thanks for your help. I can find my way out."

Joanna walked back across the laboratory to the glass cubicles. She paused to again study the plants they contained. The corn stalks were growing so tall and looked so green and healthy in the natural light. Yet if their husks were stripped away, one would find ears of corn producing their own pesticide that killed not only pests, but other forms of life, as well. And someday it might also harm humans. After all, it was a pesticide and people would be eating it. And only God knew what the pesticide might do once it got into the human body.

Joanna wondered if she was looking at a Frankenstein crop—one that had been genetically modified to help man but ended up hurting him. Some scientists considered the idea of a Frankenstein plant paranoid nonsense, but others believed it was just a matter of time before it happened and turned out to be another example of science run amuck.

Joanna sighed to herself, wondering if the two cases of cancer occurring in the artery-cleansing study had been induced by scientists tampering with something without fully realizing all the consequences.

Behind her the door to Brennerman's office slammed shut. Joanna turned and watched Brennerman and

Hoddings arguing heatedly and pointing fingers at each other. She could hear their muffled voices coming through the glass partitions of the office.

Joanna left the laboratory, thinking that there was going to be a lot of yelling and finger pointing at Memorial before everything was said and done.

9

With her binoculars Sara Ann Moore carefully studied the parking lot just inside the fence surrounding the Bio-Med Corporation. The target's car was still there. It hadn't moved since 8 A.M. Slowly she scanned the ten-foot chain-link fence with barbed wire atop it. The main gate was manned by an armed guard inside a kiosk. And soon, Sara thought, when night came, guards would be patrolling the grounds around the plant. And she had heard guard dogs barking, but hadn't seen them.

"Shit," Sara growled, unhappy with the progress she'd made in setting up the hit. The doctor seemed to spend every waking minute either here at the plant or at Memorial Hospital. He had no outside life. None. And the only reason he went home was to sleep.

Sara lit a cigarette and tried to concentrate on the doctor-scientist she had to kill and make sure the death looked accidental. The hit couldn't be done in the plant because it was too risky trying to get inside. And it couldn't be done at Memorial because the doctor worked in a genetics institute. Where everybody knew everybody, strangers stuck out and were easy to spot. *And besides*, she pondered, *how do you kill somebody accidentally in a genetics lab?*

The guy had no outside life. No girlfriends, no buddies, no hobbies, and no habits she could zero in on. She had been following him for five straight days, and all he did was work and work and work. But she would keep following him, tracking him day and night, looking for the opening she needed. It was there. All she had to do was find it.

Sara opened the window of her rented truck and felt the chilly evening air. She flipped her cigarette out and quickly closed the window. Dusk was falling rapidly, and so was the desert temperature. Sara had on jeans, a sweater, and a woolen coat, but she was still cold. Rubbing her hands together, she hoped she wouldn't have to spend another night on the desert. *Damn this place*, she thought miserably. And damn the isolation and frigid air that came with it.

She was parked at the rear of a huge empty lot across the highway from the Bio-Med plant. Her truck was actually parked on a dirt road at the far northeast corner of the barren lot. Some large boulders and scattered sagebrush in front of her partially concealed her truck from the highway. If anybody asked her why she was there, she would tell them she was a hiker, planning to camp out. In the back of the truck she had the appropriate camping equipment.

She resisted the urge to turn on the heater. That would require starting the engine, and someone on the highway might see the truck's exhaust. *Screw it!* She'd stay cold.

To pass time, Sara turned on her laptop computer and logged onto the Internet to see how her stocks were doing. Pfizer was up a point and going strong since it had announced its plan to merge with Warner Lambert. That stock would stay solid, Sara thought, as long as Pfizer kept making Viagra. Ah, Viagra! The elixir of youth for men, guaranteeing them perpetual erections. And Delta was doing fine, too. The giant airline was gobbling up smaller regional and commuter lines, solidifying its hold on the entire Southeast. Sara decided to buy more Delta with the money she'd receive for the hit on the doctor. And maybe more Pfizer, too.

A pair of headlights came on in the parking lot across the highway. Sara reached for her binoculars. The doctor's car was moving.

Sara turned on the truck's ignition and drove slowly toward the highway, her headlights off.

10

Joanna slumped down wearily onto the metal stool in the special autopsy room. It was eight o'clock and she'd just completed the postmortem examination on the Russian immigrant. They still didn't know the victim's identity, and the autopsy hadn't given any new clues. She glanced at the ten bottles on the shelf, each containing a well-preserved fetus. She wondered if she had enough energy to do a few fetal autopsies before she called it a night. Maybe one, she thought, and pushed herself up from the stool.

The door to the room swung open, and Lori McKay entered. She was wearing a green scrub suit that was stained in front with blood and perspiration.

"How are you doing?" Lori asked.

"I'm running on fumes," Joanna said, and gently stretched her back, trying to ease some of the tightness. "Did you get enough tissue from the drowning victim to make slides?"

Lori nodded. "I think I did for most of the organs, but it wasn't easy. There's so much putrefaction present after a week in the water."

"Did you get enough lung tissue for us to look at under the microscope?"

"More than enough."

"So now all we have to do is find the victim's latest skull X rays."

"I've got them," Lori said. "They're up on the view box in the big autopsy room. And I've got Harry Crowe ready to saw through the guy's skull for us."

Joanna looked over at the preserved fetuses. "Can we wait a while on that?"

"We'd better not," Lori advised. "Harry is already pissing and moaning because he had to stay so late."

They went out and down a long, empty corridor. From behind a closed door they heard Elvis Presley music, followed by high-pitched laughter. Then Elvis came back on.

Lori asked, "Did you find anything in the immigrant from the bottom of the pit?"

Joanna shook her head. "There was nothing new. He had a tattoo of a cross on his arm, a mouthful of metal teeth, and some deep calluses on his hands. He did heavy work, that's for sure." Joanna thought back to the victim's muscular arms and wondered what he had to lift to develop them. "Did we get back the analysis on the material I scraped out of the calluses?"

"It came back this morning, but I don't know how helpful it's going to be." Lori took out a stack of file cards and quickly flipped through them. Then she flipped through them a second time before finding the card she wanted. "They found some unidentifiable threads and some scattered bits of copper in the callus. Some of the copper bits were coated with a plastic-like material."

Joanna concentrated on the findings, wondering if the threads were from gloves the man wore at work. No, she quickly decided. If he had worn gloves he wouldn't have developed calluses. "The copper is the key here. Isolated bits of copper suggest he could have been a plumber or pipe-fitter. They use copper pipes and tubing."

Lori squinted an eye, unconvinced. "He could have worked in a factory, making computer parts or something."

"No, no," Joanna corrected her. "Remember, this man had muscular arms. He did heavy labor. A plumber would fit better here."

"But what about the pieces of copper covered with plastic?"

"That takes us down a different road," Joanna said. "The plastic coating on the bits might represent copper wiring with insulation, and that's something an electrician might use."

"So he could be an electrician or a plumber."

"Or both."

"And they also found grease embedded in his callus," Lori went on, turning the file card over. "You know, like some kind of lubricant."

"Like a mechanic might use?"

Lori shrugged. "I guess."

"So," Joanna concluded, "he could be a plumber or an electrician or a mechanic or a jack-of-all-trades."

"Great," Lori groaned. "That narrows our suspect list down to about a half-million."

They came to the swinging double doors of the main autopsy room. As they pushed their way inside, Joanna said, "Later tonight I'd like you to remove every callus that man has. I want them all analyzed thoroughly. In particular, I need to know the source of that copper. See if they can determine whether it came from wire or pipe. And I want them to define and characterize that grease. We need to know what it's used for."

Lori nodded as she committed the instructions to memory. But she was also thinking that again she'd missed the boat. And again her inexperience had cost her. She had failed to follow one of Joanna Blalock's cardinal rules. Milk every clue for everything it's worth because it may be the only clue you'll find. Lori had accepted the analysis of the callus at face value, not looking beyond the findings and interpreting their full meaning.

"Is anything wrong?" Joanna asked.

"Just trying to get my brain to click on all cylinders."

"You're doing fine."

As they approached a second set of swinging doors, Lori checked the bottom of the index card. "They also detected something interesting in the shoe box found at the crime scene."

"You mean besides formaldehyde?"

"They found two strands of blond hair in that shoe box."

Joanna stopped in her tracks. "From a female?"

"They couldn't tell for certain because the hair was broken off," Lori answered. "But the strands were really long, so they think it came from a female."

"So somebody else had gotten into that shoe box," Joanna deduced.

"Maybe he had a girlfriend."

"The first thing we have to do is establish beyond any doubt that this hair came from a female," Joanna said, her mind racing ahead. "I want you to go over the victim's clothes with a vacuum cleaner. We need some intact strands of blond hair that can be analyzed for gender. And while you're at it, look for anything feminine in his clothing. Things like lipstick or perfume aromas."

"This blonde has got to be involved here, doesn't she?"

"Right up to her teeth."

They pushed on into the main autopsy room. It was deserted except for Harry Crowe, who was standing beside a bloated corpse. He was impatiently tapping his foot.

"Why the hell do I have to wait to open up this guy's skull?" Harry blurted out. "I could have him opened one-two-three. But no! I must wait for you to show me how to do it."

"This is a special case," Joanna said placatingly.

Harry spat something off his tongue. "A corpse is a corpse."

"But this one has a skull fracture that I don't want you to saw through."

Joanna moved over to the X-ray view box on the wall and carefully studied the multiple views of the skull. The skull fracture was now clearly evident. It was located high up on the posterior aspect of the parietal bone near the crown of the head. Using a ruler, Joanna measured the distance between the fracture and the edge of the mastoid bone. Twelve centi-meters. She went over to the corpse and again measured the distance before marking the area of the fracture with a green dye. Well beneath the green spot, she painted on purple dye.

She turned to Harry. "You saw through at the level of the purple dye."

Harry studied the area he was going to incise. "It's too low."

"Do what I tell you."

"Yeah. Right," Harry sneered at her. "And you can be the one to put his face back together afterward."

"Do exactly as I've instructed you," Joanna said slowly and deliberately, trying to control her temper.

Harry Crowe cursed under his breath and reached for the electric saw. Once again he studied the area he'd have to saw through. Too low, he thought, too low. The man's face would end up even more disfig-ured when the top of his skull was replaced and the scalp pulled back over it. But who the hell cared? The guy already looked like a blowfish from spending a week at the bottom of the sea.

Harry tested the edge of the power saw with his thumb, making Joanna wait longer, knowing it would irritate her even more. Finally he switched on the saw. It made a loud, high-pitched noise. He smiled to him-self, pleased with her irritation.

"This guy's skull is tough," Harry said, and feigned pushing down harder on the saw. "It's like steel."

No, it's not, Joanna wanted to say. If anything, the bone would be softer because salt water leeched out calcium. Harry was just prolonging the process to make her wait longer.

Joanna leaned against the wall and briefly studied Harry's features. He was a short, stocky man, totally bald, with thin lips and very dark eyes that looked like BBs. In his case, Joanna thought, appearances weren't deceiving. He looked every bit as mean as he really was.

The screeching noise of the saw abruptly stopped.

Harry worked his fingers between the cut edges of the skull and pulled. The top of the skull came off with a loud pop.

"There," he announced. "You can put his head back together when you're done. I'm out of here."

Lori watched Harry go through the swinging doors, and then she gave him the finger. "What an asshole! I don't understand how you can put up with him."

"He's an asshole, all right," Joanna agreed. "But he's a very competent asshole."

Joanna reached down for the detached upper portion of the skull. "Now let's see if we can piece together the death of Mr. Edmond Rabb."

Lori snapped on a pair of gloves and focused her mind away from Harry Crowe and onto Edmond Rabb. She glanced down at the corpse, thinking that ten days ago Rabb was living the life everybody dreamed of. He had been a venture capitalist worth untold millions who enjoyed the best of everything. Now he was a lump of putrid flesh. She saw Joanna examining the detached piece of skull with a magnifying glass and asked, "Do you see anything?"

Joanna slowly nodded. "A through-and-through fracture of the parietal bone. And there's blood around the site, which means the fracture occurred while he was still alive."

Lori moved in for a closer look. "But that fracture didn't cause his death. Drowning did. Remember, his lungs were filled with froth and mucus, which is characteristic of saltwater submersion."

"I know," Joanna said. "What I'm trying to decipher now is how he got into the salt water to begin with."

Lori shrugged. "He accidentally fell off his yacht."

"Are you sure of that?"

Lori stared at the skull, wondering if Joanna had uncovered some subtle clue that everybody else had missed. But what? Everything pointed to an accidental death. She decided to summarize aloud what she knew about the case. Maybe the clue would pop out. "According to eyewitnesses, he was last seen standing at the rear of his yacht. He was leaning against the railing with a drink in his hand. The sea was calm that night. Approximately ten minutes later he couldn't be found. The assumption was he accidentally fell overboard.

"Why no screams or yells for help?" Joanna asked.

"Maybe he hit his head on the railing as he fell overboard. That would explain the fracture and the absence of any yells for help." Lori nodded to herself. "That would fit."

"No, it wouldn't," Joanna said at once.

"Why not?"

"The position of the skull fracture."

Lori wrinkled her brow, concentrating on the clue. "I'm not sure I follow you."

"When he struck his head, do you think he was falling forward or backward?"

"I'd guess backward, because that's more likely to cause a head injury."

"If that were the case, he would have hit the back of his head and the fracture would have involved the occipital bone—which it didn't," Joanna explained. "And had he fallen forward and struck his head, the fracture would have been in the frontal or temporal area—which it wasn't." Joanna held up the detached piece of skull and pointed to the green dye. "The fracture site was very near the crown."

"How do you think it got there?"

"I think somebody whacked him," Joanna said matter-of-factly. "As a rule of thumb, homicidal skull fractures are almost always located at or near the crown. Victims are usually hit on top of the head, you see. Accidental fractures are located elsewhere."

"That may all be true," Lori agreed reluctantly. "But I think it's going to be impossible to prove that this guy didn't die accidentally."

"Maybe, maybe not," Joanna said, and placed the segment of skull down. "I want you to make sections of the fracture site and the tissue around it. Then have them examined under routine and electron microscopy."

"What are we looking for?"

"Anything that shouldn't be there."

Joanna lifted Edmond Rabb's brain and pulled back the dura mater, exposing a pool of blood in the parietal area. "Jesus! He really got whacked good."

Lori stood on tiptoes and looked over Joanna's shoulder. "A big-ass subdural hematoma."

"Right beneath the fracture site."

"So our man gets conked on the head, which fractures his skull and causes the subdural vessels to rupture," Lori summarized. "Then he's pushed over the side and drowns—and we can't prove a damn thing. In a court of law, his death would still be considered an accidental drowning. Right?"

"I guess," Joanna said wearily, and handed Lori the corpse's brain. "Would you mind weighing the brain and sectioning it for me?"

"Not at all."

Lori expertly sliced the cerebral hemispheres apart and examined their glistening convoluted folds. "A multimillionaire's brain looks the same as everybody else's, doesn't it?"

"Yeah," Joanna said absently, still thinking about the traumatized area on the skull. Rabb was a tall man at six feet two and was struck near the crown of the head. The killer would have to be at least Rabb's height to land that blow. Unless Rabb was leaning over the railing at the time of the attack. Then anyone five feet or taller could have done it. Joanna wondered what type of weapon was used. She heard Lori asking a question. "What was that?"

"Why would somebody want to kill this guy?" Lori asked again, rapidly sectioning the brain.

For money, love, or power, Joanna thought at once. According to Jake Sinclair, those motives accounted for virtually every murder ever committed. And when it came to millionaires, the motive had to be money. "For his millions," Joanna said aloud.

"That would be my guess, too."

Joanna leaned against the wall, so tired she could barely stand. The wall clock said 9:20. The drowning victim would have to be her last case of the day. Her fatigue was growing by the minute, and soon she wouldn't be able to think at all. But her workload was still so stacked up she'd have to work through the weekend just to make a dent in it. The fetuses in the bottles hadn't even been looked at, and pressure for answers was coming from all sides. The police, the news media, church groups. And everybody wanted answers now.

"Done," Lori announced.

Joanna pushed herself away from the wall. "Let's go take a peek at those fetuses."

Lori glanced at the wall clock and gave Joanna an odd look. "You want to start on them now?"

"I only want to take a quick look," Joanna said. "I've got an important meeting tomorrow morning, and I can't just tell them that those fetuses are still in their bottles sitting on a shelf."

"I've never done an autopsy on a tiny fetus," Lori admitted. "How do you do it?"

"With a magnifying glass."

They hurried out of the autopsy room and down the deserted corridor. Everything was dead quiet. There was no music or laughter coming from behind the closed doors. Joanna decided to examine only one fetus. She'd pick the largest because it would be the easiest to do. But she would perform only a gross, cursory examination and look for obvious abnormalities. A more detailed examination would have to wait until tomorrow.

They entered the special autopsy room and went directly to the shelf that held the fetuses. Joanna picked the bottle that held the largest one. It measured about three inches. She carefully opened the bottle and waved her free hand, dispersing the pungent odor of formaldehyde. Using forceps, she gently removed the fetus from its surrounding fluid.

It was well formed with clearly defined hands that had tiny fingers and small feet that had tiny toes. Joanna could easily see its eyes and ears and mouth. There was a deep incision across its chest and abdomen.

"Jesus," Lori breathed. "This is like a horror show."

"I know," Joanna said softly.

"Do you think the cut is the result of an abortion?"

"Could be," Joanna replied. "But the incision is so straight. That's not what we usually see in a D and C. And I see only one cut."

"No, no," Lori said hastily. "There's another cut here atop the head." Lori swallowed hard. "Do you think that a fetus this age could feel anything?"

"I hope not," Joanna said, and reached for a small pair of tweezers. "Let's see how deep these incisions go."

Lori held the fetal limbs stationary while Joanna gently separated the edges of the incision that ran from the abdomen to the upper chest.

Joanna's eyes suddenly widened. "Oh, Lord!"

"What?"

Joanna looked up at Lori with a stunned expression. "This fetus has been eviscerated. Somebody has removed all of its organs."

11

Joanna could hear the rain pounding down on the patio outside her bedroom. In the distance there was a low, continuous rumble of thunder.

She snuggled up to Jake under the blankets. "You know what's strange?"

"What?" Jake asked.

"How one minute you're so tired you can hardly move," she told him. "And an instant later you've got plenty of energy for sex."

"That happens when you shut your brain off."

Joanna smiled. "Do you want to explain that to me?"

"Sure," Jake said easily. "In people like you, who think for a living, fatigue is mostly mental."

Joanna looked at him strangely. "So, if I shut my brain off, the fatigue should magically disappear?"

"Naw," Jake said. "That just pushes the fatigue aside so you can get on with more important things."

Joanna chuckled and moved even closer to Jake. She wished that time would come to a sudden stop and stay frozen in place. If only for a little while.

Outside, lightning cracked and the rain was coming down so hard it caused the sliding-glass door to rattle. Good, Joanna thought, hoping all the streets and roads would flood so badly that everybody would have to stay where they were over the weekend.

Jake's stomach suddenly growled and then growled loudly again.

Joanna looked at him. "I think somebody skipped dinner."

"Busy," Jake said, as if his mind was elsewhere.

"How does chicken pot pie and cold beer sound to you?"

"Like manna from heaven."

They put on terry-cloth robes and left the bedroom. Joanna skipped into the kitchen, humming happily under her breath. Jake went over to the fireplace, where he stoked the fire back to life and added a fresh log. The fire blazed, lighting up the living room.

Jake glanced at the clothes strewn about. On the coffee table were his pants and shorts and holstered weapon, and next to them were Joanna's skirt and blouse. Her bra and panties were on the floor, partially covered by his tie and coat. Jake had been waiting for her at the front door when she arrived home. They barely made it to the bedroom.

"Here you go," Joanna said, and handed him a frosty mug of beer. "My microwave is on the fritz, so I had to put the chicken pot pies in the oven. It's going to take a while."

"No rush," Jake said, and sat down on a bearskin rug in front of the fireplace. He lit a cigarette and inhaled deeply. "Do you want to talk a little murder?"

Joanna quickly sat next to him. "You got something?"

"Bits and pieces," Jake said tonelessly, "that may or may not add up."

Joanna reached for his cigarette and took a puff; then she handed it back. "Tell me what you've got."

"For starters, we think the Russian guy lived in the neighborhood," Jake told her. "The doughnut lady said he came into her shop two or three times a week for over a year, and a couple of times he was carrying a big bag of groceries."

"He doesn't live too far away," Joanna agreed.

"We also know the bar he was in just before he went to the convenience store," Jake continued. "It's a crummy low-class bar with a lot of regulars. They recognized his face, but he always kept to himself, so nobody knew his name."

"Damn," Joanna groaned. "He sounds like a real loner."

"And some," Jake went on. "But on the night he got iced, he was talking to somebody in that bar. He spent some time with a well-dressed woman who had never been in the place before. They left separately, but the bartender was almost certain they met up outside."

"But he doesn't know that for a fact?"

"He's pretty sure," Jake said. "He could tell from the way they left the bar. Bartenders are really good at that. In addition, he heard her propositioning the Russian."

Joanna's brow went up. "*She* did the propositioning?"

"Big time," Jake assured her. "According to the bartender, she offered him a hundred and twenty-five dollars for a bang."

Joanna thought for a moment. "Was this woman a blonde?"

Jake stared at her wide-eyed. "How did you know that?"

"Because we found two long strands of blond hair in the Russian's shoe box."

"Son of a bitch!" Jake jumped to his feet and started pacing the floor, moving articles of clothing aside with his foot. "She was inside that guy's shoe box."

Joanna nodded. "That's for sure."

"And I think she looked in it after she killed him."

Joanna looked at him strangely. "How do you figure all that?"

"Follow me," Jake said, puffing on his cigarette as he thought aloud. "We'll take it step by step. First, the Russian leaves the bar with the shoe box under his arm. She hadn't looked inside it yet. Right?"

"Right."

"Then he walks a half block to the convenience store and buys a candy bar," Jake continued. "The clerk remembers that the Russian was alone. The blonde was nowhere in sight. So far she still hasn't looked in the box."

"Maybe they did a quickie, like in her car."

"I don't think so," Jake said promptly. "There wasn't enough time. The Russian left the bar just before nine. He bought the candy bar at nine-o-five."

"She's following him," Joanna deduced.

"Had to be." Jake nodded and then flicked his cigarette into the fireplace. He started pacing again. "The Russian leaves the convenience store and walks down a dark street. She pops him with two slugs in his head and looks into the shoe box."

"She knew what was in that shoe box all along," Joanna said.

Jake tried to follow Joanna's logic, but couldn't. "What do you base that on?"

"A number of things," Joanna told him. "First, this obviously wasn't a run-of-the-mill robbery. She looked like Beverly Hills and he looked like a ditchdigger. So she wasn't after his money. Second, and most important, she removed the bottle from the shoe box and took it with her. Remember, that shoe box was open at the crime scene, and we never found the bottle it contained."

"Maybe she threw the bottle into the pit after she pushed the Russian in," Jake suggested.

Joanna shook her head. "All the bottles in the pit were buried or half-buried. She knew what was in the box, and that's why she followed him and killed him. She wanted what was in that shoe box. Otherwise we would have found it at the crime scene."

Jake thought through Joanna's line of reasoning. All of the pieces fit except for one. "But why kill him if you don't have to? Why not just conk him over the head and take the box? Keep in mind, she had the gun."

Joanna shrugged and gestured with opened palms. "That I don't know."

Jake paced the floor again, thinking through the story from start to finish. The guy was on a quiet, deserted street with poor lighting. It was a perfect place for a robbery. But why bother to shoot him *twice* and take the chance that somebody would hear the shots? That didn't make sense. Everything up to that point had been planned so—

Suddenly the answer came to Jake. He stopped in his tracks and spun around to face Joanna. "I'll be a son of a bitch!"

"What?"

"It was a hit," Jake said hoarsely. "A well-planned hit. She set the poor bastard up perfectly. She comes on to him in the bar, even offering him money for a bang. He can't believe his good luck. He's going to get laid and get paid for it. He arranges to meet her later, maybe after he does his burial business. And he ends up getting iced for his trouble."

Joanna sipped her beer slowly, her eyes fixed on the fire. "This blonde sounds like a pro, a real pro."

"Oh, yeah," Jake said, and lit another cigarette. "She had everything planned down to the minute."

"Professional hitters cost," Joanna went on. "Now, who would be willing to pay big bucks to hit some Russian immigrant?"

"Somebody who wanted to stop him from planting babies," Jake replied at once.

"Or somebody who wanted to stop him from taking babies to plant," Joanna added. She thought again about all the evidence at hand, including the cut-up fetuses. "There's some very gruesome business going on here. And we're only seeing the tip of the iceberg now."

"Are you talking about the guy's murder?"

"I'm talking about fetuses that have been cut open and eviscerated."

"What!" Jake came over to Joanna and sat beside her. "What the hell are you talking about?"

"The babies in the bottles have all been split open and their internal organs removed," Joanna said quietly.

"Jesus!" Jake hissed under his breath. "What's this all about?"

"I don't have the faintest idea," Joanna answered. "But somebody removed every organ, including their brains."

"Why would somebody do that?" Jake asked, feeling way out of his depth.

Joanna shrugged. "Who knows?"

"Cui bono?" Jake asked. "Who would benefit from it?"

"No one that I can think of."

"Can the organs be used?" Jake probed.

Joanna considered the question at length. "The brains maybe. In some medical centers they are now implanting fetal brain cells into the brains of patients with Parkinson's disease."

"Does it work?"

"Some think it does," Joanna said ambiguously.

"What about the heart and liver and things like that?"

"They have no use that I know of."

"So you couldn't transplant them into kids or adults?"

"No way."

"Could they be used in some type of experiment?"

Joanna thought for a moment. "I don't think so. In this country, experiments on fetal tissues are closely monitored. And even if they weren't, I don't know what you'd do with a fetal heart or liver. You can't keep the organs alive for very long."

"How long are we talking?"

"Hours."

"Well, somebody sure as hell wanted those organs." Jake was back on his feet, pacing. "Where did those fetuses come from? That's the key here."

"We're going to check out all the local hospitals and abortion clinics, but chances are we'll come up with a big nothing."

"You figure the people responsible would cover their trail pretty good, huh?"

Joanna nodded. "You can lose track of tissue specimens real easy, particularly in a clinic setting."

Jake continued to pace the floor. "Where the hell did those fetuses come from?"

"I'll bet the blond hitter could lead us to it."

"And so could the Russian," Jake said. "But he's dead and she's disappeared."

"You've got to find her, Jake."

"Tell me about it," he growled. "We scoured every bar and motel in a five-mile radius, thinking she was just some well-heeled housewife looking for some action. And of course, we found nothing because she's not some damn housewife. She's a professional hitter." Jake ran a hand through his hair absentmindedly. "Who the hell could have ever guessed that?"

"Not the Russian," Joanna commented. "That's for sure."

"And we're running into dead ends with him, too," Jake said sourly. "Nobody in the neighborhood knows who he is or where he lives. And on the occasions he went into some store, he always paid in cash. If the guy had a credit card, he never used it."

"My kingdom for a credit card," Joanna muttered.

"What?"

"Nothing."

Joanna got to her feet and went into the kitchen to check on the chicken pot pies in the oven. She opened another bottle of beer, still thinking about credit cards and how valuable they were in tracking down an individual. A credit card yields a person's name, address, place of employment, income, bank, and work history. It detailed what a person bought and where he bought it, what his tastes were, where he traveled, and in some instances it would tell you all about a person's habits and vices. Credit cards had tracked down more criminals than fingerprints ever would.

But the Russian didn't have one. He was just a poor working stiff. The expensively dressed blonde, on the other hand, would have a purse full of cards. And Joanna had an idea where the blonde might use them. She hurried back into the living room and handed Jake a fresh beer.

"Let's talk about the blond hitter," Joanna said.

"Okay." Jake carefully poured beer into his mug and sipped it. "What aspect?"

"Where she'd be most likely to use her credit cards."

Jake looked up quickly. "How do you know she had any?"

"Oh, I think the odds are pretty good that a well-dressed woman would have credit cards. Don't you?"

Jake nodded, wondering where Joanna was headed. "Okay. Let's assume she had them."

"So, where would she use them?"

"Not in that goddamn neighborhood," Jake said. "You don't use credit cards in cheap bars and doughnut shops. And last I looked, there weren't any Neiman Marcus stores in south Santa Monica."

"But there are gas stations."

Jake blinked rapidly as the pieces suddenly fell into place. "Like you said, she was really well dressed, which means she wasn't a local. She drove in from Beverly Hills or the west Valley. And she did it at least two or three times a week, so she could track the guy and learn his routine."

"She might have gassed up in this area," Joanna opined. "She wouldn't want to run out of gas on the freeway on her drive back."

"Or run out of gas following the Russian," Jake added. "Hell, she didn't know where he was going at first. He could have led her to the next county." Jake nodded firmly. "She gassed up nearby. And maybe, just maybe, one of the service station guys will remember her. They don't see many expensively dressed blondes in this area. She'd stand out."

"It's a long shot," Joanna told him. "And it's also a ton of work. There are dozens of gas stations in that area."

"But at least it's a possible trail to follow, and who knows what might turn up." Jake looked over at Joanna and gave her a big wink. "That gas station idea was damn good. You're pretty sharp after a roll in the hay, aren't you?"

"Well, I've had a chance to turn my brain back on now," Joanna said demurely.

Jake grinned. "I hate quick women."

"How about quick women who make great chicken pot pies?"

"Those I can't live without."

Joanna went into the kitchen and removed the well-done chicken pot pies from the oven. She placed them on a tray and reached for napkins and forks and fresh beers. Life was going so good, she thought contentedly. Joanna came back into the living room and placed the tray on the lower ledge of the brick fireplace. She used a fork to break the crusts of the pies. Small puffs of steam seeped out, carrying a wonderful aroma with it.

"Want to talk a little more crime while we wait for these to cool a bit?" Joanna asked.

"Sure," Jake said as he stirred the crust into the steaming pie. "What do you have?"

"I finished the autopsy on the drowning victim."

"And?"

"And I don't think it was accidental."

Jake smiled thinly. "I knew it. I just knew it. What'd you find?"

Joanna told him about the skull fracture and the large subdural hematoma beneath it. "I think somebody conked him on the head and pushed him overboard."

"Would it stand up in a court of law?"

"Probably not," Joanna had to admit. "The findings are suspicious, but suspicions don't prove a damn thing."

"His wife did it," Jake said with certainty. "The young brunette with the big boobs and the cute ass either iced him or had him iced. I'd bet on it."

"Is she a lot younger than he?"

"Try thirty years." Jake tasted a small piece of the

chicken pot pie. It was still too hot. "And it wasn't only the age difference. There were other things."

"Like what?"

"Like the way she tried to act sad when she wasn't," Jake answered, remembering. "And there were her eyes. She tried to look straight at me and Farelli, but her gaze kept drifting to the young studs passing by in the marina. She just couldn't control it. She's got hot pants, and she'll be ready to ride as soon as they bury her ex."

"And she's going to have a ton of money to ride with," Joanna said. "What do you think she'll be worth?"

Jake hesitated. "It's hard to determine exactly how much because his will is so complicated. Apparently he was into a dozen different ventures. Most of them go to his two sons from a prior marriage. Some go to family charities and some to Miss Hot Pants. Then there are all sorts of options on who can buy out who and what they'll have to pay for it."

"Roughly, what does she stand to inherit?"

"Somewhere in the vicinity of twenty million dollars."

"That's a lot of reasons to murder someone."

"And don't forget the two-million-dollar life insurance policy she gets."

"That gives her even more reasons."

"And chances are the little bitch will walk," Jake said sourly. "With twenty-two million tax-free dollars."

"We might get lucky," Joanna said with little optimism. "I still haven't looked at the microscopic slides. Maybe they'll turn up something."

"She's going to walk," Jake said again.

"You're probably right," Joanna agreed. "But let's touch all the bases. Can you arrange for me to take a look at Edmond Rabb's yacht?"

"Yeah, I guess so." Jake chewed on a hot piece of crust and washed it down with beer. "What are you going to be looking for?"

"I want to see if I can find some mechanism to

explain how Edmond Rabb tripped at the back of his yacht, cracked his head open, and still managed to fall overboard."

"And even if you can't, do you think that would stand up in court?"

"Probably not."

"Like I said, she's going to walk."

The cell phone in Jake's coat chirped. He reached for it and spoke briefly. Then he switched it off. He stared into the fire for a full thirty seconds, his face expressionless, his mind obviously somewhere else. Slowly he pushed himself up from the fireplace and began gathering his clothes. "I've got to go."

"What's wrong, Jake?"

"Billy Cunningham just died."

12

The desert wind gusted strongly, blowing sand and loose sagebrush across the highway. Joanna leaned over the steering wheel of her car and tried to see the center dividing line. All she saw was brown. Everything was brown. The sky, the air, the ground. A sudden blast of wind shoved her car sideways, and she had to fight to control it. Joanna slowed down more and hoped no one would crash into her from behind. The visibility was less than twenty-five feet.

Joanna concentrated on the road ahead, looking for the Bio-Med facility. The person who had given her directions said she couldn't miss it. Just follow the highway out of Lancaster, turn left at the big intersection, and drive until she came to the plant that was surrounded by a big chain-link fence. She couldn't miss it. But in a sandstorm like this, Joanna thought miserably, she could miss the Empire State Building.

Up ahead the air seemed clearer, but all Joanna could see was desert. And more desert. Again she wondered why Bio-Med had built their facility in such an isolated location. Eric Brennerman had told her that the land was cheap and security easy to maintain. But still, why come way out to the edge of the Mojave Desert? There were other places in Los Angeles County they could have used. She considered the possibility that the dry climate was somehow important to genetic research. No, she quickly decided. It was easy to control the temperature and humidity inside a research laboratory. One didn't have to come out to the desert for that.

Suddenly the wind died and the sky cleared. The desert was colored a light tan, the sky a deep blue. Off to her right, Joanna saw the chain-link fence. Atop the fence were large coils of barbed wire. Maybe security was the reason for the plant's locale, Joanna thought again, remembering that the science of genetic engineering had become a multibillion-dollar business. And with the human genome about to be deciphered—in essence, the product of every human gene determined—the genetic industry would be worth trillions. The money involved was staggering. Just isolating the gene that produced human insulin had already generated billions of dollars in the marketplace.

Ahead Joanna saw a tall metal gate with a kiosk adjacent to it. She slowed, turning to the right, and lowered her window.

"I'm Dr. Blalock, here to see Dr. Brennerman," Joanna told the uniformed guard.

"I'll need a photo ID," the guard said.

Joanna handed him her driver's license and noticed that he was armed. Inside the guard's kiosk was a panel of electronic switches and buttons, and above that a bank of small television monitors.

The guard handed her license back and pushed a button. The metal gate slowly opened. "Follow the road straight in. You can park in the VIP spaces next to the front entrance."

Joanna drove in slowly on a narrow asphalt road that was still covered with sand from the windstorm. In the rearview mirror, she saw the gate closing and the guard in the kiosk talking on the phone.

Joanna brought her attention back to the grounds around the plant. Everything was barren with no grass or trees or any attempt at landscaping. Off to her left was a paved parking lot, but the rest of the ground was covered with a gravel-like material.

She pulled into a parking space in front of a huge building that looked like a storage shed. Its walls were made of corrugated metal with no wood or trimming of any kind. There were no windows.

Joanna left her car and entered the building. She went through one set of glass doors and then passed another set before coming to an empty reception area. The room was small, with no furniture or decorations. On the white plaster wall in front of her was the blue logo for Bio-Med. It was a globe of the world surrounded by the words *Bio* and *Med*.

A side door opened and an armed guard came over. He handed her a visitor's card and watched her pin it on. "Please wear that at all times."

She followed him through the door and down a narrow corridor with no side doors or windows. Overhead she hear a soft whirring sound and looked up. A surveillance camera mounted on the ceiling was following her. At the end of the corridor they came to a panel on the wall. The guard punched numbers into the panel and stepped back as the door opened automatically.

Joanna entered an enormous laboratory that was an exact replica of Eric Brennerman's lab at the Biogenetics Institute, except that it was at least three times larger. Joanna scanned the spacious glass cubicles that lined the walls. The colors of the plants and vegetables growing inside the cubicles were so bright they were almost blinding.

"Hey, Joanna," Brennerman called out as he walked over. "Welcome to Bio-Med."

"Sorry I'm late," Joanna apologized. "I got caught in a sandstorm."

"We get them all the time," Brennerman said. "They come and go pretty fast."

"Does the sand ever seep into the labs?"

Brennerman shook his head. "It can't get through two layers of corrugated steel. And the skylights are made of Plexiglas that is sealed into the metal roof."

Joanna glanced up at the skylight, which was large and circular. Each cubicle seemed to have its own natural light source. The cubicle nearest her contained green shrubs laden with brown beans. "Are those coffee beans?"

Brennerman nodded. "A special kind."

"What's so special about them?"

"They don't contain caffeine."

Joanna leaned up against the cubicle for a closer look. The glass felt warm and dry, but everything inside the cubicle appeared moist and cool. "How did you manage that?"

"By snipping out the plant's gene that produces caffeine."

"How does the coffee taste?"

"Like what you buy in the store."

They moved on to the next cubicle. It was freezing inside with ice forming on the walls and floor. A researcher wearing a winter coat was tending to the tomato plants. The tomatoes looked ripe and delicious.

"Doesn't the freezing temperature kill the tomatoes?" Joanna asked.

"Nope." Brennerman knocked on the Plexiglas and got the researcher's attention. He motioned for the man to pick a tomato and pass it out.

The cubicle door opened. Joanna felt a blast of cold air as the researcher handed her the tomato.

"Feel it," Brennerman said.

Joanna gently squeezed the tomato. It was ripe and soft. There wasn't even a speck of ice on its outer coat. "Amazing."

"Not really," Brennerman explained. "It's done by gene transfer. There is a winter flounder that can swim all day long in freezing water, and it never ices up. That's because the flounder makes an antifreeze which protects it. We isolated the fish's antifreeze-producing gene and transferred it to tomato plants. The end result is a tomato that can withstand very low temperatures."

"Impressive," Joanna said, and meant it. But the idea of transferring genes between totally unrelated species—fish to tomato—bothered her. Creating a Frankenstein monster was now well within reach, particularly in the private biotechnology section where there was so little federal monitoring or regulation.

"And here is a real problem," Brennerman said, guiding her along to the next cubicle. Inside was golden wheat bathed in natural light that was coming from the skylight above. "This wheat has been genetically modified to increase its protein content. In essence, that allows the farmer to plant less, yet feed more people."

"So what's the problem?"

"The wheat also produces something which makes it very resistant to antibiotics."

Joanna furrowed her brow as she tried to think through the problem. Slowly she looked up at Brennerman. "Are you suggesting that the plants may be able to transfer this resistance?"

Brennerman nodded. "Maybe to the bacteria that feed on them in the ground. And if that's the case, you'll end up with a group of antibiotic-resistant bacteria, and that would be very bad for man."

"Jesus," Joanna breathed softly.

The quiet in the laboratory was broken by a loud, angry male voice. Joanna and Brennerman turned to watch a scientist in a long white coat as he berated an Asian American technician. He glared down at the woman and shook a finger in her face, making her cringe. The technician looked as if she wanted to run and hide. Joanna couldn't help but feel for her.

"That's Alex Mirren," Brennerman said. "He's the senior scientist I mentioned to you last week."

"Does he always embarrass his technicians in public?" Joanna asked.

"Alex is not much on civility," Brennerman replied. "But he's a very fine scientist who has made some important discoveries. He's the one, by the way, who did the animal studies on the lipolytic enzyme."

"Let's go talk to him."

Walking over, Joanna could hear Mirren complaining about the technician's sloppiness which had caused an experiment to fail. It was her fault that the cell line hadn't continued to grow and replicate.

"I followed your instructions exactly, Dr. Mirren," the technician said defensively.

"Then why the hell did the cells die?" Mirren snapped.

"I do not know."

"Because you screwed up," Mirren grumbled. "That's why."

Brennerman cleared his throat loudly. "Alex, have you got a moment?"

"Not really."

"This is Dr. Joanna Blalock," Brennerman went on. "She's here to look over the animal studies we did on the lipolytic enzyme."

"Well, she'll have to wait," Mirren said curtly, and then turned back to the technician. "Now you've cost us a week of valuable time because you couldn't set up a simple cell line. It seems you're not even competent enough to do that."

The technician's lower lip quivered. "But I—"

"Don't interrupt me," Mirren barked. "Just listen, and maybe you'll do the damn experiment right."

The technician bowed her head in shame. She brought a hand up and involuntarily covered her name tag that read NANCY TANAKA.

"I'm going to look over your shoulder and watch you do every step of the experiment," Mirren continued on. "We're going to find out where you screwed up. And I don't give a damn if it takes all day and all night to do it."

"Yes, sir," Nancy Tanaka said weakly.

Mirren turned abruptly to Joanna. "Now, what do you want?"

"I want to see all the data on the lipolytic enzyme," Joanna replied.

"You mean the animal studies. Right?"

"For starters."

Mirren motioned with his head to a nearby workbench. "The microscopic slides are over there."

Joanna glanced over at the workbench. Dozens of

slide boxes were stacked up haphazardly. Some had typed labels. Others were marked with Roman numerals printed in ink. "What do the Roman numerals stand for?"

Mirren stared at Joanna as if she were a simpleton. "What do you think they stand for?"

"I don't know," Joanna said patiently. "That's why I'm asking."

"Christ!" Mirren growled under his breath. "The numbers indicate the chronological sequence in which the experiments were done and the slides made."

"Good," Joanna said. "That will make things easier. Now, I'll also need all the experimental data books that go along with those slides."

"Those books stay here," Mirren said quickly. "They go nowhere."

"I need those books to guide me," Joanna told him.

"Too bad."

Joanna took a deep breath, trying to control her irritation; then she looked over to Brennerman for help.

Brennerman shrugged. "Those books really do have to stay here, Joanna. They are the originals, the only copies we have."

"And the slides should stay, too," Mirren added. "We don't have copies of those, either."

"Fine," Joanna said evenly, but inwardly she was fuming. "Everything should stay here. It'll make things easier for the FDA when they move in to investigate."

Brennerman's face suddenly lost color. "What do you mean? The FDA is not involved with this."

"But they soon will be," Joanna informed him. "Because as soon as I get back to Memorial, I'm going straight to Simon Murdock's office, and together we'll compose a letter to the FDA, telling them about your lipolytic enzyme study and how two of the patients have developed malignancies which may be related to their treatment. We'll also send a copy of the letter to the NIH. They'll swoop down on this place faster than you can blink. And, of course, they'll shut it down while they investigate. But that won't bother you, will it? Because while the investigators are tearing this place apart, you'll have the warm and wonderful feeling which comes with knowing that your data books and slides never left this facility." Joanna turned to leave. "I can find my way out."

"Whoa!" Brennerman said at once. "Let's not be hasty. Let's think this matter through."

"I've already done that," Joanna said tersely. "And I've already told you what I need. The books and the slides. Now, all I want from you is an answer. Yes or no?"

Mirren's lips started to form a word, but he reconsidered.

Joanna glared at him. "You had something you wanted to say?"

"No."

"Good," Joanna said. "Because now is not the time to be shy." She continued to stare at him, disliking everything about him, down to his appearance. He was a stocky man with a round face, thick lips, and thinning black hair. His aftershave lotion smelled as if he had bought it at a dime store.

Mirren stared back at her, his fists involuntarily clenching.

They continued to exchange hard looks, neither person blinking or budging an inch.

Nancy Tanaka watched out of the corner of her eye. A faint smile came to her face. She quickly raised a hand to cover it.

"Ah, perhaps there is a middle ground," Brennerman suggested, breaking the tense silence. "You can, of course, take the slides with you, Joanna. And we'll make Xerox copies of the experimental data books. How does that sound?"

"Fine," Joanna agreed. "As long as I take the original books with me."

Brennerman hesitated for a brief moment and then nodded. "That sounds like a plan to me."

As he gave instructions to Nancy Tanaka about which data books to have copied, Joanna glanced around the immense laboratory. She wondered why the two scientists had so strongly resisted giving up the experimental data books. One possibility was that they really had only one copy and were afraid it would get lost. On the other hand, Joanna thought, maybe there was something in those lab books they didn't want her to see. She planned to study those books very carefully. And have a scientist-physician like Wallace Hoddings double-check them.

Her gaze went to the metal door at the far end of the laboratory beyond the glass cubicles. A sign on the door read:

RESTRICTED AREA
NO ADMITTANCE

"What's in there?" Joanna asked, pointing at the rear door.

"That's where we do our stem cell work," Brennerman answered.

Joanna looked at him quizzically. "Why would you need a restricted area to work with stem cells?"

"Because every time we got a good stem cell line growing, it ended up infected with some damn virus. So we had to set up a lab that looks like a hot zone area." Brennerman took her arm. "Come on. I'll show you."

"Do you do a lot of stem cell work?" Joanna asked.

"Everybody does," Brennerman told her. "Stem cells represent the answer to the greatest mystery of all."

"Which is?"

"How do human beings form and develop from a single cell?"

Joanna wondered if that question would ever be answered, with or without stem cells. Like most people, it was beyond Joanna's imagination to conceptualize the end result after one sperm and one ovum combined to form a single cell with a total of forty-six chromosomes. Within the forty-six chromosomes of that cell were one hundred thousand genes that would dictate every feature of the person-to-be. The earliest dividing cells were called stem cells because they were undifferentiated and were not yet committed to become one tissue type or another. But then some factor within the stem cell activated the appropriate genes and that cell's destiny was determined. It would become liver or heart or lung or whatever the genes directed the cell to become.

Scientists now knew how to harvest human stem cells from adult subjects. If they could learn how to make those cells differentiate into one organ-cell type or another, medicine would be changed forever. It would then be entirely conceivable to grow human hearts and livers and kidneys in a laboratory and transplant them into people.

"Where do you get your stem cells from?" she asked.

"Mainly from peripheral blood, but sometimes from bone marrow," Brennerman said. "Marrow is the best source, but we have to pay our marrow donors a thousand dollars for each specimen."

Not enough, Joanna was thinking. Bone-marrow aspirations hurt like hell, and the site of the aspiration could be sore for weeks afterward.

"Here we are," Brennerman said, and punched numbers into the wall panel. The door clicked open.

They entered a small viewing area with a large Plexiglas window that looked into the laboratory. It did look like a lab in a hot zone, Joanna thought. The technician inside had on a bulky space suit with hood and dark visor. A tube ran from the ceiling to the technician's hood, supplying oxygen.

"Every cell line we established got infected with some adenovirus," Brennerman told her. "So we had to set up this laboratory at a cost of over a million dollars. Before our technician gets into that space suit, she walks through a room flooded with ultraviolet light. That kills every virus hanging onto her clothes or skin. Then she puts on double-thick gloves. It's not foolproof, of course, but so far all of our stem cell lines have stayed clean."

Joanna watched the technician carefully pipetting liquid into small vials. Her latex gloves were taped tightly around the sleeves of her space suit. "Have you had any luck turning out stem cells? You know, making them turn into one specific cell type or another?"

"I wish," Brennerman said. "One infected batch of stem cells formed small pockets that looked like premature lung tissue. But we couldn't be sure and we couldn't get it to grow in long-term cultures."

"Did you actually see alveoli?"

Brennerman shrugged. "It had some features that resembled alveolar membranes. But, as I said, it appeared to be quite primitive."

Joanna moved in closer to the Plexiglas window. The technician was now transferring a creamy red fluid into test tubes. "It's hard for me to envision a human lung growing from stem cells in a petri dish."

"Oh, it'll happen," Brennerman said confidently. "I just hope Bio-Med is the first to do it."

I'll bet you do, Joanna was thinking. That discovery would be worth a Nobel Prize and untold billions in revenue.

The technician inside the laboratory stepped on a floor pedal and a side door opened. She disappeared through it. The door closed automatically after her.

"All traffic in this specialized lab is designed to go one way. You can only enter from here, and you can only leave through the sliding door." Brennerman turned and pointed to the panel on the wall next to him. "And you have to know the code to get into the lab."

"How many technicians work in there?"

"Just one. And she can enter only after either Mirren or I punch in the code."

A small beeper attached to Brennerman's laboratory coat buzzed softly. He reached up and silenced it. "They've finished photocopying the data books."

They went back into the main laboratory. The dozens of slide boxes were now neatly stacked on a side table. And next to them were four thick data books. A uniformed armed guard stood nearby.

"Eddie will carry all of this material to your car," Brennerman said. "If you need anything else, please let me know."

"I will," Joanna said, watching the guard pack the slides and books into a cardboard box. He hoisted the box onto his shoulder.

Joanna followed the guard across the laboratory. Out of the corner of her eye she saw Alex Mirren hovering over the Asian American technician. He was still yelling. There was so much about the man to dislike, Joanna thought. She really felt for Nancy Tanaka, who had to work with the obnoxious boor on a daily basis.

They walked through the reception area and out into a dull day. The wind was blowing again, kicking up sand and clouding the air.

"Not another sandstorm," Joanna complained.

"Yeah," the guard muttered, obviously not wanting to make conversation. He quickly loaded the box into the car.

Joanna looked at her windshield. It was caked with dirt. "Could you please fetch me a damp rag so I can clean my windshield?"

"Use the windshield washer in your car," the guard said gruffly.

"All that will do is make mud," Joanna told him. "Now, either you get a rag or I will."

The guard hesitated. Then he turned away and said, "You stay here."

Joanna watched the guard walk rapidly to the side of the building and disappear. She eyed the deserted highway and the barren land beyond. Everything seemed so bleak and desolate with no sign of life. She wondered why anyone would choose to work here. The pay had to be fabulous, she decided.

Joanna felt like stretching her legs before the drive back to Los Angeles. She slowly strolled along the paved road to the large parking lot. All the cars were covered with dust. And some of their surfaces were badly pitted from sandstorms that could abrade the paint off a car. Another reason not to work out here, Joanna told herself.

Joanna turned back, looking down the side of the Bio-Med plant. A door was open at the rear of the building with an unmarked van backed up to it. At first Joanna thought it was a delivery van. But there was no ramp or loading dock. And there was no paved road leading up to it.

She saw the armed guard come from behind the van and hurry toward her. He seemed to be waving her away from something. Joanna looked around quickly and saw nothing but cars and black asphalt.

"This is a restricted area," the guard called out.

Joanna looked at him oddly. "What? The parking lot?"

"Not so much the lot, ma'am," the guard said, toning down his voice. "It's the rattlesnakes that get in here. They like warm places, so they crawl under the cars and stay there."

Joanna studied his face, not at all sure he was telling the truth. But she knew that rattlesnakes were cold-blooded creatures whose body temperature depended on the environment. After a night in the cold desert, snakes would seek out a warm place to increase their body temperature. "Were you able to find a rag?"

"Here you are," the guard said, and handed her a piece of worn-out towel. "Turn left at the gate, and that'll take you to the highway. Then go right."

Joanna walked to her car, head down, watching every step. *Nasty damn snakes*, she thought, *to go along with everything else in this godforsaken place*. And again she wondered why anyone would put a high-tech plant way out in the middle of nowhere.

She cleaned her windshield with the damp cloth; then she drove out through the main gate and turned left. The wind was picking up and sagebrush was being blown across the deserted highway.

Through her rearview mirror, Joanna could see the expanse of the Bio-Med complex. A strange place, she kept telling herself. Very strange. Particularly the specialized laboratory where the technician wore a space suit. Something in there was wrong. Something in there was off. But Joanna couldn't put her finger on it. Damn! What was it?

The wind suddenly gusted and blew giant puffs of sand across the highway. The air turned a murky brown color. Joanna leaned over the steering wheel and concentrated on the road, her train of thought broken. All she could think about was getting through the sandstorm and finding her way safely back to Los Angeles.

13

Lou Farelli was drawing a big zero. So far he'd covered an eight-square-block area, starting at the mini mart where the Russian immigrant had last been seen alive. Farelli had canvassed dozens of shops and apartment houses and over a hundred private homes. Nobody knew or recognized the Russian.

Farelli was standing outside Young Mi's grocery store, sipping a Diet Coke while he waited. The store owners were Korean, and their English was so bad Farelli couldn't understand more than a few words. But their daughter was due home shortly from a nearby high school she attended. Farelli decided to wait for her, although he doubted the store owners would be helpful. Purchases at the store were placed in plastic bags, not paper. And the doughnut lady had told Farelli that the groceries the Russian carried were always in a paper bag.

Farelli finished his soda and tossed the can into a nearby trash container. It was a warm, muggy day, and he was sweating beneath his suit. He pulled out his collar and again surveyed the lower-middle-class neighborhood. The houses were made of stucco and all windows facing the street had iron bars over them. BEWARE OF THE DOG signs seemed to be everywhere. Directly across from him was an old apartment building, two stories high, with an exterior that was covered with rust streaks and gang graffiti.

Farelli checked his watch. It was almost three o'clock and he still hadn't turned up a single clue about the dead Russian. He leaned against the wall of the store and again pulled his collar as perspiration ran down his neck.

Across the street, a small postal truck drove up to the front of the apartment building. The postman got out and stretched his back.

Farelli pushed himself away from the wall and quickly crossed the street. "Hey! How are you doing?" he called out.

"Doing good." The postman was a tall, thin African American with prematurely gray hair. "Can I help you with something?"

"Maybe." Farelli took out a snapshot of the dead Russian and held it up. "Have you ever seen this guy?"

The postman studied the photograph carefully. "Why is his head shaped so funny?"

"Because it's got two slugs in it," Farelli told him. "You ever seen him?"

"No."

"Do you work this area on a regular basis?"

The postman nodded. "Every day but Sunday for the past five years."

"Thanks for your time," Farelli said and placed the snapshot back in his pocket. He wasn't put off by the postman's failure to recognize the Russian. The Russian was believed to be a workingman and wouldn't be around the neighborhood during the day when the mail was delivered. Out of the corner of his eye Farelli saw a teenage girl with Oriental features enter the grocery store.

He hurried across the street and went in. The teenager was behind the counter, speaking to her nervous parents in Korean. She turned to Farelli and took a deep breath, like someone gathering up courage. "Is—is there something wrong, Officer?"

"No," Farelli said, keeping his voice friendly. He took out the snapshot of the Russian and showed it to them. "I just need to know if they've ever seen this man. He was the victim of a crime, and we're trying to identify him."

The girl spoke quickly in Korean to her parents and waited for them to put on their reading glasses. After carefully studying the photo, the parents shook their heads.

"They have never seen him," the girl reported.

"Okay." Farelli put the photo away and exhaled wearily. "Tell me, are there any other small grocery stores nearby?"

The teenager pointed to the west. "There is a health food store one block down the street."

"Thanks for your help."

The girl stepped over to Farelli as he turned to leave. "Officer, I hope you will forgive my parents' poor English."

"You don't have to apologize," Farelli said, and meant it. "My grandmother was in this country for twenty-five years before she could put a decent sentence together."

The girl looked over to her parents, smiled reassuringly, and then came back to Farelli. "They work fourteen hours a day, and there is very little time for them to study. But they try so hard."

"You tell them to keep at it."

The girl bowed gracefully as Farelli left.

Outside, the day was becoming gloomy with an overcast sky. The humidity seemed to be increasing by the minute. Farelli opened his coat and fanned himself with it. He decided to make one last stop before checking in with Jake.

Farelli started up the street, which had a slight but definite incline. That made him put more weight on his right leg—the bad leg—and that caused it to throb. He walked on, trying to ignore the pain and wondering if it would ever go away as the doctors had promised.

Two years ago Farelli and Jake had been ambushed by some mean bastard with an AK-47. One of the slugs had torn into Farelli's quadriceps muscle. The bullet had been surgically removed and the wound had healed. But any sort of strain on the muscle brought back the pain. The doctors had assured him that the pain would eventually disappear. Well, Farelli thought miserably, eventually hadn't arrived yet.

Up ahead he saw the health food store and next to it a small hardware store. Farelli would have bet dollars to doughnuts that the Russian never went into the health food place. The Russian was a real drinker. He had been guzzling down double shots of vodka two or three nights a week. That wasn't the type of guy who worried about his intake of vitamins and minerals.

The owner of the health food store looked like Mr. Universe with muscles that bulged out of his white T-shirt. He had never seen the Russian. He tried to sell Farelli a new antioxidant vitamin preparation that stopped aging. Only $12.95 a bottle. Farelli politely declined.

Farelli walked next door and entered Herman Rucker's Hardware and Supplies. The store was small and cluttered. Merchandise was stacked on shelves that went from floor to ceiling. The place smelled like something metallic was burning.

"What can I do for you?" Herman Rucker yelled out from behind a wire cage at the rear.

"I need you to look at a picture for me," Farelli yelled back.

"You a cop?"

"Yeah."

Rucker came out from behind the wire cage. He was a short, thin man with horn-rimmed glasses and hawklike features. "What's the guy done?"

Farelli ignored the question and held up the snapshot of the Russian. "You know him?"

"Sure," Rucker said. "That's Vladie. What'd he do?"

"He got in the way of two thirty-eight slugs."

"Shit," Rucker growled. "This fucking neighborhood ain't safe for nobody."

"Was Vladie his first or last name?"

Rucker considered the question carefully. "First—I think. I figured it was short for Vladimir. The guy was Russian, you know."

"Yeah, I know." Farelli took out a pen and note-pad. "You got a last name for this guy?"

"He never gave it."

"What about an address?"

"Didn't give that, either."

"Did he pay in cash or use a credit card?"

Rucker pointed at a sign on the wire cage near the cash register. It read CASH ONLY—NO REFUNDS.

"What'd he usually buy?" Farelli asked.

"Electrical things," Rucker answered. "Wiring, plugs, jacks, fuses. It was mainly simple stuff, but he knew his way around electricity, I'll guarantee you."

"How do you know that?"

"Because we used to talk a lot. You know, about capacity and voltage and things like that."

"You figure him to be an electrician?"

Rucker thought about that before nodding slowly. "I guess. I know for sure he did electrical work around the house. He would always say, 'I have to fix this for the old lady or do that for the old lady.'"

Farelli pricked up his ears. "Old lady" was a term usually used by the lower classes to denote their wives. "Was he married?"

Rucker shrugged. "I guess."

"You ever see a ring on his finger?"

"Never looked."

Farelli rubbed at his chin, thinking. If the Russian had a wife, she would have surely called the police or Bureau of Missing Persons by now. But she hadn't. "You said he did electrical work around his house."

"Right."

"Did he ever tell you where his house was?"

"Nope."

"But you were sure he was talking about his house?"

"It sounded like that to me," Rucker told him. "He

said he was going to fix the television cable, and that sounds like a house to me.''

"Me, too.''

"The cable company in this area ain't worth a shit," Rucker continued on. "Everybody bitches and complains about the poor-quality picture they get on their TV sets.''

Farelli's eyebrows suddenly went up. "Wait a minute! Wait a minute!''

"What?''

"You said he had cable TV?''

"That's right," Rucker said, wondering what the big deal about cable was. "Everybody around here has got it. You can't get a good picture on your screen without it.'' He shrugged to himself. "Hell, you can't get a decent picture with it, either. People are always bitching about the cable service. You call them, they come and don't do a damn thing. The picture is still crummy.''

"Was that why Vladie was going to fix his own cable?''

"That's what he told me," Rucker answered. "His old lady called the cable company two or three times, and they sent a repairman out to fix it. But the picture still wasn't worth a damn. That's why Vladie bought all that stuff from me. He was going to fix it himself.''

"Do you know the name of the cable company?''

"Centurion.''

"Spell it.''

"*C-e-n-t-u-r-i-o-n,*'' Rucker spelled it out slowly, wondering what was so important about a cable company. "Do you think they had something to do with Vladie getting killed?''

Farelli ignored the question. "Where's your phone?''

14

"Jesus," Joanna marveled, "that's more than a yacht. It's a ship."

Joanna and Jake were walking on a wharf at Marina del Rey. Securely moored alongside was the *Argonaut*, a gleaming, white 110-foot oceangoing vessel. It was manned by a crew of eight and owned by a corporation that controlled the assets of a dead Greek shipping tycoon. Edmond Rabb had been leasing the vessel from the corporation for the past year.

"For two thousand dollars a day," Jake was telling her.

"And I'll bet that doesn't include everything," Joanna said, studying the thick ropes that secured the vessel to the wharf.

"It doesn't. Booze, parties, and special foods are extra."

They passed by open portholes. From inside they could hear the sound of high-pitched voices and the hum of a vacuum cleaner. Music was playing somewhere in the background.

Joanna glanced up at the side of the vessel and saw the polished brass railing. In the sunlight it shined like gold. "I guess two thousand dollars a day doesn't matter very much when you're worth a hundred million."

"It didn't matter a damn to Edmond Rabb," Jake said. "According to the harbor master, the ship never went out more than a couple of times a month. The rest of the time it just sat here."

"At two grand a day."

"Plus docking fees."

They came to the gangplank leading up to the ship. A large, heavyset man with a shaved head stood guard. He was dressed entirely in white and wore dark wraparound sunglasses.

Jake flashed his shield.

"You got papers to go with badge?" the guard asked, not budging. His accent was foreign—maybe Eastern European.

"No," Jake said.

"Well, you come back when you got papers."

It happened so fast Joanna almost didn't see it. In an instant Jake shoved his forearm into the man's throat, pinning him up against the gangplank. The guard began to choke and suck for air, his face turning a bright red.

"Next time you see that shield, you move your ass to the side," Jake said, his voice grating.

The guard tried to nod, but Jake pushed even harder against the man's throat.

"And you do it real quick," Jake went on. "Otherwise I might get upset."

The guard's face was turning purple.

Jake released his hold and stepped back, watching the guard gasp and wheeze for air. "When I come back down this gangplank, you'd better be standing right here. I might have some questions for you."

The guard nodded, but it was hard to see because he was bent over like a man about to throw up.

Jake took Joanna's arm as they went up the gangplank. Two heads that had been peering over the railing quickly disappeared.

"That guard looked really mean," Joanna commented.

"So?"

"So he looks like the type who could push a man overboard and not lose a wink of sleep over it."

"Are you thinking he might be the one who did the deed on Edmond Rabb?" Jake asked.

"Maybe," Joanna replied. "Of course, he would do it only on orders from somebody else."

"Naw," Jake said at once. "He's too stupid. They'd never trust him to do that."

They reached the gangway and stepped onto the deck of the *Argonaut*. A seaman dressed in tan shorts and a white T-shirt led them aft along a shiny deck made of teak. Joanna glanced at the brass railing and the teakwood ledge beneath it. Both were plenty hard enough to crack a skull.

Beyond the wheelhouse was a spacious area with lounge chairs and a portable bar. An exquisite brunette was stretched out on a blanket sunning herself. Standing next to her was a tall, handsome, deeply tanned man wearing a dark blue Armani suit with white shirt and yellow tie.

"I think we've met before, Lieutenant," the man said easily, not bothering to offer his hand.

"Yeah," Jake said sourly, disliking everything about the lawyer. "You took a cold-blooded murderer and got him off on involuntary manslaughter."

"He was tried by a jury of his peers."

"Well, you go tell that to the parents of the girl he killed."

Mervin Tuch shrugged, unmoved. "The case has already been tried, Lieutenant."

"Wonderful," Jake muttered, and turned toward the strikingly attractive brunette. "Mrs. Rabb, I—"

Tuch moved in between the detective and Lucy Rabb. "There are some matters which my client is concerned about."

Jake groaned to himself, thinking that the longest distance between two points was called a lawyer.

"To begin with," Tuch continued, "the guard you just manhandled is employed by Mrs. Rabb to protect her. Mrs. Rabb feels, and I agree, that the amount of physical force you used on that man was excessive and unjustified."

"You talking police brutality?" Jake asked evenly.

"It looked that way from here."

"Ah-huh." Jake took out his shield and held it up.

"Here's my number. Write it down so you can give it to them when you file your complaint."

Tuch started to reach inside his coat for a pen.

"Of course," Jake went on, "you'll have to come downtown to fill out a bunch of forms and you'll be interviewed by the investigating officer. Then there's the hearing itself, at which you'll have to testify. We're talking a lot of hours here for both you and Mrs. Rabb."

Tuch withdrew his hand from his coat, leaving his pen where it was.

"And while you're thinking about what you want to do, Dr. Blalock and I can take a look around."

"That's the second matter Mrs. Rabb wanted me to discuss with you," Tuch said. "She feels her privacy is being invaded unnecessarily. She has asked me to see to it that your search warrant is a limited one."

Jake's jaw tightened noticeably. "When I talked with Mrs. Rabb yesterday, she said a search warrant wouldn't be necessary."

Jake glanced over at Lucy Rabb, who quickly looked away and began studying her fingernails. Jake growled to himself because he'd made a stupid mistake by not obtaining the search warrant. He had taken Lucy Rabb's word, and that was really stupid.

Tuch read the detective's face. "You do have a warrant, don't you?"

"No," Jake had to admit.

"Then I would advise you to obtain one. Otherwise there'll be no search."

"All right." Jake sighed and reached for his cell phone. "It shouldn't take more than four or five hours."

Tuch suppressed a grin. "Come back when you've got the warrant."

"Oh, I will," Jake said, and began punching numbers into his cell phone. "Just give me a second to call a black-and-white unit to seal this ship. We don't want anything or anybody to leave this vessel while we're waiting for the warrant."

Tuch raised an eyebrow. "Surely you don't expect me to sit here for hours."

"You were aboard this ship the night Edmond Rabb was killed. Right?"

"I was a guest at the—" Tuch stopped in midsentence and stared at Jake. "You used the term 'was killed.' That implies his death was not accidental."

"You were at the party, weren't you?"

"That's correct."

"Then we'll have to question you about that night," Jake said. "You can walk us around the ship and show us exactly where you were and what you were doing when Mr. Rabb dropped overboard."

Tuch and Lucy Rabb looked at each other intently, as if they were exchanging a silent message. A seagull squawked overhead and then flew away.

"Well?" Jake demanded.

"Could we agree to a limited search?" Tuch asked.

"No, we couldn't," Joanna told him and stepped forward. "I'll look wherever I want or I won't look at all."

Tuch narrowed his eyes. "And just who are you?"

"I'm Dr. Joanna Blalock," she said, "and I represent the Coroner's Office. For your information, we don't do limited searches."

Tuch studied her briefly, recalling that he'd seen her being interviewed on television once. She was even prettier in person. "A limited search is better than no search at all."

"Let me tell you how this is going to work," Joanna said, talking to both the lawyer and Lucy Rabb. "Either I search now or I come back in a few hours with a dozen medical examiners from the Coroner's Office. We'll go over this ship from bow to stern with a fine-tooth comb, and it'll take days for us to do it. And while we're doing that, Lieutenant Sinclair and his men will search every one of Mr. Rabb's homes and business offices. Every personal and business effect he has will be put under a microscope."

"You need a stack of court orders for that," Tuch challenged.

"That'll be no problem," Joanna shot back. "Judges are very accommodating when we tell them we're dealing with suspected murder."

"Murder!" Lucy Rabb almost came off her seat on the deck. Her eyes darted back and forth between Tuch and Joanna. "Are you saying my husband was murdered?"

Joanna looked down at Lucy Rabb, wondering if she was acting or really shocked.

Tuch asked, "Are you suggesting you have evidence to indicate murder?"

"You can hear about it at the inquest," Joanna said, bluffing.

Jake smiled to himself. Tuch was being outfoxed and outclassed and didn't know it. He let the lawyer squirm a little longer and then said, "If I were you, Counselor, I'd allow Dr. Blalock to do her search. Judges don't like to hear that somebody is trying to impede a murder investigation."

"What kind of bullshit is this?" Lucy Rabb barked out. "You can't just rummage through my dead husband's things."

"Sure we can," Jake said, thinking that class always showed. Or lack of it. Lucy Rabb was gorgeous with a body that wouldn't quit. She was okay as long as she kept her mouth shut.

"Mervin," Lucy Rabb said angrily, "will you tell these ass—?"

Tuch quickly brought a finger up to his lips, silencing her. He turned to Jake. "I'd like to confer with my client for a moment."

"All right," Jake said, watching Lucy Rabb get to her feet and walk over to the far railing with Tuch. She was tall with shapely legs and an ass so tight it looked as if it were molded on. But her boobs seemed too big and stood out too straight. Silicone, Jake thought.

Joanna moved in close to Jake, keeping her voice very low. "What do you think?"

"I think she's perfect, except maybe for the boobs," Jake said absently.

"She's got cellulite," Joanna spat out softly.

Jake studied the backs of Lucy's thighs. They were noticeably dimpled. He smiled to himself, thinking it was curious what a woman noticed. "Not so perfect, after all."

"Will you get your mind back on business?" Joanna chided him gently.

"It is on business," Jake said in a whisper. "I was thinking that old man Rabb had a hundred million dollars so he could easily buy something real exquisite. And something real exquisite had him iced."

"She wasn't exactly torn up over his death, was she?"

"Christ!" Jake said louder than he'd intended. Tuch looked over and Jake lowered his voice. "The poor bastard has been gone for only a couple of weeks and she calls him 'my dead husband.' She doesn't even have enough sense to act sad."

"Maybe," Joanna said. "But there's a really good chance she's going to walk and take a ton of money with her. And, of course, her handsome lawyer will be right by her side."

Jake studied the couple by the railing and then turned back to Joanna. "You think they're a couple, huh?"

"I'd bet on it."

Tuch and Lucy Rabb came back to the lounging area. Jake noticed that their arms were almost touching.

"Mrs. Rabb has decided to allow you to search the ship without a warrant," Tuch said. "If her husband was murdered, she wants the person responsible caught and punished to the fullest extent of the law."

Yeah, right, Jake thought. If old man Rabb were to suddenly return from the dead, Lucy Rabb would have a shit hemorrhage. "We'll start in the stateroom."

Joanna and Jake went through an open door and down carpeted stairs that led into a spacious stateroom. All the furniture was neatly stacked against the walls. A team of Mexican cleaners were vacuuming the floor while listening to Latino music on their radio.

"Qué?" the eldest of the cleaners asked.

Jake motioned with a hand, indicating he didn't need the Mexican. The old man went back to vacuuming.

Joanna asked, "Why do you think they were so anxious to delay our search?"

"Either they wanted to discard something or maybe rearrange things."

"Like what?"

Jake shrugged. "Who knows?"

They walked across the big stateroom, heading for the master bedroom.

"And what is Lucy Rabb doing with a high-priced criminal defense lawyer?" Joanna asked.

"Tuch is a regular lawyer who handled all of Edmond Rabb's legal affairs," Jake told her. "But if a high-profile murder case comes along, he jumps right in. Then he brings in a team of top-notch defense lawyers to actually handle the case."

"He still must be pretty good to put a team like that together."

"I guess so," Jake conceded. "He's got a damn good reputation for getting people off."

"Like the murderer who got off with involuntary manslaughter?"

"Yeah," Jake growled.

"Tell me about the case."

"The asshole son of a rich investment banker decided to slip his date a heavy dose of ecstasy," Jake said hoarsely. "While he's pulling her panties off, she starts having trouble breathing. So he takes her to the front of an emergency room, dumps her out, and splits. By the time they find her, she's choking to death on her own vomit."

"Oh, Lord!"

"It should have been murder two," Jake went on.

"But the snotty little bastard got manslaughter. He served three years and walked."

"But he gave her the ecstasy and she was still breathing when he dumped her," Joanna argued. "If he had taken her into the ER, he could have saved her life."

"Tell that to Mr. Armani upstairs," Jake said disgustedly.

They entered the master bedroom. The king-size bed was unmade, its sheets and comforter wrinkled up. The pillows showed that two heads had rested there during the night.

"Cute," Joanna said, seeing two bathrobes draped over a chair. "Chances are those two have been a pair for a while."

"Oh, yeah," Jake agreed. "They were banging each other when the old man was alive." He motioned with his head to the chair. "Brand-new lovers don't take the time to neatly fold their bathrobes."

Joanna stared at the crumpled-up sheets that looked as if they'd been kicked back. "I guess it's possible some other couple used the bed."

"Like who?"

Joanna shrugged. "Just thinking out loud."

Jake walked over to the chair and examined the white terry-cloth bathrobes. One was embroidered with the initials ER on the front pocket. The other had the initials LR. He took hair samples from the backs of each. LR had brunette strands. ER had black strands. "Edmund Rabb had gray hair, didn't he?"

"Almost white," Joanna replied.

"We'll see what these show." Jake placed the strands in separate plastic envelopes, then picked up the bathrobes and carefully sniffed their collars.

Joanna watched Jake, now recalling that he had a remarkable sense of smell. He could detect and identify odors that most people barely noticed.

"Tuch was wearing a heavily scented aftershave lotion," Jake said. "Did you notice it?"

Joanna nodded. "It smelled like Polo."

"So does the back of Edmond Rabb's robe."

Sleeping with your lover so soon after your husband's death was really stupid, Joanna thought. And stupid people usually made careless mistakes. Slowly Joanna moved around the bedroom and methodically inspected every heavy object that could be hand-held. A pair of brass lamps, a phone with answering machine attached, a small metal replica of Michelangelo's *David*. All were spotless. "No blood," she observed.

"Whoever conked him on the head deep-sixed the weapon," Jake said. "It's sitting on the bottom of the ocean now."

"I know." Joanna stepped back and gazed around the room once more. "And whoever conked him wouldn't carry a bloody weapon through a stateroom full of guests just to get back to the bedroom. But still . . ." Her voice trailed off as she walked over to an open porthole and carefully examined the metal sill. "No blood," she reported again.

Jake's gaze went from the open porthole back to the king-size bed. He envisioned Lucy Rabb and Tuch screwing their brains out. Then, over cigarettes, they decided the best way to whack the old man. Greed, Jake thought. It had no end. It was a goddamn bottomless pit.

Spotting the telephone, he walked over and checked the machine for messages. There were none. Then he looked for the phone number. "Let's see who Lucy Rabb called the most after her husband got whacked."

"I'll bet on Mervin Tuch," Joanna said.

"Oh, yeah," Jake agreed. "And since he was her lawyer, I'll bet all those calls were strictly professional and privileged."

"Of course."

They went into a large bathroom. Everything was done in dark wood, including the toilet seat. The counter next to the basin was covered with feminine things. Atop it were hand lotion, cosmetics, perfumes, and a small basket of Crabtree & Evelyn soaps. The medicine cabinet looked like it belonged to an old man. There were vitamin preparations for seniors, dental adhesives for false teeth, testosterone patches, and a bottle of Viagra.

Jake took out the bottle of Viagra and examined it. "The label says the tablets are one hundred milligrams each. Is that a big dose?"

"The highest you can buy," Joanna said.

"Well, at least the old guy was trying."

Jake closed the medicine cabinet. "A big nothing. Let's go look at the deck."

They walked out and across the stateroom where the cleaning men were still busy vacuuming and scrubbing. Jake slowed, watching them, and then went over to the oldest of the crew. "Do you speak English?"

"Oh, yes," the thin gray-haired man said.

"Have you cleaned up any blood from this ship?"

"No, señor."

"Did you ever see blood in the bedroom or bathroom or up top?"

The man shook his head three times.

Joanna and Jake went topside into bright sunlight. Lucy Rabb had put on a wraparound skirt over her bikini bathing suit. Tuch had his coat off and slung over his shoulder. He was drinking Coca-Cola from a small, thick bottle.

Jake asked, "Do you always serve Coke in those bottles aboard ship?"

"Yes," Lucy answered. "It was Edmond's favorite drink."

And a perfect weapon to crack somebody over the head with, Jake was thinking. "We're going to take a look at the stern. That's where your husband was standing before he went overboard. Right, Mrs. Rabb?"

"I believe so," Lucy Rabb said without emotion.

Cold, Jake thought. So damn pretty and beneath it nothing but ice. He took Joanna's arm and guided her to the back of the vessel. When they were well out of earshot, he asked, "Did you see that Coke bottle? You could really bash in a skull with that."

"And toss it overboard in the wink of an eye."

"That, too," Jake said as a seagull flew over them. "Is there any way to check Edmond Rabb's skull to see if he might have gotten conked with a Coke bottle?"

Joanna thought for a moment. "I guess it's possible that a little piece of green glass chipped off and embedded itself into bone."

"Check it out." Jake put on dark sunglasses and walked to the brass railing at the very rear of the vessel. "Let me show you where Edmond Rabb was seen just before he died. According to an eyewitness, he was leaning forward with one hand on the railing and the other holding a drink." Jake assumed the position for Joanna and then straightened up. "No one was near him. The sea was calm. There was no wind. They were traveling at five knots per hour."

"Is it possible that he was sitting on the railing?"

Jake shook his head. "Rabb wasn't that stupid. As a young man he was in the merchant marine. He knew ships and he knew the sea."

Joanna carefully inspected the brass railing and the hard wood below it. There was no protruding ledge or anything else jutting out. She peered down over the railing to examine the stern of the ship. It was smooth and flat with nothing protruding. She couldn't see the propeller beneath the blue water. She gazed back at the deck. She searched the area around her, looking for hiding places. There weren't any.

Joanna stepped away from the railing, trying to envision the murder of Edmond Rabb. He was leaning on the rail, yet his body was a safe distance from it. He was probably staring out at the sea. Everything was calm and quiet, so he would have heard someone coming up behind him. Rabb turned, but he was unconcerned because he knew his murderer. He again assumed his position, leaning over the railing. Then he got his head bashed in. He fell forward onto the railing and the murderer shoved him overboard.

"Well?" Jake broke into her thoughts.

"It's got to be murder," Joanna told him. "There's no other way to explain the skull fracture near the crown of his head."

"No way it could have been accidental, huh?"

"Not that I can see," Joanna said, and pointed at the brass railing. "If he'd slipped and hit the railing, the skull fracture would have been at the front or back of his head."

"Could he have taken a header and hit the propeller?"

Joanna shook her head. "They were moving at five knots an hour. The propeller blades would have chewed him up."

"And you're telling me that a coroner's inquest would never buy murder here?"

"It would be a long shot," Joanna replied. "Somebody would raise the possibility that he took a header and hit a piece of log floating in the water. That would cause a skull fracture near the crown."

"Is that really a possibility?"

"Sure. But it's not what happened."

Joanna and Jake walked back across the deck. The day was becoming hotter, with virtually no breeze at all. Atop the wheelhouse, a string of flags drooped down motionless.

Jake nodded to Lucy Rabb and her lawyer. "Thanks for your time."

"Mrs. Rabb hopes that no further searches of her ship will be necessary," Tuch said formally.

"I can't promise you that," Jake said.

"If you do return, she will insist on your having a search warrant."

"I'll keep that in mind."

Jake and Joanna went down the gangplank and onto the wharf. The bald man in the white suit was still standing guard.

"Were you working here the night of the party?" Jake asked the guard.

"Yeah."

"Did you go aboard that night?"

"No," the guard said, his eyes avoiding Jake's stare. "I stay on dock."

"You sure of that?"

"Anybody who say I was on the boat is a liar," the guard growled.

"We'll see."

Jake and Joanna walked away, each lost in their own thoughts for a moment. Behind them they could hear Lucy Rabb shouting down orders to the guard. She wasn't happy about something.

"What do you think?" Joanna asked.

"I think they're going to walk."

The breeze suddenly picked up, blowing in from the harbor. The flags on the pole above the wheelhouse of the *Argonaut* began to unfurl. There were three flags: the American flag, the State of California flag, and a third one that showed a corporate logo. It was a blue globe of the world on a white background. The word BIO-MED surrounded the globe.

Joanna and Jake left the wharf without looking back. They didn't see the Bio-Med flag blowing in the wind.

15

"Oliver Rhodes could have lived forever," Lori McKay said, moving her chair aside. "Take a peek at this."

Joanna leaned in and studied the slide under the microscope. The cardiac muscle cells appeared young and healthy with no evidence of scarring or atrophy. Small arterioles were wide open without a hint of atherosclerosis. "It looks like the heart of a twenty-year-old."

"And it performed that way, too." Lori pointed over at a stack of medical records on a nearby table. "Check out his cardiac function studies, and it'll blow your mind. His EKG and thallium stress test were absolutely normal, and his cardiac ejection fraction was a hundred and ten percent of the expected value. Hell, this heart could have beat for another fifty years."

"If it hadn't developed rhabdomyosarcoma."

"It's the same story here," said Dennis Green, the specialist in oncologic pathology. He pushed himself away from a microscope near the wall in the forensic laboratory. "You examine the brain tissue from this patient and you'll swear it came from a teenager. There's no scarring or infarcts or atrophy—yet she'd had multiple strokes in the past."

"Did her brain function return as well?" Joanna asked.

"It was unbelievable," Green answered. "All of her motor and sensory functions were completely restored. And perhaps most remarkable of all, she had been suffering from a progressive form of dementia, like Alzheimer's. That, too, was reversed."

"Like magic," Lori commented.

"Like black magic," Green went on. "Because right in the middle of this woman's brain was an astrocytoma, which is just about the nastiest tumor you can find."

Joanna sighed deeply. "And we still don't know why."

"It could be happenstance," Lori suggested. "That's a possibility here. Remember, we're dealing with only two patients."

"No way." Green shook his head at Lori. "We've got two very rare tumors occurring in a group of thirty patients. That's not a coincidence. I'd bet it's somehow related to that lipolytic enzyme they received."

He turned in his swivel chair to Joanna. "Did you find out anything at Bio-Med?"

"Everything looked fine," Joanna told him. "They have very good quality control. In one lab they even had a—" She interrupted herself, thinking back to the lab with the technician wearing a space suit. And plain latex gloves. That's what had bothered Joanna. The plain latex gloves wouldn't protect the wearer in a supposed hot zone laboratory. "Excuse me for a moment."

Joanna went to a wall phone, spoke briefly, and returned.

"What was that all about?" Green asked.

"A virus was contaminating one of the labs at Bio-Med," Joanna replied.

"So?"

"So the technician in that lab was wearing a space suit."

Green looked at Joanna strangely. "A space suit?"

"We'll talk about it in a little while," Joanna said. "I just spoke with Mack Brown down in virology research. He's on his way up. Maybe he can explain it to us."

"A space suit?" Green asked again.

"Let's wait for Mack."

Joanna reached in her white laboratory coat for a chocolate bar. She unwrapped it slowly, her thoughts now going back to the rare cancers. "Let's focus in on the enzyme made by Bio-Med. They had plenty of quality control in place. Their enzyme preparations should have been pure. But we'll check them out ourselves to make sure."

Green asked, "You think there may be a contaminant in the preparation?"

"It's possible," Joanna said. "I think we all remember the L-tryptophan story."

Green and Lori nodded at the memory of the medical disaster.

L-tryptophan, a naturally occurring amino acid, was found to be helpful in inducing sleep and relaxing muscles. It was eventually produced by a Japanese pharmaceutical company using a gene-splicing technique and sold in large quantities at health food stores all over America. Soon some of the patients taking L-tryptophan showed signs of a progressive, devastating neurologic disorder. A number of them died as a result. The disease was caused by a contaminant that was present in the L-tryptophan preparations. The pharmaceutical company was sued for hundreds of millions of dollars. L-tryptophan was pulled from the shelves.

"So," Joanna said as she nibbled on the candy bar, "a contaminant in the Bio-Med preparation remains high on the list of possibilities. But the enzyme itself could still be the causative agent."

Green waved off the idea. "There's never been an enzyme shown to induce cancer. Not one."

"Right," Joanna agreed. "Except this enzyme was produced by a genetically altered bacteria. This may not be your run-of-the-mill enzyme."

"You've got a point," Green conceded.

Joanna licked the chocolate from her fingers. "But this doesn't bring us any closer to the answer, does it?"

"Well, whatever it is," Green said, "I think we can all agree that the causative agent is in that enzyme preparation."

Joanna nodded firmly. "You can bet your house on that."

"Two patients already dead from cancer," Green said, more to himself than to the others. "And more sure to come."

Lori asked thoughtfully, "Can you imagine how those other twenty-eight patients will feel once they find out what's going on? They'll just be sitting there, waiting for a cancer to pop up and kill them. And there's not a damn thing anybody can do about it. Our study is not going to help them."

"I know," Joanna said softly, thinking how frightened and angry the patients would be. One day they're feeling great and sitting on top of the world, and the next day they're without hope and waiting for a deadly cancer to appear.

Joanna pushed the sad thoughts from her mind and focused again on the study to find the causative agent. She pointed to boxes and boxes of slides stacked high on a nearby table. "Those are the slides on the experimental animals who received the enzyme preparation at Bio-Med. We've got to review every one of them."

"Jesus," Lori groaned. "There must be a hundred boxes on that table. It's going to take us weeks to go through all of them."

"More," Green said miserably.

"Whatever," Joanna said, ignoring their objections. "Each of us will review a box of slides per day. Don't just scan them. Look at them carefully and concentrate on the heart and brain."

"Should we get some pathology fellows to help out?" Lori suggested.

"No," Joanna said at once. "We can't afford inexperience here. And remember, subtle changes may be important, particularly if they indicate early malignant transformation."

The door to the forensic laboratory opened, and

J. Mack Brown entered. He was a tall, lanky Texan with a square jaw and tousled brown hair that never stayed in place no matter how often he brushed it. Everybody thought he looked like the Marlboro man. And they weren't far off. Named after the famous movie cowboy Johnnie Mack Brown, he was born and raised on a ranch near Del Rio, Texas. He was also a renowned virologist and the world's expert on Lassa fever, an illness caused by one of nature's deadliest viruses. Mack Brown had spent a lot of time doing research in a space suit.

"How you doing, Joanna?" Mack asked in a soft Texas drawl.

"Just fine."

"You look real good," Mack said, scratching his ear. "How do you manage to stay so young?"

"Clean living." Joanna grinned.

Mack grinned back. "Ha!" He sat in a swivel chair and propped his feet up on a table. His boots were old and worn, but well polished.

"I think you know Dennis and Lori," Joanna said, sitting on the counter that held the microscopes.

"Sure do." Mack nodded to them and then looked at Joanna. "What's all this business about a space suit?"

"What I'm about to tell you has got to be held in strict confidence."

"Fire away."

Joanna told him about the lipolytic enzyme and how it appeared to have induced malignant tumors in two patients. She described her visit to the Bio-Med plant, giving Mack all the details of the laboratory where the technician wore a space suit.

Mack squinted an eye at Joanna. "A space suit, with a visor and everything?"

Joanna nodded. "And a tube connected to the helmet to supply oxygen."

"What the hell were they doing back there?"

"They said that their cell lines were being contaminated with an adenovirus," Joanna told him. "They thought the virus was being transmitted into the lab by the personnel who worked in there. The space suit was meant to prevent the individual from contaminating the cell lines."

Mack slowly digested the information and then ran a hand through his hair. "Something is wrong here."

"Like what?"

"Like you usually wear a space suit to keep nasty viruses away from an individual," Mack explained to her. "For example, if you were working with the Ebola or Marburg virus, you'd wear the space suit to keep the virus *out* and not let it get in to the person. But at Bio-Med it seems they're using the space suit to prevent a person from transmitting a virus into the lab." He slowly shook his head. "I've never heard of any laboratory doing that. Why spend all the money when you don't have to?"

"Are you saying they don't need the space suit to contain the adenovirus?"

"Not in my book," Mack said. "All that technician needed to wear was a mask, surgical gown, and latex gloves. That keeps out the HIV and hepatitis viruses. It sure as hell would keep in an adenovirus."

"Maybe that's why the technician was wearing plain latex gloves rather than the big bulky ones you usually see with the space suit outfit," Joanna said, thinking aloud. "But it still doesn't tell us why she wore a space suit."

Mack tilted back in his chair and rocked gently, considering the various viruses that could contaminate an in vitro cell line. Usually it was the Epstein-Barr virus, not the adenoviruses, that caused the contamination. Then Mack remembered that sometimes strange, modified forms of adenoviruses were used in genetics laboratories. "Did you ask about the type of adenovirus that was causing them trouble?"

"No," Joanna replied. "Is that important here?"

"It could be," Mack explained. "Genetic labs often

use a modified form of adenovirus to serve as a vector which transfers genetic information from one cell to another."

He saw the puzzled looks on their faces and went into more detail. "Let me give you an example. Say you wanted to transfer DNA or genes from cell A to cell B. It can be done using a virus as a carrier. First, you take an adenovirus and modify it by removing its disease-producing portion. Next you take a sip of DNA from cell A and attach it to the modified virus; then expose the mixture to cell B. The virus carrying DNA from cell A then penetrates cell B. And voila! You've effected the transfer of DNA or genes from cell A to cell B."

Joanna let the information sink in before saying, "I'm not sure they do that kind of work out at Bio-Med."

"Every genetics lab is doing it," Mack said promptly. "They believe it represents the key to the magic kingdom. You see, you can use the same technique to transfer genes from one animal to another animal."

"Assuming that's all true," Joanna said, "why would the Bio-Med people be so concerned with a modified adenovirus that can't cause disease?"

"Maybe the modified virus turned out to be something they didn't expect," Mack theorized. "Maybe it turned out to be something vicious as hell."

Joanna nodded as the pieces began to fall into place. "So the real reason for the space suit might be to prevent the modified nasty virus from infecting the technician?"

"That'd be my guess," Mack said carefully. "But keep in mind, it's only a guess."

"And there's no way to prove or disprove it."

"You might ask them straight out."

"They'd never admit it."

"Then question the personnel out there," Mack advised. "See if some of them have come down with terrible virus infections."

"Questions and more questions," Joanna grumbled. "With no answers. And chances are, this virus has nothing to do with the cancers caused by that damn enzyme."

Mack shrugged. "You never know until you look."

The door to the forensic laboratory opened, and a secretary stuck her head in. "Dr. Blalock, Dean Murdock would like to see you as soon as possible. He's in the conference room."

Joanna turned to Mack. "Thanks for your help. I'll let you know if anything else turns up."

"If you want me to go out there and snoop around with you, just give me a call," Mack offered. "I'm real good at that."

Joanna hurried out of the laboratory and into the corridor, hoping that Simon Murdock wasn't bringing more bad news. Which would mean even more work. She was already overloaded to the max, working sixteen-hour days and making absolutely no progress. None. Nada. The only things she was uncovering were more questions she couldn't answer.

A modified virus! Goddamn it! What did that have to do with anything? Probably nothing. But she'd have to track it down and see where it led. She wondered where she'd find the time to do it.

Joanna entered the conference room. Simon Murdock was pacing around a big oval-shaped table. The blinds in the room were drawn, the phone buttons flashing on hold.

"Lock the door, please," Murdock said in a somber voice.

Joanna turned the lock and looked over at Murdock. He had a worried expression on his face, the lines deeper than ever. "Bad news?"

"The worst," Murdock replied. "It seems we have another cancer in the enzyme-treated group."

"Oh, Lord!" Joanna groaned and sat in a high-backed chair. "Where is the cancer located?"

"Kidney."

"And he had his renal arteries cleaned out with the lipolytic enzyme. Right?"

"Exactly."

"It's a nightmare, Simon," Joanna said softly. "A medical disaster."

"There's still a glimmer of hope," Murdock told her. "The presence of the cancer hasn't been proved yet."

Joanna reached for a pen and a file card. "Give me all the details."

Murdock continued to pace. "He's a sixty-year-old patient who had extensive atheromatous plaques blocking his renal arteries. As a result, he was hypertensive and his kidneys were starting to fail. He underwent the arterial cleansing procedure and everything reversed. He was doing wonderfully well until yesterday when he began to urinate blood. X rays show a mass in his right kidney."

"It's cancer," Joanna said.

"But they haven't proved it yet," Murdock argued. "He'll have surgery next week, and they'll do a biopsy then."

Joanna looked up from her file card. "Why the delay?"

"Because he has pneumonia from which he is now recovering."

Joanna thought through the case again, concentrating on the patient's renal mass. "Was the mass present in X rays done before the patient received the lipolytic enzyme?"

"They don't think so."

"It's cancer," Joanna said again. "We may as well face up to it."

"But it's only in one kidney," Murdock said hopefully. "So if we remove that cancerous kidney, perhaps he'll be cured."

"Maybe for now," Joanna told him. "But remember, that enzyme preparation was squirted into both renal arteries. It's only a matter of time before the other kidney develops a cancer. That patient is sitting on a time bomb."

"Shit," Murdock muttered, allowing himself a rare obscenity. "And to make matters worse, this patient also sits on the editorial board of the *Los Angeles Times*."

Joanna watched Murdock slump into a chair at the far end of the table. He looked like a very tired, very old man. "There's no way you can keep this nightmare under wraps any longer. You'll have to issue some sort of statement."

"Saying what?"

"The truth," Joanna advised. "Make it plain and to the point so everybody understands it."

Murdock sighed sadly. "Another scandal at Memorial. Another black mark against our good name."

"It would be foolish to try to cover up any of this," Joanna warned. "That will only make it worse later on. You should tell the public exactly what we know."

Murdock nodded slowly. "I'd like you to look at the statement before it's issued."

"Of course."

"You'll be around all day?"

"And all night."

Joanna left the conference room, for once feeling sorry for Simon Murdock. There was no way to sugar-coat the press release. It was a medical nightmare no matter how you phrased it. Memorial had, in fact, given people cancer. It was more than a scandal. It was a catastrophe that would stain Memorial's name for years to come.

Joanna entered the forensic reception area, poured coffee into a plastic cup, and walked into the laboratory at the rear. Mack and Green were gone. Lori was hanging up the wall phone.

"Guess what?" Lori asked.

"What?" Joanna asked, hoping it wasn't more bad news.

"They found some peculiar-looking material in Edmond Rabb's skull fracture," Lori reported.

Joanna put her cup down, her eyes glued on Lori. "Who found it?"

"The people who did the electron microscopic study," Lori said. "They discovered some slivers of a foreign material embedded in the fracture site. And they were able to get some of it out."

Joanna's mind went back to the *Argonaut* and the thick bottles of Coca-Cola served aboard the ship. She wondered if there were chips of glass in Edmond Rabb's skull. "Were they able to identify the foreign matter?"

"That's the strange part," Lori said. "They think the material is regular old leather."

Joanna's eyes widened. "They zapped him."

"They *what*?"

"They zapped him with a blackjack."

Joanna reached for the phone and dialed Jake's office number. He wasn't in. He was attending Billy Cunningham's funeral.

Lori watched Joanna hang up, not certain what a blackjack was. She had heard the term used but had never really seen one. "Without sounding too stupid, can I ask what a blackjack looks like?"

"It's a short, leather-covered club," Joanna said darkly. "It's the perfect weapon to crack open someone's skull with."

16

Sara Ann Moore watched the doctor's house from her parked car, wondering if the woman who had gone inside an hour earlier was going to spend the night. The woman wasn't carrying an overnight case and had left her car on the street rather than in the driveway. She was probably visiting.

Bright headlights suddenly appeared in the rearview mirror. Sara quickly slumped down under the steering wheel and stayed there until the car passed by. The residential neighborhood was upper middle class and quiet, with very little traffic. There were no sounds except for an occasional barking dog.

Sara checked her watch. It was ten and it looked as if this was going to be another wasted night. For seven days she had been following the doctor, and all he seemed to do was eat, sleep, and work. He appeared to have no social life until tonight.

Sara's mind went back to the woman who had gone into the house just before nine. Her appearance was tawdry and cheap. She was wearing boots with high heels, a miniskirt and a short coat that was made from some type of animal fur. She could easily have passed for a hooker. A hooker! Maybe the woman *was* a hooker.

Sara's gaze went to the woman's car. An old beat-up Ford that stood out like a sore thumb in a neighborhood full of Mercedes and Lexus. A hooker, Sara thought again. Maybe part of some escort service. It all fit together now. The doctor was so busy he ate only take-out food, and he probably only screwed take-out women. If this woman was a call girl, it opened up all sorts of possibilities on how to set up the doctor's accidental death.

Sara opened the car door and quietly closed it behind her. She waited for some overhead clouds to pass in front of the moon. Then she darted across the street and up the doctor's driveway. She crept along the side of the house, keeping within the shadows. The adjacent house was dark except for a lighted upstairs window. Sara could hear a child's voice and a small dog yapping, but they seemed to be away from the window.

In the doctor's house the lights were on. Pressing herself against the house, she moved silently up to the first window and peered in. It was a small library with a desk and swivel chair and bookshelves. One wall was covered with framed certificates and photographs.

Sara heard a female voice and rapidly ducked down. There was more talking—then laughter. A big dog barked in the night, but it was houses away. The moon was bright again, casting shadows everywhere.

Sara waited for the clouds to block out the moonlight before moving on to the next window. Now the voices were louder. She heard a man's voice say, "Don't tell me you forgot the goddamn menthol."

"I swear I put some in my bag before I came over," the woman said.

"Shit!"

Very slowly Sara rose up and peeked in from the corner of the window. She quickly dropped back down, not believing what she had seen. Holy Christ! A freak show! Again she slowly rose and peeked in.

Alex Mirren was lying spread-eagled on his bed with all his extremities tied securely to the bedposts with black silk stockings. Someone had drawn red circles around his nipples and genitals with lipstick.

"I know the menthol cream is in here somewhere," the hooker said as she rummaged through her purse. She was a tall, thin woman with bushy red hair and small breasts. A cigarette dangled from her lips. She was wearing boots with spike heels, pink panties, and fishnet hose. "I must have lost it."

"Well, go get some, goddamn it!" Mirren demanded.

"I live out in the Valley," the hooker complained. "It'll take me an hour to get there and back."

"There's an all-night drugstore at Wilshire and Dorsey," Mirren said. "Go get the stuff and get the hell back here. And make sure it's the double-strength menthol cream."

"Yeah, yeah," the hooker said unhappily. "I know."

Sara watched the hooker dress, praying that the woman wouldn't untie Mirren before she left. The setup was so perfect. Alex Mirren would die in what looked like an accident, and someone else would be blamed for it. So perfect. Just leave his freaky ass tied up to the bedposts.

The hooker was tucking her blouse into her miniskirt. "This is going to cost you extra, you know?"

"Just get the damn menthol!"

Sara knew what the mentholated cream would be used for. One of her girlfriends at Columbia had performed the menthol trick on her boyfriend regularly. The menthol cream was gently rubbed over the man's scrotum and penis. As the man achieved an erection, the woman mounted him and began to slowly ride him. The warmth of the woman's vagina turned the menthol on his genitals into an erotic heat that went on and on. The boyfriend had gone from having one orgasm per night to three.

"I've got to get some cigarettes anyhow," the hooker said, picking up her purse.

"You want to untie me?" Mirren asked submissively.

The hooker hesitated. "How far away is the drugstore?"

"About five blocks."

The hooker tapped Mirren's penis with her index finger. "Should I or shouldn't I?"

"Please."

The hooker grabbed his testicles and squeezed,

making Mirren groan loudly and hump up against her hand. "You stay right where you are, Tiger."

Sara watched the hooker leave the room. Mirren remained tied to the bedposts. Like a chicken ready to be plucked. The front door slammed loudly. The door wouldn't be locked, Sara thought. There was no way Mirren would give his key to a hooker.

The clouds moved away from the moon once more, causing eerie shadows. Sara glanced up at the lighted window in the adjacent house. For a moment she thought she saw something—then it was gone. She waited and waited. Whatever had moved was no longer there. Maybe it was a shadow from the moonlight, Sara guessed, still watching the window. The clouds passed over and blocked out the moon completely.

Sara dashed to the front entrance of the house and quickly entered through the unlocked door. She studied herself in the mirror in the foyer and adjusted her blond wig to make certain it was on straight. Then she hurried across the living room and down a narrow hallway. Sara took out her revolver and attached a silencer to it.

She took a deep breath, calming herself, and then burst into the bedroom.

Mirren looked over, momentarily dumbfounded. "Wha—?"

Sara pointed the revolver at Mirren's head. "You make a sound and you're dead. Understood?"

Mirren nodded quickly, his eyes glued on the silencer attached to the weapon. *She's going to kill me*, he thought. *She's going to blow my head off.*

"I'm here for your money," Sara said coolly. "Do as you're told and you won't get hurt."

Mirren continued to stare at the blond woman, not believing her. She and the hooker had planned the robbery. And he could identify both. They were going to rob him, then kill him.

"Where's your wallet?"

"In—in the top drawer of the dresser," Mirren stammered.

"Good," Sara said agreeably. "And where's the money you hide?"

"In the closet," Mirren croaked, his throat so dry he could barely form the words. "In the blue blazer."

"Good," Sara said again. "Now open your mouth so I can stuff some Kleenex in. I don't want you screaming your head off after I leave."

Mirren breathed a silent sigh of relief. She wasn't going to kill him after all. "How am I going to get myself untied?"

"Oh, I'm certain you'll think of a way."

Sara reached for the box of tissues at the bedside. "Open wide."

Mirren did as he was told. One tissue after another was forced into his mouth. His cheeks bulged out like someone holding his breath underwater.

Sara went into the bathroom and came back with a pair of scissors. At the foot of the bed she grabbed the end of a black silk stocking and stretched it out. She cut off a two-foot length of stocking and pocketed the scissors. Then she held the piece of stocking by its ends and began to twirl it until it became ropelike.

"Wh—fo—?" Mirren garbled through the mouthful of tissues.

"What's it for?" Sara asked him back. "Why, it's for fun and games. Here, let me show you."

Mirren suddenly realized something was terribly wrong. She hadn't bothered to look into his wallet or to search the closet for hidden money. Now she was walking toward him, still twirling the black stocking.

Quickly Sara placed the black stocking around his neck and crossed the ends over each other. "So far so good, huh?"

Mirren's eyes were bulging out of his head.

"Now watch."

Sara tightened the stocking around his neck, cutting off Mirren's air supply.

Mirren's eyes bulged out even farther, his face turning a purplish red. He twisted and turned so violently that the bed came off the floor, but the bonds held him in place. Gagging and choking, he tried to spit out the Kleenex tissues that were stuffed in his mouth.

Sara tightened the noose even more and rode him, as if she were on the back of a bucking horse. Slowly his resistance weakened, and then he stopped moving altogether. He died with his eyes and mouth wide open.

Sara quickly removed the Kleenex tissues from Mirren's mouth and flushed them down the toilet. She took the scissors from her pocket and placed them back in the medicine cabinet where she'd found them.

Returning to the bedroom, she carefully scanned Mirren's body to make certain everything was set up perfectly. Her gaze went to the area of the sheet just beneath Mirren's crotch. There were small pools of drying semen on the sheet from his earlier encounter with the hooker. That made for a very nice touch, Sara thought.

Once more she surveyed the room, looking for anything that might be out of order. Satisfied, she went back into the bathroom and searched for any mistakes she might have made. Everything was fine. And for added good measure, some strands from the hooker's red hair were in the basin. Perfect.

Sara hurried out of the house, closing the front door behind her. She used a handkerchief to wipe the doorknob clean of fingerprints.

The moonlight was bright, even brighter than before. And the clouds around the moon weren't moving. Sara ran for her car and started the engine. As she was about to switch on the lights, she saw approaching headlights in her rearview mirror. She slumped down in her seat, keeping the engine running.

An old Ford pulled into Alex Mirren's driveway. The hooker got out carrying a package and hurried into the house, slamming the door behind her.

Sara drove away slowly with her lights still off.

17

"Why?" Girish Gupta, the medical examiner, asked in astonishment. "Why risk everything for this kind of nonsense?"

"I don't know," Jake said, circling the body of Alex Mirren. The doctor was still tied to the bedposts and spread-eagled. His face was colored a deep purple, his eyes bulging out.

"I mean, this fellow had everything in the world," Gupta went on. "And he throws it all away for a few moments of sexual gratification."

"So you figure it was all fun and games?"

"Most certainly." Gupta pointed at the black stockings that tied the corpse to the bedposts. "It's a straightforward case of bondage. And the man was a willing participant."

"How do you know he was so willing?"

"Two findings," Gupta said, his tone now clinical. "First, there was no sign of a struggle. Second, the red circles around his nipples and genitals are evenly drawn. Had he resisted, the lipstick lines would have zigzagged a bit."

"Good points," Jake agreed, examining the ligature around the corpse's neck and the deep imprint it made into the skin. Then he went to the foot of the bed and inspected the cut-off end of a black stocking. "But there is something here that bothers me."

Gupta moved in closer. "What is that?"

"The stocking has been twisted into a rope. And that would be sure to leave a deep indentation in the skin. A pro would never do that. He or she would use a flattened-out stocking. That would leave less of a mark."

"Maybe she was inexperienced," Gupta suggested.

"I guess," Jake said, still unconvinced. He studied the corpse of Alex Mirren and wondered about the mind-set of people who shut off their air supply for sexual gratification. Orgasms were supposedly magnified by momentarily depriving the brain of oxygen. But sometimes people went too far and ended up dead, like Dr. Alex Mirren.

Jake glanced at the area beneath Mirren's genitals. On the sheet were two dried semen stains. A hell of a price to pay for an orgasm, Jake thought. And then there was the price Mirren's family would pay. The public embarrassment and humiliation would last for the rest of their lives.

"We are very fortunate that his maid came in today." Gupta broke into his thoughts. "She comes in only once a week, and had she not come in this morning the body would have lain here for six days. He would have ended up being a pile of jelly. And that would have been bad for us. Very bad."

Jake nodded, hating cases that had become putrid. Not only was most of the bodily evidence destroyed, but the smell that came from the remains stayed in Jake's nostrils for days afterward.

His mind drifted back to the maid who had found the corpse just after 10 A.M. The Mexican woman had screamed her head off until the neighbors came running. They saw what the maid had seen and called the police. At least five neighbors had entered the house, and all swore they had touched nothing. Which was bullshit, Jake thought. They had touched the phone and the door and the night table and trampled over any evidence that might have been on the carpet or floor. The neighbors were all visibly upset, but at least one of them had taken the time to call a local television station.

The first black-and-white unit arrived on the scene just before a television truck pulled up to the curb.

And the news had spread like wildfire. Now a circus was going on outside the Mirren home. Television trucks with antennas were parked across the street, and news reporters were yelling out questions to anyone who entered or exited the house. A goddamn circus, Jake thought sourly, with Alex Mirren the freak show.

Jake walked into an adjoining bathroom and quickly glanced around. Everything was in order. The towels were neatly folded, the soap dish clean and dry. The medicine cabinet contained the usual—a bottle of aspirin, shaving materials, toothbrush and toothpaste, a pair of scissors. Closing the cabinet door, Jake glanced down at the basin and saw several strands of hair. They were long and coarse and red. Alex Mirren's hair was short and black. Jake carefully placed the red strands in an envelope.

Jake returned to the bedroom, where Girish Gupta was holding a thermometer up to the light.

"From a temperature standpoint," Gupta reported, "he's been dead approximately twelve hours."

Jake counted back in time. "So he died at about eleven last night?"

"Correct."

Jake grumbled under his breath. Eleven p.m. was late. Most people would be in bed asleep. Witnesses would be hard to come by.

"Are there any particular studies you would like, Lieutenant?"

"The usual," Jake said, and slowly walked around the bedroom, checking to see if he had missed anything. The phone was next to the bed, and beside it was an unopened box of Kleenex. Jake looked into a nearby wastebasket. An empty box was inside. Nothing wrong about that. Jake looked under the bed and, seeing nothing, moved on.

The dresser drawers were closed, the clothes in the closet neatly hung. There was nothing to suggest robbery. He went back to the bed and again inspected the sheet. Between Mirren's knees was another long strand of red hair. The hooker had red hair, Jake told himself, and that narrowed the list of suspects down to about ten thousand.

Jake's eyes drifted over to the dresser. A small, white plastic bag was atop it. He strolled over and looked into the bag. It contained a bottle of mentholated backrub cream. Double strength. The sales receipt stated that the cream had been purchased at 10:20 the evening before at a nearby drugstore. Jake could think of at least a half-dozen ways the hooker might use the mentholated cream on Alex Mirren.

Lou Farelli hurried into the room and came over to Jake. He paused a moment, catching his breath. "We might have gotten lucky."

"You got a witness?" Jake asked quickly.

"Maybe," Farelli said. "The woman who lives next door—the one who called the police—told her son that something bad had happened to Alex Mirren during the night. And the little boy told her he saw two women leave the Mirren house late last night."

"Two women?"

"That's what the kid told his mother."

Jake shook his head. "That doesn't make sense. Unless the guy was doing a double-header."

"The mother says the kid has a real active imagination, like any eight-year-old would," Farelli said. "So the mother isn't sure how much the kid says is going to turn out to be fact."

"You talk to the kid?"

"Can't," Farelli told him. "The boy has got real bad asthma, and his doctor is over there now. They're treating the little guy with inhalers and all that kind of shit. The doc says we might be able to talk to the kid in an hour or so."

Jake rubbed his chin, wondering if the little boy's story would be valid. And even if it was, what could the boy have clearly seen at night from a distance of forty or fifty feet? Still, an eyewitness was an eyewitness. "What time did the little boy say he saw the women?"

"About ten-thirty."

Jake nodded to himself. That fit. The sales slip said the mentholated cream had been bought at 10:20. The drugstore was less than ten minutes away. Jake squinted an eye at Farelli. "Ten-thirty is kind of late for an eight-year-old to be up, isn't it?"

"Like I told you, the little boy has got bad asthma," Farelli explained. "He was having an attack last night, and it kept him up. The mother says the boy will sometimes watch TV until past midnight. She said it takes his mind off his trouble breathing." Farelli gave the matter a moment's thought. "It sounds right to me."

"And me," Jake said. "Put a uniformed cop outside that house. Nobody but family and police gets in."

Jake and Farelli walked out into the narrow hallway. The crime scene unit was dusting everything for fingerprints and vacuuming the carpet in the living room for possible evidence not visible to the naked eye.

Jake said, "Some of the pieces don't fit together here."

Farelli's brow went up. "Did you find something?"

"Just a lot of little things that don't add up to much yet."

"Maybe the little boy will help."

"Maybe," Jake said, sensing that he was overlooking something. What the hell was it? It had to do with the two women the boy saw. He pushed the question aside for a moment. "You've got to canvass every house on the block on both sides of the street. See if anybody saw an unfamiliar car parked at the curb." He handed Farelli the sales receipt for the mentholated cream. "I think the hooker bought this cream last night at this drugstore. See if anybody remembers her."

"Maybe she used a credit card."

Jake smiled crookedly. "In your dreams."

Jake watched Farelli hurry away, still thinking about the something he might have overlooked. It had to do with the two women, and it was right on the tip of his tongue. But he couldn't come up with it.

Jake stepped into Mirren's small library and sat on the edge of the desk, lighting a cigarette. A side wall was covered with framed diplomas and certificates and photographs. Mirren's medical degree was from the University of Michigan, his Ph.D. in genetics from Stanford. A distinguished physician, Jake thought, who played with fire and got burned.

Jake looked over at a large framed photograph and did a sudden double-take. Slowly he rose from the edge of the desk and stepped in closer. The photograph showed Alex Mirren shaking hands with Edmond Rabb. Lucy Rabb was looking on proudly. Below the photograph was a metal plaque. It read:

THE RABB AWARD FOR EXCELLENCE IN GENETICS
ALEXANDER MIRREN, M.D.

"Son of a bitch," Jake muttered under his breath, and reached for the phone.

A television reporter across the street recognized Joanna Blalock as she got out of her car.

"Dr. Blalock," the reporter shouted, "can you tell us why you're being called into this case?"

Another reporter yelled out, "Aren't you and Dr. Mirren colleagues at Memorial?"

Joanna ignored the questions and hurried up the lawn of the Mirren house. Neighbors and workers were watching the goings-on from nearby yards. Uniformed police were everywhere. Overhead a helicopter from Channel 14 was circling, getting pictures to feed back to the local television station.

Joanna ducked under the crime-scene tape and went past a thick hedge. The policeman guarding the door recognized her and gave her a half salute. Jake was waiting for her in the living room.

"It's a zoo out there," Joanna said, stepping over a vacuum cleaner.

"Tell me about it." Jake's voice was raspy from too many cigarettes. He crushed out the one he was smoking in an oversize ashtray. "You mentioned on the phone that you'd met Mirren a few days ago. What was that all about?"

"An experimental procedure gone bad."

Joanna told him about the lipolytic enzyme used to clean out arteries and how it appeared to induce cancer in three patients. She described in detail her visit to the Bio-Med plant where she had met Mirren. "So far we have no definite proof to link the enzyme to the cancers, but I think it's only a matter of time before we do."

"So this enzyme was actually manufactured by Bio-Med?"

Joanna nodded. "And injected into patients at Memorial."

"Man, oh, man! The lawyers are going to have a field day with this one."

"I guess."

Jake thought for a moment about Bio-Med and the enzyme they produced and the lawsuits and the huge amounts of money that were going to change hands. He wondered if Mirren was somehow involved in all this. "Did Mirren actually make the enzyme?"

"No," Joanna answered. "It was discovered by Eric Brennerman. He's the head scientist and one of the founders of Bio-Med."

"So Mirren was just a worker there?"

Joanna hesitated and then shrugged. "As far as I could tell."

"What kind of a guy was Mirren?"

"A big bully," Joanna said at once. "He was the type who liked to come down hard on people who couldn't defend themselves."

That fit, Jake was thinking. In his experience, the bondage freaks often appeared tough on the outside, but deep down they were submissive little assholes who enjoyed being rendered helpless. Like a Jekyll-and-Hyde personality, a police profiler had once told Jake.

"If I had to guess," Joanna went on, "I'd say he

was the type who wouldn't have any friends. I doubt if anybody would want to get real close to him."

"Well, somebody got real close to him last night."

Jake took her by the arm and guided her to the hallway. "I want you to look at a picture."

They went down the hallway and entered the compact library. Jake pointed out the framed photograph on the wall.

Joanna moved in closer and carefully studied the photo of Mirren and Edmond Rabb shaking hands. They were standing in the courtyard outside the Biogenetics Institute at Memorial. Lucy Rabb was smiling, standing close to her husband. The proud and adoring wife. Joanna wondered if Lucy was already planning her husband's murder when the photograph was being taken.

"Nice, huh?" Jake commented.

"Real cute," Joanna said, reading the plaque beneath the framed photograph. "I wonder why the Rabbs established an award for research in genetics."

Jake shrugged. "What's the usual reason for people setting up that type of award?"

"Because either they or somebody in their family have a serious genetic disorder," Joanna replied. "So they want research done on the treatment and maybe even the prevention of the disease."

"Well," Jake said, thinking aloud, "we know that Rabb's first wife died of some kind of cancer and he didn't have one of those genetic diseases, did he?"

"No."

"And his two sons that I talked to seemed okay to me," Jake went on.

"And you can bet Lucy Rabb wouldn't give a penny of her future inheritance for research."

"That's for damn sure."

Joanna mulled over the question at length. "There has got to be a reason for his genetics grant. Multimillionaires don't give away money without a very good reason."

"Is there any way to check it out?"

Joanna nodded and then pointed at the framed photograph. "That was taken on the grounds at Memorial Hospital. That means the award was given there. I'll ask Simon Murdock about it. He'll know."

Jake moved in next to her, still staring at the photograph. "Edmond Rabb looks real young there, doesn't he?"

"He probably made them take a dozen shots, then picked out the one he looked best in."

Jake grinned to himself. Only a woman would think like that. "Well, he doesn't have to worry about getting old anymore."

"He certainly doesn't," Joanna said. "Murder is one sure way to stop the aging process."

Jake jerked his head around. "You got proof?"

"Beyond any doubt." Joanna told him about the bits of worn leather that were embedded in Rabb's skull fracture. "And the blow was struck when Rabb was still alive. Those little pieces of leather were soaked in blood."

"A blackjack," Jake said, rubbing his hands together. "A damn blackjack. It's the perfect weapon here. You can hide it in your pocket or purse, you can generate a lot of force without much of a swing, and when you drop it in the ocean it doesn't make much noise and it sinks right to the bottom."

"You're going to have to requestion all the people who were aboard the *Argonaut* the night Rabb was murdered."

"Including Lucy Rabb and Mervin Tuch."

"Them most of all."

Jake smiled to himself. "This gets more and more interesting, doesn't it? We've got two men in this photograph. One was definitely murdered, the other possibly."

Joanna asked quickly, "Does Gupta think Mirren was murdered?"

Jake shook his head. "He thinks it was fun and games gone wrong."

"But you don't?"

"Let's say there are some pieces here that don't fit."

Jake led the way out and into the bedroom. Gupta was leaning over the corpse, scraping off a sample of red lipstick for further analysis. The air was filled with the smell of a sickly sweet deodorizer.

Gupta glanced up and waved. "Ah, Dr. Blalock! How nice to see you again. And so soon, too."

"I hope you don't mind me taking a look," Joanna said amicably.

"Mind?" Gupta dismissed the notion with a flick of his hand. "Your expertise is always welcomed."

"Thank you."

Gupta stepped back from the bed and watched and wondered—as always—what he had overlooked. Joanna Blalock had a knack for seeing things that other people didn't. And she always seemed to make so much from such a small finding. It was as if the clue was sitting there, waiting just for her. Nonsense, Gupta told himself. His eyes were connected to his brain, just like Joanna's. The difference was that her cerebral connections were more finely tuned.

Joanna slipped on a pair of latex gloves and walked around Mirren's body, checking the ligature around his neck and the deep indentation it had left. His face was deep purple, congested with blood. She pulled down Mirren's lower eyelids and saw the small petechial hemorrhages that indicated death by strangulation.

She studied his genitals and saw the semen stains on the sheet beneath them. Next she went to his abdomen and chest. Joanna saw the lipstick circles, but no whip or belt marks. Her gaze went to the black stockings that bound the corpse's arms and legs. She noticed the cut-off end on one of the leg ligatures. Quickly she looked over at the black stocking around Mirren's neck. It was shorter than the others and it, too, had a cut-off end. Finally she went back and carefully examined the ligatures around Mirren's limbs.

"Well?" Jake asked.

"I can't be sure," Joanna said hesitantly. "But I'd guess it's more than just fun and games."

"Are you talking murder?"

"Maybe."

It had to be, Jake thought. It had to be murder. Three people in the photograph and two die under suspicious circumstances within weeks of each other. They had to be connected. "Tell me why."

"First of all," Joanna began, "there's the ligature around his neck. It was twirled into a cord, so it left a very deep mark for all the world to see. A pro would never do that."

Right, Jake thought. She was thinking the same way he had.

"Perhaps the hooker was inexperienced," Gupta suggested again.

"I don't think so," Joanna explained. "The bindings on his wrists and ankles are done exactly right. They're neatly tied and secure, but not too tight. And she left him just the right amount of wiggle room. So we can say he was tied up by a pro, but it looks as if he wasn't strangled by one."

Jake's eyes narrowed, remembering the little boy next door who had told his mother he saw two women. "Are you saying there were two women here?"

"I'm saying that's a possibility," Joanna said carefully. "It's also possible that the hooker who tied him up became angry and lost her cool and in a fit of rage killed him."

Gupta was having trouble putting the pieces of evidence together. It still didn't look like murder to him. "But surely he would have had an inkling that they were doing something wrong. At some point he would have known his life was in danger. Why didn't he scream for help? Perhaps the neighbors would have heard and come to his aid."

"He didn't scream because he couldn't," Joanna told him. "Assuming your scenario is correct, he wouldn't have realized that something was wrong until it was too late. The stocking would already have been around his neck. And people being strangled can barely make a gurgling sound, much less scream."

Gupta considered all the clues uncovered so far, weighing them carefully. "So it could well be murder. But our evidence for that is still weak. Very weak indeed."

Joanna nodded. "It would never stand up in a court of law."

"Perhaps the autopsy will tell us more."

"Don't bet on it."

Joanna peeled off her gloves and dropped them in the wastebasket. She glanced back at the corpse of Alex Mirren, wondering if there was any way to track down the hooker involved.

Farelli hurried into the room and nodded to Joanna. "Hi, Doc," he said genially, and smiled at her. "How are you doing?"

"Just fine." Joanna grinned back.

"Nasty business, huh?"

"The worst."

Farelli turned to Jake. "The little boy's asthma is better. He's ready to talk with us."

"What's this about?" Joanna asked.

"An eyewitness, we think," Jake told her. "Want to come along?"

"You bet!"

Mikey Sellman looked like a little boy out of a Norman Rockwell painting. He was a thin eight-year-old with tousled blond hair and deep blue eyes. His legs dangled over the side of his bed, not yet long enough to reach the floor. Next to him was his dog, a beagle named Sparky.

"How you doing, Mikey?" Jake asked.

"Okay," the little boy said.

Jake eased himself down on a small stool so that his eyes were on the same level as the boy's. "I heard you weren't feeling so good last night."

"My asthma."

"But your mom says you're feeling better now."

"Yeah."

"Good," Jake said, nodding. But he could still hear

a few wheezes coming from the boy's chest. "I'm Detective Sinclair, and these people over here are some other detectives." Jake pointed with his thumb to Joanna and Farelli. "Do you feel up to answering some questions for us?"

"Sure."

"Late last night your mom said you saw some people coming out of Dr. Mirren's house," Jake began, his voice soft like that of a storyteller. "Is that right?"

"Uh-huh."

"What did you see?"

"A lady came out."

"What did she look like?"

The boy shrugged. "It was dark."

"Do you remember anything about her?"

Mikey started scratching the dog's stomach, smiling as the dog stretched out happily. He looked back at Jake. "She had real bushy hair."

An Afro? Jake wondered. "Was she black?"

Mikey shook his head. "And she had real long legs."

"Good," Jake said encouragingly. "That really helps us. Now, how bushy was her hair?"

Mikey held his hands up to his head and kept them over a foot apart. "Like that."

Jake remembered the long, coarse red hair he'd found in Mirren's basin, thinking they probably came from the hooker's bushy hair. "What time was that?"

Mikey turned to his mother, who was standing by the door. "It was in the middle of *Dragnet*."

"Dragnet?" Jake raised an eyebrow. The popular television series hadn't been on for over thirty years.

"Uh-huh."

"Mikey watches the TV Land channel," Mrs. Sellman explained. "They show a lot of old reruns."

Jake asked, "What time does *Dragnet* come on?"

"Ten o'clock."

It's a half-hour show, Jake recalled. "So that would make it about ten-fifteen."

Mikey nodded.

Jake nodded back. The hooker had purchased the mentholated cream at 10:20. The drugstore was about five minutes away from the Mirren house. "What happened next?"

"That's when the other lady went in," Mikey said without hesitation.

Son of a bitch, Jake was thinking. There were two women involved. "The other lady went in right after the first lady left?"

"Uh-huh. She came from the side of the house."

"And what did she look like?"

"Her hair was like mine."

"You could see it real good, huh?" Jake asked.

Mikey nodded again. "When the moon came back out."

"And you're sure her hair was blond?"

"Uh-huh," Mikey answered.

Jake quickly put the pieces of the boy's story together. A blond woman was on the side of the house, waiting for the hooker to leave, maybe even watching the show through a side window. The hooker leaves, the blonde moves in real quick and ices the doc before the hooker returns. Yeah. It had to be the blonde who— Son of a bitch! A blonde whacked the doctor. Maybe the same blonde who iced the Russian. Just maybe. But how could Mirren and the Russian be connected? They came from such different worlds. Jake hurriedly thought of other possibilities. Maybe the hooker and the blonde worked as a team. No, no, he decided quickly. The hooker came back with the menthol cream because she thought Mirren was still alive.

"You feel okay?" the little boy asked, studying the expression on the detective's face.

"Yeah. I just got a cold," Jake said, bringing his expression back to neutral.

"I get them all the time, too."

"Now, I really want you to think hard on this one, Mikey," Jake said. "How long did the blond lady stay inside the house?"

"Just a few minutes."

"Then she left?"

Mikey nodded. "And then the lady with the bushy hair came back."

"What time was that?"

Mikey's gaze went to his mother. "Just before *Gunsmoke* started."

"That would make it a little before ten-thirty," the mother told them.

"When the bushy-haired lady came back, was she carrying anything?" Jake asked.

Mikey thought for a moment. "She got out of her car carrying a bag of something."

The mentholated cream, Jake thought. She was bringing back the— His mind suddenly flashed back to the hooker's car. "Did you see the bushy-haired lady's car?"

Mikey nodded. "In the driveway."

"What did the car look like?"

Mikey shrugged. "It was kind of old. That's all I remember."

"Thanks, Mikey," Jake said, and moved aside, letting Farelli step in.

"You know, Mikey," Farelli said easily, "I have a son about your age, and he watches a lot of television."

"What's his favorite show?" Mikey asked.

"Beavis and Butthead."

Mikey nodded quickly. "I like them a lot, too."

"Now, when my boy watches TV," Farelli went on, "I can't pull him away from the set. Do you think there could have been more people in that house and you just missed them because you were watching TV?"

Mikey shook his head firmly. "If anybody comes, Sparky starts barking and jumping around. We see everybody who comes and goes."

"I'll bet you do."

Jake glanced over at Joanna. "You got any questions for Mikey?"

"Just one or two."

Joanna sat on the bed next to the little boy and scratched the beagle's ear. "Do you know that a dog once saved my life?"

Mikey was immediately interested. "How?"

"Once I got caught in a mudslide and got all covered up. They couldn't find me, so they brought in a bloodhound and he started digging into the ground at the exact place I was buried."

"Wow!"

"I didn't like dogs so much before that, but I like them a lot now."

Mikey picked up his dog and allowed it to lick his face. "I love Sparky."

"I know," Joanna said, hearing Mikey's wheezes and thinking what a cruel fate it was for a little boy to have severe asthma. "Can I ask you a few quick questions?"

"Sure."

"How can you be so sure that the blond lady was on the side of the house?" Joanna asked. "Maybe she just walked across your lawn to get to the Mirren house."

Mikey shook his head. "I saw her come up Dr. Mirren's lawn and go to the side of the house. That's when Sparky really started barking."

"Was she carrying anything with her?"

Mikey shook his head again.

"And you're sure her hair was blond, huh?"

"Just like mine."

"Was it pulled back?" Joanna asked. "Like mine is?"

"No. It was straight down." Mikey pointed over to his mother. "It kind of looked like Mom's."

Jake nodded to himself. Blond hair, shoulder length. Maybe she left some of it behind for the crime scene unit to find.

"Mikey, you really helped us a lot," Joanna said, getting to her feet. "I know your mom is very proud of you."

Mrs. Sellman walked them down the stairs to the

front door. As Joanna and the detectives stepped out, reporters began yelling out questions from across the street.

Jake turned to Mrs. Sellman. "Ma'am, I'm going to leave a police officer at your door for a while to make sure the press doesn't bother you."

"Thank you, Lieutenant."

The detectives and Joanna walked across the lawn, heading for Alex Mirren's house. They ignored the reporters who continued to shout questions. Three television trucks with antennas were parked at the curb.

"A zoo," Farelli commented as they approached the Mirren driveway. "A big, damn zoo."

Jake signaled to a member of the crime scene unit and quickly walked over. "Did you find any blond hairs?"

"Not yet," the investigator replied. "Why?"

"Because a blond woman was seen on this side of the victim's house last night," Jake told him. "Check around, particularly by the window looking into the victim's bedroom. You're searching for long blond hair and maybe fingerprints on the window or window-sill."

"I'll get right on it."

Jake watched the investigator leave, thinking about other places the blonde might have left her finger-prints. The front doorknob, the Kleenex box, maybe the night table. He made a mental note of the places and then turned to Joanna and Farelli. "Are you two thinking what I'm thinking?"

"Regarding what?" Joanna asked.

"I'm thinking Los Angeles may be a big city, but I'll bet we've got only one young, blond, female hitter running around."

"The blond hitter," Joanna said, nodding to herself. "A pro who tries to cover up her hits."

"It's almost got to be," Jake agreed. "She carefully set up the hit on the Russian and did the same with Alex Mirren."

"And I'll bet she had him staked out," Farelli picked up the story. "And she just waited. Then the bondage hooker comes along and gives the hitter a golden opportunity."

Jake nodded. "That's why the ligature around Mirren's neck was all wrong. Our hitter doesn't have much experience in bondage games." Jake looked toward the rear window of Mirren's house. The hitter could have been in and out in under five minutes. It doesn't take long to strangle a tied-down man. "And the timing was perfect. According to Mikey, the hooker left the house at ten-fifteen or so, and we know she went to the drugstore to buy the mentholated cream. She made the buy at ten-twenty. While the hooker was away, the blond hitter moved in for the kill."

Joanna stared out into space, thinking aloud. "What in the world does Alex Mirren have to do with a Russian carrying around dead fetuses?"

"I don't know," Jake said. "But they were both killed by the same blond hitter and that connects them to one another." He glanced over at Farelli. "Anything new on the Russian?"

"Nothing so far," Farelli answered. "The cable company in that area isn't doing such a good job. They've had hundreds of complaints. We're running them down one by one."

"You check their workbooks for Russian- or Middle European–sounding names?"

"Nada. A big blank."

They crossed the lawn to Alex Mirren's house and entered. The crime scene unit was finishing up in the living room and starting to pack away their equipment. Jake led the way into the kitchen, where he turned on the water and took a swig from the faucet.

"We've got to find that hooker," Jake said, wiping his lips with a finger.

"You figure she's involved?" Farelli asked.

"Probably not," Jake said. "But she might have

seen something we can track. She and that blond hitter might have crossed paths, if only for an instant."

"Shit," Farelli grumbled. "We'll have to interview a million hookers. And chances are, we'll still come up empty."

"There might be an easier way," Joanna suggested.

"We're listening," Jake said.

Joanna pointed at a messy countertop that was covered with empty boxes and containers for pizza and take-out Chinese food. Receipts from the food deliveries were still attached to the empty boxes. "This guy called out to have his food delivered. He might have done the same thing for the hooker. There must be a dozen escort services listed in the yellow pages."

Farelli smiled at her and then at Jake. "She's getting pretty good at this, isn't she?"

Jake looked at Joanna admiringly. "And he probably called from home."

"Or on his way home," Farelli added and pointed out the window at Mirren's car in the driveway.

Atop its rear window was a car-phone antenna.

18

Jake and Farelli trudged up the stairs to the third floor of the old office building. The wooden steps creaked loudly under their weight.

"And of course, the prick has got to have his office on the third floor," Farelli grumbled.

"Of course," Jake said.

"And of course, the elevator in this piece-of-shit place ain't working."

"I wouldn't use it if it was."

"You got a point."

Everything about the building in North Hollywood was old and run-down. The exterior was covered with pink paint that was cracked and peeling. Inside, the floors were scuffed and worn, the ceiling spotted with watermarks. And its elevator looked like an antique. It was a brass cage with its door chained shut. An OUT OF ORDER sign was attached to it.

At the third-floor landing, Farelli stopped and leaned down to massage his thigh. It felt as if there were a hot poker inside it.

"Is your leg still bothering you?" Jake asked.

Farelli downplayed it. "Some."

"Maybe you ought to go back and see the doc about it."

"I did. He said to keep exercising it."

Farelli straightened up and pushed the pain aside. Reaching for his notepad, he said, "Let me tell you about the guy who runs this escort service. He's a hustler named Frankie White. According to Vice, he's a small-time operator who runs a string of five or six girls. He does his business out of this office and contacts the hookers by beeper."

"Any rough stuff?"

"None recently." Farelli turned to a page in his notepad and referred to it briefly. "He once did five years in the slammer for armed robbery. But that was in the early seventies."

"And since then he's gone on to bigger and better things."

"Yeah," Farelli said, closing his notepad. "Now he runs a stable."

They walked down a narrow, stale-smelling corridor to Suite 302. ECSTASY ESCORTS was painted on the glass panel in the door. Inside, someone was coughing loudly. Jake knocked and entered, Farelli a step behind him.

A middle-aged man talking on the phone behind the desk looked up. He had a cigar clenched between his teeth. "Yeah? What?"

Jake flashed his shield. "You Frankie White?"

The man spoke quickly into the phone. "I'll get back to you," he said, and hung up. His gaze went back to the detectives. "Yeah. I'm White."

"We need to talk to you about your girls," Jake said.

"I guess I'd better call a lawyer," White said unhappily.

"Why? Have you done something wrong?"

White glanced back and forth between the two detectives. "What do you want?"

"We want to look at the list of girls you sent out last night, and we want to know where you sent them," Jake said.

"I don't keep records." White was a short, wiry man, totally bald except for a fringe of hair just above his ears. His eyes were dark and lifeless, his teeth stained brown from tobacco. He tilted back in his straight wooden chair and puffed on his cigar. "I got no records. So it looks like I can't help you."

Farelli moved in next to White. "No record book, huh?"

"How many times I got to say it?"

Farelli kicked the chair out from under White. The cigar went flying into the air as Frankie White landed flat on his back with a loud thud. His head bounced off the wooden floor. "Oww! Goddamn it!"

"You've got to watch those chairs," Farelli said coldly. "Sometimes they slip."

"I ain't got no damn books." White picked himself and his chair off the floor. Then he searched around for his cigar. "If you don't want to believe me, too fucking bad."

"We can do this the easy way or the hard way," Jake said, and waited for White to relight his cigar.

"I've had my balls busted plenty of times before," White spat. "One more time ain't going to matter."

"That's the easy way," Jake went on. "The tough way would be for me to have to round up your girls and question them individually. And after I've questioned them, I'll have a cop tag along with them wherever they go. That won't be so good for business."

White shrugged, unmoved.

"And then I'll have the girls talk to the people over at the IRS. I'll bet those girls have been paying you a cut, and I'll bet you haven't been reporting that to the IRS as income."

White's eyes slowly widened.

"Then the girls will give evidence against you for tax evasion, and they'll be let off. But not you, Frankie." Jake lit a cigarette and inhaled deeply. "And let me remind you, those IRS guys are real bastards. They'll send you away for ten years if you try to fuck them out of a nickel."

White reached inside his coat pocket and took out a black book, his eyes still on Jake. "No IRS, right?"

"Right."

"And no tags on my girls."

"No tags."

White opened the black book. "What do you want to know?"

"You sent somebody to two-five-two Royal Drive last night," Jake said. "We want her name."

White carefully flipped through pages. "She calls herself Princess."

"You know where she lives?"

"Close by," White answered. "But I got no address."

"Does she turn tricks during the day, too?"

"Sure."

"Then beep her and get her ass up here."

Jake and Farelli waited for Princess in the corridor outside Frankie White's one-room office. White continued to conduct business over the phone even though the door was open and the detectives could hear. He tried to speak in code, but it sounded like he did some bookmaking on the side in addition to running whores.

"That guy has got balls the size of an elephant's," Farelli said, listening to White talk about a horse named Sunrise. "We're standing here and he's taking bets."

Jake shrugged. "He knows we're not interested in him."

"His code is so simple an idiot could understand it." Farelli glanced into the small office, studied White briefly, and then looked back at Jake. "You think he might have passed a code word to Princess and she split on us?"

"He's not that stupid," Jake said, taking out his notepad and turning pages. "Did you get anything from Alex Mirren's neighbors?"

"Not much," Farelli reported, reaching for his own notepad. "A surgeon who lives down the street was driving by about ten o'clock last night. He saw a car parked across from the Mirren house. The doc doesn't remember seeing anybody in it."

"Was the car old or new?" Jake asked at once, recalling that Mikey Sellman said the hooker's car was old.

"Pretty new," Farelli replied. "Maybe a Chevrolet or Buick. And all of Mirren's neighbors own foreign cars."

"It could have belonged to the blond hitter."

Farelli nodded. "It's the place I would have picked for a stakeout." He paused and scratched the side of his head. "You know, Jake, we're taking for granted that the blonde who whacked the Russian is the same one who whacked the doc. There are a hell of a lot of blondes in this city."

"Yeah, but damn few of them are professional hitters."

"I guess," Farelli said, still not convinced. He went back to his notepad. "Anyhow, the blonde covered her tracks pretty good in Santa Monica. Nobody remembers selling her gas, and we checked out all the women who bought gas with credit cards in the immediate area. A shitload of work that turned up a big nothing."

"What about the motels and bars?"

"Again a big nothing," Farelli went on, quickly flipping pages. "But I might have turned up something at the bar where the Russian was last seen. Do you remember the old female boozer at the end of the bar?"

Jake nodded. "The one with caked-on makeup?"

"Yeah. Well, I questioned her again, and she starts talking about the blonde who walked out with the Russian. The boozer called the blonde a real phony."

"Why a phony?"

"Because the boozer believes the blonde was wearing a wig." Farelli held his hand up to his head and demonstrated. "The blonde kept doing this to her hair, like she was adjusting a wig."

"Smart," Jake said. "So damn smart. The hitter knows that everybody notices blond hair. So if anybody makes her, all she has to do is throw away her blond wig, and she loses her identity."

"So now we're looking for a sometimes blonde."

Jake lit another cigarette and inhaled a lungful of blue smoke. "Life isn't easy, is it?"

"And we're batting zero on the Russian."

"Did you check the Russian Orthodox church?"

"Two of them," Farelli said. "They don't know him."

"We've got to track down that Russian," Jake said. "He could be the key to everything."

Farelli looked at Jake oddly. "I figure the Russian to be a bit player here. You know, like the delivery man who gets caught carrying the wrong goods."

"Oh, he's a bit player, all right," Jake agreed. "But he's also the link between the blond hitter and the dead babies."

Farelli nodded to himself as he put his notepad away. "And since the blonde also whacked Dr. Mirren, you figure the Russian is somehow connected to that, too?"

"He's got to be." Jake puffed at his cigarette, wondering why the Russian was proving so difficult to track down. The immigrant had to live in the neighborhood. He just had to. "You say the Russian was married?"

"That's what the guy at the hardware store told me."

"And his wife hasn't reported him missing, huh?"

"Not to the Santa Monica police or to the Bureau of Missing Persons," Farelli said. "And we double-check every day."

Jake shook his head. "That doesn't make any sense."

"Tell me about it."

They heard the click of high heels coming up the stairs.

Jake crushed his cigarette out in a standing ashtray and hurried back into Frankie White's office. Lou Farelli closed the door behind them and motioned for White to stay seated.

A moment later the door opened, and Princess entered. She glanced at Jake and Farelli and immediately recognized them as cops. Her face suddenly lost color. "Oh, shit!" she said hopelessly.

Frankie White grabbed some papers from his desk and quickly headed for the door. "Lock up when you leave."

Princess glared at him. "You could have warned me, you prick!"

"I ain't in the warning business," White said, and closed the door behind him.

"Sit," Jake told her, pointing at the soiled director's chair in front of the desk.

"I guess I'm going to need a lawyer," Princess said, sitting and crossing her long legs in a single motion.

"Maybe, maybe not." Jake studied the hooker at length. She looked exactly as the little boy had described her. Tall and thin with bushy red hair. But her face was not what Jake had expected. Her features were soft with a small nose and perfectly contoured lips.

"I think I'm going to need a lawyer," she said again.

"Listen and listen up good," Jake said, "because I'm only going to say this once. You give us the information we need, and you'll walk out of here. If you lie, twist, or hold back the truth, I'll charge you with being an accessory to murder and make it stick. And a pretty girl like you wouldn't do very well in the slammer. Believe me when I tell you that you won't get paid for the tricks you do in there."

Princess swallowed hard. "I didn't kill him."

Jake ignored her plea of innocence. "How many times have you serviced this guy?"

"Three times."

"Last night was the third?"

Princess nodded.

"What time did you arrive?"

"A little after nine."

"Did you get right to it?"

Princess shook her head slowly. "He showered first," she said quietly.

"Then?"

"Then I tied him to the bedposts and we started."

"With what?"

She turned and looked out the window. "With oral sex. He liked to perform oral sex on me while he was tied down."

"Then what?"

"He wanted me to do the menthol trick, but I had—"

"Forgotten to bring the cream," Jake filled in. "Is that why you went to the drugstore? To buy some cream?"

Princess's eyes widened. "How did you know that?"

Jake didn't answer.

Princess suddenly nodded to herself. "You were in that damn car across the street, weren't you?"

"What car?" Jake asked at once.

"The Toyo—" Princess stopped in midsentence, thinking as her lips moved silently. Slowly she shook her head. "You wouldn't have been in that car. If you had, you would have caught the person who did it."

"You said it was a Toyota."

"That's right," Princess told them. "A new Toyota."

Jake and Farelli exchanged quick glances; then they turned back to the hooker and stared at her.

"It was a goddamn Toyota," she insisted, thinking they thought she was lying.

Farelli asked, "Why did you pay so much attention to that car?"

"Just being careful," Princess explained. "Maybe some of your Vice buddies had the place staked out and were waiting for me."

"So you looked at the car real hard?" Farelli pressed on.

"Damn right! Wouldn't you?"

"Did you see a driver?"

Princess hesitated, thinking back. "Not then. But maybe later."

"What did you see?"

"When I came back from the drugstore, I pulled

into the john's driveway," Princess recounted. "As I got out of my car I looked across the street to the parked car. I thought I saw something move in the front seat. Then it was gone. I couldn't be sure anyone was there."

The blond hitter had gotten back to her car by then, Jake was thinking. The doctor was stone-cold dead.

"And then you went back into the house?"

Princess nodded. "And got the hell out when I found the doctor dead."

"Was the Toyota still there when you left?" Jake asked.

Princess shrugged. "I didn't notice. All I wanted to do was get the hell away."

Jake decided to try a long shot. "Did you ever see a blond woman around the doctor's house on any of your visits there?"

"Sure," Princess said without hesitation. "I saw a blonde the night he died."

"Where?"

"In the driveway next door," she said. "When I was driving away to pick up the mentholated cream, I saw a blond woman in the driveway by the house next door. I thought she was the next-door neighbor."

Jake and Farelli glanced at each other and exchanged nods. The hooker's story fit perfectly with the things Mikey Sellman had seen. The blonde in the driveway was the hitter.

"Are you positive that the parked car was a Toyota?" Jake asked.

"Yeah," Princess assured him. "I've been thinking about buying a new car, and I've been checking out all the new models. That car was a new Toyota."

"What color?"

"Dark. Maybe black or deep green," Princess said, thinking back. "With a California license plate."

Jake's eyes narrowed. "You wouldn't happen to have the license number?"

"It started with the number four," she said. "Then came some letters. I don't recall what they were."

Jake stared at her skeptically. "You just happened to remember that, huh?"

"Uh-huh," Princess said easily. "I looked closely at the license plate because most unmarked cop cars have a public employee designation. It's a little *E* that comes just before the numbers. That license number started with a four. There was no *E*."

"You're more than just street-smart," Jake commented, thinking the hooker was sharp and observant and spoke like someone with an education. "You're plenty bright. What the hell are you doing hooking?"

"You want the long or short version?"

"The short one."

The hooker fluffed her red hair while she considered how much to tell. "Well, it starts this way. You're making twenty-four grand a year teaching kindergarten and you're barely scraping by. A girlfriend tells you about a way to make extra money. You do it, promising yourself you'll only do it once, that you can always step back across the line. But the money is good and easy, so you do it again and again. You do it enough times and the line I just talked about becomes invisible."

"Your line is not invisible," Jake said.

"Sure it is," Princess said resignedly, and got to her feet. "You got any more questions?"

"No. That's it."

The detectives watched the hooker walk out of the office. She closed the door softly, barely making a sound.

"What do you think?" Farelli asked.

"I think our blond hitter just made a big mistake."

19

Joanna hurried up the gangplank and onto the deck of the *Argonaut*. Jake was standing near the stern, giving orders to two uniformed policemen.

"And bring his ass back here," Jake was saying.

"What if we can't find him?" the shorter cop asked.

"You keep looking until you do," Jake told him. "Start at the bar across from the entrance to the marina. That's where his girlfriend works."

Joanna waited for the policemen to leave. Then she walked over. "What's this all about?"

"One of the male guests lost a shoe on the yacht the night Rabb was killed."

"So?"

"So a shoe can make a pretty good weapon to conk somebody over the head with," Jake explained.

Joanna wrinkled her brow, now envisioning a man's shoe as a weapon. "The killer would grab the shoe by the toe end so that the heel would strike the victim's head."

"Right."

"But the heels in most boat shoes are made of rubber, and the foreign material in Rabb's skull was leather."

"True," Jake said. "But every now and then I've seen heels that are at least part leather or have a leather trim."

"I think you're more likely to see that in custom-made shoes."

Jake nodded. "This crowd could afford that."

"You sent the cops for the guy who lost the shoe?" Joanna asked.

"No," Jake said. "They went for the guy who found the shoe."

Jake explained how one of the female guests remembered that some man had misplaced a shoe. A security guard on the vessel had found it.

"Do you want to guess who the guard was?"

Joanna shrugged.

"Mr. Clean," Jake went on. "The bald guy dressed in white who was guarding the gangplank on our first visit here."

Joanna thought back. "And he told us he didn't set foot on the ship the night Rabb was murdered."

"We're going to ask him about that, too."

There was a sudden burst of laughter from the stateroom below and then a few chuckles followed by loud conversation.

"Apparently they're not in mourning anymore," Joanna observed.

"Life goes on," Jake said dryly.

"With this bunch you wonder if it ever stopped." Joanna lifted her head up to the sun and felt its warm rays on her face. In the distance she heard a boat's horn. "Jake, I hope you didn't bring me down here just to talk about a lost shoe and the security guard who found it."

"You're busy, huh?"

Joanna sighed wearily. "You've got no idea how busy. I started today looking at dead fetuses and trying to determine why somebody would eviscerate them. By noon I gave up on that one and switched over to the enzyme preparation to see if I could uncover how and why it was inducing cancer in patients. I was in the process of drawing another big blank when I received your phone message. So if there's nothing more for me here, I'd like to get back to my lab where I can continue to come up with big zeroes."

"There's more," Jake said.

"Like what?"

"Like an invitation list." Jake reached into his coat pocket and took out a long sheet of paper. "Pay particular attention to the last two names on the list."

Joanna quickly scanned the list of twenty. Her eyes widened as she came to the final two guests.

Wallace Hoddings, M.D., Institute of Biogenetics, Memorial Medical Center

Eric Brennerman, M.D., CEO, Bio-Med Corporation

"Jesus," Joanna breathed softly.

"I figure these two will know all about Edmond Rabb and the genetics award he gave to Alex Mirren."

"That's for certain," Joanna said, handing back the list. "And for them to be invited to the party, they must have been pretty chummy with the Rabbs."

"It gets more and more interesting, doesn't it?"

Jake signaled over to the policeman standing near the passageway to the stateroom; then he came back to Joanna. "Remember, it's the genetics business that's important here. It's the link between Rabb and Mirren. Don't give these two guys coming up any wiggle room with their answers. Nail them hard if you have to."

A moment later Brennerman and Hoddings came up on deck. They waved to Joanna and walked over. Their expressions were relaxed and unconcerned.

Joanna extended her hand to them. Hoddings took it, shaking it firmly. Then Brennerman did the same. Both men's hands felt cool. "I hope we're not inconveniencing you," she said.

"Not at all," Hoddings said promptly. "This is such an awful business. A fine man like Edmond Rabb getting murdered on his own yacht." Hoddings paused, raising an eyebrow at Joanna. "It is murder, isn't it?"

"Oh, it's murder," Joanna assured him.

Hoddings kept his eyes on Joanna, waiting, as if he expected her to give him all the clinical findings. Several awkward seconds passed. "I take it that the autopsy results were absolutely conclusive," he prompted.

"Quite," Joanna said tonelessly, letting both men know that this was not going to be some friendly academic discussion between colleagues. "The night of the party, when was the last time you saw Edmond Rabb alive?"

Hoddings's face tightened around the jawline. "As I told the detective, we were at the bar having a drink."

Joanna looked over at Brennerman. "And you?"

"The same," Brennerman replied. "I believe we were discussing some recent advance in gene splicing. Mr. Rabb was surprisingly well informed in genetics for someone having no training in the field."

"Was there any particular reason for his interest in genetics?" Joanna asked.

"He had twenty-five million reasons," Brennerman said, and pointed at the flag blowing in the breeze above the wheelhouse. It had the Bio-Med logo emblazoned on it. "Edmond Rabb provided the venture capital to establish Bio-Med. He owned the vast majority of the stock."

"I see," Joanna said, trying to keep her expression neutral. The amount of money involved in this murder was almost too much to count. Bio-Med was thought to be worth hundreds of millions of dollars, and Rabb owned most of that. Joanna nodded to herself, remembering that big money always attracted big crime. "Who else has substantial holdings in Bio-Med?"

Brennerman hesitated, looking over at Hoddings. If the two men exchanged a silent message, Joanna didn't see it.

"Well?" Joanna insisted.

"Is that also part of this investigation?" Brennerman asked back.

"It sure as hell is," Jake growled. "Anything with Edmond Rabb's name on it is a part of this investigation."

"I guess it is," Brennerman had to admit. "Mr. Rabb owned seventy-five percent of the shares, and I owned twenty percent. The remaining five percent was divided up among several others."

Jake's ears pricked. "Tell me about the others."

Brennerman swallowed noticeably. "The Jeanette Hoddings Family Trust owns four percent and Mervin Tuch owns one percent."

Joanna stared at Wallace Hoddings with contempt, making the man blush and turn away. So the high and mighty had been bought out, too, Joanna was thinking. Hoddings had placed the stock in his wife's trust, hoping to hide it away from the public eye. That way he could have ownership in an outside medical enterprise and still hold on to his tenured professorship at Memorial.

"My—my wife's family decided to invest," Hoddings said apologetically.

"A wise investment," Joanna said with a hint of sarcasm, all respect for the man gone. "What happens to the shares of an owner who dies?"

"That's somewhat complicated," Hoddings replied.

"Well, uncomplicate it for us," Jake said.

"Th-there are buy-out clauses which I don't fully understand," Hoddings stammered, and looked over to Brennerman for help.

"They really are complicated," Brennerman told them. "The stock passes to the heirs of the deceased, but the other shareholders have the option of buying the stock at fair market value. But no such purchases could occur without Edmond Rabb's approval. And it would be Edmond Rabb who determined what the fair market value was."

"So Edmond Rabb controlled everything?" Jake concluded.

"With an iron fist," Brennerman added.

"But now it's Lucy Rabb who has all the control," Jake said, thinking aloud.

"Only if we decide not to buy her out."

Jake looked at Brennerman quizzically. "But that has to be okayed by Lucy Rabb, right?"

Brennerman shook his head. "She inherits the stock, but not her husband's veto power on stock purchases. That's one of the complexities Wallace was just alluding to."

A tugboat was coming into the harbor, its diesel engine chugging loudly.

Jake lit a cigarette, digesting the new information as the tugboat passed by. Everybody had their hands in this pot. There was a ton of money here, and a lot of hands were grabbing for it. Edmond Rabb had the biggest chunk, and that was now Lucy's. Then there were Hoddings and Brennerman, two fine and distinguished physicians who were making millions on the side from their science. And there was Mervin Tuch, who got his one percent while screwing Edmond Rabb's wife.

Jake puffed on his cigarette, while waiting for the noise of the tugboat to fade. *Who benefits from Rabb's death?* he asked himself. *Cui bono? Lucy Rabb for sure and probably the lawyer she's screwing.* And maybe the two doctors standing in front of him, too. Because with Rabb dead, they would control Bio-Med. Although Lucy Rabb owned most of the stock, she was too much of a twit to become involved with the scientific business.

Jake flipped his cigarette into the water and turned to Brennerman. "Was Rabb a good guy to work with?"

"Really good," Brennerman said at once.

"Did he ever get in the way?"

"How do you mean?"

"Well, you mentioned earlier that he had some knowledge of genetics," Jake said. "Did he ever insist on things being done his way?"

Brennerman shook his head. "Never. You have to understand something, Lieutenant. Edmond Rabb was first and foremost a venture capitalist. His only concern was making money, and he had the perfect formula to do it. He would pick the right people, set them up in the right environment, and turn them loose. His interest in genetics was money, not science."

"But he must have had *some* interest in science," Jake countered. "After all, he did set up a genetics award at Memorial."

Brennerman smiled. "That was window dressing. Like most wealthy people, Edmond Rabb wanted to show the world that underneath all those millions was a pretty decent guy."

"Was there?"

"Yes, I think so."

Lucy Rabb came up on deck and walked quickly over to the group. She was wearing a yellow sundress, low cut to expose as much cleavage as possible. "Lieutenant, I hope you're not going to be a lot longer. It's becoming very stuffy in the stateroom."

"We're almost done," Jake said, straining to keep his eyes off her breasts.

"The sooner the better."

"Right," Jake said, thinking that Edmond Rabb was already a distant memory to his widow.

Lucy turned to Eric Brennerman. "My lawyer and I would like to meet with you as soon as possible."

Brennerman bowed his head slightly. "At your convenience, Mrs. Rabb."

"Yes," Lucy Rabb said condescendingly. "At my convenience."

Jesus, Jake groaned to himself, wondering if Brennerman had any idea how much bullshit he was going to have to put up with.

The group looked over to the gangplank. The bald security guard accompanied by two policemen was stepping onto the deck. Jake waved them over.

The security guard glanced at Jake and swallowed hard. He gazed down at the deck submissively.

"You lied to us," Jake said hoarsely.

The guard's jaw dropped. "About what?"

"About not coming aboard the ship the night of the party."

The guard thought back, concentrating. "I stayed at my post," he said, raising his right hand. "I swear to God I stayed on the dock."

"You came aboard to look for a shoe."

The guard thought back again. "Yeah, yeah. But

Mr. Rabb yelled down for me to come up. I'll bet I wasn't aboard two minutes before I found the damn shoe."

"Where did you find it?"

"Right there." The guard pointed at the stairs leading up to the wheelhouse. "Some old geezer had lost a tennis shoe."

"A regular tennis shoe?"

"Yeah. You know, the white kind with the rubber sole."

"Then Mr. Rabb told you to go back to your post?"

"He didn't say nothing to me," the guard answered. "He was busy talking to the blonde."

The guard pointed at the brass railing at the stern. "They were standing there, Mr. Rabb and the blonde. They were looking out at the harbor."

Jake turned to Lucy Rabb. "Did any of your female guests have blond hair?"

Lucy nodded. "There were a few—"

"She wasn't no guest," the guard interjected. "She was part of the catering crew."

Jake asked, "How do you know that?"

"I let them up the gangplank. There were three or four guys and her."

"What did she look like?"

"Tall, thin, blond hair," the guard recalled easily. "I'd guess she was in her early thirties."

"Was there anything special about her?"

"Naw. She was kind of plain."

Jake and Joanna exchanged glances, both thinking about the blond hitter from the other murders.

"I'm telling you the truth," the guard insisted. "I found the shoe and got the hell back to my post. Then the boat went out to sea and came back later. And I'll swear to that on a—"

"All right, all right," Jake said hastily, his mind elsewhere.

"Can we please leave now?" Lucy Rabb asked, losing patience.

"Yeah," Jake said with a wave of dismissal. "Everybody can go. But don't leave town without letting us know. We may have more questions for you."

He turned to Lucy Rabb. "I need the name and telephone number of the catering company you used for the party."

"For what?"

"Just get it."

Lucy Rabb walked away in a huff, muttering under her breath.

Joanna waited for Lucy to be out of earshot and then asked in a whisper, "You think it's the blond hitter again?"

"It sounds like her," Jake said, keeping his voice low.

"If it is, she's batting three for three: first Rabb, then the Russian, then Mirren." Joanna ran a hand through her hair and then patted it in place. "An entrepreneur, a scientist, and a Russian immigrant carrying around dead fetuses. And somehow they're connected to one another. But how?"

"You tell me and we've got all three cases solved."

Jake glanced up as a squawking seagull flew over. "Are you having any luck finding the source of the dead babies?"

"We checked out the local hospitals," Joanna told him. "They weren't missing any fetuses."

"Nor were the abortion clinics we looked at." Jake waited for another squawking gull to pass overhead. "Where the hell did those fetuses come from?"

"Well, he sure didn't find them in a Dumpster."

Jake nodded. "He wouldn't have gotten himself killed over that."

Joanna concentrated on the well-planned murders. "This blond hitter really does her homework, doesn't she?"

"Oh, yeah," Jake agreed. "And she's damn good at what she does."

"I wonder how many other supposedly accidental deaths were in fact caused by this woman."

"A lot, I'd bet."

Lucy Rabb returned and gave Jake a slip of paper. Then she went back to her guests in the stateroom.

Jake used his cell phone to call the catering service. He spoke briefly and then hung up.

"Well?" Joanna asked.

"There was no blond woman on the catering crew that night," Jake reported.

20

Dennis Green entered the forensic laboratory and wearily slumped down into a swivel chair. Perspiration was seeping through the front of his scrub suit and surgical cap. "I've got bad news from the OR."

"What?" Joanna asked, looking up from her microscope.

"We now have three patients who developed cancer after receiving the enzyme preparation," Green said, and propped his legs on another chair. "The guy's kidney contained a highly malignant tumor. They're trying to resect it out now."

"Has it spread?"

"All over the retroperitoneum," Green told her. "He's as good as dead."

Joanna pushed away from her microscope and walked over to a huge blackboard that listed all the data on the three patients who had received the enzyme preparation and had come down with cancer. She erased the question mark after the name of the third patient.

Stepping back, she carefully studied the data. The three patients were all Caucasian, all middle-aged, had received the enzyme preparation, and had cancer. Otherwise there were no common denominators. Joanna slid the front blackboard aside, exposing another blackboard. On it were written the physical properties of the various enzyme preparations the patients had received. The protein concentrations and biological activities of the preparations were almost identical. Her gaze went to the section on the preservative used in the preparations. The spaces were blank.

Joanna reached for the intercom button and asked Lori McKay to come back to the main laboratory. Glancing over at Green, she asked, "Was there anything unusual about the renal malignancy you just saw?"

"Not really," Green replied.

"Did it have any similarities to the rhabdomyosarcoma or astroblastoma we saw in the initial two patients?"

Green shook his head. "They were totally different tumors. But they all looked nasty as hell."

"And they're all one hundred percent fatal," Joanna added.

"That, too."

Lori McKay came into the laboratory carrying a stack of medical records and sucking on a cherry-flavored lollipop. She plopped the charts on a countertop and moved the lollipop over to the side of her mouth. "We've got more bad news."

"Don't tell me we have another patient with cancer," Joanna said quickly.

"Nope." Lori sat on the countertop and let her legs dangle. "But still bad news. One of the patients who received the enzyme preparation has reclogged his coronary arteries."

"So soon?"

"Ten months after the procedure," Lori said. "He's being admitted to the CCU for observation now."

Green said, "Well, nobody thought the treatment would be perfect."

"And nobody thought it would cause cancer, either."

Joanna walked over to the blackboard, pointed at patient number three, and then said to Lori, "Dennis has just come from the OR where they're operating on this man. He has a definite renal malignancy."

"Shit," Lori hissed under her breath. "That's three out of thirty patients for sure. And more to come."

"I'm reviewing the enzyme preparations that these three patients received," Joanna went on. "And I saw something a little unusual. Maybe you can explain it."

Lori leaned forward, studying the blackboard. "I'll try."

"Direct your attention to the column that deals with the preservative in the enzyme preparation."

"Okay."

"The spaces are blank."

Lori slowly nodded. "That means none was present."

"But I was told they used benzyl alcohol as a preservative in their enzyme preparations."

"Not in those batches they didn't," Lori informed her. "We didn't detect alcohol or any other preservative."

"I wonder why."

Joanna thought about preservatives and their uses. They were added to either stabilize patients or to prevent contamination with microorganisms. In the case of the enzyme preparations, it would be used to kill any microorganisms that might be present. "Why leave it out?" She put the question more to herself than to the others.

Lori shrugged. "Maybe it wasn't needed. They could have purified the preparation by other means, such as ultrafiltration."

"Maybe," Joanna said, making a mental note to ask Brennerman about it. But, she reminded herself, the absence of something wasn't going to help her with the problem. It was something *in* the enzyme preparation that was causing the cancers. But what?

Green pushed himself up from the swivel chair. "Well, it's back to the coal mines for me."

Joanna walked back over to the blackboards and studied them. Carefully she scrutinized the data on the patients and the enzyme preparations. Why did they develop those cancers? What set it off? Maybe the enzyme itself was a carcinogen. Maybe with time each of the patients who had received it would develop a bizarre malignancy. Joanna shuddered at the thought.

There was a loud knock at the door.

Joanna turned as Jake Sinclair entered the laboratory. He was carrying a cardboard box under his arm.

"Got a minute?" Jake asked.

"Sure," Joanna said, eyeing the box Jake had set down on the countertop. "What do you have?"

"Pajamas and stuff."

Lori looked up at the detective, hoping that he'd let her stay in the room, but knowing he wouldn't. He tended to exclude her from the special cases he and Joanna worked together. He considered her a novice, someone who never really contributed. And then there was the personal problem between them. From day one, Sinclair hadn't liked her, nor she him. Screw it! She had plenty of other things to do. She began to push herself off the countertop. "I guess you'd like me to leave?"

Jake glanced over at Joanna. "Does she know about the Mirren case?"

"Every detail."

Jake motioned Lori back down. "Stick around."

Lori sat and quickly removed the lollipop from her mouth, placing it in a nearby glass mug. Jake Sinclair opened the cardboard box. He took out two sheets of paper and laid them side by side on the countertop.

Each sheet was plain white paper with a large square drawn in the center. Within the squares were scattered red dots. One sheet was labeled SMV, the other CC.

Joanna studied the papers carefully, trying to decipher what they represented. "What are they?"

"Sheets of paper I found hidden under some shirts in Mirren's closet," Jake said.

"Hidden, you say?"

"Oh, yeah. They were in the back between cellophane-wrapped shirts," Jake told her. "He didn't want anybody to find them."

"Why?"

Jake shrugged. "You tell me."

Joanna studied the white sheets of paper again. The squares were really more like rectangles that had been drawn in blue ink. The red dots were also done in ink. There was no lettering or explanation other than the SMV and CC at the tops of the sheets.

Joanna held each sheet up to the light and inspected them at length. Then she turned the pages sideways, still holding them up to the light.

Jake asked, "What do you see?"

"Nothing," Joanna reported. "I thought that maybe the dots were arranged in some sort of pattern or code."

"They're not," Jake said. "We've already looked for that. And the people in the crime scene lab examined the dots and letters under a microscope. There's no message or inscription in them."

Joanna pointed at the letters at the top of each page. "That's the key."

"How do you know that?" Lori asked.

"Because it's the title," Joanna explained. "It tells us what the square represents. And he used—" She interrupted herself and turned to Jake. "Are we sure this is Mirren's handwriting?"

Jake nodded. "We had an expert compare it to other things Mirren had written. It's his handwriting."

"Anyhow," Joanna continued, "it seems as if Mirren used letters or abbreviations so that only he could decipher them."

"Got any ideas?"

Joanna shrugged. "The initials most likely represent a person's name or maybe an address. That's just a guess, of course."

"That's what we figured, too," Jake said, picking up the sheets. "We're running it against the names of all the people he worked with at Memorial and Bio-Med to see if there's a match."

"It must have been really important to Mirren," Joanna said thoughtfully.

"Oh, yeah," Jake agreed. "It was doubly important.

Not only did he write it in code, he tried his damnedest to hide it away."

Lori asked, "Why didn't he just put it in a safety deposit box?"

Jake hesitated for a moment, giving the question thought. "For some reason he didn't want to."

"Or maybe he did," Joanna suggested. "Maybe there's a copy in a bank deposit box."

"And maybe," Jake said, "there's some clue in that deposit box that'll tell us what these initials mean." He looked over at Lori. "Good thinking."

Lori beamed. She brought up a hand to cover her blush.

Jake reached back into the cardboard box and brought out a pair of black silk pajamas. On the top section, embroidered in yellow, was exquisite Japanese calligraphy. "What do you think of these?"

"Beautiful," Joanna said admiringly. "Where did you get them?"

"From the top drawer of Mirren's dresser."

Joanna groaned. "Don't tell me he was a cross-dresser, too."

Lori choked back a laugh.

"I don't think so," Jake said. "They're way too small for Mirren. And there's a small laundry tag near the collar. It has the letters *NT* on it."

"Jesus," Joanna hissed. "This can't possibly get any stranger."

"What?" Jake asked.

"There's a Japanese American technician whom I saw out at Bio-Med," Joanna went on. "She worked under Alex Mirren and her name is Nancy Tanaka."

Jake's eyes brightened. "Is she kinky, too?"

Lori leaned in closer, not wanting to miss a word.

"I'd say not," Joanna said carefully. "But who knows?"

Jake asked, "Did you get the feeling anything was going on between Mirren and this technician? You know, secret looks or subtle touching?"

Joanna shook her head. "It was just the opposite.

He belittled and humiliated her in front of others. He was a real bastard."

"Maybe that was part of the games they played," Lori said. "You know, like a master-slave type thing."

"Or maybe he really hated her," Joanna said. "Maybe they were once lovers and she dumped him."

Jake waved away the sexual speculations. "This is what we know for sure. Nancy Tanaka spent more than a few nights there. We found all sorts of feminine things in the bathroom, and she was seen a few times by neighbors. So we can figure that they were sleeping together. And people who sleep together talk a lot. This woman may know one hell of a lot about Alex Mirren." Jake rubbed his palms together. "I think Nancy Tanaka and I are going to have a little chat."

"I'd be very careful, Jake," Joanna cautioned. "Women don't like to talk with men about their sexual escapades."

"Are you saying women are more comfortable talking to other women about those things?"

"Exactly."

"Makes sense," Jake said, placing the pajamas back inside the box and closing the lid. "How's nine o'clock tomorrow morning?"

"For what?"

"For me to pick you up and take you out to the Bio-Med plant?" Jake lifted the cardboard box and headed for the door. "You're going to be the one who questions Nancy Tanaka."

21

"What do you think?" Joanna asked.

"It looks like the perfect place to build a prison," Jake said, glancing around the grounds at the Bio-Med plant.

"Because of its isolation?"

"It's more than that," Jake told her. "The land is flat with no place to hide. And there's only one road in and out. Anybody on the move would stand out."

"I guess a person could try the desert if he was desperate enough."

Jake shook his head. "He'd be looking at a hundred miles of sand and certain death. There's no water, no food, nothing to support life. And anybody dressed in ordinary clothing would die from exposure in a matter of days. Like I said, this is a perfect place for a prison."

They walked across the parking lot, both hunched up against the chill. It was a cold, cloudy morning with a strong wind gusting in intermittently from the desert. They came to a pile of dog manure and stepped around it.

"Big dogs," Jake commented. "And barbed-wire fences and armed guards. What the hell are they protecting out here?"

"Genetic research that's worth billions of dollars," Joanna said. "You'll see some of their products when we go inside."

They entered through the front door and went into the reception area, where a security guard awaited them. He handed them visitor's cards and watched as they pinned them on. Then he led the way down a narrow corridor. An overhead surveillance camera made a whirring sound as it tracked them. At the end of the corridor the guard punched numbers into a panel on the wall. The door opened automatically.

Joanna and Jake walked through. The door closed silently behind them.

"Jesus H. Christ!" Jake said, taken aback by the lush vegetation growing inside the big glass cubicles. "What is all this?"

"The world of tomorrow."

Joanna pointed out each of the genetically modified plants, including the coffee beans that grew free of caffeine and the tomatoes that resisted freezing because they contained a new gene that produced an antifreeze substance. The tomatoes interested Jake the most.

"How do they taste?"

"Pretty good," Joanna replied, "according to Dr. Brennerman."

They moved down to a new cubicle that was separate and much larger than the others. It took them a moment to realize that they were looking at a huge fish tank. Giant pink salmon were gracefully swimming around in it.

"Don't tell me they're growing these, too," Jake said, awestruck.

"I guess."

Joanna stared at the giant salmon, not liking what she saw. Genetically altering plants was one thing, but doing it to living creatures was another. And if they could do it to a fish, they could do it to humans.

"How do they grow them so big?" Jake asked.

"We genetically modify them," Brennerman said, coming up behind them. "We splice a growth hormone gene into their DNA, and that doubles their growth rate."

Jake watched a fish do a belly roll and then dive to the bottom for food. "Is there any limit to how big they can get?"

Brennerman considered the question carefully before answering. "We could probably double their size again if we wished."

"And how the hell are giant fish like that going to feed themselves?"

"That's a major limiting factor," Brennerman said, surprised at the detective's insight into a biological matter. "The bigger they become, the more food they require. Eventually they could eat so much that the smaller creatures in the food chain would suffer."

Kind of like humans in Latin America, Jake was thinking. The big ones at the top ate so much there was damn little left for the others. He gave the fish a final look and then turned to Brennerman. "Thanks for seeing us on such short notice."

"No problem," Brennerman said, and then he glanced over his shoulder to make sure no one was close enough to hear the conversation. "This Alex Mirren business is shocking beyond words. Can you even begin to envision the embarrassment to his family?"

"How much family has he got?" Jake asked.

"A divorced wife and a daughter living in Florida."

"Well, with any luck the kinky details of his murder won't reach the press there."

"Murder!" Brennerman said loudly and then quickly looked around to see if anyone had overheard. The technicians still had their heads down, apparently busily working away. Brennerman lowered his voice. "No one said anything about murder."

"Tune in the six o'clock news tonight," Jake said, and brought out his notepad. "It seems somebody decided to strangle him while he was tied to his bed."

"Will the news media give out all the details?"

Jake stared at him incredulously. "Are you kidding? Chances are, they'll call it the Silk Stocking Strangler."

Brennerman shook his head sadly. "Bad for the Mirren family, bad for Bio-Med."

And particularly bad for Alex Mirren, Jake thought humorlessly. "Did Mirren have any enemies you know of?"

"None," Brennerman said promptly. "He tended to be a loner, but he had no real enemies."

"Did he get along with the people here at Bio-Med?"

"As far as I know."

Bullshit, Joanna was thinking. "He was kind of rough on Nancy Tanaka, wasn't he?"

Brennerman shrugged. "That was just Alex's temperament. He demanded perfection from everybody, including himself."

"Mmm," Joanna murmured, unconvinced.

"Look," Brennerman said, his voice harder now. "Alex may have been tough as hell, but he was a good scientist, and people liked to work with him, including Nancy Tanaka. If she was so miserable, she could have left here at any time."

"Good point," Joanna said. But it wasn't. Because Nancy was sleeping with Mirren and maybe playing all sorts of sexual games with him. And maybe she liked that part of it.

"Do you know of anybody who would gain financially from Mirren's death?" Jake asked.

"No one."

"Maybe his ex-wife?"

Brennerman shook his head. "She cleaned him out at their divorce two years ago. It was so bad Mirren had to borrow money against his Bio-Med stock options." Brennerman shook his head again. "No, Lieutenant, nobody gained from Alex Mirren's death."

Sure somebody did, Jake wanted to say. That's why they had him whacked. "So, only Bio-Med ends up losing here?"

Brennerman nodded. "He was our very best scientist. He was responsible for a half-dozen patents that Bio-Med owns."

Jake asked quickly, "Was Mirren entitled to royalties from those patents?"

"Absolutely," Brennerman replied. "He would have received two percent of the net profit from each patent."

"*Would* have?"

"The patents had not become commercially viable yet, but they would have some time down the road."

"How much money are we talking about here?" Jake asked.

"Perhaps as much as two million a year."

Jake whistled softly. "That's a lot of money."

"He earned it."

Jake wrote a note in his notepad. "Who will eventually get those royalties now that Mirren is dead?"

Brennerman gestured with his hands, palms out. "I have no idea. You'll have to check his will."

"Oh, we'll do that," Jake assured him.

A technician came over and handed Brennerman a message. He read it rapidly before crushing it into a ball. "Would you excuse me for a moment? I have an urgent phone call."

Joanna watched him walk away; then she turned to Jake and spoke in a low voice. "What do you think?"

"I think he's covering up for Mirren."

"Covering what?"

"The fun and games," Jake said, gazing up at the sunbeams coming through the skylight. "He knows everything about Mirren—his divorce, his ex-wife, his money problems, everything. I suspect he knew about the freaky sex games, too. That's why he wasn't too bothered about the Mirren business. That was the word he used. *Business*. And he only really got upset when I mentioned murder, didn't he?"

Joanna nodded. "And he wanted us to believe everything was fine between Mirren and Nancy Tanaka."

"That, too," Jake agreed. "And remember, we found her pajamas in Mirren's bedroom. She may have been part of his sexual games. That being the case, Brennerman is doing his best to cover up this sex business."

"But why?"

"I don't know," Jake said, lowering his voice as Brennerman approached. "But Nancy Tanaka might."

"Sorry about the interruption," Brennerman told

them. "That was a call from our Canadian colleagues who are working with us on the giant salmon project. The Canadian government has given its approval for us to start a fish farm in Nova Scotia." A pleased look came over Brennerman's face. "The number of people this project will be able to feed is incredible."

Almost as incredible as the number of dollars you'll make from it, Joanna thought. *And the only people it will end up feeding are those who can afford salmon.*

Joanna brought her mind back to business and reached into her purse for a stack of file cards. She studied the top one briefly. "Eric, I'm afraid Alex Mirren is not the only disaster you're going to have to face up to. We've run into more problems with the lipolytic enzyme preparation."

Brennerman's face grew very serious. "What's happened?"

"Another patient has developed cancer."

Joanna described the sixty-year-old man who had come down with a high-grade kidney cancer after the enzyme preparation was injected into his renal arteries. "This is the third malignancy to occur in the thirty patients who received the preparation," she said. "That's a ten percent incidence. There can be no doubt that this preparation somehow induces cancer in humans."

"I can't believe the enzyme is a carcinogen," Brennerman said, visibly shaken. "Enzymes just don't do that. There's never been an enzyme in nature that caused cancer."

"Well, then, we may be looking at a first."

Brennerman rubbed at his chin worriedly. "I guess it's possible that a contaminant got into the preparation somehow. But if it was there, we never detected it."

"Nor did we," Joanna said, and went to another file card. "But we did notice something unusual about the preparations given to the patients who later developed cancer. They didn't contain any preservative. There was no benzyl alcohol in them."

Brennerman wrinkled his brow, concentrating and thinking back. Slowly he nodded. "There was one batch of the enzyme preparation that we decided to purify by ultrafiltration. That process removed any bacteria or viruses and obviated the need for a preservative."

"Was there some reason why ultrafiltration was used on just that one batch?"

Brennerman thought again. "I believe that Mirren had read a recent publication that indicated benzyl alcohol might denature or interfere with the activities of certain enzymes. But fortunately that didn't turn out to be the case here. So we went back to using benzyl alcohol as a preservative, which was cheaper and much less time consuming than ultrafiltration."

"Did Mirren do all the work on the preservatives?"

Brennerman nodded. "He and Nancy Tanaka. We can check with her on that later."

"I'd like to check with her right now," Joanna said, seeing her opening. "While I'm doing that, you can give Lieutenant Sinclair some more background information on Alex Mirren."

"Yeah," Jake said immediately. "There's a bunch of things I need to know about Alex Mirren."

"Fine, but—" Brennerman was about to say something to Joanna but changed his mind. "If you require any technical details, just let me know."

"I will," Joanna said.

She walked across the expansive laboratory, feeling the eyes of the technicians on her. They kept their heads down, but they were following Joanna in their peripheral vision, waiting to see who she wanted to question. And about what. Joanna could sense an air of tension in the laboratory. But no sadness. Not even an iota.

Joanna approached the workbench where Nancy Tanaka was carefully pipetting a clear liquid into a row of test tubes. A young brunette technician was seated nearby, hunched over a microscope, her hearing obviously focused so as not to miss a word.

Joanna tapped the brunette gently on her shoulder. "I wonder if you could excuse us for a few minutes."

"Sure," the technician said, wanting desperately to stay within earshot. "Would you like me to move down a few rows?"

"I want you to go get a cup of coffee," Joanna said firmly.

"Okay," the technician said, pushing herself away from the microscope.

Joanna waited for the young woman to walk away, and then she sat next to Nancy Tanaka. "Do you remember me from my first visit to Bio-Med?"

"Of course," Nancy said quietly. "It's nice to see you again, Dr. Blalock."

"We have to talk."

Nancy nodded slightly. "I know."

"About Alex Mirren."

Nancy hesitated, her eyes looking away from Joanna's. "He was not a bad person. I think you saw him on a day when things were not going well for him."

"So you liked him?"

"He was a very good scientist."

Joanna stared at Nancy, trying to read her expression. "That's not what I asked you."

"We got along all right," Nancy said, her eyelids fluttering involuntarily.

She's lying, Joanna thought. Jake had once told her that fluttering eyelids were a sure sign of lying. "Did you see him socially?"

"No," Nancy said hastily.

Joanna leaned in closer to Nancy and lowered her voice. "So far you've told me three lies in less than two minutes."

"I have not," Nancy said defiantly.

Joanna counted the lies on her fingers. "One—you told me he wasn't a bad person, and he was. Two—you said you got along with him, and you didn't. Three—you told me you didn't see him socially, and you did."

"I didn't—"

Joanna held up an index finger, interrupting her. "You're not a suspect here, but if you keep lying to me you'll become one. And then there'll be a detective who questions you and not me. Believe me when I tell you how unpleasant that can be. Particularly when they sit you in an interrogation room that has a one-way mirror so half the world can spy on you."

Nancy took a deep breath and swallowed audibly. "He was a mean bastard. He seemed to take delight in belittling those who worked around him."

"Why did you put up with that?"

"The money," Nancy said matter-of-factly. "I made fifty thousand a year plus benefits and stock options. That's very good for somebody with a master's degree in microbiology."

"But you saw him socially, too."

Nancy's eyes narrowed into slits. Her lips stayed shut.

"We found your pajamas in the dresser in Alex Mirren's bedroom," Joanna went on. "And a kimono in the closet. And there were personal items in the bathroom that will no doubt have your fingerprints on them."

"I—I'm so ashamed," Nancy whispered.

"You slept with him?"

Nancy nodded. "Five or six times. But there was no real feeling. Nothing was there."

Did you do it for the money? Joanna was about to ask, but decided not to. "Was he into kinky things?"

"The last time I was with him, he wanted me to tie him up and hit him," Nancy said, her voice barely above a whisper. "With a damn whip."

"Did you?"

Nancy shook her head. "I ran out as fast as I could and left all my things behind. That's why you found my pajamas and kimono there."

"And I'll bet that's when he became really mean to you in the laboratory."

"It became almost intolerable," Nancy said. "The littlest mistake would cause him to rant and rave. If anything went wrong, it was always my fault. And to be doubly mean, he transferred me out of the stem cell·lab and back into the general laboratory. That cost me five thousand a year."

"Why did it cost you that?"

"Because the technician who works in the hot zone lab receives a bonus," Nancy explained. "You know, you have to put on a space suit and hook yourself up to an oxygen supply. It was a fucking pain in the ass."

Joanna grinned at the unexpected profanity. But good, she thought. Nancy was loosening up and the truth would flow out now. "Did Mirren give you a reason for transferring you out of the hot zone lab?"

"There was no good reason," Nancy said sharply. "So he just made one up. One day I went into the side room off the hot zone to look for some equipment. Mirren caught me in there and went wild, yelling and screaming about contamination—which was so much crap."

Joanna asked, "What was in the side room?"

"Nothing except for a small steel table with some surgical instruments on it. Things like scissors and scalpels and stuff like that."

"What would they use surgical instruments for?"

Nancy shrugged. "I guess for the experimental animals they work on. We do a fair amount of research on mice and rats. Anyhow, they transferred me out and dropped my salary by five thousand per year."

"Just because you walked into that side room?"

Nancy shook her head. "That was the excuse. The real reason Mirren transferred me out was because I wouldn't sleep with him anymore."

"He wasn't a very nice person," Joanna said as she reached for her file cards. "I appreciate your being so honest with me."

"Will I still have to talk with the detective?"

"That won't be necessary now."

Nancy Tanaka breathed an audible sigh of relief.

Joanna looked at the file card on enzyme preparation. "I need a little bit of information from you on the lipolytic enzyme made by Bio-Med."

"Sure," Nancy said, obviously happy to change the subject. "What do you need?"

"All of the enzyme preparations had the preservative benzyl alcohol added to them. Right?"

"As far as I know."

"But one batch didn't," Joanna went on. "It had no preservative at all."

Nancy wrinkled up her face. "That's strange."

"According to Brennerman, this batch was supposedly purified by ultrafiltration," Joanna added. "Does that ring a bell?"

Nancy thought for a moment, and then slowly nodded. "Yes. I remember now. They were concerned that the alcohol preservative might somehow interfere with the enzyme's activity. So we purified several batches by ultrafiltration. We triple-checked to make certain nothing was growing in those preparations, so I can guarantee you they were free of microorganisms."

"And you added nothing else to those batches?"

"Nothing," Nancy assured her. "And we eventually found that the alcohol really didn't interfere with the enzymes, so we went back to using it as a preservative."

"Good," Joanna said, but her mind was now back in the hot zone and the side room next to it. She wondered how many more side rooms there were in the hot zone area and what kinds of experiments they did back there. Perhaps Nancy Tanaka could provide more details if she really thought about it.

Nancy was glancing nervously over her shoulder. Brennerman and the detective were slowly making their way across the laboratory.

Joanna said quickly, "Nancy, I'd like to talk with you some more, but away from here. Would that be possible?"

"Sure."

"Do you live close by here?"

"Not too far. My house is in Canyon Country."

Joanna wrote down the address. Canyon Country was a pleasant middle-class neighborhood that was located south of Lancaster. "Why don't we do lunch? That way you can teach me all about the enzyme preparation and the hot zone laboratory. And we'll bill Memorial Hospital for it."

"Sounds good," Nancy said as if she meant it. "Let me jot down my phone number for you."

"Well, thanks for your help," Joanna said, loud enough for the approaching Eric Brennerman to hear. She placed the file cards back into her purse and stood.

"Did Nancy clear up the benzyl alcohol business for you?" Brennerman asked.

"She certainly did," Joanna answered. "It was exactly as you said. There was some concern that alcohol might interfere with the enzyme's activity."

"And the preparation was purified by ultrafiltration," Brennerman added. "Right, Nancy?"

Nancy nodded. "Correct. There were no contaminants present and no preservative was used."

Brennerman turned to Joanna. "If you'd like more of that particular batch of enzyme to test in your laboratory, we'll be glad to provide it."

"Please do," Joanna said, picking up her purse. "I don't want to miss anything here."

Brennerman escorted them across the laboratory and past the glass cubicles where a security guard was waiting. The guard was holding two small boxes of microscopic slides.

"I almost forgot," Brennerman said, snapping his fingers. "We found two more boxes of slides on the experimental animals that were injected with the enzyme. I guess Mirren must have overlooked them."

Joanna took the slide boxes and placed them in her oversize purse, wondering what else Alex Mirren might have conveniently overlooked.

"If there's anything else we can do," Brennerman continued, "just let us know. We want to get to the bottom of this disaster every bit as much as you do. And if there are any new developments, we'd appreciate hearing about them as quickly as possible."

"You'll be one of the first to know."

Joanna and Jake followed the guard down the narrow corridor to the reception area where they returned their visitor's cards. Then they walked out into a cool, overcast day.

"Did you learn anything?" Jake asked.

"Nothing that we didn't already know," Joanna replied. "She admitted she was sleeping with him."

"Did he try any kinky stuff on her?"

"Once, but she didn't go for it. She ran like hell and never came back."

"Smart girl."

The wind kicked up, blowing sand directly at them. Joanna turned and waited for it to die down. "If Nancy wanted to, she could sue Bio-Med for millions for sexual harassment."

"He was that big of a bastard, huh?"

"More than you'll ever know," Joanna said. "But that doesn't bring us any closer to finding out who killed him. All we seem to be doing is running into one frustration after another with no real answers. And my investigation into the cases of cancer caused by that damn enzyme isn't going any better."

"No luck at all?"

"Not even a hint," Joanna said wearily. "You know, Jake, for once I really feel overwhelmed. It's like I've got way too much on my plate."

"Then take a break and step back."

"That's what I plan to do," Joanna said, nodding to herself. "But only for a night. Tonight I'm going to busy myself in the kitchen, making veal marsala and a spinach soufflé. With maybe a nice red wine to wash it down. Are you interested?"

"Oh, Lord! I wish I could," Jake said. "But I've got police business tonight. Can I take a rain check?"

"I'll think about it," Joanna said, and gave him a playful elbow in the side.

They moved across the asphalt parking lot, heading for their car. Both kept their eyes on the ground, looking for any creatures that might have crawled in from the desert during the night. In her peripheral vision, Joanna saw a truck parked at the rear of the Bio-Med plant. Again she noticed there was no loading dock or road along the side of the building.

Joanna pointed at the side of the building. "Why would they have a delivery area with no road leading up to it?"

Jake studied the area briefly. "I'd guess for security," he said. "When you're going through sandy ground, vehicles can't go very fast. Nor could a person on foot, for that matter."

"In some ways this factory resembles a fortress, doesn't it?"

Jake nodded. "Like I said before, it's the perfect place to build a prison."

They hurried to their car as the wind kicked up again.

22

Lucy Rabb and Mervin Tuch were locked in a tight embrace. They were humping each other so hard that the bed almost came out of the bolts that secured it to the floor. Tuch's body suddenly stiffened.

"Oh, Jesus! Oh, Jesus!" he groaned over and over again.

"Yes! Yes! Yes!" Lucy rose to meet him, arching her body acutely.

They fell together in a heap, breathing hard, still embracing. Outside they could hear seagulls squawking overhead and small waves rocking gently against the side of the *Argonaut*. A cool breeze came in through the open porthole.

"It doesn't get any better than this," Tuch gasped, catching his breath.

"I hope not." Lucy sighed deeply and moved from under him. "I don't know if I could stand it if it got any better."

"You'd stand it," Tuch chuckled.

"Damn right I would!"

Tuch swung his legs over the side of the bed and reached for his cigarettes. He lit two, handing one of them to Lucy Rabb. "This is the life, isn't it?"

"It's perfect."

"Not quite yet," Tuch said, exhaling blue smoke. "It'll be perfect when this mess is over and done with."

"We're almost there," Lucy said, unconcerned.

"No, we're not." Tuch got up and put on a terry-cloth bathrobe. He looked down at his abdomen, where an obvious paunch was protruding. He sucked in his stomach. "We're not out of this by a long shot."

"I don't know what you're so worried about."

"I'm worried about a detective who's clever as hell. He knows your husband was murdered. And I can tell you that Sinclair is the type who won't stop until he finds out who killed your husband, and why."

Lucy shrugged. "He can try all he wants. All he's got is some blonde he can't identify."

"And she was supposed to be such a pro," Tuch spat out. "We were guaranteed Edmond's death would look like an accident."

"You were the one who hired her," Lucy said.

"*We* hired her," Tuch corrected her. "And it was your money that paid for it."

"Do we get our money back, since the pro screwed up?"

Tuch stared at her in disbelief. Here was a woman soon to be worth millions, and she was grasping for a $15,000 refund. "Let it go," he advised.

"Fifteen thousand is fifteen thousand," Lucy snapped. "And I want it back."

"Don't be stupid," Tuch retorted. "The smart move is to distance ourselves as far away from the killer as possible. All it takes is one mistake and we could spend the rest of our lives in prison."

You mean you *could spend the rest of* your *life in prison,* Lucy thought. *You were the one who set up the hit on my husband, and you were the one who paid for it with money from one of my husband's accounts. And although you told me all the details—who, how, where, and how much—I'll say I know nothing and swear to that with my right hand on a stack of Bibles. I was just the grieving widow who you took advantage of. Lawyers aren't supposed to screw recently widowed women they represent.*

Tuch studied her expression, reminding himself that she was greedy and could be cold as ice when it came to money. "All I'm saying is that now is the time for you to be very careful."

"And you should be careful, too," Lucy said tonelessly.

"Oh, I plan to be."

Tuch lit another cigarette and began pacing around the cabin. He glanced over at Lucy Rabb, who was lying nude on the king-size bed, her brunette hair swept over the side of her face. She was so beautiful and her body so perfect. And she could fuck a man to death and make him smile while she was doing it. But was she greedy! Just like most women, including his wife, who was fifty and plump and constantly bitching about her life.

Tuch felt a twinge of guilt as he thought about his wife, whom he'd married twenty-two years ago, and his two sons, who were doing so well in college. But soon he'd leave all that behind for a new life with Lucy Rabb—and her money. Oh, how much he needed the Rabb millions! Tuch was near bankruptcy from bad investments and stock market speculation. His house in Brentwood and his condominium in Palm Springs were heavily mortgaged. He had even borrowed the maximum against his pension plan. The only thing he had of value was his Bio-Med stock, and that hadn't paid off a nickel. All profits were still being spent on expansion and new equipment. Tuch's thoughts went back to the Rabb millions. Just thinking about them made him feel better.

Lucy watched the handsome lawyer pace around the cabin. He was so smart, she thought. But like a lot of smart men, he had a boring wife and a boring life and nothing to look forward to but more of the same. So damn smart, she thought again. And he fit so perfectly into her plans.

Tuch sat on the bed next to her and kissed her shoulder. "You're beautiful."

"I know," she said, breathing in his ear.

Tuch felt himself stirring. "Are you ready for another round?"

"I think I could manage that," Lucy said, and pulled him down on top of her.

*   *   *

Lori McKay looked up from her microscope. "Joanna, you won't believe what you see when you look at this guy's kidney."

"Are you talking about the cancer?" Joanna asked.

Lori shook her head and moved aside to make room for Joanna. "I'm talking about the normal renal tissue next to it."

Joanna peered through the microscope and carefully studied the kidney biopsy. She slowly moved the slide back and forth, seeing large clumps of bizarre, malignant cells. Adjacent to the cancer was normal renal tissue that looked surprisingly young. "How old was this patient?"

"Sixty."

Joanna focused in on the glomeruli, the small cluster of capillaries through which the blood is filtered. They were fine and delicate with no evidence of atrophy or scarring. The renal tubules appeared equally healthy. "The normal part of this kidney looks as if it belonged to a teenager."

"And it functioned like one, too," Lori said. "He had a creatinine clearance rate of a hundred and forty cc's a minute."

Joanna leaned back. "It's hard to believe this is all due to a procedure that unplugged his renal arteries."

"I can't think of another reason for it," Lori said. "Can you?"

"Not offhand." Joanna strummed her fingers against the countertop, trying to think through the problem. "Did this patient have a kidney biopsy before he received the lipolytic enzyme?"

Lori nodded. "Two years ago. It showed widespread atrophy and scarring, and his creatinine clearance was down to forty cc's per minute. He was rapidly becoming a candidate for hemodialysis. Then he gets treated and ends up with super kidneys. It's like the enzyme preparation brought about a miracle."

"It also brought on cancer," Joanna said, now thinking about the similarities in the three cases of cancer associated with the lipolytic enzyme. All had their arteries unblocked so that their organs suddenly received a markedly increased blood supply. And that would have resulted in more oxygen and nutrients flooding into the diseased organs. Those events would have surely improved organ function but wouldn't have removed every sign of aging and disease. Nothing in modern medicine did that. But something here had. The heart, brain, and kidneys of these patients looked as if they belonged to teenagers.

"I'm so far behind on the experimental animal slides," Lori complained, breaking into Joanna's thoughts. "I've barely made a dent in them."

"Same here," Joanna said absently.

"And I haven't even begun to study the fetal tissue slides."

"I've looked at them. There's really nothing there."

And that was the absolute truth, Joanna told herself. The slides only revealed what they already knew. The fetuses had been eviscerated, and what was left behind showed no abnormalities or any clues as to where the fetuses had come from. There was no mutilation, just careful evisceration. Why? Why eviscerate? Why bury the remains? Why kill a Russian immigrant at the burial site? And why did the blond hitter who killed the Russian also kill Edmond Rabb and Alex Mirren?

More questions and more questions, Joanna thought wearily. And none being answered. It seemed as if the deeper she dug, the darker it became. She was getting nowhere, and it was taking up more and more of her time. And to make matters even worse, her workload at Memorial was now badly backed up.

Abruptly, Joanna pushed herself away from the desk. "That's enough!"

"What?" Lori asked, startled.

"I said that's enough for now," Joanna repeated. "Let's go home."

Lori glanced up at the wall clock. It was 8:40. "My boyfriend is going to think something is strange when I come home this early."

Joanna grabbed her coat and purse and took the elevator to the main floor. She hurried across the almost deserted lobby and went through sliding-glass doors into a cool, clear night. The moon was full, the stars around it twinkling in the black sky.

Near the front entrance to Memorial, Joanna saw a sport-utility vehicle pull up to the curb. She watched Elaine Dent, a pediatric cardiologist, peck her husband's cheek and climb out on the passenger's side of the front seat. In the back seat, twin boys were jumping around and waving to their mother. Joanna felt her biological clock ticking, and for the thousandth time wondered what life would be like with a husband and children.

In the parking lot Joanna's fatigue became more noticeable, and she wondered if she had the energy to do a big number in the kitchen. Veal marsala and a spinach soufflé took time, and the nearest supermarket was out of her way. Maybe she'd just grab some fast food somewhere. She shook her head at the notion. *Do the damn veal.*

Joanna drove down Wilshire Boulevard toward Santa Monica. She decided to make the veal but to buy a frozen spinach soufflé rather than starting from scratch. That way she wouldn't fall asleep on her feet while she was in the kitchen.

Up ahead she saw Flannigan's, a cop bar that Jake had taken her to a number of times. It was a fun place where police people could really relax and tell their incredible stories.

Joanna stopped at a red light, smiling at the thought of one of the more famous stories to come out of Flannigan's. A stupid, mean thug decided to rob the bar, not knowing it was a cop hangout. He made the customers empty their pockets. Then, to show how tough he was, he hit a waitress across her forehead with his gun, opening up a two-inch gash. He was almost to the door when the cops opened up. Eighteen slugs found their mark. The liberal newspaper and minority groups raised hell, claiming excessive police force was used. Jake tended to agree, telling anyone who would listen that seventeen slugs should have been enough. Joanna chuckled. Only Jake could get away with something like that.

The smile on Joanna's face faded as she thought about Jake and where he might be tonight. He had told her that he had police business to take care of, and that usually meant he was on some dangerous assignment, like a stakeout. Joanna tried her best not to worry about Jake when he was in those situations, but she always did. For the hundredth time she wondered what life would be like if Jake were a doctor or a lawyer rather than a homicide detective. It would probably be secure but very dull. Because then Jake wouldn't be Jake, and she'd miss out on all the high-profile crime cases. Joanna sighed to herself. Life was full of trade-offs.

Joanna's stomach growled loudly, and her fatigue began to worsen. Now she was having trouble keeping her eyes open. Just get some fast food, she decided finally. Then go home and go to sleep. And try not to dream about blond hitters and dead babies.

23

Mervin Tuch exited the elevator on the tenth floor of the Century City Tower. The entire floor was occupied by the law offices of Matlin, Mason & Silverstein. Tuch strolled past the large reception desk where two receptionists wearing headsets were busily answering phones.

One of the receptionists called after him, "Mr. Tuch, Mr. Matlin needs to see you as soon as possible."

"Right," Tuch said, and walked down a long corridor lined with offices that housed the firm's sixty attorneys. Mervin Tuch was one of ten senior partners. In addition, there were fifty associates and a dozen paralegals. There were so many in the group now that Tuch couldn't remember all their names.

He entered his suite and stopped by the bubbling aquarium to sprinkle in some fish food. He checked the pH of the water and made sure ammonia wasn't accumulating. That could kill exotic fish with remarkable rapidity.

His secretary hurried over. "Mr. Tuch, I—"

Tuch held up a hand. "Let me get settled first."

"I'm not sure you'll have time for that."

"Oh," Tuch said easily, "there's always time for that."

Tuch walked into his spacious office and went over to a wet bar where he poured coffee into a plastic cup. Then he stepped over to a large window and admired the view of West Los Angeles stretching out to the Pacific Ocean. It was a crystal-clear day, and

Marina del Rey was visible in the distance. His mind drifted back to Lucy Rabb with her incredible body and the wonderful things she could do with her mouth.

"Mr. Tuch," the secretary said gravely. "You really have some important matters to deal with."

"Okay," Tuch said, and reluctantly turned away from the window. "Fire away."

"Mr. Matlin is on his way down now," the secretary began.

"Did he say what it's about?" Tuch asked.

"No, but it must be very important," his secretary said. "They've been calling every five minutes to see if you had arrived."

Tuch lit a cigarette, thinking. "It must be a new case they want me to handle."

The secretary shrugged, but she knew it was more than that. Matlin's secretary had told her that the old man had been furiously pacing his office all morning. And David Matlin, the founder of the law firm, was known for his even temperament. Tuch's secretary looked down at her steno pad. "Are you aware that the police were up here all afternoon yesterday?"

Tuch waved away the information, unconcerned. "They were looking through Edmond Rabb's file. Right?"

The secretary shook her head. "They were examining our record of your phone calls. They also had a printout from the phone company that listed all calls you made."

"Goddamn it," Tuch growled, irritated. "Did they have a warrant for all that?"

The secretary nodded and then referred back to her steno pad. "They kept asking me about a call to a place called Club West."

Tuch's face paled. "Wh-what?"

"A place called Club West," the secretary repeated. "We don't have any file on them."

Tuch remembered making the phone call to Club West to set up a meeting with David Westmoreland. *Stupid! Stupid!* It would have been smarter to have used a pay phone. He'd have to make an excuse for that call. It was a good bar in a respectable part of Los Angeles. He could have called to find out what time they opened so he could meet a client there for drinks.

"All right," Tuch said finally. "What else have you got?"

"Your banker called. He needs for you to send him information on the stock you own in Bio-Med."

Tuch almost choked on his coffee. "What did you tell him?"

"That I'd bring it to your attention."

Tuch held his expression even, but his gut was twisting and churning. The Bio-Med stock was the one asset he'd managed to hide from the bank and his other creditors. Everything else was gone or mortgaged. All he had was the Bio-Med stock, which one day would be worth millions. Although it had never shown a profit, its potential was mind-boggling, particularly with the discoveries that were about to come to fruition. My God! The ability to make people's organs young again. How much was that worth? But now his Bio-Med stock would be gone. The bank had somehow found out about the stock, and they would easily find a buyer for it. And the money would all go to his creditors and he'd be left flat broke. Tuch felt the acid burning in his stomach.

There was a sharp rap on the door, and David Matlin entered.

"You'll excuse me," Matlin said formally to the secretary. "Make certain we are not disturbed."

"Yes, sir."

David Matlin watched the secretary close the door behind her; then he sat on the edge of Tuch's desk. Matlin was a tall man with chiseled features and wavy gray-white hair. He was impeccably dressed in a dark pin-striped suit. "We have some important matters to discuss."

Tuch poured himself more coffee. "So I hear."

"We had a meeting of the partners yesterday afternoon," Matlin began. "Apparently you were unable to attend."

"I was tied up with the Rabb estate," Tuch explained.

"All afternoon?"

"There were extenuating circumstances."

"Such as?"

"The police now believe Edmond Rabb was murdered."

Matlin's eyes narrowed. "But he fell overboard."

"With someone's help, according to the police."

"Do they know who did it?"

"I don't think so," Tuch said. "But everyone who was on the yacht that night is a suspect, and that includes me."

"Is that why they're looking through your phone records?"

Tuch nodded. "I think they're digging into everything and everybody associated with Edmond Rabb."

Matlin studied his manicured fingernails. For a tall man, his hands were remarkably small. "Do you think Lucy Rabb is involved?"

"I doubt it," Tuch said. "The money might be tempting, but I believe she really loved the guy."

"Well . . . ," Maitlin said, letting his voice trail off, always suspicious of young, beautiful women who marry old men. "Let's return to the partners meeting yesterday. It seems that your draw is now substantially higher than the amount of money you generate for the firm. After calculating overhead, you are at least twenty percent off."

"It's the high-profile cases," Tuch told him. "As you know, one spends a lot of time doing things in those cases that you can't bill for."

"We took that into consideration."

"Maybe we should assign someone else to the high-profile cases," Tuch suggested, knowing that no one in the firm could handle such cases nearly as well as he could. "That way I could concentrate on more lucrative matters in the practice."

"We'll leave things the way they are for now," Matlin said. "But you must generate more income if you expect to continue receiving your current draw."

"Fine," Tuch said, glancing out the window to the ocean and wishing he were aboard the *Argonaut* with Lucy Rabb. "Is there anything else?"

"I'm afraid so," Matlin said, his voice very somber. "Our accounting firm has gone over all of our books, including your old escrow accounts. They've found some serious irregularities."

Tuch felt a streak of fear shoot through his body. He strained to keep his expression even. "Regarding what?"

"Three of your dormant escrow accounts," Matlin went on. "In particular, the accounts of Mary Marshall, Benjamin Stone, and the Charles Warring Trust. There is over four hundred thousand dollars missing."

"And that's been double-checked?"

"Triple-checked."

"There must be some mistake," Tuch said, and walked over to refill his coffee cup. "Or perhaps some funds were transferred into other, special accounts."

"Do you recall doing that?"

"Let me think back."

Tuch lit a cigarette, his hand shaking despite his efforts to control it. He stared up at the ceiling as if concentrating to remember. But he remembered all too well. Tuch had gone into the accounts to cover his stock market losses. The escrow accounts had been dormant for so long. No one had touched them in years. So Tuch had stuck his fingers in, fully intending to return the money he had taken. But his losses and debts continued to mount, and he found himself taking more and more from the accounts. But he hadn't realized he had taken so much. "I think I do recall some transfers," Tuch said finally.

"Give me the particulars," Matlin demanded.

"I—I'd have to review the files," Tuch stammered.

Matlin pushed himself off the edge of the desk. "Then review them. Today being Friday, you'll have the entire weekend to do it. I'll expect your answers Monday morning. Ten o'clock sharp in my office.''

Tuch waited for the door to close, and then he ran over to the wet bar. He held his head over the small sink and began to retch, bringing up bile and coffee-tinged vomit. And when there was nothing more to bring up, he dry-heaved over and over again. Finally it stopped.

Tuch rinsed out his mouth and splashed cool water on his face, trying to compose himself. His whole world was collapsing. And it wasn't just the money. It was his whole life. Tuch was guilty of embezzlement, and for that he could be disbarred and lose his livelihood. It was also possible he would spend time in jail. Unless he could come up with the money.

Four hundred thousand, he thought miserably, *might as well be forty million*. He had nowhere to go for the money. His Bio-Med stock would probably have covered it, but that, too, was gone now. The banks would suck it up like a vacuum cleaner. He wouldn't see a dime from it. And he couldn't transfer funds out of other escrow accounts, either. The accountants would be watching those accounts like hawks. "Where the hell do I find four hundred thousand dollars?"

Tuch went over to the window and looked out at the blue Pacific. *Enjoy the view while you can*, he told himself. *You won't have it much longer*. His gaze drifted over to the marina in the distance. The good life, he thought, with Lucy Rabb and yachts would soon be a thing of the—

Suddenly his eyes brightened. Lucy Rabb and the Rabb millions! Lucy would be his way out. Oh, yes! Easy as pie. She'd do exactly as she was told. And if she refused, Tuch knew how to make her change her mind. A little fear could work wonders.

Tuch quickly rinsed his mouth out with mouthwash. He straightened his tie in the mirror behind the wet bar; then he ran a hand through his hair and patted it in place. He smiled at his reflection in the mirror. *You're one clever son of a bitch, aren't you?*

Tuch left his office and hurried past his secretary's desk.

The secretary looked up. "Is everything all right, Mr. Tuch?"

"Couldn't be better."

Lucy Rabb was putting on diamond earrings when Tuch walked into her bedroom aboard the *Argonaut*. She was wearing faded jeans and a white turtleneck cashmere sweater.

"We have to talk," Tuch said.

"I'm kind of in a rush, Merv," Lucy said, reaching for a blue blazer. "I've got a luncheon date in Ancien."

"With who?"

Lucy smiled at his jealousy. "With a girlfriend."

"She'll have to wait."

Lucy looked over and studied his face. "Is something wrong?"

"I've run into some financial problems," Tuch said. He sat on the side of the bed and lit a cigarette. "I need a loan, and I need it now."

"How much are we talking about?"

"A half-million dollars."

"Ha!" Lucy exclaimed. "What the hell do you think I am, a bank?"

"You've got it."

"Not until my husband's will clears probate."

"There are ways around that."

Lucy eyed him carefully. "What do you need that kind of money for?"

"To cover a bad investment," Tuch lied easily. "And since my wife owns over half of everything, I'd have trouble hocking anything without her permission." He suddenly realized his mistake and backtracked. "But to be totally honest, there's not much left to hock. Except for my Bio-Med stock."

"Why not borrow against the stock?" Lucy asked suspiciously.

"Because my wife doesn't know about the stock, and I want to keep it that way," Tuch said, making it up as he went along. "I don't want it to become part of a community property settlement when we divorce. You and I know how valuable that Bio-Med stock is going to be."

"Billions," Lucy said breathlessly.

"And billions," Tuch agreed. "And I'm going to do everything under the sun to protect my stock. It'll be that much more we can add to the ton of money we're going to enjoy together."

"Yes," Lucy said, smiling at the words *a ton of money.* "It's going to be so good."

"You bet." Tuch reached over and pulled her to him, burying his head between her breasts. "I just can't get enough of you."

"Oh, I wish I had time to jump in bed with you," Lucy said, her voice huskier.

"Make time."

"I really can't." Lucy sat on his lap and quickly kissed his lips and nose. "Tell me how we can get to my dead husband's assets before his will goes through probate."

"Just show the bank your husband's will and what he left you," Tuch explained. "They'd be delighted to have the Bio-Med stock you'll inherit as collateral."

Lucy stiffened. "I'm not going to put that up. That's my future fortune."

"It's just temporary," Tuch said soothingly.

"Temporary, hell!"

Lucy stood and went over to the mirror, where she angrily ran a brush through her hair. "I'm not going to risk that for anything or anybody."

"You're going to put it up whether you like it or not," Tuch said hoarsely.

"Oh? Are you going to make me?"

Tuch gave her a hard stare. "Don't forget, we're partners in this. We've had a man killed, and that can send us to jail for a very long time."

"Are you threatening me?"

Tuch shook his head. "I'm just telling you the way things stand. If I don't cover these loans, I could be disbarred and sent to prison. I'd lose everything and become very desperate. And desperate people do desperate things. They might even turn state's evidence in a murder case, provided they were given total immunity. Of course, I'd hate to see that happen because we'd all still lose. And all those millions would be long gone."

Lucy stared back at him for a moment. Then she dropped her head submissively. "Let's not fight. We've got so much going for us."

"That's what I've been trying to tell you."

"Sometimes I don't listen very well," Lucy said apologetically. "Tell me what I have to do to get the loan."

"I'll make all the arrangements," Tuch said, smiling at her. So easy, he was thinking, so damn easy. He'd gotten a half-million dollars in about five minutes. He wondered how long it would take him to get all her millions.

Tuch reached out for her. "Come here!"

"I don't have time to get undressed and all," Lucy said, resisting as he pulled her to him.

"Oh, I was thinking of something else."

Lucy smiled seductively and got down on her knees. She unzipped his pants and pulled down his underwear, then buried her face in his crotch, flicking her tongue everywhere.

"Yeah, yeah," Tuch moaned, and leaned back against a pillow. He watched her head bobbing up and down, immensely pleased with himself. He would end up controlling the Rabb millions and have Lucy Rabb as a plaything. *The best of all worlds.* Outside, small waves were gently bouncing off the side of the *Argonaut. The best of all worlds*, he thought again.

Tuch suddenly felt himself throbbing inside Lucy's mouth. "Oh, Jesus!" he groaned loudly, grabbing the bedpost.

Lucy looked up at him, swallowing. "I like doing that."

"I know."

"Want me to do it again?"

Tuch forced a laugh. "You'll kill me."

"Oh, I wouldn't do that," Lucy said, and got to her feet.

Tuch went into the adjoining bathroom and washed himself over the basin. He talked to Lucy through the open door. "I'll run by the bank this afternoon and get everything set up."

"Good."

"Then you can sign the papers and the money will be transferred into my account."

"Good."

Tuch walked back into the bedroom. "And believe me, your Bio-Med stock will be absolutely safe."

"I know that." Lucy came over and hugged him tightly. "You're not angry at me, are you?"

"No way," Tuch assured her and kissed the tip of her nose. "I have to run now."

"You'll call me later?"

"For sure," Tuch promised.

Lucy blew a kiss to him as he left, and then she went into the bedroom. She put on new lipstick and brushed her hair again, her eyes studying her reflection in the mirror. She wondered if she looked anywhere near as stupid as Mervin Tuch thought she was.

Lucy returned to the master bedroom and picked up the phone. She quickly punched in numbers.

"I have a big problem," she said into the receiver without identifying herself. "And it needs fixing."

24

Farelli was still drawing a blank tracking down the Russian immigrant. The Centurion Cable Company had given him a list of all customers in the area who had reported their television cable malfunctioning over the past three months. Farelli had checked each one personally. There were a hundred and four complaints. A hundred and one knew nothing about the Russian. Of the remaining three households, two were middle-aged couples away on vacation. And one was a seventy-two-year-old widow who had been recently hospitalized. Nothing, Farelli thought sourly. A big nothing. But Farelli knew the Russian had to have lived in the area. Had to. But where?

As Farelli drove by Rucker's Hardware Store, he saw up ahead a Centurion Cable repair truck. He thought of a question he hadn't asked. It was a question the company couldn't answer, but a cable repairman might. Farelli quickly pulled over to the curb.

He walked back to the Centurion truck and waved to the repairman. "Hey, you got a minute?"

"Sure." The cable repairman was a tall young man with brown hair pulled back in a ponytail. "What do you need?"

Farelli flashed his shield and showed the repairman a snapshot of the Russian. "Have you ever seen this guy?"

The repairman studied the photo and then shook his head. "Nope."

"You certain?"

"Positive."

Farelli decided to try another tack. "Did you ever have to repair a cable that somebody else tried to fix by themselves?"

The repairman thought about the question for a few moments before answering. "Nope."

"Do you know of anybody around here who tried to fix their own cable?"

"Just one."

Farelli's eyes lit up. "Tell me about it."

"Some old lady had underground wires that had rotted through," the repairman recounted. "It would have been a big mess to dig up the wire and replace it, so the company put it off. She apparently got some outside guy to do it for her."

"Did he do a good job?"

"Damn right," the repairman said. "He didn't dig up anything. He just strung the wire alongside her house."

Farelli took out his notepad. "Give me the woman's name."

"Mrs. Anderson." The repairman turned and pointed at a stucco house on the far corner. "That's her house right there."

Farelli studied the house briefly, recalling that it belonged to the seventy-two-year-old widow who was recently hospitalized. Some sort of heart problem, Farelli had been told by a neighbor. "You wouldn't happen to know what hospital she's in?"

The repairman looked at Farelli oddly. "She's not in the hospital. At least she wasn't this morning."

"You know that for a fact?"

"Yeah," the repairman said. "I was there a few hours ago. She called because her picture wasn't so good. But it wasn't the cable. It was the picture tube in her television set. It's going bad."

"I appreciate your help."

"Any time."

Farelli hurried across the street, hoping he'd found the right house. All he needed was the Russian's full name. With that, Farelli could obtain the man's Social

Security number. And that would open up the immigrant's whole world to them.

Farelli walked up the lawn to the front door. He rang the bell and stepped back.

The door cracked open, its chain still in place. An elderly woman peeked out. "Yes?" she said in a weak voice.

Farelli showed her his shield. "Ma'am, I'm from the police department. I'd like to ask you a few questions, if I could."

"About what?"

"About the Russian who did some work for you."

"I haven't seen him for so long," the woman said. "Is he all right?"

"It might be best if we talked about it inside."

She unchained the door and led the way into a small living room. The furniture was very old, but nicely polished. A brick fireplace was filled with red-hot ashes and bits of charred wood. The room seemed very warm to Farelli. He waited for her to sit in a padded rocking chair. Then he took a seat on the sofa across from her.

"I'm afraid I've got some bad news," Farelli began. "Vladie was shot to death by some robbers."

The woman nodded slowly. "I was afraid of that. You know, this is not a safe neighborhood."

"Yes, ma'am." Farelli glanced over at the bars on the window and the chains and locks on the front door. "I understand Vladie fixed your TV cable?"

The woman stared at the detective briefly. "That's not against the law, is it?"

"No, ma'am," Farelli said. "I'm just trying to make sure we have the right fellow." He reached into his coat pocket for the snapshot of the Russian. "Is this Vladie?"

"That's Vladie," she said softly.

"Do you know his last name?"

"Belov," she told him, and then spelled it out. *"B-e-l-o-v."*

Farelli jotted down the information in his notepad. "Did he live around here?"

The woman motioned with her head to the rear of the house. "He lived in a small apartment in the backyard. When my husband was alive, he used it as a workshop. After he passed away, I made it into a small apartment to rent out."

"Could I take a look at it?" Farelli asked eagerly.

"I don't see why not," she said. "But let me call the dog first."

The woman let out a sharp whistle. Farelli heard thumping sounds on the floor of the nearby kitchen. A moment later a huge rottweiler ran into the living room. He sat on his haunches next to the old woman and carefully measured Farelli.

"This is Taffy," the woman announced. "He makes sure nothing bad happens to me."

"I'll bet," Farelli said, thinking that Taffy was such a sweet name for a dog that could bite the ass off an elephant. "Why didn't he bark when I came to the front door?"

"Because I told him to be quiet."

The rottweiler came over and sniffed Farelli's shoes. Apparently satisfied, he went back to his mistress.

Farelli asked, "Will I need a key to get into Vladie's apartment?"

The woman shook her head. "Vladie never felt the need to lock his door with Taffy around."

Farelli walked through the kitchen and out into a well-kept backyard. The green lawn was closely cut, the hedges evenly trimmed. Off to the side was a small wooden structure with a door but no windows. Farelli went inside.

There was only one room, and the furnishings were spare and old. There was a stained sink and counter on one side of the room, a fold-out sofa and scarred coffee table on the other. A phone was on the floor atop a phone book. Farelli peeked into the tiny bathroom and saw a basin and toilet, but no tub or shower. A dirty towel hung from a hook on the wall.

Farelli stepped over to the coffee table and examined a stack of opened letters. Most were sent from

Russia and addressed in English to Vladimir Belov. The letters themselves were written in Russian. Farelli got to the last envelope. It was unstamped with only Belov's name typed on it. Inside was an employee pay statement. Vladimir Belov worked for the Family Planning Medical Center.

Farelli quickly reached for the phone book and flipped through the yellow pages until he came to the ad for the medical center. It read:

FAMILY PLANNING MEDICAL CENTER
ABORTIONS UP TO 24 WEEKS

"Son of a bitch," Farelli muttered, ripping the yellow page out of the book.

25

Mervin Tuch was driving down Pico Boulevard toward Century City, the sunroof on his BMW open. He whistled happily, all of his problems fading away. With Lucy Rabb's Bio-Med stock as collateral, the bank was delighted to give him a loan of five hundred thousand dollars. The bankers were particularly delighted when they learned that one hundred thousand of the loan would go to pay down the note Tuch already owed them. And had today not been Saturday, the transaction would have been signed and sealed and the money transferred. But that was no problem, Tuch thought contentedly. Monday would be soon enough.

Let's see now, Tuch thought on as he planned his weekend activities. Today he'd go to his office and doctor the files on the escrow accounts so they showed that funds had been inadvertently transferred to his account. An honest mistake. His law partners might not believe him, but they would accept what he told them as long as the money was repaid. It would take at least two hours for him to fix the files, Tuch decided. Maybe as much as three hours. Whatever. After he was done, he'd reward himself with lunch at the Beverly Wilshire. He'd have the barbecued chicken salad with mustard sauce. His favorite. Then he'd call Lucy and go over to the *Argonaut* for a quick screw.

He felt himself stir as he thought about Lucy Rabb and her fantastic body and even more fantastic mouth. She was so great in bed. And she was also so stupid, so easy to manipulate. All he had to do was keep screwing her and she'd do whatever he wanted.

Tuch turned left onto the Avenue of the Stars, then made another wide left and entered the underground parking of the Century Tower. He didn't notice the black Toyota behind him.

Tuch drove down to the second level and parked in his reserved space. The whole area was empty with no cars in sight. Lazy people, Tuch chuckled to himself. If they were as ambitious as he was, they, too, could get their hands on five hundred thousand dollars for a few hours' work.

Tuch heard a noise that sounded like a popping lightbulb. Then a car door nearby slammed shut. Tuch glanced from side to side and, seeing nothing unusual, looked in the rearview mirror. A black car was approaching.

The car pulled up beside him in David Matlin's space. But it wasn't David Matlin. It was a young blonde. Probably some dumb secretary, Tuch thought. She got out of the Toyota and waved to him. Tuch waved back, undressing her with his eyes. Too thin. And no breasts. She approached him with a wide smile.

"Do I know you?" Tuch asked, opening the door of his BMW to exit.

"Stay right where you are," Sara Ann Moore said, and pointed a revolver with a silencer at his head.

"Wh—!"

"Keep your mouth shut and nothing will happen to you." Sara glanced down toward the far end of the underground parking. A car was going down the ramp to the next level. She waited for it to disappear and then turned back to Tuch. "I want your watch and wallet."

"Sure, sure," Tuch mumbled nervously. He quickly stripped off his gold Rolex and handed it to her, along with his wallet. "I'll give you whatever you want. Just don't shoot."

"Are your credit cards in your wallet?"

Tuch nodded hastily. "Everything is in there."

"Now turn and face the passenger side with your hands behind your back," Sara ordered.

"Do-don't hurt me," Tuch stammered, so frightened he passed a small amount of urine.

"I'm going to tie you up and gag you," Sara told him. "Somebody will find you later."

"All right," Tuch said submissively, and turned, keeping his hands behind him. "Is this okay?"

"Perfect," Sara said, reaching into her oversize purse.

She took out a large kitchen knife and plunged it deep into Mervin Tuch's back.

26

Joanna ducked under the crime scene tape and headed down the ramp to the underground parking garage at the Century Tower. Police and medical examiners were everywhere on the second level, combing the area for clues and evidence. Joanna saw Jake Sinclair and Girish Gupta in conversation beside a dark BMW. She waved and walked over to them.

"Hey, Joanna," Jake said, giving her a subtle wink.

"Hi," Joanna said warmly, and turned to Gupta. "I hope I'm not barging in on your case."

Gupta shook his head. "Not at all. The lieutenant has told me about this murder's connection to the others you've been working on. I'm delighted to have your help, although Mr. Tuch's death seems straightforward."

Joanna looked down at the corpse of Mervin Tuch. He was lying facedown, his arms by his sides, his palms turned outward. His coat and shirt had been cut away to expose the gaping wound between his shoulder blades. There was congealed blood over most of his back as well as on the seat and floor of the car. Joanna slipped on a pair of gloves and probed the large wound in Tuck's back. "Is this the only wound?"

"Yes," Gupta answered. "Although there is a fair amount of blood around his nose and mouth."

Joanna turned Tuch's head and examined the front of it. There was frothy blood everywhere, but most of it was concentrated about his oral cavity. His lips were twisted and distorted in a permanent grimace. The handsome face of Mervin Tuch was barely recognizable.

"His wallet and watch are missing," Gupta went on. "According to his partners, he wore a Rolex Presidential."

"Gupta thinks that robbery was the motive here," Jake said, giving Joanna a half-smile. "What do you think?"

"Let me look at a few more things first," Joanna said noncommittally, and went back to her examination.

Jake stepped back, thinking this was murder regardless of what Joanna did or didn't find. It had to be. All three victims—Edmond Rabb, Alex Mirren, and now Mervin Tuch—were interconnected, and all had been iced in a matter of weeks. Somebody wanted them dead. But who and why?

Gupta saw the hard look on Jake's face. "You don't think it was just robbery?"

"I think it was murder made to look like robbery," Jake said.

"But there's no real proof of that," Gupta argued mildly. "It still looks like robbery. To say otherwise, one would have to be guessing."

"But it's a pretty good guess," Jake told him, "because there are some things here that don't fit. Let me count them off for you. First, it's the murder itself. Most perps don't kill their victims during a simple robbery. Armed robbery gets you five to ten, murder gets you life. And every perp knows that. Second, why kill him? There's no need for it. You can bash him over the head or lock him in the trunk or keep him quiet in a dozen other ways."

"And then there's the wound itself," Joanna said from her crouch. "That's not a simple knife wound."

Gupta moved in for a closer look at the gaping laceration. He saw nothing unusual except for perhaps its length. "Are you referring to the size of the wound?"

"Exactly," Joanna told him. "And there's more. If

you carefully examine the edges at the top of the wound, you'll see that they are smooth and even, like a clean cut from a knife. But the edges from the middle of the wound on down are chewed up and ragged. What do you make of that?"

Gupta thought for a moment, then his eyes brightened. "The killer used a knife with a serrated edge. Maybe a kitchen knife."

"That would be my guess, too," Joanna said. "And the killer didn't simply stab the victim. When the knife was in, he sawed away, trying to inflict as much internal damage as possible. The perpetrator wasn't interested in just incapacitating or silencing Mervin Tuch. He wanted him dead."

Jake leaned over the corpse and studied the lower portion of the wound where the edges were ragged. Like Gupta, he had missed that, too. "So that's why the guy bled out like a stuck pig."

Joanna nodded. "And the bleeding internally was even more massive. He had a big pulmonary hemorrhage, for sure. That's why the blood around his mouth is so frothy. It was mixed with the air in his lungs."

"He probably didn't have time to cry out for help," Gupta surmised.

"Even if he did, nobody would have heard him," Joanna said. "Trying to yell when your lungs are filled with blood is like trying to scream when your head is under water."

Gupta stared at Joanna admiringly, again wondering if she was some sort of psychic or simply had a sixth sense for putting subtle clues together.

A uniformed policeman hurried up to the group. "Lieutenant, Farelli would like to see you in the security room."

"Has he got something?" Jake asked.

"He didn't say," the policeman said, and walked away.

Jake turned to Joanna. "Do you want to go look at some surveillance film?"

"Sure." Joanna peeled off her gloves and tossed them into a nearby container. "But I can only stay for a little while longer."

"Busy, huh?"

"The work just keeps piling up."

"Did you ever make that veal dinner?" Jake asked.

"I settled for fast food," Joanna said. "An overdone pizza."

"Bad, huh?"

"The worst. Let's go look at the film."

"Thank you for your help," Gupta called after her.

"It's always a pleasure working with you," Joanna said, and waved good-bye.

As they walked away, Jake took Joanna's arm. "None of this makes any damn sense."

"I know."

"There's no common thread to connect all these murders."

"I know that, too."

They went up some metal steps and entered a darkened room with a small screen on the far wall. The moving picture on the screen was in black-and-white. In the lower right corner of the film was the date and time.

"You'll never guess what we got," Farelli called out.

"What?" Jake asked.

"The hitter's car on film."

Jake looked at Farelli incredulously. "Are you telling me the hitter didn't bother to take out the surveillance camera?"

"Oh, she took out the one she saw," Farelli said. "We found bits and pieces of one camera on the floor. My guess is she put a slug through it."

"But there was a second camera, huh?"

Farelli nodded. "It was partially hidden by a light fixture. That's why she missed it."

The projectionist rewound the film to Saturday morning at 10:30 and then played it forward. The picture on the screen showed Tuch's BMW at a distance as it enters his parking space. A moment later a dark

Toyota pulls in alongside him. A thin blond woman exits the Toyota and walks over to the BMW. The BMW's front door opens, but Tuch stays inside. The blonde and Tuch appear to be talking. She reaches in her purse. They talk more. Then she pulls out a large knife and holds it high above her head.

Everyone in the security room leaned forward to watch the actual murder on film.

The knife comes down. Tuch's body jerks abruptly and disappears from view. The blonde hurries back to her car and drives away.

"Son of a bitch," Jake murmured under his breath.

"The car is definitely a Toyota," Farelli told them. "But we couldn't get a license number. The plate is small and blurred on the screen."

"Let's see the frames where the hitter is walking over to Tuch's car," Jake requested and moved in for a better view. He kept his eyes on the screen, watching the film running backward. "Stop! Right there."

The still frame showed the blond hitter at the rear of her car. The license plate. It looked like a small white square. Its numbers were so indistinct they appeared to be a smudge.

"Let the FBI people, who do photo image enhancement, study this frame and see if they can come up with a number for us." Jake peered at the hitter. She was thin and blond, but her features weren't sharp enough for Jake to accurately gauge her age. Early thirties, he guessed. "Also see if they can enhance the hitter's face and give us a better picture of her."

"She looks so young and harmless," Joanna said in a low voice.

"That's what her victims probably thought," Jake told her. "Right up until the time she murdered them."

He took her arm and led her out of the security room. On the metal steps, Jake stopped and said, "You'll never see a human being more cold-blooded than that. She's a natural-born killer."

"Be careful, Jake," Joanna warned. "If you come up against her, be very, very careful."

Jake's eyes turned cold. "Oh, I have a special rule when it comes to hitters."

"What's that?"

"The second I can't see both of their hands, I shoot."

"Good rule," Joanna said, and walked on.

27

The receptionist at the Family Planning Medical Center placed her hand over the phone and then looked up at Jake and Farelli. "Dr. Decker is not available this morning. He's really tied up."

"We'll he'd better untie himself real quick," Jake said. "Otherwise I'll come back with a bench warrant."

"What's that?" the receptionist asked innocently.

"It's something that can march him out of here in handcuffs."

The receptionist spoke rapidly into the phone, her eyes avoiding Jake's. She waited for a response, wondering why the police were here and hoping the clinic hadn't done something that could involve her in any way. She never even peeked into the back rooms where they did the things they did. And that was the God's truth. She'd swear to it.

The receptionist pressed the phone to her ear and listened intently; then she nodded and looked up at the detectives. "Dr. Decker is in the middle of a procedure. He'll be with you in a few minutes."

Farelli led the way over to a water cooler in the corner of the room. He sipped water from a conical paper cup, keeping his back to the receptionist. "The doctor is doing a procedure," Farelli said gruffly in a low voice. "They make it sound like he's doing something good back there."

"It's legal," Jake reminded him.

"That doesn't make it right." Farelli crushed the cup into a tight ball and threw it into a nearby wastebasket. "You should have seen the ad in the phone book, Jake. It read 'Abortions up to twenty-four weeks.' That comes out to six months of age. Don't tell me that baby is not alive and moving then."

"I guess," Jake said, and glanced around the well-appointed reception area. The walls were covered with pale yellow grass cloth, the furniture upholstered in dark leather. On a couch near the window a teenage girl was sitting next to her mother. They were holding hands, their expressions a mixture of fear and sadness.

"You don't think the doc is going to split out the back door on us, do you?" Farelli asked.

"He can't be that stupid," Jake said, reaching for a cup of water. "Did you check to see if the Russian worked anywhere else other than this clinic?"

"Only here, according to his W-2 forms," Farelli reported.

Jake shook his head slowly. "How the hell is Mervin Tuch tied into a Russian immigrant?"

Farelli shrugged. "I haven't gotten that far yet. But they've got to be connected somehow."

Jake thought about the question at length. Other than the blond hitter, there was no common denominator between Tuch and the Russian. And there were no possible witnesses to tie the two together. A paper trail would be their best hope, Jake decided. And lawyers generated plenty of papers. "You've got to triple-check everything Tuch was involved in, and I mean everything. His law practice, his financial dealings, even his phone calls. Somewhere along the line Tuch and the Russian crossed paths."

"Talking about phone calls," Farelli said as he turned pages in his notepad, "we did find something interesting in the phone records from Tuch's office. He called a bar named Club West."

"So?"

"So somebody called the same bar from the *Argonaut*," Farelli said, and then added, "twice."

"Did you check it out?"

"We're on it now."

"It'd be nice if we could somehow put the Russian in that bar."

"That ain't going to happen," Farelli said sourly. "It's an upgrade bar. The Russian would never go in there."

"Shit," Jake growled.

"Yeah." Farelli quickly flipped to another page. "We got a little luckier with the blond hitter's license plate. It's a California plate, and the first number is a four. After that there are letters we can't be sure of because of mud splatter."

"Even with photo-image enhancement?"

"Even with that," Farelli replied. "The FBI guys think the mud was smeared on intentionally to cover up the plate. Our blond hitter isn't that stupid."

"Could they give us any more information on the hitter's car?"

"It's a Toyota Camry," Farelli said, and put away his notepad. "It's this year's model with a California license that starts with a four. The FBI thinks the next letter may be a *W* or *V* or *U*. At least, that's their best guess."

"Assuming they're right, how many cars are we talking about?"

"According to the Department of Motor Vehicles, there are over two thousand Camrys that fit that description."

Jake's eyes narrowed. "In Southern California alone?"

"Right."

"Narrow it down," Jake advised. "Look for female owners who are under the age of forty."

"And blond?"

"No," Jake said quickly, remembering that the hitter could be wearing a wig. "Don't limit it to blondes. Women can change hair color faster than you can blink."

"Tell me about it."

Jake refilled his water cup and sipped it. It tasted lukewarm. "Anything else?"

"Just a phone call this morning from Alex Mirren's ex-wife in Florida," Farelli answered. "You don't want to hear about it."

"Why not?"

"Because she's a real nutcase," Farelli said disgustedly. "She spent the first five minutes telling me why she went back to her maiden name, which is Faye Plum. 'Just like the fruit,' she told me—as if I gave a shit."

"Did she tell you anything about Alex Mirren?"

"Oh, yeah," Farelli said. "Apparently old Alex didn't want Faye to invite one of her favorite aunts to the wedding. That caused a feud that goes on to this day. She holds Alex responsible for all the turmoil in her family."

Jake flicked his hand. "Spare me."

"It gets better," Farelli went on. "Because Alex was so mean, Faye put a curse on him, and that's why Alex got whacked. She wasn't unhappy over his passing, I'll tell you that."

Jake scratched his head. "Did she benefit any from his death?"

"Not according to Alex's will," Farelli replied. "Everything goes into a blind trust that pays child support until his daughter reaches twenty-one. Then the daughter inherits everything."

Jake nodded knowingly. "And I'll bet Faye Plum wants it all now so she can control it."

"That was the phone call," Farelli said, nodding back. "But of course, she also wanted me to know why she changed her name to Faye Plum. That was very important."

"She sounds crazy as a loon."

"And mean on top of it. Getting close to that is like getting close to a rattlesnake."

"Well, Mirren isn't going to have to worry about that anymore, is he?"

"Not in this world."

They turned as a heavyset nurse came through the door by the receptionist's desk. She signaled the detectives over, but stood squarely in the middle of the doorway.

"I hope this won't take long," the nurse said, not the least bit intimidated by the detectives.

"We just have a few questions for Dr. Decker," Jake told her.

The nurse made a guttural, disapproving sound. Then she turned and said, "This way."

Jake and Farelli followed the nurse in and down a wide corridor. All the doors were closed. In the distance Jake thought he heard a muffled groan, but he wasn't sure. As they turned onto another corridor, Jake could detect the odor of anesthetic gas. He heard the groan, clearer this time.

The nurse led the way into the doctors lounge and closed the door behind them. The lounge was drab with light green plaster walls and furniture upholstered in well-worn Naugahyde. A noisy refrigerator was in the corner. Dr. Ted Decker was seated at a dinette table, munching on a jelly doughnut. He ate hurriedly and washed the food down with bottled water. Decker dusted off his hands and looked up at the detectives, not bothering to stand. "What can I do for you?"

"We need some information on Vladimir Belov," Jake began. "We understand he used to work here."

Decker jabbed his thumb toward the nurse. "She hires the help in the clinic."

Jake turned to the nurse. She was a stocky, unattractive woman with her hair pulled back severely into a bun. "When did you see Vladimir Belov last?"

The nurse thought for a moment. "It's been almost three weeks now. He just disappeared."

"Had he ever done that before?"

"Never," the nurse said at once. "And he would certainly never do that around payday."

"So you still have his last paycheck?"

"As far as I know."

Jake took out his notepad and flipped pages. "What was his job here?"

"He was a janitor-handyman," the nurse answered. "May I ask what this is all about?"

"Vladimir Belov was murdered," Jake said evenly.

"Oh," the nurse said with no emotion.

Dr. Decker looked up briefly and then started on another doughnut. Jake noticed that the young, curly-haired doctor was wearing tennis shoes along with his scrub suit.

"Did he do a good job for you?" Jake asked.

"He was okay," the nurse said carefully, more guarded now.

"Did you know anything about his life outside the clinic?"

The nurse shook her head. "He came to work, did his job, and left when we closed. That's all I know, and that's all I wanted to know."

Farelli asked, "Did he leave a number or name to call in case of an emergency?"

"We don't ask for that information," the nurse replied.

"What are you going to do with his last paycheck?"

The nurse shrugged. "That will be up to the owners."

"Who owns this place?" Jake asked.

The nurse hesitated, eyeing him suspiciously. "Why do you need to know that?"

"Just answer the question," Jake said, his voice harder.

"A group of doctors," the nurse answered.

"Are there any outside investors?" Jake asked, thinking about Mervin Tuch and any possible connection he might have had with the Russian.

"I think it's only doctors," the nurse said, not certain. "Maybe Dr. Decker knows."

Jake turned to Decker, who was licking jelly off his fingers. "Well?"

"Well, what?" Decker smirked.

Jake put his knuckles on the dinette table and leaned forward, giving the doctor a long stare. "If I were you, I'd listen carefully to each question, and I'd answer it as accurately as I could. Because if you give me one wrong answer, I'll run your ass in and turn your life into a living hell. By the time I'm done, you'll never practice medicine in the state of California again."

Decker's face went pale. "Wh-what's this all about?"

"Dead babies."

"What!"

"Dead babies," Jake repeated. "Have I got your attention now?"

"What we do here is legal," the nurse blurted out. "You have no—"

"Put a lid on it!" Jake snapped at her. "You answer questions when they're directed to you. Understand?"

The nurse nodded weakly, wondering whether she should call the owners.

Jake glared down at Decker, resisting the urge to drive his fist through the young doctor's arrogant face. "Now, let's get back to dead babies."

Decker tried to gather himself, but his legs were shaking under the table. He reached down to steady them. "Are you talking about babies or fetuses?"

"You tell me the difference."

"Fetuses are in the womb until they're nine months old," Decker explained. "When they're born they're called babies."

"Well then," Jake said, "we're talking about dead fetuses."

Decker shrugged, wondering what all the fuss was about. "Look, Lieutenant," he said calmly, "we do abortions here. The fetuses are nonviable when they're removed from the woman's uterus."

"What do you do with these nonviable fetuses once they're removed?"

Decker shrugged again. "That's not my department."

Jake slapped the top of the table with an open palm, hard enough to cause the bottle of water to rattle. "You goddamn well better make it your department."

"I just work here," Decker said defensively. "I do abortions, get paid, and get the hell out."

"Who handles the dead babies?" Jake persisted.

"I put the fetuses in an aluminum pan," Decker answered. "That's the last I see of them."

"And who takes the pan?"

Decker motioned with his head to the nurse. "She does."

Jake turned to the nurse. "What do you do with those babies?"

"They are disposed of appropriately," she said in a clinical tone.

"Uh-huh," Jake said, sensing that the woman was lying. "Let me spell things out for you. If you obstruct a murder investigation in this state, it's a felony. You go to jail for that." Jake narrowed his eyes into a hard squint. "With that in mind, let's try again. What do you do with those babies?"

The nurse hesitated but finally caved in. "We sell them."

"To whom?"

"Dr. Alex Mirren."

Jake blinked, caught totally off guard. He reached for his notepad and turned pages, buying time as he collected his thoughts. So Mirren was purchasing dead babies, or fetuses, or whatever the hell you wanted to call them. And that meant Bio-Med was involved. "Did Mirren say why he wanted the fetuses?"

The nurse shook her head. "He only said that the fetuses had to be fresh and intact. And if they were, we would receive five hundred dollars for each fetus."

Jake, clearly out of his depth, looked over to Farelli, who looked back blankly. Fresh and intact, Jake kept thinking. What the hell did that mean? "Wouldn't all the babies be intact? Aren't they usually intact?"

"Not in abortion clinics," Decker explained, relieved that the nurse hadn't mentioned that he received half of every fee from Mirren. "If abortions are done by D and C, as they usually are, the fetuses are often cut and sometimes dismembered. So, they wouldn't be intact."

"So how do you keep the fetuses intact?" Jake asked.

"We don't abort with D and C," Decker went on. "We induce miscarriages with Ru-486, that new abortion pill. Then we remove the fetus intact with a vacuum device. It's really a lot easier on the mothers."

"And Mirren gets his intact babies," Jake added.

"It's the only type he wanted," Decker said, as if he were talking about some kind of produce. "They had to be intact or Mirren wouldn't buy them from us."

Jake stared at the doctor. So the little prick was in on it, too. A goddamn black market for dead babies. Jake thought that he had seen it all until now. "Did Mirren pick up the babies himself?"

Decker shook his head. "We never saw him."

"Then how did he get the babies?"

"We had them delivered."

"Who did the actual delivery?"

"Our handyman," Decker told him. "Vladimir Belov."

28

Nancy Tanaka picked at her salad with a fork while she considered Joanna's question about Alex Mirren. What kind of a person was he? At last she said, "Actually he could be pretty interesting when he wasn't in the lab. He read about a lot of things."

"Like what?" Joanna asked.

"About immortality and how one day science would allow man to live on and on indefinitely."

"Do you think he was talking about the lipolytic enzyme and how it could clean arteries to improve organ function?"

"It wasn't that," Nancy said thoughtfully. "It was more along the lines of genetic manipulation that would keep people disease-free and maybe double their life spans."

"Did he think that was really possible?"

"From a hypothetical standpoint he thought it was possible," Nancy went on, nibbling on a small tomato. "But that, of course, would greatly expand the earth's population, and Alex was concerned about how all those people could be fed."

"Did he have an answer for that?"

Nancy nodded. "He was convinced that one day all crops would be genetically modified so they would grow in abundance in virtually any soil in virtually any climate. Thus, genetic manipulation of crops would provide the food for the ever-expanding, genetically manipulated population."

"That doesn't sound very appealing to me."

Nancy Tanaka shrugged. "It was all hypothetical. But it was interesting to talk about."

They were sitting in a large, family-style restaurant on the outskirts of Lancaster. All the tables and booths were occupied by the lunchtime crowd. A line of people was waiting patiently for seats.

Outside, the day was bright and sunny. And for once, Joanna thought as she looked out the window beside their table, the desert looked beautiful. But she could never work or live out here, never in a million years. It was too isolated, too monotonous. She was a big-city girl and always would be.

Joanna brought her mind back to Nancy Tanaka and Alex Mirren. She decided to dig deeper.

"So," Joanna said, breaking the silence, "most of your conversations were about science?"

"Almost all of them were."

"Did he ever talk about himself or personal things?"

"Rarely," Nancy replied. "Except for the nightmares. He'd talk about those some."

Joanna leaned forward across the table. "Tell me about his nightmares."

Nancy looked around to make sure no one was listening. Then she, too, leaned forward. "It had to do with dead babies."

"Tell me everything he said." Joanna lowered her voice even further. "I want his exact words."

"He'd say something like, 'They're dead, they're dead.' Then he'd twist and turn and wake up sweating and really nervous."

Joanna wondered if Mirren was referring to the dead fetuses found at the construction site in Santa Monica. But Mirren had no connection to the Russian as far as she knew. "Did you ever ask him about the dead babies?"

"A couple of times, but he wouldn't talk about it," Nancy answered. "He would only say that it was personal."

"Maybe when he was married his wife had a miscarriage," Joanna suggested.

"I asked him that," Nancy said, nodding. "But all he'd say was that his wife was crazy and he didn't want to talk about her."

"So he could have been dreaming about a miscarriage his wife had?"

"I guess." Nancy stared down at her salad, lost in thought; then she pushed her plate away. "You know, I don't want it to sound like he was an ogre. He really wasn't a bad guy."

"Until he decided to go kinky on you?" Joanna coaxed.

"Jesus," Nancy hissed softly. "I couldn't believe it. Who needs that kind of stuff?"

"Apparently Alex Mirren did."

Nancy nodded again, her face hardening. "He became such a bastard after that. He literally threw me out of the back lab, and that hurt."

"Are you talking about the cut in salary?"

"It was more than that," Nancy told her. "The back lab really represented the future of medicine. It was fascinating, absolutely fascinating. Particularly the stem cell work."

A waitress came by to refill their coffee cups. Joanna waited for the waitress to leave, and then asked, "How far along had their stem cell work progressed?"

"Not very far," Nancy said. "They had gotten the stem cells to grow in culture, but they had difficulty making them differentiate into other cell types."

"They had no luck at all?"

Nancy hesitated, thinking back. "One of the cell lines had grown into something that looked like lung tissue, but the cells died off. I think that was the closest they came to cell differentiation."

Joanna recalled Eric Brennerman telling her the same thing during her tour of the hot zone laboratory at Bio-Med. In her mind's eye she could see the technician wearing a space suit with its oxygen tube attached. And behind the technician there was a door that led to another back room. "Did you do much work in the back room of the hot zone lab?"

"You mean the one that has the little surgical table?"

"Yes."

Nancy shook her head. "I did very little in that room. Most of the work back there was done by Brennerman and Mirren."

"What'd they work on?"

"Ears," Nancy replied. "They were implanting plastic ears covered with human skin cells into the backs of rats. The rats were genetically programmed to accept the human skin cells as their own. Once the ears were sufficiently encased in human cells, they could be removed and transplanted onto a human who was missing an ear."

"I saw something like that in a genetics laboratory at Memorial," Joanna said. "As a matter of fact, it sounds identical to the work they were doing."

Nancy nodded. "I think it's a collaborative venture between Memorial and Bio-Med."

Just like the damn lipolytic enzyme that was causing cancer, Joanna thought sourly. The third patient to develop cancer had died at Memorial the night before from a massive pulmonary embolus. Joanna was scheduled to do the autopsy on him tomorrow morning.

She brought her mind back to the hot zone laboratory at Bio-Med. Something was wrong in that laboratory. She knew it. Mack Brown knew it. But what was it? "I'd love to get into that lab and look around," Joanna said, thinking aloud.

"They'd never let you in," Nancy said. "And you couldn't sneak in because you don't know the entry code."

"And I'd have to put on that damn space suit, too."

"Maybe, maybe not," Nancy said quietly.

Joanna leaned forward. "I thought everybody in there wears those suits."

"Not everybody," Nancy informed her. "The technicians always wear space suits, but I've seen Brennerman and Mirren walk through there and go into the back room with only surgical masks on."

"How many times did you see that?" Joanna asked.

"At least twice."

"And you're sure the technician was wearing a space suit at that time?"

Nancy nodded firmly. "I was the technician wearing the space suit."

"This gets stranger and stranger," Joanna said, glancing at her watch and reaching for the check. "There are a few things more I need to ask, but I've really got to run. Maybe we could have lunch again next week?"

"I'd like that."

The women walked over to the cashier's counter, where a line of people were still waiting for tables. At the rear of the line, a man carefully studied the profiles of the two women. When he was certain who they were, he abruptly turned and left the restaurant.

The security guard from Bio-Med punched numbers into his cell phone as he hurried back to his car.

29

Joanna was taking off her makeup when the doorbell rang. She dabbed on some lipstick, wondering who it could be. It was after eleven, and outside the weather was foul with wind and rain. The doorbell rang again. She hurried into the living room and peeked through the peephole. Jake was standing in the rain with no raincoat, his hair dripping wet.

Joanna quickly opened the door and stared at him. "Is anything wrong?"

"Nope," Jake said. "I just need some questions answered."

Joanna looked at him strangely. "At midnight in the middle of a thunderstorm?"

"Wait until you hear the questions."

Joanna stepped aside. "You'd better get in here before you catch pneumonia."

Jake went directly to the fireplace and stood close to the dying flames. "I tried to call you, but all I got was a busy signal."

"I was talking to Kate in Paris."

"For over two hours?"

"We had a lot to talk about."

"Is she all right?" Jake asked, concerned.

"She's fine," Joanna said, but that wasn't true. Her sister Kate was having marital problems. Kate's husband was cheating on her with his secretary. And this wasn't the first time it had happened. Joanna wondered for the thousandth time why men and women could never seem to get things right in a relationship.

"Would you like a brandy?" she asked.

"Beer sounds better."

Joanna turned and headed for the kitchen.

"You might want to put another log on the fire," she said over her shoulder.

Jake added a small log and then used an iron poker to stir the red-hot coals and get the fire blazing again. He sat on the couch and lit a cigarette, thinking about the abortion clinic and the Russian immigrant who worked there. The threads of the case were starting to come together, but there were still large gaps that needed to be filled in. And there were important questions that could be answered only by a medical expert. Maybe Joanna could help.

"Here you are," Joanna said, handing him a beer and sitting beside him on the couch. "Now, tell me what brings you out near midnight in the middle of a rainstorm."

Jake sipped his beer—ice cold and delicious. "It seems that Alex Mirren was into some crazy business."

"Like what?"

"Like buying the dead babies that the Russian was burying."

Joanna almost choked on her beer. "What!"

Jake opened his hands wide. "Is that worth a midnight visit in a rainstorm?"

"Holy Christ," Joanna said softly, her mind racing ahead. "I want all the details. Don't leave anything out."

Jake told her about the abortion clinic where the Russian worked and how they were selling infant fetuses to Alex Mirren for five hundred dollars each. He explained how the Russian was a handyman at the clinic and also acted as a deliveryman for the fetuses. Nobody knew or admitted to knowing what Mirren was doing with the dead babies. "So, what do you think?"

Joanna quickly sorted out the facts that fit together from those that didn't. "You said Mirren demanded that the fetuses be intact?"

"Absolutely," Jake said. "Otherwise he wouldn't buy them."

"But why?" Joanna asked, searching her mind for possible answers. "What could he have been doing with them?"

"Maybe some type of experiment," Jake suggested.

"On a dead fetus?" Joanna asked back. "There's nothing you can do with those tissues and organs except look at them."

Jake shrugged. "All I know is that the fetuses had to be intact."

Joanna thought through the problem again. Dead fetuses were of no value to an experimental geneticist. Dead organs couldn't function. They had no physiological or biological capabilities. Dead was dead. Yet Mirren wanted intact fetuses so he could remove their internal organs.

Joanna's eyes narrowed as she wondered if the fetal organs were really dead. "Find out if the fetuses were packed in ice until they were handed over to Mirren."

Jake took out his notepad and hurriedly jotted that down. "Why is the ice important?"

"Because organs that are packed in ice can retain their physiologic function for at least twelve hours," Joanna explained. "That's why organs for transplants are placed on ice before being shipped out."

Jake raised an eyebrow. "Do you think the baby organs are being used for transplants?"

"I don't see how," Joanna said. "But if Mirren had those fetuses packed in ice, it tells us he wanted those fetal organs while they were still viable."

"And you're sure you can't transplant them, huh?"

"Maybe some of the brain cells," Joanna told him. She explained how fetal brain cells could be implanted into the brains of patients with Parkinson's disease and how in some cases it seemed to help. "But that wouldn't explain why Mirren removed the fetuses' hearts and lungs and all their abdominal organs. Those have no use in transplantation."

"So why the hell did he want them?"

"That I don't know." Joanna sipped her beer slowly, trying to come up with answers. "For starters, let's see if Mirren wanted those fetuses packed in ice. That would give us a hint as to where to go next."

Jake shook his head, confused by facts that contradicted one another. "Packed in ice or not, why would anybody want to save dead baby bodies? Why pickle them in a bottle and bury them? That just doesn't make sense."

"The smart move would have been to destroy them," Joanna agreed, nodding. "Why leave evidence like that lying around?"

"In a preserved state, so it would last forever," Jake added. "It doesn't make sense."

He stood up and began pacing across the living room, hands behind him holding his notepad. At the door he stopped and turned, about to say something. But then he discarded the idea and started pacing again. He slowed at the fireplace, staring at the blazing log as if it might give him the answer.

"Let's back up," Jake said finally. "Let's say the bodies had belonged to live babies. Why would somebody preserve them in bottles and bury them? What purpose would that serve?"

"Well, they surely have no value scientifically," Joanna said thoughtfully.

"Oh, but they have some value to somebody," Jake countered. "Otherwise they wouldn't have saved them."

"But it's so risky," Joanna said. "If somebody finds them, like we did, it points to an illegal activity."

"Yeah. Why risk—?" Jake stopped in midsentence and spun around. "Son of a bitch!"

"What?"

A smile spread across Jake's face. "Blackmail. It's got to be blackmail."

Joanna nodded slowly as she put the facts and clues together and weaved them into a chain of events. "So you think the Russian was blackmailing Mirren, and Mirren got tired of it and had the Russian killed?"

Jake nodded back at her. "That's exactly how I figure it. The Russian probably found out that the doctor and nurse at the clinic were getting five hundred dollars a head for the fetuses, so he decided to cash in and make a little bundle for himself."

Joanna shook her head. "There's one big problem with your theory."

"What?"

"How did the Russian get those fetuses back after Mirren finished with them? Remember, the Russian was just a deliveryman. Mirrren would have never given him the cut-up fetuses to dispose of, would he?"

"Good point," Jake said, rethinking his theory. "Mirren would have never shown the Russian those cut-up babies, never in a million years. That would have exposed him to even more blackmail."

"And things would have gotten totally out of control," Joanna added.

"Right," Jake agreed. "Mirren may have been a mean bastard, but he wasn't stupid."

"Then how did the Russian get those fetuses?"

Jake pondered the question at length before saying, "Maybe there's somebody else involved at Bio-Med. Maybe somebody else slipped those cut-up babies to the Russian."

"But who?"

Jake shrugged his shoulders. "Who the hell knows? But this is blackmail for sure, and it somehow involves Mirren and the Russian."

Joanna shook her head disgustedly. "The things people will do for money."

"Particularly when they're hard up," Jake said. "And we know the Russian needed money badly."

"How do we know that?"

"From the letters Farelli found in the Russian's apartment," Jake said. "We had them translated. It seems he needed twelve thousand dollars to bring his mother and brother over here from Russia. The letters sounded like his family was getting pretty desperate."

"So he blackmailed Mirren for twelve thousand dollars?"

"Damn near," Jake answered. "And the Russian wasn't stupid, either. He stretched the blackmail out, getting two hundred and fifty dollars per baby. His bank account showed a lot of two-hundred-and-fifty-dollar deposits over the past year." Jake lit a second cigarette and blew smoke up at the ceiling. "We wondered where all those deposits had come from. And now we know. Blackmail."

Joanna's eyes brightened as she smiled up at Jake. "What?"

"How many deposits did the Russian make?" Joanna asked.

"A lot."

"Give me an exact number."

Jake quickly flipped through his notepad until he reached the information he wanted. "The Russian made thirty-two deposits."

"And how many red dots were present on the two sheets of paper you found in Mirren's closet?"

Jake grinned broadly. "Thirty-two."

"So those papers were really maps showing where the fetuses were buried," Joanna went on. "By the way, how many dots were present on the sheet labeled SMV?"

Jake checked his notepad again. "Twelve."

"And that's the number of fetuses discovered at the construction site in Santa Monica."

"But the label read SMV."

"I think that means Santa Monica-Venice," Joanna told him. "The construction site borders those two cities."

"And the CC on the other sheet could be Culver City," Jake suggested.

"Or Century City, or a dozen other places."

Jake started pacing again. "But why did Mirren hold on to those maps?"

"To keep a tally, I guess."

"But after he had the Russian killed, he didn't need those maps," Jake said, flicking his cigarette into the fireplace. "Most people would have destroyed them."

"Maybe he just hadn't gotten around to it."

"Maybe," Jake said, unconvinced. "Or maybe there was a reason he wanted to keep them."

"Like what?"

Jake shrugged. "I don't know. But I'll bet the person Mirren was in cahoots with does."

"What makes you so sure there was somebody else?"

"Because somebody had Mirren iced by a pro," Jake explained. "Somebody else was right in the middle of this."

They sipped their beers in silence, both trying to fit all the pieces of the puzzle together. The log in the fireplace cracked loudly and split in two, sending sparks flying upward. For a moment the blaze intensified. Then it died down.

"Everything points to Bio-Med," Joanna said quietly. "Everything."

"You got proof?"

"No," she had to admit. "But this baby trail leads right to Bio-Med. And there are some very peculiar things going on out there."

Joanna told Jake about the hot zone lab and the space suits that seemed to have no function. Then she described the back room behind the hot zone lab where a small surgical table was located and where no technicians were allowed.

"What the hell do they do back there?" Jake asked hoarsely.

"Nancy Tanaka says they work on experimental animals in there."

"You believe that?"

"Not now," Joanna replied. "I think they're working on something other than experimental animals."

"Like fetuses?"

"Like human fetuses."

"But you got no proof. Right?"

"Right," Joanna conceded. "But I'll bet I could find some proof if we could take a look around in there. Particularly if we showed up unexpectedly."

Jake's eyes narrowed. "Are you talking about a search warrant?"

Joanna hesitated. "I guess."

"Forget it," Jake said at once. "We'll never get a search warrant based on hunches. That'll never fly."

"But you know I'm right."

"Knowing you're right and proving it are two different things."

"Just a quick look around," Joanna said, more to herself than to Jake.

Jake studied her face at length, trying to read her expression and her mind. "Don't do anything stupid. Breaking and entering is a felony, regardless of why you do it."

"Oh, I'd never do that," Joanna said lightly.

"Don't even think about it," Jake said, his voice dead serious.

"Why think about something that can't be done?" Joanna asked. "Nobody is going to get through the high security they have out there."

Jake studied her face again, hoping she wasn't going to try something foolish. She's got more sense than that, he tried to convince himself. She wouldn't be that dumb.

Jake was looking at Joanna's profile as the blazing fire illuminated it in flashes. Her features were striking and soft, her hair pulled back into a ponytail. She appeared so young and pretty, so unchanged by the years. She seemed ageless to him.

"What?" Joanna asked, returning his stare.

"Nothing," Jake said, reaching for her and drawing her close. "Just don't do anything stupid."

30

Lucy Rabb and Eric Brennerman were sitting across from each other at the noisy, crowded restaurant in Encino. Their knees were touching under the table.

"Isn't it dangerous for us to meet like this?" Lucy asked. "You know, out in the open?"

"It's the perfect place," Brennerman told her. "I run Bio-Med and you are now its major stockholder. Why shouldn't we be having lunch at a fine restaurant? We're talking business. We have nothing to hide."

Lucy pressed her knee up against his inner thigh. "I wish we were aboard the *Argonaut*."

"Me, too."

The waiter came over, refilled their wineglasses, and then placed the 1992 Mondavi chardonnay back in the ice bucket. "Would you like to see a menu, sir?"

"Later," Brennerman said, and waved him away.

Lucy watched the waiter leave. She leaned forward, keeping her voice low. "Is everything going all right out at Bio-Med?"

"All of our experiments are on track."

"What about the side effects?"

"They can be dealt with," Brennerman assured her.

"Cancer can be dealt with?" Lucy asked too loudly. Heads turned, and she lowered her voice once more. "How the hell are you going to deal with that?"

"I know what the problem is," Brennerman said quietly. "And it can be readily fixed."

Which was a half truth. He knew the mechanism that induced the organs to become malignant, but fixing it was another matter. That could take a lot of time to sort out and eventually remedy. But it was doable. A purified preparation that could transform old organs into new ones was entirely doable.

"How long will it take?" Lucy asked.

"A few months," Brennerman lied easily. "And from then on, it's smooth sailing."

"And it's going to be worth billions," Lucy said dreamily.

"And billions," Brennerman added. "It'll produce an ocean of money."

Lucy made a wry face. "But so far I haven't seen a penny."

"Bio-Med is making plenty of money from our genetically modified plants, but we're putting all the profits back into research and development," Brennerman said. "That way we'll become incredibly profitable in the future."

"But I still haven't gotten any money out of it," Lucy complained.

Brennerman nodded, knowing exactly how to play Lucy Rabb. "If you wished, you could declare a dividend on all Bio-Med shares."

Lucy brightened up. "I could?"

"Sure. You're the majority stockholder. All you've got to say is, 'I want to declare a dividend of a quarter a share,' and we'd have to do it."

Lucy licked her lips. "Have we got enough money to do that?"

"I think so."

"And how much money would I end up getting?"

Brennerman tilted his head back, as if he were calculating in his mind. He made up a number. "Probably a couple of hundred thousand a year."

"That's not bad," Lucy said, wondering if she should declare an even bigger dividend. Say a dollar a share.

"But if you plowed the money back into research and development, your annual draw would eventually be a lot more."

"How much more?" Lucy asked hastily.

"As much as two million dollars a year."

"Jesus," Lucy breathed. "That's a ton of money."

"Isn't it, though?"

Brennerman watched the greed on Lucy's face grow. He knew her answer before she gave it.

"I think I'll wait," she said.

"That's the smart move."

"Yeah. I'll wait," Lucy said again, trusting Brennerman more than any man she'd ever known, which wasn't very much. But he owned 20 percent of Bio-Med, and he loved money every bit as much as she did. Like everybody else in the world, he'd act in his own best interest. And his best interest just happened to be her best interest. "You'll tell me when it's the right time to declare a dividend?"

"I sure will."

The waiter returned with menus and handed them out. "Would you like to hear our specials for today?"

"Yes," Lucy answered before Brennerman could say no.

"We have a delicious lobster salad," the waiter began. "It's made with chunks of fresh Maine lobster on a bed of . . ."

Brennerman tuned out the waiter's voice and watched Lucy Rabb over the top of his menu. She was stunning and sexy and brighter than most people gave her credit for. A lot brighter. She was smart enough to know the value of Bio-Med stock and smart enough to know what to do when her husband had decided to turn over all his Bio-Med holdings to a charitable foundation for ovarian cancer, the disease that had killed his first wife.

That would have been a disaster, Brennerman thought, shuddering at just the idea. They would have controlled everything and had an oversight committee looking over his shoulder twenty-four hours a day. But Lucy knew exactly how to handle that. She ensnared Mervin Tuch with her beauty and body, and made him do everything she wanted him to do. Tuch was able to delay the transfer of Bio-Med stock to charity and also made sure Edmond Rabb's will remained unchanged until the old man could be dropped off the end of his yacht. And then Lucy made her smartest move. She picked Eric Brennerman to be her partner. Oh, yeah. *She could be plenty smart enough when she wanted to be*, Brennerman told himself. *And cold-blooded as well.*

Brennerman felt Lucy's big toe running up his shinbone under the table.

"The mussels sound delicious, don't they?" Lucy asked.

"Absolutely," Brennerman said absently.

"They're brought in fresh from Australia," the waiter went on, "and cooked in a . . ."

Brennerman tuned out the voice again and watched the waiter, who was now peeking down at Lucy's cleavage. She could do that to men. She could make them look even when they tried not to.

That was how it had started between himself and Lucy. A look. Instant attraction. They were good together and better yet in bed. But their relationship hadn't turned into love and never would. But that was all right with Brennerman. He knew they would stay together because they needed each other. And need was much more dependable than love.

"What do you think, Eric?" Lucy asked.

"I'll have the lobster salad."

"Me, too."

As the waiter retrieved the menus, he stole one more peek at Lucy's breasts.

"It's terrible what happened to Mervin Tuch," Lucy said, making conversation.

"Terrible," Brennerman agreed.

"The streets aren't safe anymore."

"And getting worse."

The waiter nodded his agreement and checked the wineglasses. Then he withdrew.

Lucy leaned forward, keeping her voice down. "The pro did a good job this time, didn't she?"

Brennerman quickly brought a finger to his lips and hushed her. "Shhh!"

Lucy glanced around, making certain no one was within earshot. "But it was a good job."

"Maybe, maybe not."

She glanced around again and leaned in even closer. "What do you mean?"

"On the local TV news last night, a reporter said the police were looking into the possibility that Tuch was killed by a professional."

"Shit," Lucy spat disgustedly. "This hitter keeps screwing up."

"We're still okay," Brennerman whispered reassuringly. "Nothing points to us. And remember, all lawyers have enemies. It comes with the territory."

"The police aren't stupid," Lucy whispered back. "They know Edmond and Mirren were murdered. And now Tuch gets it. Somebody is going to put everything together."

"Nobody is going to put anything together unless they first find out what's going on out at Bio-Med," Brennerman said quietly. "We're the only two left who know. And neither of us will talk, will we?"

"God, if they find out," Lucy said worriedly. "I guess we should be thankful the cops aren't scientists."

"The cops could never figure this out," Brennerman told her. "Our only concern is Joanna Blalock. If she digs long enough and deep enough, she could come up with the answer."

"But you said she wasn't making any more visits to the Bio-Med plant."

"She's not," Brennerman said, his voice barely above a whisper. "But she's been meeting secretly with one of our senior technicians."

"Oh, shit," Lucy moaned softly.

"And it's the same technician who was sleeping with Mirren."

"Oh, shit," Lucy said again. "And Blalock is smart enough to put everything together, too."

"Not if she's dead."

Lucy's eyes widened. "Not another one!"

"It can't be helped."

"But if she's murdered, the police will never let go of the investigation."

"What if she just disappears?"

"How can you do that?"

"There are ways."

Lucy gave the matter more thought. "But the police will still come looking for her."

"Let them."

"Her disappearance will cause big trouble for us," Lucy said, shaking her head disapprovingly. "Is there any other way to deal with her?"

"We have a backup plan to get rid of her that may be even better."

"That's still murder. Remember, the police aren't stupid."

"In the backup plan we don't murder her."

"Then how are you going to do it?"

"We'll let nature do it for us."

"Nature? What the hell are you talking about?"

Brennerman reached for the wine bottle in the ice bucket. "You'll see."

31

The woman who managed the Mail Boxes Etc. store refused to accept the search warrant from Jake Sinclair.

"I'm sorry, Lieutenant," the manager said apologetically, "but I can't let you near any post office box without permission from the postal inspector or the FBI."

"Can you at least describe the person who rents out a box?" Jake asked.

"Not without an okay from the higher-ups."

"How about if it's a murder investigation?"

"Still can't do it."

"Never even for murder, huh?"

The manager extended her arms, palms out. "What can I do? The post office sets the rules, and I've got to follow them. People pay for their confidentiality, you see."

Yeah, Jake was thinking, particularly professional hitters.

"Sorry."

Jake nodded and turned to Farelli. "Put a uniformed officer behind the postal boxes and tell him to ID anybody who opens one."

"Wait a minute!" the manager said hastily. "I've got a business to run here."

Jake extended his arms, palms out. "What can I do? The police authorities set the rules. I just follow them."

"Christ," the manager grumbled, and went back behind the counter.

Jake and Farelli walked out of the store and into the bright sunshine. The traffic on Wilshire Boulevard was heavy, the smog in the air dense and irritating. Jake glanced around at the stores adjacent to Mail Boxes Etc. There were no parking lots.

"When the hitter comes, she'll have to park on the street," Jake told Farelli. "Keep your eyes peeled for a black Camry. You've got the license number?"

"Right here," Farelli said, patting his coat pocket. "Thanks to the DMV computer."

Jake lit a cigarette, thinking about how many man-hours they had saved by using the computer at the Department of Motor Vehicles. They told the computer technician they were looking for a new, dark Toyota Camry with a license number that started with a 4, followed by the letter *W*, *U*, or *V*. The computer gave them a list of over a thousand names. Then the computer was given the information that the car was owned by a woman under the age of forty who lived in the Los Angeles area. That narrowed the list down to thirty-six names, each of whom had to be carefully checked out. In less than two days, the police had the name and address of the hitter. A cold-blooded bitch, Jake was thinking, who had already killed God knows how many people.

He turned to Farelli. "Don't take any chances with her. Slam her ass down hard on the sidewalk, face down, hands out."

"Oh, she'll be spread-eagled," Farelli said. "Don't worry about that."

Jake nodded. "And kick her purse away. That's where she'll be carrying."

"Got you."

Jake started to walk away. Then he turned back. "And tell the cop inside to stay out of sight. We don't want to spook the hitter."

"How long you figure it'll take you to get to the postal inspector?" Farelli asked.

"A couple of hours, if we're lucky."

Farelli watched Jake drive away, and then he

walked over to his car, an unmarked two-year-old Chevy that was parked two doors down.

He waited in the front seat, watching the Mail Boxes Etc. store and thinking how smart the hitter had been. She was a pro who knew how to cover her tracks. Even though they had a street address for her, they still might not get her. Because she might have never used the address—which was really a front for a P.O. box—for any mail other than that which came from the Department of Motor Vehicles. The DMV wouldn't accept a P.O. box number as an address. They required a street address to register a car. And the hitter wasn't about to put her real address on any official document that could be traced. So she went to a Mail Boxes Etc. facility that gave a Wilshire Boulevard address and not a P.O. box number to its customers.

Smart, Farelli thought again, *so damn smart*. But they'd eventually catch her, and she'd talk her head off to save herself from sucking cyanide in a gas chamber. Oh, yeah, they'd catch her. Because now they had her name. Sara Ann Moore. And if she had a car here, that meant she lived here. And somewhere they'd find a real address. Maybe from records at the phone company or electric company. Somewhere they'd find her.

Farelli slouched down behind the steering wheel to wait for her.

Sara Ann Moore couldn't find a parking space near the Mail Boxes Etc. store, so she went to a car-wash facility two blocks away. They had a $24.95 special on a quick wax job that took an hour to perform. And that was fine with Sara. She had the whole afternoon to kill before her meeting with David Westmoreland.

Walking away from the car wash, Sara put on oversize sunglasses to protect her eyes from the bright sunlight. It was a very warm day, and she was glad she hadn't worn her blond wig. It was too hot for that, she thought. And besides, her short brown hair was growing out, the blond streaks not nearly so pronounced. She liked it much better at this length, and men were noticing it more, too.

Her thoughts returned to David Westmoreland, and she wondered again what the meeting was about. Maybe it was another hit, which would be nice. Particularly if it was going to be a high-priced, high-profile job. Another possibility was that some of her recent customers were demanding refunds because the deaths were found to be premeditated murder and not accidental. Like the Edmond Rabb hit. How in the world did they discover that the old fart hadn't just dropped overboard and drowned accidentally? Maybe they were only guessing, with the insurance company doing anything and everything to hold up payment. The bastards were good at that.

She came to a busy intersection and waited for the light to change. She gazed at the row of stores where Mail Boxes Etc. was located. The shop on the end, run by Vietnamese, did manicures and pedicures. Sara decided to treat herself and get her nails done. That would take up at least an hour, and by then her car would be ready. But first she'd check her mail.

The light changed and Sara crossed the street.

She stopped in the manicure shop and made an appointment, promising to be right back. She hurried down to Mail Boxes Etc. and entered, paying no attention to the Chevrolet parked two doors down or to the man slouched down behind the wheel.

Sara had to wait. A heavy-set, middle-aged woman was at the wall lined with postal boxes, struggling with the combination to her box.

"Damn," the woman said after another unsuccessful try.

A uniformed policeman stepped out from behind the postal boxes, saying, "Ma'am, may I see your ID, please?"

"Wh-what?" the woman stammered.

"May I see your ID?" the policeman repeated.

Sara turned quickly away and looked at a rack of

greeting cards, picking one and studying it intently, all the while watching the cop in her peripheral vision.

"What's this all about?" the woman asked, handing over her driver's license.

"We've had some problems with the mail boxes here," the policeman lied lamely.

Bullshit, Sara thought, her face buried in the birthday card. If they had problems with the mail boxes, they'd call a postal inspector, not a cop.

"Thank you, ma'am," the cop said, returning the license. He disappeared back behind the wall of postal boxes.

Sara glanced over at the manager, who was busily talking on the phone at the rear of the store. She carefully placed the birthday card back on the rack. Then she took a deep breath and began to inch her way to the door.

Sara moved aside as another woman entered the store—a tall young woman with blond hair. The young blonde approached the postal boxes.

In an instant the cop appeared from behind the wall, gun drawn. "Freeze! And don't even think about moving!"

A plainclothes cop rushed through the door, brushing past Sara. He had his gun out and pointed at the blonde. "Get your hands up against the wall and keep them there!"

"Wh-what have I done?" the blonde shrieked, petrified with fear.

"Just do as you're told," the plainclothes cop ordered, his gun trained at the blonde's head. "Now, get those goddamn hands up!"

Sara slipped out of the store. She walked slowly past the manicure shop and turned the corner. Ahead two sightseeing buses had stopped and were offloading passengers. Most of the people were blond and fair-complected with cameras around the necks. Sara hurried toward the buses and disappeared into a crowd of German tourists.

32

Lori McKay went to the blackboard and put check marks by the names of the three patients who had received the lipolytic enzyme and had developed cancer.

"We've retested the enzyme preparations from Bio-Med for the third time and found nothing," she told Joanna. "They contain no preservatives, and there's no contamination of any kind."

"Oh, something is there," Joanna said, sipping coffee as she studied the blackboard. "We just haven't found it yet."

"Well, we'd better find it soon, because we're running out of specimens and places to look."

"Did you restudy the microscopic slides?"

"Until my eyes dropped out," Lori replied. "There was nothing new. The normal tissue in their organs appears to be incredibly healthy, and the cancers look bizarre and mean as hell."

"What about the electron microscopic studies?" Joanna asked.

"Dennis Green is checking on that now," Lori answered. "But when you hear nothing from those people, it usually means they've found nothing."

Joanna sighed wearily. "We're not making any progress here. We're just fumbling around in the dark."

"Well, we'd better shed some light on something real quick, or the newspapers are going to eat us alive."

Joanna nodded. "I just saw yesterday's front-page article."

"It's not as bad as today's editorial," Lori went on. "They flat-out say we experimented on desperate patients without warning them of all the possible side effects. They said the public should expect more from doctors, particularly those at Memorial."

"No doubt that was written by the colleagues of the editor who developed renal cancer."

"No doubt."

"And you know what the sad part is?" Joanna asked.

"What?"

"What they wrote was true."

The phone rang. Lori picked it up and spoke briefly. Then she placed her hand over the receiver. "It's Simon Murdock."

Joanna groaned and reached for the phone. "Yes, Simon."

"I may require your assistance in a somewhat delicate matter."

"Tell me how I can help."

"The news media is demanding we have a press conference on this cancer-causing drug," Murdock told her. "They want details, and I want you to be there to answer the scientific questions."

"I'd put that conference on hold for now," Joanna advised.

"That's easier said than done." Murdock described the intense pressure being put on him to hold a public hearing. The pressure was coming at him from all sides. Even his own board of directors at Memorial was demanding a full and open disclosure.

Joanna listened patiently, feeling sorry for Murdock and knowing he had no way out.

A second line on Joanna's phone began to blink. Quickly she signaled to Lori, pointing at the wall phone.

Lori hurried over and picked up the phone. She spoke for a moment and then waved to Joanna. "It's Lieutenant Sinclair."

Joanna covered the receiver with her hand, mentally blocking out Murdock's voice. "Take a message," she called over softly.

Joanna returned to her conversation with Murdock, but she kept her eyes on Lori and tried to overhear her conversation with Jake.

Lori was saying, "She's on the other line. Can I take a message? . . . Uh-huh, uh-huh. . . . No more than six hours. . . . Uh-huh. . . . Okay. I'll make sure she gets the message."

Lori hung up.

Joanna turned her full attention back to Simon Murdock. "Here's my best advice, Simon. Delay the press conference. Tell them we're now finishing our investigation, and once that's done we'll be glad to meet with them and discuss our findings."

"Given more time, do you think you can come up with an answer?" Murdock asked hopefully.

"I wouldn't bet on it," Joanna said. "But if I'm going to stand up in front of a news conference, I'll want every bit of information at my fingertips."

"I doubt if they will agree to a delay."

"They will if you don't give them any other choice."

"I'll get back to you later."

Joanna put the phone down and looked over at Lori. "Well? What did Jake want?"

"He said to tell you that the fetuses were packed in ice," Lori reported. "That was a mandatory requirement. Otherwise the fetuses were not bought."

Joanna asked quickly, "What about the six hours?"

"The fetuses had to be delivered within six hours," Lori said. "That, too, was mandatory."

Joanna had other questions that only Jake could answer. Where were the fetuses delivered? Did Mirren actually pick them up from the Russian? Was there any way to show beyond a doubt that the fetuses ended up at Bio-Med? Damn, Joanna cursed to herself, now wishing she had talked to Jake.

"Why pack the fetuses in ice?" Lori asked, breaking into Joanna's thoughts.

"They wanted fetal organs," Joanna said, focusing her mind on the problem.

"But for what?" Lori persisted. "Fetal organs have no use."

"Those organs are important to somebody," Joanna assured her. "That's why those fetuses were packed in ice and had to be delivered within six hours."

"Maybe they wanted fetal bone marrow," Lori suggested. "Maybe they wanted undifferentiated blood cells for some reason."

"Then why eviscerate the fetuses and take their brains as well?"

Lori nodded. "You've got a point."

"But that doesn't bring us any closer to an answer."

Lori wrinkled her brow, concentrating. "Do you think it's possible that they discovered a way to transplant fetal organs into patients?"

Joanna shrugged. "Bio-Med is not involved in transplantation. That's not what they do." She gave the matter more thought, gauging it from a commercial standpoint. "And they don't have the know-how or facilities to do it."

"Maybe they're transplanting the fetal organs into experimental animals."

Joanna shook her head at the idea. "That has no commercial value. They wouldn't be the least bit interested in that."

"Why not take the easy route?" Lori asked. "You know, just ask the people at Bio-Med. Maybe there's a simple answer."

"They'd deny any knowledge of it," Joanna said. "And remember, Mirren was the only one we can prove was involved with the fetuses, and he's dead."

"How about getting a search warrant?"

"You're dreaming."

The door opened, and Dennis Green walked into the forensic laboratory. "They found something interesting in the electron microscopic studies on Oliver Rhodes's heart. I'm not sure what the hell it means, though."

Joanna leaned forward. "Within the cardiac muscle cells?"

"Right," Green went on. "They found viral particles scattered throughout, both in the malignant and nonmalignant cells."

Joanna's eyes widened. "Are they positive those are viral particles?"

"Positive."

"Could they explain the presence of these particles?"

"Not really," Green replied. "Somebody suggested Rhodes might have had a viral myocarditis. But that wouldn't explain why he developed a malignancy of the heart."

"Viruses are known to cause some cancers," Lori said. "For example, in cats a virus causes feline leukemia."

"But viruses have never been proved to cause cancer in man," Green countered. "Except maybe for the Epstein-Barr virus in Burkitt's lymphoma. And this patient surely doesn't have a lymphoma."

Joanna listened to the scientific exchange, but her mind was elsewhere. She was trying to concentrate on the viral particles and what their presence meant. What were those viral particles doing there? And how did they get into the cardiac muscle cells? Was it just a case of viral myocarditis? Was the finding simply a red herring that had no relationship to the malignancy?

"No," Green was telling Lori, "they couldn't identify the type of virus from the particles."

"Too bad," Lori said. "There are some viruses that are known to cause myocarditis with some frequency. Viruses like Coxsackie usually—"

"Wait a minute!" Joanna interrupted. "What makes you so certain this was a viral myocarditis?"

"I'm not certain," Green said. "But the virus was present in the cardiac muscle cells and—"

"No, no!" Joanna interrupted again. "You're missing the point. Maybe the virus is involved in *all* these patients."

"But we can't prove that," Lori argued.

"Maybe, maybe not," Joanna said, and turned to Dennis Green. "Do we have the electron microscopic results on the other two patients with cancer?"

"I haven't seen them," Green answered.

"So we don't know whether there are viral particles present in the other two patients with cancer, do we?"

"There's one way to find out." Green reached for the phone and punched in numbers. He spoke briefly and then waited for a response.

Joanna began pacing the floor of the laboratory, thinking about viruses and cancers and the relationship between the two. And how could viral particles be related to a lipolytic enzyme that seemed to cause cancer?

Green put the phone down. "I'll be a son of a bitch. All three tumors contained the same viral particles."

"Jesus," Lori hissed softly. "How did that virus get into these patients?"

"Take a guess," Joanna said.

Lori thought hard, her brow furrowed. "Well, we know it couldn't have been in the enzyme preparations the patients received."

"How do you know that?"

"Because we didn't detect any virus in the enzyme preparations we received from Bio-Med."

Joanna smiled, then asked, "Are you sure the enzyme preparations they sent us to test are the same ones they gave to the patients?"

Lori still couldn't make the connection. "Why would viral particles be mixed in with the lipolytic enzyme?"

"I don't know," Joanna said. "But I think I know somebody who does."

Joanna reached for her personal phone book and flipped pages until she came to Nancy Tanaka's number.

33

Sara puffed on her cigarette and stared into space. "They're on to me. They know who I am, and they're looking for me."

"Do you know that for sure?" David Westmoreland asked.

Sara nodded firmly. "There was a cop waiting behind the postal boxes where I pick up my mail. He was checking IDs."

"So?"

"So a blonde who resembled me walked in, and the cop jumped all over her. Then a plainclothes cop ran in with his gun drawn. They treated her like she was armed and dangerous." Sara puffed again on her cigarette. "*Shit!* They were looking for me. It was just pure luck I wasn't wearing my blond wig."

"Did they ask you for your ID?"

"No," Sara said. "I slipped out of the place during all the commotion."

Westmoreland gave her a hard look. "And you're certain you weren't followed here?"

"Positive," she assured him. "I drove around for two hours, off and on the freeway and down back streets. There was nobody following me."

"Good," Westmoreland said, but he still wasn't convinced. A real pro could have tailed her, and she would have had no idea he was there.

"What should I do?"

"Play it cool," he advised her. "That way you won't make more mistakes."

"The mistakes are happening because you're giving

me too many hits too fast," Sara complained. "If you and your client don't allow me enough time to prepare, the hits aren't always going to come off perfect."

"You were given plenty of money to make those hits look good," Westmoreland said, an edge to his voice. "You didn't have any trouble taking those big bucks, did you?"

"The money was fine," Sara said. "It's just these damn rush jobs. I've made mistakes by hurrying things."

Damn right you have, Westmoreland wanted to say, but he held his tongue. He pushed himself up from the corner booth at Club West. "I'm going to get a beer. You want anything?"

"No, thanks."

Westmoreland walked over to the front window and cracked the venetian blinds to look out. Traffic was moving nicely, and there were no cars parked nearby. Across the street a truck was delivering produce to a Chinese restaurant. And next to the restaurant was a newsstand with two people browsing through magazines. An old man and a kid. No cops there, Westmoreland decided.

He went behind the bar and opened a bottle of imported beer. Carefully he poured the beer into a mug, thinking about the predicament Sara Ann Moore had placed them both in. Somehow they had ID'd her. And they damn well knew she was a hitter. Otherwise the cops wouldn't have come at the blonde with their guns drawn. They had her made, and it was only a matter of time before they tracked her down. And she could lead them right back to him.

"I think I will have that beer," Sara called over.

"Coming up," Westmoreland said lightly, but his mind was still working on the problem at hand. He knew the cops were close to Sara, but he didn't know how close. They didn't have her home address yet, because if they did, they would have picked her up there. The cops only had her postal box number. But now that they had her name, the chase would be a straight line and they would quickly zero in on her. She had just a few days left.

Westmoreland brought the beers to their booth and

sat across from her. He studied her face briefly. She looked scared and tired, like prey about to be captured. He knew how he would handle her—and all the rest of this mess. "You've got to get out of town," he told her.

"I know," Sara said. "When should I leave?"

"Soon," he said. "Within thirty-six hours."

"That's not much time."

"You've got to get while the getting's good."

Sara began organizing things in her mind. Leave the car and the condominium as is and catch a plane out. Make the reservations at a ticket office and pay in cash. Don't go home tonight. Stay at a motel. Only that airline ticket would cost a lot. She had no credit cards and only a hundred in cash. "Do you think I should chance going to my safety deposit box?"

"I wouldn't."

"You're right," Sara said, nodding. "It's just that I'm a little short on cash."

"Me, too," Westmoreland lied. "I just paid off a big gambling debt."

"I think I'll take a chance and go back to my condominium after I leave here." Sara lit another cigarette off the cigarette she was smoking. Her hands were no longer shaking. "I have to grab a few personal things and download stuff off my computer."

"It'll be risky."

"I've got to do it," Sara told him. "The information in my computer is very important to me. And I've also got some cash stashed away up there."

"Be very careful," Westmoreland warned. "Call the front desk and talk with your doorman before you go there."

"That's my plan."

"And grab only what you absolutely need and get out."

Sara sighed deeply. "I wish I had more cash I could get to. I'm going to be on the move for a while, and that costs."

Westmoreland slowly twirled his beer mug between his palms, studying the foam as it rose. "I know somebody who's willing to pay really big bucks for a quick hit."

"Jesus!" Sara blurted out. "Not another rush job."

"I'm talking really, really large bucks."

Sara fixed her eyes on Westmoreland. "How much would I get?"

"Your end would be forty thousand."

Sara whistled softly and repeated, "Forty thousand."

"And that's a lot of traveling money."

"Who's the hit?"

"Joanna Blalock."

Sara shook her head. "If we hit her, half the world will come looking for us."

"Not if she just disappears."

"Has the hit already been planned?"

Westmoreland nodded. "For tomorrow night. You could do it and be on your way with forty large in your purse."

Sara considered the proposition carefully, weighing the pros and cons of a quick hit. Things could go wrong without appropriate planning and usually did. But the forty thousand was irresistible.

"Well?" Westmoreland pressed.

"I need to know the details before I can give you an answer."

Westmoreland gave her an icy stare. "If I tell you about it, you're committed."

Sara hesitated, still unsure what to do. The money was great, but so was the risk. Killing Joanna Blalock could set off a firestorm of trouble. Again she thought about the forty thousand dollars. With that kind of money, she could avoid the firestorm. Finally she said, "Okay, I'm in."

"Good," Westmoreland said approvingly. "Here's how it will work. We know where Blalock lives and where she parks her car at home. It's an outdoor parking space at the north end of the condominium complex. When she gets out of her car, you pop her. Two to the head. Make sure you use your silencer."

"And how does she disappear?"

"My friend Scottie and his cement truck will be close by. Blalock will be put in a body bag and taken

to a place where she'll be covered up in wet cement."
Westmoreland ran an index finger across his throat
and smiled humorlessly. "She disappears and she's
never found."

"And I walk away with forty grand?"

"Right," Westmoreland said. "Let me call Scottie
and tell him it's a go."

As Sara watched him walk to the phone, she considered the things she had to do back at her condominium.
The most important task was to download her computer
and retrieve all the information on her stock portfolio.
Once she did that, she was safe. The accounts were all
untraceable because everything was bought in her mother's name using her mother's Social Security number.

Sara sighed sadly as she thought about her mother,
who was withering away with Alzheimer's disease and
for whom Sara was conservator. The poor woman couldn't
even recognize her daughter anymore. A picture of her
mother flashed into Sara's mind. She pushed it aside and
went back to tallying money. There was a half-million
in stocks and another fifty thousand in cash, including
the fee for the upcoming hit. Not a fortune, but enough
to get by on until she inherited her mother's estate. And
that wouldn't be long now. Maybe it was time to get
out of the hit business while—as David had said—the
getting was good.

David returned to the booth and handed Sara a slip
of paper. "Everything is set. Here's the location where
you meet Scottie tomorrow at six p.m."

"You sure he's reliable?"

"Absolutely," Westmoreland said. "And he's the
best cement man we've got."

Sara shuddered. "I don't want to see any of this
cement business."

"Oh, you'll be long gone by then," David reas-
sured her.

34

It was early evening when Joanna arrived at the large, busy shopping mall on the west side of the San Fernando Valley. The ground level was crowded with shoppers who were there for the semiannual red-letter sale. Moviegoers—mainly teenagers—were lined up for the horror show at the mall's theater.

Joanna waded through the crowd until she spotted Nancy Tanaka standing outside Nordstrom. She waved and strolled over. "Thanks for meeting me here on such short notice," Joanna said.

"I'm glad you called," Nancy told her. "It gave me a chance to get away from Bio-Med for a while."

Joanna detected the unhappiness in the technician's voice. "I thought things would go better for you now that Alex Mirren is no longer there."

"If anything, it's gotten worse," Nancy said. "I think they now consider me persona non grata."

Two screaming children dashed by, followed by two more who were screaming even louder.

"Let's get away from this noise."

Joanna took Nancy's arm and guided her into the giant department store. They strolled down an aisle that was lined with ladies leatherware. "Tell me more about this persona non grata business," Joanna inquired. "Have they said something to you?"

Nancy shook her head. "It's not what they say, it's what they've done. I've now been taken off all projects dealing with the enzyme preparation. They've even taken my laboratory data books away."

"Without explanation?"

"Oh, they say the projects are nearly completed, but that's not true. That's a bunch of bull."

Nancy stopped and picked up an expensive lizard-skin purse. She studied it closely and then made a face at its three-hundred-dollar price tag. "And on top of everything else," she said, "they're giving me not so subtle hints that I soon may be let go."

"Oh, goodness," Joanna lamented, feeling bad for the attractive technician. "This may well be my fault. My investigation may have cost you your job."

"Not really," Nancy said, putting the expensive purse back on the shelf. "I think the handwriting was on the wall when Alex Mirren died. You see, I worked almost exclusively with him."

"They could have found you another position."

"Well, they apparently chose not to."

Joanna thought for a moment and then asked, "Would you be interested in a position at Memorial?"

"In microbiology?"

"Yes."

"I'd love it," Nancy said sincerely. "But I hear they've got a waiting list a mile long."

"I know a few shortcuts."

Nancy smiled. "I'd be indebted to you forever."

"No," Joanna told her. "That would just make us even."

They walked on, passing the cosmetic counters where women were lined up to try a new brand of lipstick. To their right was the perfume area with clerks dressed in sharp white coats. A lovely fragrance filled the air.

"I want to ask you a few more questions," Joanna said in a low voice.

"Fire away."

"Did you know that Alex Mirren worked with fetuses?"

Nancy jerked her head around. "Human?"

"Yes."

"Jesus," Nancy hissed under her breath. "I never saw it."

"Can you think of anybody or any experiment that used human fetuses?"

Nancy shook her head emphatically. "Not even animal fetuses."

"Could they have worked on fetuses in the back room in the hot zone lab?" Joanna asked. "You know, where they have the small surgical table?"

"I guess," Nancy said with uncertainty. "But I never saw any evidence of it."

"But you were rarely in the back room. Right?"

"Almost never."

Another blank wall, Joanna thought. But Mirren was working with human fetuses—she was sure of that. And she knew that the abortions were done during the day and that the fetuses had to be handed over within six hours. Six hours. That meant the fetuses had to be delivered to Bio-Med during the day or early evening. "Did you ever see any unusual deliveries? For example, things packed in ice and rushed in?"

Nancy thought back and then slowly shook her head. "I don't remember anything like that. But, of course, all deliveries are made at the back of the plant."

"You mean, the deliveries are made on the side of the building."

"No," Nancy said at once. "At the back where they have a large loading dock."

"I see," Joanna said, recalling the side entrance where the delivery van had pulled up. There was no road leading to it and no loading dock.

Nancy lowered her voice to a whisper. "Was he really working with human fetuses?"

"We have our suspicions," Joanna said vaguely.

"I'm glad I'm getting the hell out of there." Nancy glanced over her shoulder to make sure no one was listening in. "Human fetuses, for chrissakes!"

Joanna gave her a long look. "What we talk about here remains confidential. You understand that. Right?"

"Of course."

They came to the ladies shoe section. A big sale was on. A sign read 50% OFF. The shoes were stacked up on a table in no particular order. A group of women were busily rummaging through them.

"Did you do any work with viruses out at Bio-Med?" Joanna asked quietly.

"Some."

"Tell me about it."

"We were taking adenoviruses and modifying them so they wouldn't cause disease." Nancy explained how the modified virus was then used as a vector to carry genetic information into a cell. "So you take a piece of DNA and hook it onto the virus, and then you take that and mix it with the cells. The virus penetrates the cells and carries the DNA in with it. The end result is that new genetic material has been transferred into the cell."

"So, you're talking about gene transfer."

"Exactly."

"What kind of genes were you transferring?"

"One that might induce the stem cells to produce heparin, which, of course, is a widely used anti-coagulant."

"Did it work?"

"No," Nancy replied. "It was a complete bust."

"And I take it that everything was done in vitro?"

Nancy nodded. "No animals were used."

"Is there any way those modified viruses could have found their way into the lipolytic enzyme preparation?" Joanna asked.

Nancy thought about the question at length before answering. "I don't see how."

"Were you the only one working with viruses?"

"Just me."

"What about Mirren?"

"Him, too. But I did most of the hands-on work."

Joanna carefully worded her next question. "If he had to, could Mirren have modified the virus by himself?"

"Probably not," Nancy said. Then she looked over

at Joanna and studied her for a moment. "Why all the interest in viruses?"

"Because we found viral particles in the tumors of the three patients who developed cancer after receiving the enzyme preparation."

Nancy's eyes widened. "Are you saying that the viruses were present in the lipolytic enzyme preparation the patients received?"

"It almost had to be," Joanna told her. "There's no other way to explain the presence of the virus in the three tumors and in the tissues around them."

"And you think that the virus is somehow associated with the development of the cancers?"

"It seems that way."

Nancy's face paled. "Don't tell me they injected my virus into three patients and caused them to come down with cancer."

"We can't prove that."

"But you think so."

Joanna nodded. "I think so."

Nancy swallowed hard, obviously shaken. "I had no idea they were going to do this."

"I know," Joanna said softly.

Nancy turned away and stared out into space. "You try to do good research and help people. And along comes a bastard like Mirren who . . ." Her voice trailed off.

"What use could that virus have had in the enzyme preparation?" Joanna asked. "Why was it there?"

Nancy shrugged. "I have no idea."

"We've got to find out," Joanna said, lowering her voice as a group of shoppers passed by. "If we knew what they were doing out at Bio-Med, it might give us a clue on how to deal with patients who have already been injected."

"It would all be in Mirren's laboratory data books."

"And where are they?"

"Probably in his office. Or maybe in the back lab."

Joanna sighed hopelessly. "And we'll never get in there without knowing the code that opens the door."

"I think I know it," Nancy whispered.

Joanna moved in closer. "How did you get it?"

"As bright as Mirren was, he had a terrible memory for numbers," Nancy said. "So he wrote down things like telephone numbers on his sleeve. The other day I passed by the place at Bio-Med where Mirren hung his laboratory coat. It had two sets of numbers written on the sleeve. I knew one of them. It was the code to the front door. I'll bet my last dollar that the second set was the code to the hot zone lab."

"Did you write down the second code?" Joanna asked quickly.

Nancy smiled mischievously. "I just might have."

"So you could get in there any time you wanted, couldn't you?"

"Not during the day," Nancy answered. "They watch me like hawks."

"What about the night?"

"I guess it's possible," Nancy said hesitantly. "But it would still be risky." She took a deep breath and exhaled, trying to make up her mind. "It'd be really risky."

"What if I came with you?" Joanna coaxed.

"There's so much security," Nancy said uneasily.

"There are ways around that," Joanna pressed on.

"It's going to take a lot of planning," Nancy cautioned. "And a lot of luck to pull it off."

"This is really important," Joanna emphasized. "People's lives might be at stake here."

Nancy looked Joanna squarely in the eyes. "You'd really go in there with me?"

"Absolutely."

Nancy smiled faintly. "You're braver than I am."

"Or maybe not as smart."

Nancy took Joanna's arm. "Let's go up to the café on the second floor. We can get some coffee and talk more."

As they rode the escalator up, they heard a medley of Gershwin tunes being played on a nearby piano. Neither woman noticed the man following them.

35

Sara was ten minutes late for her meeting with Scottie and his cement truck. She sped up as she took the Mulholland Drive exit off the freeway and drove westward along the winding road. Glancing in her rearview mirror, she saw a dark Chevrolet a dozen car lengths behind her. It wasn't the car that she thought might have been following her, but to make sure she pulled over to the side of the road and pretended to be studying a map. The car behind her passed and disappeared around a curve ahead.

Sara continued on, watching for the off-road rest area that was 1.8 miles from the freeway exit. She checked the rearview mirror again. No one was behind her. The road was clear. She lit a cigarette, less tense now. *Only one more thing to do,* Sara thought, *and I'm out of here. I whack Joanna Blalock, get my forty grand, and scoot.*

Everything else had been taken care of. She had gotten back into her condominium unseen, collected some personal things and downloaded her computer. And she'd done it all in under twenty minutes. Her only possessions were in the overnight bag on the seat beside her. Again she glanced into the rearview mirror. Nothing. Her odometer showed she'd traveled 1.6 miles from the freeway exit.

Sara rounded a sharp curve—then another and another. Up ahead she saw the off-road rest area. A huge cement truck was parked there, and next to it was a new Cadillac. Something about the setup made Sara feel uneasy. Why a car and a cement truck? Two vehicles meant two people. She was supposed to meet only *one* man called Scottie. Sara reached into her purse and made certain the safety on the weapon was in the off position.

She pulled off the road and stopped in the rest area. Slowly she got out of the car, her open purse in her hand.

A big, heavyset man with dark hair and a barrel chest came over. He was wearing blue jeans and a leather bomber jacket. "I'm Scottie. And you're late. Where the hell you been?"

"I thought somebody might be following me," Sara explained. "So I got off and on the freeway a couple of times to make certain nobody was on my tail."

Scottie was instantly on guard, his senses sharpened. Quickly he peered down the winding road and saw no cars or lights. "You sure nobody was there?"

"If he was, I lost him."

Sara glanced around the deserted area and then up at the cement truck. A man was behind the steering wheel, but Sara couldn't make out his face in the twilight. "Why is the truck here?"

Scottie looked at her strangely. "You expect me to park a big-ass cement truck outside a ritzy condominium complex in Brentwood?"

"I guess not," Sara said.

"All right. Let's go through the numbers here." Scottie took out an unfiltered cigarette, lit it, and inhaled deeply. He blew smoke into the cool evening air. "This is David's plan. We follow it to the letter. Got it?"

"Got it."

"We've checked out this Blalock broad and she never gets back to her condo until after eight every night. Her parking space is on the outside of the building near a side gate. There's a light there, but I fixed it so it ain't working now."

Sara asked, "Are there any units or windows close by?"

"Nothing but a brick wall," Scottie answered. "I'll

park in a space for guests that's a few rows back. You'll be right next to her in a handicapped parking space." He reached into his back pocket and handed her a handicapped-parking permit. "You put this in your window. If anybody gives you any shit, you tell them you're waiting for your mother who's walking on crutches."

Sara nodded, now understanding why Scottie had brought a car along with the cement truck. "When do I make the hit?"

"All right, all right," Scottie said, moving his hands as if he were talking with them. "The Blalock broad gets out of her car and I start my car. I turn the lights on bright so she's sure to look around. That's when you jump out and whack her. Two shots to the head. And don't stand around to admire your work. Get in your car and leave. Don't drive fast. Just go nice and slow. I'll take care of all the rest."

Sara thought through the plan, searching for risks and flaws. "What if somebody else is nearby? You know, a jogger or somebody walking their dog?"

"I'll handle it," Scottie said.

Sara glanced up at the man in the cement truck. "And what does he do?"

"He stays here until I come back with Blalock in a body bag," Scottie replied, taking a final drag on his cigarette before crushing it out on the ground. "Then we drive to a real lonely spot and make the body disappear."

"Good," Sara said, nodding her approval and wondering where she would pick up her forty-thousand-dollar fee. She didn't want to leave Los Angeles without it. Sara didn't believe in IOUs. "Did David leave any instructions for me?"

"A bunch," Scottie said as headlights appeared in the distance. He took Sara's arm and guided her behind the cement truck. "If somebody stops and gets nosy, you just stay put. Let Louie up in the cab take care of it."

"Suppose it's a highway cop?" Sara asked worriedly.

Scottie shrugged. "We'll put him in cement, too."

The headlights came closer and closer—then sped past without slowing down.

Sara breathed easier. "You were saying David left some instructions for me?"

"A whole bunch. So listen up, because I don't want to go through all this shit again." Scottie lit another cigarette and spat a piece of tobacco from his lip. "You make the hit and you drive away nice and slow. You take the San Diego Freeway to the airport and get off at the Century Boulevard exit. A couple of blocks down you'll see a big neon sign that says Safety Valet Parking. You got that?"

"Safety Valet Parking," Sara repeated.

"You give your keys to a guy named José, and he'll give you a small suitcase that you can carry on the plane. When you open it, it'll be empty except for your new passport. Throw all your personal stuff in there. The lining in the suitcase will be kind of thick because that's where David left the money he owes you. Any questions so far?"

Sara thought for a moment and then asked, "What do I do with my gun? I can't carry it with me because it'll set off the metal detector at the airport."

"Leave it in the glove compartment," Scottie told her. "José will lose it for you."

"What happens to my car?"

"We've already sold it to some guy in Tijuana," Scottie said. "It'll be across the border before dawn."

"Nice," Sara said, thinking that David was good at details and planning. That's why he's never been arrested, much less caught committing a crime.

"Your cut from the sale of the car is also in the lining of the suitcase," Scottie went on. "We didn't get as much as we usually do because we had to unload it real quick. You picked up an extra two grand."

Sara smiled to herself. *Good old David.* He had been a real friend to her, and she would always be indebted to him for that. Sara wondered if they'd ever see each other again.

"So, José will put you on one of those airport buses," Scottie continued. "And you'll get off at the Delta counter."

"My ticket is on United."

"Tear it up. The Delta ticket matches the name on your passport."

Scottie studied the indecision on her face, suspecting that she was thinking about cashing in the United ticket. "Tear the damn thing up! That's what David said to do."

"Okay," Sara agreed, but the ticket to New York had cost nearly two thousand dollars because she had to make the reservation on such short notice. She'd cash it in. "Is my new ticket to New York?"

Scottie shook his head. "To Miami. David said for you to stay there for a while, then think about taking a trip to Costa Rica."

That was a secret message from David. Costa Rica had excellent plastic surgeons who charged only a fraction of what their American counterparts charged. She and David had talked several times about what to do if either of them was on the run and in real trouble. Go to Costa Rica and get a face job and a new passport photo to match. Then come back to the United States with a new identity. "Costa Rica, huh?"

"Yeah," Scottie replied. "That's what David said. He told me the beaches were real good down there."

"I'll think about it."

"And David said for you to wait a year or so and then maybe give him a call."

"In New York or here?"

"He didn't say." Scottie threw his cigarette to the ground and stamped it out. "All right. One more thing and we're out of here." He rapped on the door of the cement truck. "Hey, Louie!"

Louie climbed out of the cab carrying a set of license plates and a screwdriver. "Can I just do the back?"

"Do both," Scottie ordered. "We don't want some

highway cop deciding he hasn't filled his quota of tickets for the month yet."

Sara turned to watch Louie change the license plates.

"Oh, there's one more thing," Scottie said, tapping her on the shoulder.

Sara turned back. "What?"

Scottie reached into his pocket for a slip of paper and handed it to her. "David said to give this to you. It's the phone number of some doctor in Costa Rica. In case you get sick down there, I guess."

Sara grinned slightly. It was probably the number of a very good plastic surgeon.

"I'm done here," Louie called over, tightening the last screw on the Nevada license plate.

"Let's go," Scottie said, motioning to Sara. "I'll follow you."

36

"Are you okay back there?" Nancy Tanaka asked.

"I'm fine," Joanna called, but she felt really claustrophobic in the blackness of the car's trunk.

"We'll be at Bio-Med in a few minutes."

Joanna tried to stretch her legs out, but couldn't. The Honda's trunk was small, and it was made smaller by the thick blanket covering her. And the smell of gasoline fumes made it even more unpleasant. She wiggled her ankles in an attempt to get the blood moving, wondering what she'd do if the guard at the gate decided to search the car's trunk.

The car hit a big bump in the road. Joanna bounced up and down a few times before settling. Then the car slowed and made a sharp turn to the left. In her mind's eye, Joanna retraced the trips she'd taken to Bio-Med. She guessed they were turning off the main highway and onto the narrow road that led to the plant's isolated location.

The car's radio came on loudly. It was tuned to a country-and-western station and some cowboy was singing a song with the words "Bubba shot the jukebox last night." Joanna groaned at the song, but she knew it had a purpose. According to Nancy, the night guard at Bio-Med's main gate loved country music and listened to it constantly while in his kiosk. Whenever Nancy pulled up to the gate, she and the guard always chatted about country music and its latest hits. He usually waved her through with only a cursory look into her car.

Joanna felt the Honda slow again and gradually turn

to the right. Then it stopped altogether. Joanna curled up in the blanket, her heart thumping away in her chest. The volume on the car radio dropped, and she heard Nancy Tanaka talking.

"Good evening, Will," Nancy said.

"Hi, young lady," the guard replied genially. "I see you're listening to some mighty fine music."

"I've got my radio dial glued there."

"Did you hear that Garth Brooks is giving a concert down in Anaheim this summer?"

"I hadn't heard that."

"Well, you'd better get your ticket real quick before they sell out."

"I will."

There was silence.

Joanna thought she heard footsteps approaching on the driver's side. She held her breath.

"You carrying any contraband?" the guard asked.

"Just a case of Bud Light."

The guard laughed. "Get out of here."

Nancy drove on slowly, gradually turned to the left, and then to the left again. The car stopped. The radio went off. A moment later the trunk opened.

"Are you all right?" Nancy asked.

"I'm cramped as hell back here," Joanna complained.

"You're going to have to stay that way for a little longer." Nancy rubbed her arms against the chilly night air. "Jesus! It's getting colder out here."

Joanna pulled the blanket down to her chin. "Won't the guard be suspicious that you came back at night?"

Nancy shook her head. "I do it a lot. And besides, I told him when I left this afternoon that I'd have to come back later to take something out of the incubator. I really bitched about having to return at night. I think he bought it."

The wind blew in from the desert and seemed to lower the temperature even further. It gusted again, and Nancy turned her back against it.

Joanna shivered. "Let's get this over with."

"You stay put," Nancy said, reaching up for the lid of the trunk. "I'll be back in a few minutes."

Joanna was in blackness again, but it had grown colder, much colder. She huddled up under the blanket and checked her luminous watch in the darkness. It was 8:40. Outside, the wind was howling and Joanna could hear the desert sand peppering the side of the car.

She'd have to wait ten more minutes. That's how long it would take Nancy to get things set up. The technician would punch in the code and enter the main laboratory. Then she'd walk to the rear and open the side door to the back lab using the code she'd copied from the sleeve of Alex Mirren's white coat. Then she'd come back for Joanna. That way they'd avoid the surveillance camera that constantly scanned the corridor leading into the main laboratory. Once inside, Joanna would study the experimental data books. That's where all the information was. Those data books would tell her exactly what Bio-Med was doing with enzyme preparations and viruses and dead fetuses.

She heard footsteps approaching. They were coming closer and closer. Quickly Joanna checked her watch. It was 8:44. Only four minutes had passed since Nancy left. That wasn't enough time for the technician to get inside and do all the things she had to do. Now the footsteps were right outside the trunk.

Joanna curled up and froze, barely breathing under the blanket. She prayed that Nancy had locked the trunk.

The trunk lid opened, the blanket jerked away.

It was Nancy Tanaka.

"Come on," she said quickly. "We got lucky."

Joanna climbed out and stretched her aching legs. She glanced at her purse in the rear of the trunk and decided to leave it. "What happened?"

"The surveillance camera is broken."

"Are you sure?"

"Positive," Nancy answered. "It's not moving on its tracks, and the lens is pointed at the ceiling."

Joanna thought for a moment and then asked, "Can the guard see us go in the front door?"

"Not if we do it when his back is turned."

Joanna reached up for the trunk lid and quietly closed it. "Let's go."

They moved quickly across the paved parking lot. The light was poor, the wind blowing and kicking up sand. Both women were wearing boots as protection in case they came too close to snakes. They were still watching the ground carefully, however.

They stopped in the darkness at the corner of the building and waited. The guard in the kiosk was facing their way, but not looking at them.

"What the hell is he doing?" Joanna asked.

Nancy focused in on the kiosk. "I think he's changing the cassette in his tape player."

They waited for the guard to turn away. Then they hurried toward the front entrance, stepping around a pile of dog manure.

"What about the guard dogs?" Joanna asked.

"They're not let out until midnight."

They dashed up the steps and entered the reception area, closing the door behind them. Walking on their tiptoes, they went down a narrow corridor, their eyes on the surveillance camera above. It was tilted awkwardly up and not moving. They reached the far door, where Nancy punched the code into the wall panel. The door clicked open automatically.

They entered the main laboratory.

Everything was dark except for the small lights in the glass cubicles along the wall. The giant plants and bushes gave off eerie shadows. Joanna grabbed Nancy's arm and froze in her tracks. She pointed to a moving shadow. It took them a moment to realize the shadow was being cast by a huge salmon swimming in the lighted fish tank.

"Christ, it's spooky in here!" Joanna whispered.

"Get used to it," Nancy said, "because we're not turning on the lights."

"Why not?"

"The lights are controlled by some type of computer," Nancy told her. "If you try to override it, an alarm goes off."

"How are we going to see?"

Nancy reached for a flashlight in her coat pocket and switched it on. They walked cautiously past the glass cubicle housing the coffee beans that contained no caffeine, then past the tomatoes that wouldn't freeze even at low temperatures. The giant salmon swam up to the side of their tank and seemed to be staring at the intruders.

"Should we start in the back lab?" Joanna asked.

"No," Nancy said. "We'll begin in Alex Mirren's old office. That's where the data books are most likely to be."

"I still want to look in the back lab."

"We'll do that on our way out."

They continued on, passing workbenches and large centrifuges and incubators. At the end incubator, Nancy stopped and took out two flasks that contained a milky fluid. She gently agitated the flasks before transferring that to another incubator.

"The cells grow better if you put them at thirty-seven degrees centigrade for a while."

"So you really did have to come back tonight to take something out of the incubator?"

Nancy nodded. "It's convenient the way things sometimes work out, huh?"

They walked on, passing more workbenches until they came to a glass-enclosed office. The door was closed. Nancy tried it. It was locked.

"What now?" Joanna asked.

Nancy reached into her pocket for a key and opened the door.

Joanna smiled thinly. "Should I ask you how you got that key?"

"Alex and I used to—" Nancy stopped herself in midsentence and waved the question away. "It's past history."

They went into Mirren's darkened office. A cluttered desk took up the center of the room. Bookshelves were located on the right, file cabinets on the left. The wall behind the desk was covered with framed pictures, but there wasn't enough light for Joanna to make out what they were.

Nancy shone her light on a large file cabinet and walked over. She placed the flashlight atop the cabinet, quietly opened a drawer, and began rummaging through it.

Joanna glanced around the office of the dead scientist. In many ways it resembled hers. Books. Papers. Files. Framed pictures of people and events gone by. Mirren's white laboratory coat was hanging on a wall hook. She stepped over to look at it. The inside of its collar was filthy and probably hadn't been washed in weeks. One side pocket was empty, the other filled with pages that had been torn out of a scientific journal.

She held the pages in front of the flashlight and studied the article briefly. It described a new method for growing stem cells. As she returned the pages to Mirren's side pocket, she saw the numbers written on the sleeve of his coat. 60-50-42. 60-50-52. Joanna repeated the numbers to herself, thinking they shouldn't have been that difficult to remember, particularly if one had to use them every day. She wondered why someone as brilliant as Mirren had so much trouble memorizing numbers.

"There's nothing here," Nancy reported, closing the file cabinet. "Let's try his desk."

Joanna opened the large center drawer of the desk and searched through it. There were pencils and paper clips and memo pads. But no data books. "Nothing here, either."

"Try the side drawer," Nancy suggested.

Joanna felt around for the side drawer of the desk but couldn't find it. "Can you shine the light over here?"

Nancy focused the beam on the desk. "How's that?"

"Better," Joanna said, but she still couldn't find the side drawer. There was only a center drawer with solid wood adjacent to it. "Are you sure there is a side drawer?"

"I'm certain," Nancy said. "I remember him opening it."

Joanna knelt down and reached beneath the desk. She felt something small and metallic, but couldn't see it. "Shine the light down here, would you?"

Nancy directed the beam of light over Joanna's shoulder. "Did you find something?"

"Maybe." Joanna peered under the desk and saw a red button. She pushed it in. Nothing happened. Then a second time. Still nothing. She pushed it a third time as hard as she possibly could. The hidden side drawer clicked open. Joanna got to her feet. "This guy had a lot of secrets, didn't he?"

"Too many." Nancy emptied the side drawer. It contained two experimental data books and two sheets of paper. The sheets were labeled SMV and CC. On each was a large square that contained scattered red dots. Nancy looked at the sheets, trying to decipher them. "I wonder what these represent."

"Cemetery maps," Joanna said.

"What!"

"I'll tell you about them later." Joanna took the sheets and folded them. "Now, let's see what's in those data books."

Nancy quickly flipped through the pages of the first book. "This deals with the lipolytic enzyme preparation and purification," she said, more to herself than to Joanna. "There's nothing about viruses or fetuses."

Joanna picked up the second data book and opened it. The first section was titled FETAL TRANSFORMING FACTOR. She pointed out the title to Nancy. "Do you have any idea what this is?"

"Not even a clue."

"Hold the light a little higher so I can see the small print." It took Joanna a moment to make out Mirren's handwriting. Then she read aloud softly: "To prepare the factor, the fetal heart was first dissected out and washed thoroughly with sterile saline. The pericardium and large blood vessels were removed, and the remaining myocardial tissue was subjected to ultra sonication to disrupt all cell membranes."

Nancy looked at Joanna quizzically. "If you break open the cell walls, you kill the cells. What in the world do they want with dead heart tissue?"

"We'll see," Joanna said, and read on. "The cardiac emulsion was centrifuged at twenty thousand rpm for twenty minutes and the supernatant carefully removed. The supernatant was then subjected to Sephadex G-100 chromatography and finally passed through an immunoabsorbent column to yield purified fetal transforming factor." Joanna turned to Nancy and asked, "What kind of transforming factor would be present in dead heart tissue?"

Nancy shrugged. "You got me."

The lights suddenly came on, lighting up the entire laboratory.

"It's the magic factor," Eric Brennerman told them. "It's going to revolutionize medicine."

He was standing in the doorway of Alex Mirren's office. Two armed guards were standing just behind him.

Joanna was stunned speechless. The experimental data book dropped from her hands.

"I'll tell you all about it," Brennerman went on. "It'll save you the time of going through all of Alex's data books. His handwriting was atrocious, wasn't it?"

Joanna cleared her throat and tried to gather herself. "I know we're trespassing, but it—"

"We'll get to that in a minute," Brennerman cut her off. "Let's get back to the fetal transforming factor. I think it's the last clue you need to put everything together."

Joanna tried to read Brennerman's face. He seemed so calm and collected, but his eyes were ice cold. And the guards behind him had their hands on their weapons. Joanna forced herself to concentrate and think of a way out.

"Have you ever wondered how early fetal stem cells can differentiate into dozens of different organs? How can one cell type be transformed into a dozen others? How does this miracle actually happen?" Brennerman asked the questions in a dispassionate scientific tone. "Well, the answer is amazingly straightforward. It seems that early stem cells produce a transforming factor that converts the stem cell into a distinctive cell type, like a heart or brain cell. And the fetal heart cells you were just reading about continue to produce this transforming factor until the fetus is six months old. So, each dividing heart cell has its own transforming factor."

Brennerman rubbed his chin pensively. "I guess that's nature's way of making sure that each new cell remains a heart cell and doesn't become something else. So, anyway, we then take the isolated transforming factor and mix it with human stem cells. This, of course, instructs the stem cell to become a brand-new heart cell. We then take the newly instructed stem cell and remove its DNA which contains the gene that induces the formation of new heart cells."

Joanna nodded slowly, now understanding. "And the stem cell DNA is then attached to a modified virus and injected into patients."

"Exactly," Brennerman said, nodding back. "You're very bright, Joanna. I knew it was just a matter of time before you figured it all out."

"And it was easy for you to make certain that the genes hooked onto the virus were delivered to the diseased organs of patients," Joanna continued, struck by the scientific brilliance of the experiment. "When someone with a diseased heart underwent coronary arterial cleansing, you simply mixed the genes in with the lipolytic enzyme. The mixture went directly to the heart and the modified virus carried the genes into the cardiac cells. And old heart cells were suddenly instructed to become new heart cells."

"We did the same to selected patients who underwent the arterial cleansing procedure on their diseased brains and kidneys," Brennerman said proudly. "It brought about a miracle."

"It also brought about cancer," Joanna snapped.

"I know," Brennerman sighed, showing a hint of regret. "All great science has a price."

"Which you don't mind someone else paying."

Brennerman's face hardened. "You make it sound like these were all young people with long lives in front of them. They weren't. They were all sick and would have died in a year or two."

"Just the lipolytic enzyme would have kept them going," Joanna argued.

"Bullshit!" Brennerman bellowed. "Those arteries started to reclog within a matter of months. And do you know why? Because the basic disease process is still in place and because patients go back to their old habits of smoking and eating the wrong foods and not exercising. And before you know it, those arteries are filled with cholesterol plaques again."

He paused and took a deep breath to calm himself. "And as far as the cancer matter is concerned, I believe there are ways around that. Obviously some factor in the genetic material induced the cells to undergo malignant transformation. It wasn't the virus. It had to be the genes themselves." Brennerman shrugged indifferently. "We'll sort it out as we go along."

Joanna's brow went up. "Do you think they're going to let you continue this project?"

"Who's going to stop me?"

"Memorial will," Joanna said. "As more and more patients come down with cancer, they—"

"There won't be any more cancers," Brennerman interrupted. "You see, we gave the stem cell genes to only three patients in the group. And those were the ones who developed cancer. That's why you found the viral particles in their tumors."

"Jesus," Joanna hissed, disgusted with Brennerman and what he'd done.

"If you have any more questions, now is the time to ask them," Brennerman went on. "You won't get another chance."

Joanna suddenly realized her mistake. She had been talking with Brennerman as if he were just a scientist. But he was really a killer who had cold-bloodedly ordered the executions of Rabb and Tuch and Mirren. It had to be him. Everybody else associated with Bio-Med was dead except for Brennerman and Lucy Rabb, and Lucy wasn't smart enough to pull everything off. Joanna tried to keep her voice even, but it still quavered. "Wh-what are you going to do with us?"

"First, I want to find out how much you know," Brennerman told her.

"Not very much," Joanna said weakly.

"Oh, I think you know a lot," Brennerman pressed on. "You're a smart girl, and you've already put some of the pieces together, haven't you? You knew the diagrams hidden in Mirren's desk were really maps showing where the fetuses were buried. And you probably figured out that Mirren had hired the Russian to bury the babies so he could blackmail Bio-Med. You see, Alex wasn't satisfied with stock options. He wanted a percentage of the corporation."

Joanna swallowed hard. She and Jake had it wrong. It wasn't Mirren who had the Russian killed. It was Brennerman.

Brennerman studied Joanna's expression and then nodded. "So you did figure it out. Now I need to know what else you figured out. I need to know exactly what you and your colleagues have uncovered."

"We don't know any—"

"Don't waste my time!" Brennerman cut her off. "I need exact information on how far along your investigation has gotten. I need specifics. That way I'll know whether to shut down the project for a while until things cool off, or shut it down permanently and remove any evidence that it ever existed."

He turned abruptly to Nancy Tanaka. "And you're going to tell me everything you learned from Alex Mirren while you two were under the sheets together. And you're also going to tell me where he hid the other copies of his experimental data books."

Nancy was frozen with fear. She clenched her hands into fists to keep them from shaking. "And if I tell you, what then?"

"We'll see."

Brennerman turned to the guards. "I want to question each woman separately. Nancy in the small surgical suite and Blalock in the room next to it."

Joanna and Nancy were marched out of the office and toward the rear of the laboratory. The guards were so close Joanna could smell their cheap aftershave lotion. She glanced around the huge laboratory, searching for windows or doors or any other way of possible escape. There weren't any. She slowed and looked at the ceiling to see if there was a ladder of steps leading up to the roof. The guard behind her gave her a hard shove and said, "Move it!"

They came to the door that led into the hot zone laboratory. Brennerman punched the numbers into the panel on the wall. Joanna watched in her peripheral vision. The numbers were 60-50-42. The door clicked open automatically.

Joanna hesitated, not wanting to go into the hot zone lab unprotected.

"This setup is just a sham," Brennerman said, grinning. "We used it to keep everybody out except for Mirren and me and the technician who was unwittingly working on the fetal project."

Exactly as Mack Brown had predicted, Joanna thought, now wishing she had paid more attention to his comments. It was the big clue that something important was being hidden in the hot zone laboratory.

Brennerman stepped on a floor pedal in the lab and a side door slid open. They entered a small room that was flooded with blue ultraviolet light. There was a door on the right, another on the left.

"Put Blalock in there," Brennerman said, pointing to the left.

Joanna was pushed into a dark room. The door closed and everything went black. She paused and tried to get her bearings. Behind her she felt the door. There was no knob or lock or hinges. And there was no pedal on the floor. Probably another automatic door, she guessed. But she couldn't find the wall panel.

Cautiously she moved along the wall, feeling the way with her hand. Joanna came to a window of some sort. It seemed to be made of Plexiglas. But there was no sill or lock. A built-in Plexiglas window, she decided, wondering what was on the other side. She moved on and reached another wall, but this one was bare. No shelves, no windows, no switches. Her hand touched a corner and next to it was another door. It too had no knob or locks, but there was a wall panel close by. Joanna fingered the buttons in the darkness.

The room suddenly lighted up.

Joanna quickly moved away from the wall panel and looked over at the source of the light. It was coming through the Plexiglas window from the adjoining room. An overhead speaker came on.

"You'd better answer every question carefully," Brennerman was saying, "if you want to stay alive."

Joanna went over to the window and peered in.

Nancy Tanaka was strapped onto a surgical table, her hands and ankles and body firmly secured. Her face showed absolute terror.

"What did Mirren tell you about his work?" Brennerman asked.

"He never talked to me about his fetus business," Nancy squealed. "I swear it."

"Never?"

"Never," she repeated weakly, starting to cry.

Brennerman shook his head as if he knew she was lying. "But you made the modified adenovirus for him. You knew it was going to be used as a vector to transport genetic information. Didn't you?"

Nancy nodded rapidly. "But he told me it was only going to be used in animal experiments."

"But you knew better than that," Brennerman prompted her. "You were making up big batches of this modified virus. A smart technician like you had to realize that something else was going on."

"I was suspicious," Nancy admitted. "But I never really knew for sure."

"Sure you did," Brennerman pressed on. "And you told Joanna Blalock about it. Didn't you?"

"I didn't! I swear it!"

"Oh, I think you did," Brennerman said easily. "And once Blalock heard about it, she put that together with the viral particles in the tumors. And suddenly she knew she was on the right trail. She figured out that somehow the patients were being injected with your goddamn virus."

"No! No!" Nancy pleaded desperately. "I never told her. I swear to God!"

"Well, we're not getting very far here," Brennerman said, losing patience. "So we'll do it another way. Let's see if you do better when you have to face imminent death."

"What are you talking about?" Nancy asked breathlessly.

Brennerman signaled to a guard, who brought over two small plastic cages. The guard held the cages up so Nancy could see the rattlesnakes inside.

Nancy's eyes almost bulged out of her head.

"You'll receive bites from two rattlesnakes," Brennerman said, his tone clinical. "The total amount of venom injected into you will be approximately two hundred milligrams. That's over twice the lethal dose."

Nancy strained with all her might against the straps

holding her on the surgical table. The table began to bounce off the floor. The other guard came over to steady it.

"Within the first hour," Brennerman went on, "the places where you were bitten will become red and edematous and painful. Then you'll develop thirst and fever and parts of your body will start to go numb. That's the bad sign. Once the numbness occurs, you've reached the point of no return."

Joanna stared through the window motionless, transfixed by the horror show she was about to see.

"If you decide to tell the truth," Brennerman continued, "I'll give you the antivenin and you'll live. If you keep on lying, I'll let you die."

He signaled to the guard again and stepped back.

The guard placed a plastic cage next to Nancy Tanaka's bare upper arm. He pulled a latch up and a small door opened. He pressed the cage against Nancy's skin. The snake struck and Nancy screamed at the top of her lungs.

The other guard hurried over and clamped a towel over Nancy's mouth, dampening her screams.

Joanna pounded on the Plexiglas window with her fists, trying to stop the guards. She yelled at them as loud as she could, but her voice stayed in the soundproof room.

The guard placed the second cage up against Nancy's other arm and opened its small door. A second rattlesnake lunged forward and dug its fangs into Nancy's deltoid muscle. She screamed again and again, but her screams were muffled by the thick towel over her mouth. She started shaking, her entire body convulsing.

Joanna couldn't watch anymore. She turned away and covered her face.

"We'll be back in a half-hour," Brennerman was saying, his voice coming in clearly over the speaker. "I suggest you tell us the truth then."

The sound system clicked off.

Joanna looked back into the room. The guards and

Brennerman were gone. Nancy was crying uncontrol-
lably, tears streaking down her face. She seemed to
be screaming, "Help me! Help me!" But Joanna
couldn't hear her screams in the soundproof room.

Oh, God! She's going to die!

Joanna took off her boot and swung it with all of
her might against the Plexiglas window. She struck it
again and again, but the rubber heel didn't even
scratch the Plexiglas. Then she pounded on the window with her fists and pushed against it with her
shoulder, but it didn't budge. Nancy seemed to be
convulsing again. A frothy liquid was coming out of
her mouth.

Joanna backed away from the gruesome scene,
scared out of her wits and not knowing what to do
next. Her back hit the wall behind her hard and she
slid down to the floor, still seeing a terrified Nancy
Tanaka in her mind's eye.

*She's going to die, and I can't do anything about it.
And I'm next! They'll kill me with rattlesnakes the same
way they're killing her.*

Joanna took deep breaths, trying to calm herself
and get her brain working. *Think! Think! There's got
to be a way out.* She tried desperately to come up with
an avenue of escape, but her mind stayed on Nancy
and the horrifying death she faced. Two bites from
two big rattlesnakes were more than enough to kill a
human. And unless Nancy received the antivenin,
she'd be dead within hours.

Joanna shook her head at herself. *Stupid! They're
not going to let Nancy live, regardless of what she tells
them. She's now the real danger to Brennerman because what she knows could send him to jail forever.
No. They'll kill her. Then they'll kill me.*

Joanna pushed herself up from the floor and went
back to the window. Nancy was still crying, but less
violently. The frothy material had been cleared from
her mouth. Joanna knocked on the window and tried
to get Nancy's attention, but the sound didn't seem to
carry into the adjoining room.

She gazed past Nancy and around the small surgical suite. It was like the room she was in. No windows to the outside, two doors. Abruptly Joanna spun around and looked at the door behind her and at the wall panel next to it. She stared at the door, wondering if it led to the outside of the building where she and Jake had seen the delivery truck. If so, it was a way out.

She hurried over to the wall panel, trying to remember the code she'd seen Brennerman punch in. The numbers flashed into her mind. 60-50-42. Quickly she punched the numbers into the wall panel. Nothing happened. There was no click. The door didn't open. Joanna tried it again, but the result was the same. Nothing.

Shit! The door had another code, she thought despondently. *How many codes can they have in this damn place? Nobody could remember all those—*

She suddenly flashed back to the sleeve of Mirren's white lab coat and the numbers written on it. Two sets of numbers, she recalled instantly. One set was 60-50-42, the same numbers Brennerman had used to enter the hot zone laboratory. What was the second set?

Joanna closed her eyes and envisioned the numbers written on the sleeve. The first code was 60-50-42. Yes. But there was another code, very similar to the first. She concentrated, thinking back.

Gradually the numbers came into focus. The initial number was 60 and the second was 50. But what was the third number? She concentrated even harder, but the last number remained a blur. It was a double-digit number, but that was all she could remember. It could be 10 or 99 or any number in between.

She'd have to try them all until she hit the right combination. And then hope that the second set of numbers on Mirren's sleeve was the code to the back door.

Joanna glanced at her watch. It was 9:50 P.M. Brennerman and his goons would be back in twenty minutes.

Not enough time! Not enough time to go through all the numbers! Oh, Christ! Help me!

Quickly Joanna began punching numbers into the wall panel, starting with 60-50-10.

37

The butler led Jake and Farelli into the elegant living room of Lucy Rabb's Bel Air mansion. She was standing near a white marble fireplace, dressed in a pale blue silk hostess gown. Her dresslike garment was form-fitted to show off her curves.

"Will that be all, madam?" the butler asked.

Lucy flicked her wrist in a wave of dismissal.

Jake said to the butler, "You stick around the kitchen. I might have some questions for you."

"Very good, sir," the butler said, backing out.

Jake glanced over at the white marble fireplace and the unlighted logs inside it, thinking they were every bit as cold as Lucy Rabb. A Renoir hung on the wall behind her. He wondered if she would inherit that, too.

"You'd better have a good reason for barging in here at ten o'clock at night," Lucy snarled.

"How does murder grab you?" Jake sat on a French antique sofa without being asked to. "You'd better sit down, Mrs. Rabb. We're going to be here for a while."

"I'm going to call my lawyer," Lucy threatened.

"Your lawyer is dead. Remember?"

Lucy reached for the cell phone on the coffee table. "I'm sure there's another lawyer in that firm who will be happy to represent me."

"Give him a call," Jake said agreeably. "Tell him to meet us downtown."

Her hand moved away from the phone. "Why are we going there?"

"Because that's where we take people who are charged with first-degree murder."

"What!"

"Oh, yeah," Jake said easily. "It took us a while to put everything together, but I think we got it set up pretty good now." He looked over at Farelli. "Don't you think so, Lou?"

Farelli nodded. "Rock solid, if you ask me."

"This is insane!" Lucy screeched.

"A judge and jury won't think so," Jake went on. "Not when they hear what we've got."

"And exactly what do you have?" Lucy challenged, not backing down.

"Oh, a whole lot." Jake stared at her, waiting for her to start squirming. She didn't. "Let's start with the cell phone calls made from the *Argonaut*. Two calls were made to a bar called Club West. It's a known front for a New York-based gang that specializes in professional hits."

"So?" Lucy shrugged.

"So, the first call was made a week before your husband was murdered. And the second call was made a day before Mervin Tuch got whacked. Now, we can't just chalk that up to coincidence, can we?"

Lucy wasn't fazed. "Anyone could have made those calls. I certainly didn't."

"Uh-huh," Jake said evenly. "And I guess you didn't know the blond hitter who came aboard the yacht and murdered your husband. Right?"

Lucy shook her head. "I didn't know her."

"Her?" Jake said at once. "I didn't say the hitter was a female."

"Oh," Lucy mumbled, thinking fast. "I thought you did."

"When?"

"When you questioned all of us aboard the *Argonaut*."

She's good, Jake was thinking. Lucy Rabb wasn't smart, but she was quick. And she knew how to lie.

"Naw," Jake continued. "You knew her. And you brought her aboard the yacht."

"I did not," Lucy denied firmly.

"Sure you did. And let me tell you how we know that." Jake paused to light a cigarette, his eyes never leaving her. She uncrossed and recrossed her legs twice rapidly. "You ordered the caterers for your yacht party, didn't you?"

"I believe so," Lucy replied, being more careful.

"You arranged just about everything for that party. Right?"

"Just about."

"Now, this hitter knew exactly when the caterers would be arriving at your party. And she knew what they'd be wearing, so she could put on a similar white jacket and blend in with them. That's how she got aboard the yacht."

Lucy remained silent. *Let him talk,* she thought. *He's got nothing. He's guessing.*

"How did she find all that out?" Jake asked, blowing smoke at the ceiling. He waited a moment before answering his own question. "Well, there's only one way the hitter could have known all those details. Somebody on the inside had to tell her."

"It wasn't me."

"It was you, all right," Jake pressed on. "You brought her aboard the yacht and you introduced her to people who remembered the hitter from the photograph that was taken."

"There were no photographs taken aboard the *Argonaut* that night," Lucy countered.

"You're absolutely right."

Lucy nodded, pleased at catching him in a lie.

"The photograph we showed them came from the surveillance film taken in the parking garage where Mervin Tuch was murdered. The hitter was actually caught on film whacking Mr. Tuch. And the FBI did a great job enhancing her picture from the tape. Would you like to see her photograph?" Jake asked, and reached into his coat pocket.

Lucy turned her head away.

"No? Okay. Maybe later."

Jake crushed out his cigarette in a Chinese porcelain ashtray atop the coffee table. He decided to push harder, but not too hard. He didn't want her to lawyer up. "There's a lot more that connects you to the hitter. You remember Mr. Clean? You know, the bald security guard who was on duty the night of the party. Well, his memory suddenly improved a lot. He recalls seeing you and the blond hitter and your husband talking and laughing together. It was almost like the three of you were old friends. Did you do the introductions?"

"The guard is mistaken," Lucy said.

"I don't think so." Jake waved away her answer. "You see, he remembered too many details. Like he recalled how strange it was for you and your husband to be so chummy with the hired help."

"That proves nothing."

"Oh, it gets better," Jake went on. "When Mervin Tuch got iced, we had to go through all the things in his office. He left some interesting notes and papers behind. And to tell you the truth, Mrs. Rabb, you don't come out looking so good. There was a lot of real personal stuff that—Well, you know . . ." Jake let his voice trail off.

"There was nothing between us," Lucy said hastily.

"There was plenty between you, business and otherwise."

Jake decided that now was the moment to crack Lucy Rabb wide open. He'd have to tell some lies and half-truths, but that didn't bother him. Just as long as she gave him the whole story. "And it was all spelled out in Mervin Tuch's files," he said. "He talked about the plans you and he had and how nice things would be once your husband was out of the way. You two would control Bio-Med, and all those millions would be yours. Hell, he even talked about old man Rabb's plan to give Bio-Med to some charity. Boy, that must have been a shocker, huh? All that money flying out the window."

Lucy's face went ashen.

"Funny how a smart lawyer like that would leave something so incriminating in his files." Jake shook his head at the lawyer's made-up stupidity. He glanced over at Farelli. "It's hard to figure why he'd do something like that, isn't it?"

"Maybe he was covering his ass," Farelli suggested. "Maybe he was worried she'd point the finger at him later and try to lay it all on him."

"Well, he doesn't have to worry about that anymore," Jake said, turning back to Lucy. "Because he's dead, which leaves you, Mrs. Rabb, holding the bag."

Farelli added, "You're going to take the fall, lady. Big time."

Jake waved a hand expansively around the elegant living room. "You can kiss all this good-bye. Where you're going, they don't have Renoirs on the wall."

Lucy's face came apart. Then the tears flowed. She tried to sniff them back. "It was Mervin Tuch's idea. He planned it all. I knew nothing. Then he—he seduced me." She reached for a handkerchief and dabbed her eyes. "He took advantage of me."

Right, Jake was thinking. Like the other two hundred guys who were there before him. "So he planned it all?"

"Everything."

"He even hired the hitters, huh?"

Lucy nodded.

"Set it all up by himself, did he?"

Lucy nodded again. "Every detail."

"Then who had him killed? Who set that up?"

Lucy's mouth opened, but she said nothing.

"It was you. It had to be."

"No!"

Jake leaned forward, staring her down and making her squirm. "Why did you do it? Was he blackmailing you?"

"I think I'd better call my lawyer."

"Fine," Jake said hoarsely. "But you'll make the call from downtown."

Lucy looked at her cell phone but didn't reach for it.

"Tuch was in the process of getting a loan for a half million from his bank," Jake continued. "We know all about that, and we know you were going to sign your Bio-Med stock over as collateral. That sounds like blackmail to me." He looked over to Farelli. "What do you think, Lou?"

Farelli nodded. "That's how most juries would figure it."

Lucy Rabb suddenly saw a way out of her predicament. "It was blackmail, and I couldn't do a damn thing about it. Tuch was going to put everything off on me. And I knew nothing. That's the honest-to-God truth."

"How was he going to set you up?" Jake asked.

Lucy shrugged. "You know how smart lawyers are. They know how to screw people but good."

"Yeah. Right," Jake said flatly. "He was so damn smart he got himself killed."

"I didn't have him killed! I swear it!"

"Sure you did."

"No! I swear—"

Jake waved away her lies and glanced over at Farelli. "Read her rights. Then cuff her."

"Don't! Don't do that!" Lucy cried.

"You're not leaving us much choice."

"What if I told you everything?" Lucy bargained. "Could I get immunity?"

"Immunity from what?"

"The murders," she said, her voice barely above a whisper.

"I can't promise you anything," Jake said. "But I'll talk to the DA."

"What does that mean?"

"That means you stand a chance of getting out of prison before you're an old, wrinkled-up woman."

Lucy hesitated, trying to read the detective's face. "You promise me you'll talk to the DA?"

"I'll do what I can."

Lucy's head dropped to her chest. "Okay," she said resignedly.

Farelli read her her rights slowly and carefully.

Jake took a small tape recorder from his pocket and placed it on the coffee table. He turned it on and then looked at Lucy Rabb. "Start talking."

38

Joanna furiously punched numbers into the wall panel, still looking for the right combination to open the door. She was now up to 60-50-42.

The sound system came back on. Brennerman and the guards had returned to interrogate Nancy Tanaka again.

"Just a few more questions," Brennerman said soothingly.

Nancy started sobbing. "Please help me."

"We will," Brennerman promised. "But only if you give us the right answers."

Joanna glanced hurriedly over her shoulder, hoping she was looking through a one-way window. *It had to be one way. That's why Nancy didn't recognize me when I was pounding on the window. She couldn't see through it.*

Joanna turned back to the wall panel and punched in 60-50-43. There was no click from the door's locking mechanism.

Brennerman was asking, "Let's go back to the fetuses Mirren was working on. You knew all about that, didn't you?"

"He never told me anything," Nancy said, her voice trembling.

"Sure he did," Brennerman coaxed her along. "I'd appreciate your telling me the truth. Otherwise we'll have to let the snakes out again."

"No! Please!"

Joanna punched in 60-50-44. She waited. No click.

"That's how the police found the abortion clinic

where Mirren got the fetuses," Brennerman was saying. "He told you and you told Joanna Blalock, and she told the police."

"No! I swear I didn't!"

"We think Joanna knew all about the fetuses," Brennerman said. "And I'll bet she'll tell us everything when we question her in a few minutes. She won't be as brave as you because she knows the agony one goes through before dying from a rattlesnake bite."

Joanna was up to 60-50-46. Still no click. Her hands started shaking at the thought of a rattlesnake bite and the horrible death it caused. *Calm down, damn it! Calm down or you'll never open this damn door.* More deliberately she pushed down on the numbered buttons. 60-50-47. The door remained locked.

"And you knew exactly where the data book on the fetal research was hidden," Brennerman pressed on. "Mirren must have shown you where it was located."

"No! I just guessed."

"Are there other data books hidden away?"

"I don't know. He never showed me."

"Crap!"

"Please help me," Nancy begged, and started crying again. "Don't let me die."

Joanna was up to 60-50-48. There was still no click. She swallowed hard, wondering if the numbers she had recalled were correct. If they weren't, she was dead. Her heart began to pound in her chest. She punched in 60-50-49. Nothing.

Brennerman was asking, "And what about the extra two hundred and fifty dollars a week Mirren was giving you?"

"That was for overtime work," Nancy answered.

"That was your share of the blackmail money," Brennerman snapped.

Joanna concentrated her hearing. Was Nancy really in on the blackmail? She entered a new set of numbers as she listened.

"No," Nancy protested. "It was for overtime."

"You'd better tell the truth," Brennerman warned. "The longer the venom stays in your system, the less chance the antivenin will work."

"Please!"

"Tell the goddamn truth!"

"I am!"

Joanna was now at 60-50-50, and the door was still locked. Her hands were sweating profusely and she rubbed them against her arms to dry them. She stared at the panel, thinking about the last numbers of the code and wondering if she should not go to the uppermost number, 99, and work her way down. Maybe that would change her luck. No, she quickly decided. Keep it in sequence. She punched in 60-50-51.

"Put Nancy in the animal room," Brennerman told the guards. "She can re-think her answers while we question Joanna Blalock."

A guard asked, "Do you want Blalock strapped down on the table, too?"

"Do her the same way you did Nancy," Brennerman ordered. "And get two more rattlesnakes."

Joanna shuddered. *Oh, Christ! They're coming for me!*

Frantically, Joanna kicked against the metal door, but it hardly budged. She quickly scanned the room, looking for something that could be used as a weapon. But the walls were bare and there was no furniture. Nothing was made of glass.

Joanna glanced back through the Plexiglas window. The guards were lifting Nancy Tanaka off the surgical table. Her body was limp and offered no resistance. *She's dying*, Joanna thought. *And I'm next.*

Joanna turned back to the wall panel and tried to remember the last numbers she had punched in. Was it 60-50-50? Or 50-50-51? *Oh, Christ! Stop wasting time!* She quickly entered the numbers 60-50-50 and waited. There was no click.

"She's heavy as hell," one of the guards complained.

"That's because she's like dead weight," the other guard explained.

"Oooh," Nancy moaned weakly.

"Hurry it up!" Brennerman barked. "And get Blalock in here."

Joanna hastily punched in 60-60-51. *No! Damn it! The middle set of digits should be 50.* She entered the code 60-50-51. The locking mechanism made no sound. Joanna kicked futilely at the metal door and then glanced over her shoulder at the Plexiglas window. The guards had Nancy's body halfway through the door.

Joanna's hands were shaking again. She clasped her fingers together to steady them; then she turned back to the wall panel. *Oh, God! Let this be the right number! Please!*

She punched in 60-50-52.

The locking mechanism clicked. The door opened automatically.

Joanna dashed out, closing the door behind her. Quickly she surveyed the expansive area and tried to orient herself. She was on the side of the Bio-Med plant. To the left she saw the dimly lighted parking lot. Nancy's car was still there. Joanna ran toward the car, but her progress was slow because her boots were sinking into the sand and gravel. She prayed that Nancy had left the keys in her car. It was Joanna's only chance. *Oh, Lord! Let them be there!* Joanna's hopes started to rise. *Let those keys be in the ignition switch. I'll crash through the front gate. And then I'll come back. With Jake Sinclair.*

Joanna tripped in the loose gravel and almost fell. She regained her balance and raced on, reaching the pavement of the parking lot. Pausing to catch her breath, she glanced over her shoulder. It was dark. There was no commotion. The guards hadn't discovered her missing yet. But they soon would.

She ran to Nancy's car and flung open the front door. There was no key in the ignition or under the floor mat or behind the overhead sun visor. Joanna's hopes quickly faded. She was still trapped. In front of her was a high fence topped off with barbed wire.

Behind her was the plant and the guards. She couldn't go to the left because there was a guarded gate in her way. And to her right was desert. Nothing but desert.

I'm trapped, Joanna thought hopelessly. *Trapped with no way out. Except east through the desert. And that is certain death. I'd never survive that. I'm as good as dead. Any way I turn, I'm dead.*

Joanna noticed the automatic trunk release inside Nancy's car. Maybe Nancy had a hidden set of keys there. Joanna pulled the lever and the trunk popped open. She hurried to the rear of the car and looked inside. All she found was the woolly blanket she'd hidden under and a small plastic bottle of water that was half empty.

The side door to the Bio-Med plant suddenly swung open.

A guard stepped out yelling, "Get the dogs!"

Joanna quickly grabbed the blanket and small bottle of water. Then she ran for the darkness of the desert.

39

"You'd better warn the doc," Farelli said.

"I tried to, but there was no answer at her lab or her condo," Jake told him. "I'm going to run over to Brentwood real quick and see if Joanna is home."

"And I'll ride downtown with Mrs. Hot Pants and make sure she's booked right." Farelli gestured with his head to the backseat of the black-and-white unit where a handcuffed Lucy Rabb was sitting. "Can you believe it? She was screwing old man Rabb, Mervin Tuch, and this guy Brennerman all at the same time. She was a busy girl."

"Not that busy," Jake commented dryly. "She still found time to have two of them whacked."

Farelli moved away from the patrol car and lowered his voice. "When we get her downtown, you know she's going to lawyer up."

"Let her," Jake said, unconcerned. "We've got a nice, clear tape recording of her confession."

"They'll say we coerced it out of her."

"You can bet on that," Jake grumbled. "And then Brennerman's lawyer will say she's lying to save her own ass."

Farelli shook his head. "It's going to be a goddamn circus."

"Tell me about it," Jake said, and reached for the door to his car.

Jake drove down the winding road that led out of Bel Air and into the Brentwood area. The narrow road was poorly lighted and there were frequent deer crossing signs, so he had to go slow. He kept thinking

about Farelli's comment that the case was going to
end up being a circus. A goddamn circus. He was right
on that score. Oh, Lucy Rabb would end up going to
jail, but they would plea-bargain her sentence way
down. And they would point all the evidence at Mervin Tuch and leave him holding the bag. And nobody
would give a shit about that because Tuch was dead
and would soon be forgotten.

But Eric Brennerman was another matter. It would
be his word against Lucy Rabb's. Other than Lucy's
statement, they had nothing to really show that Brennerman was involved in the murders. He would probably walk, although he was surely in it up to his ass.

And Brennerman was plenty smart, Jake thought
sourly. He had stayed in the background and pulled
the strings to manipulate the others. The only evidence they had against him was indirect and would
never stand up in court. Oh, he was smart, all right,
and plenty dangerous, Jake concluded. One had to be
smart as hell to become a doctor and smarter yet to
become a brilliant researcher. The super-bright always
made the best criminals. They knew how to outthink
people, and that included most cops.

Jake passed through the west gate of Bel Air and
turned onto Sunset Boulevard. It was after midnight,
and traffic was light but slow because of road construction. Jake lit a cigarette, his mind still on Eric Brennerman and how bright the son of a bitch was. And
how dangerous. What was it that Lucy Rabb said
Brennerman had in store for Joanna? He was going
to kill her naturally. That was it. It would be a natural
death. And he could pull it off. But not if Joanna was
forewarned. Because she was every bit as smart as
Brennerman and every bit as tough, too.

Jake checked his watch again. It was 12:10. He figured that Joanna was probably on her way home from
the hospital. Or maybe she was enjoying one of her
hour-long bubble baths during which she refused to
be disturbed. Jake smiled, remembering the time she
wouldn't talk to him because she was in her bubble

bath, so he jumped in with his clothes still on. She was angry at first, but they ended up laughing their heads off. That was the best of times. They had just solved a difficult case involving an HMO doctor who was killing off his patients. And now, Jake thought grimly, another doctor gone bad was trying to do the same thing to Joanna. Jake's face hardened as he remembered Brennerman's threat to kill Joanna naturally. What the hell did he mean by that? How did he plan to come at her?

Jake turned onto Barrington, approaching the condominium complex where Joanna lived. He hoped she was up, because otherwise she'd be mad as hell, thinking he had awakened her for something that could have waited until morning. Well, that was just too damn bad. She was in real danger, and he was going to protect her.

Jake pulled into the visitors parking area and came to a stop. He glanced over at Joanna's parking space. It was empty. But the handicap parking space next to it was occupied by a dark Toyota with an out-of-state license plate.

Jake pushed his seat back and stretched out his legs, thinking that Joanna was probably on her way back from the hospital. He closed his eyes and began to doze while he waited for her.

Off to his left Jake heard a car door close. He looked over and saw a big, heavyset man walking toward him. The man has his right hand tucked into his leather coat, Napoleon style. The guy had *hood* written all over him.

Jake reached for his weapon and pointed it out the car window. "Freeze, asshole!"

Scottie tried to quick draw, but it was too late.

Jake fired twice. The first bullet went into Scottie's chest, the next into his forehead. Scottie dropped like a dead weight.

The windshield in Jake's car suddenly exploded, spraying glass everywhere. Reflexively, he ducked behind the steering wheel and flattened himself against the front seat. He waited for the next shot, all the while trying to gather his thoughts. *Goddamn it! There was another shooter out there! But where? Where? He had to be somewhere in front of me. Maybe near the condominium complex. Yeah, maybe up against the— Oh, shit! The dark Toyota in the handicap parking space. The blond hitter's car. She was here for Joanna.*

Jake flung the car door open and threw himself onto the ground, rolling as he hit the pavement. He heard the soft thud of a second bullet penetrating the metal of the car door. Keeping his head down, he quickly squirmed backward until he was beneath another car.

Jake looked out at the condominium complex in front of him. Off to the right and about twenty-five feet away, he saw the blond hitter's car. Jake wondered why the hitter hadn't made a break for it. Probably because she would have had to back out of the space. And it would have been easy for Jake to ram her and block her exit. So she decided to stay and take her chances.

But where was she now? She sure as hell wasn't in her car. The front door on the driver's side was open. If she had stayed in her car, all Jake would need to do was crawl out wide to his left, and she'd be an easy target. No. She wasn't that stupid. But where the hell was she?

Jake studied the dimly lit area adjacent to the condominium complex. The hitter wouldn't be there. She'd be on the move, maybe trying to circle around him. Or maybe looking for a way out. Jake heard a noise off to his left. It sounded like a twig breaking. Slowly he pushed himself sideways until he came out on the driver's side of the Ford SUV. There was no noise now, no sound at all. Jake wondered again if the hitter was circling. There were plenty of cars to hide her movements. And if she did get behind him, he was as good as dead.

Jake strained his eyes, trying to see the periphery of the poorly lit parking lot. There were no movements, no shadows to follow. But he knew that the hitter was still out there. He could almost feel her. Jake concentrated all of his senses, trying to locate the blond hitter. But again, there was nothing. Everything stayed still and quiet. Seconds ticked by. Then a cat jumped out of the darkness and ran by him.

Jake quickly moved to the rear of the SUV and crouched down low. Something or someone had caused that cat to scamper. Was it the hitter? Could be. He had to find out. Because if it was the hitter, all she had to do was keep circling, and she'd eventually get a clear shot at him.

Jake removed a shoe and tied a white handkerchief around the toe. Holding the shoe by its heel, he slowly advanced it from behind the rear fender. He heard the soft popping sound made by a weapon with a silencer. The shoe flew out of his hand.

Christ! She's close, so close. No more than twenty feet away. And she knows exactly where I am. Shit! Jake cursed at the stupid error he'd made. *I should have kept her guessing. I shouldn't have tipped off my position. But I did, and now she's got me boxed in behind this car. I'm trapped.*

Jake hurriedly glanced around the parking area, looking for a way out. There were empty parking spaces to his right and left, so he couldn't run laterally. And it was impossible for him to make it back to the condominium without giving her a clear shot.

Jake heard a sound coming from the direction of the hitter, but he couldn't make out what it was. The hitter was on the move, he thought. She'd probably go to her left, where there was virtually no light at all. Again he quickly scanned the area, searching for an escape route. There wasn't any. Jake considered crawling under the Ford SUV. *No. That's the first place she'd look.* And besides, the exhaust pipe was hanging so low he'd have trouble—

Jake stopped in midthought and stared at the exhaust pipe. It was thick and strong and at least two feet in length. It just might work for what he had in mind. He rapidly took off his coat and then ripped off the exhaust pipe. Next he inserted the metal pipe into the shoulders of his coat. The coat now hung as if it was on a hanger. Ever so slowly, Jake advanced the left shoulder of the coat from behind the car.

The hitter fired twice. Two bullets tore into the coat, nearly blowing off the sleeve. Jake went to the ground, letting go of the coat. Then he made a guttural sound of a badly wounded man. "Ahhhh! Ahhhh!"

The hitter moved in carefully, her eyes fixed on the victim's coat. He wasn't moving, but she could still hear his groans. And that meant he could still be dangerous. Now she could see more of his broad shoulder. She fired another round and the coat jumped off the ground. When it landed, it made a metallic sound.

Sara inched in closer for a better look. In the dim light she saw a rumpled-up coat and beside it a piece of metal pipe. She stared at the objects on the pavement, confused. It took her a moment to figure it out, but by then Jake had her lined up in his sights.

Sara spun around just as Jake fired off two rounds, both catching her high in the chest. She slowly dropped to her knees, with a look of total disbelief. Then she fell forward facedown onto the pavement.

Jake cautiously walked over with his gun still pointed at her. He kicked her weapon aside, watching her head and hands for any movement. Everything stayed still. Using his foot, he roughly turned her over, all the while keeping his gun trained on her.

Frothy blood was gushing from her mouth and chest. Then her lips began to move. With her last breath, Jake thought he heard her calling for someone named David.

40

Joanna felt like she was freezing to death. Despite the blanket wrapped around her shoulders, she was shivering so hard her teeth chattered. And it seemed to be getting colder by the minute.

She was standing in a shallow ravine, resting against a large boulder and trying to decide what to do next. Should she run or hide? Which would give her the best chance to survive and maybe escape? Joanna shook her head at the notion of escape, pushing it aside. She had to concentrate on surviving and staying away from the dogs. But how? She was facing an endless, barren desert with no food or shelter and damn little water. How do you survive that?

In the distance Joanna heard the dogs barking. Suddenly all her senses were heightened even more. *Oh, Christ! They're coming!* Her heart pounded at the thought of being caught and torn apart by attack dogs. And the bastards at Bio-Med would let the dogs do it, too. Joanna shuddered, remembering an autopsy she'd done on an elderly man who had been ravaged by a pack of rottweilers. They had ripped off chunks from his body. It had taken him twenty-four hours to die.

Joanna hurriedly pushed herself away from the boulder and started up the ravine, wondering which way to go. *To the left? Or right? Or straight ahead? Which way, damn it?*

At the top of the ravine she glanced around quickly and tried to get her bearings. She was totally disoriented, not knowing east from west or in what direction the Bio-Med plant lay.

The dogs barked again.

Joanna thought they were closer than before. Frantically she scanned the area around her, looking for a stick or stone or some object she could use as a weapon. But all she saw was shadows and darkness. The night seemed pitch black despite the stars and quarter moon shining above. Again she searched around, trying to pick out things in the dimness. Near her feet she spotted a narrow, straight object. A stick or metal rod, she guessed, and reached down for it. She felt its scaly surface as the object slithered away. Joanna jerked her hand back. *A snake! A goddamn snake!*

She backed away, looking at the ground and searching for the location of the snake. All she could see was sand and shadows. She wiped her hand against her jeans to get the feeling off. *That damn thing could have bitten me and I'd be dead. Be careful! There can be plenty of things that kill you in the desert other than attack dogs.*

As she backed up farther, her boot caught in a crevice. She waved her arms desperately and tried to regain her balance, but couldn't. She tumbled head over heels down the steep ravine. Her knee and thigh hit something very hard, and she felt a sharp pain shoot up and down her leg. Then something knocked the breath out of her. She lay at the bottom of the ravine, gasping for air and choking on the desert sand in her mouth and nose.

Slowly she caught her breath and sat up, spitting to clear the grit from her tongue and lips. The shooting pain continued to run up and down her leg, a little less than before. But it still hurt like hell. Carefully she moved her leg and flexed her knee to make certain no bones were broken. She reached down and touched the most painful spot. Just below the knee her jeans were torn, and Joanna could feel blood. She didn't want to put her finger on the wound and increase the chance of infecting it even more. So she took a Kleenex tissue from her shirt pocket, pressed it against the lacerated area, and then waited for the bleeding to stop and for the tissue to attach itself to the wound with dried blood.

Joanna listened intently for the dogs, but all she heard was the swirling wind.

I'm making stupid mistakes, and I'm going to get myself killed. So stupid to look for a weapon. How much good would that do against vicious attack dogs and armed guards? I can't beat them physically. They'd overpower me in a second. But mentally, that's another matter. I've thought my way out of tough situations before, and I can do it again.

Joanna shook her head despondently. She knew she was fooling herself. All the odds were against her. She was in a harsh environment totally unfamiliar to her. *Shit!* She really was as good as dead this time.

She should have listened to Jake and not tried something so risky. And so stupid. She had walked right into a trap. And all the warning signs were there. Joanna had simply ignored them. Nancy Tanaka told Joanna that the people at Bio-Med no longer trusted her and were watching her closely. Which probably meant they knew that Nancy and Joanna were meeting in secret. And Nancy told the guard at the gate she'd be coming back later that night. And the guard promptly informed Eric Brennerman. That was the tip-off. Brennerman knew they were coming, and he knew when. There were warning signs everywhere for Joanna. She just overlooked them. And that was going to cost her her life.

The bleeding from her leg wound had stopped. The Kleenex tissue was firmly stuck to it. Slowly Joanna stood and tried the leg. It still hurt, but she could walk. With effort she climbed out of the ravine and again listened for the dogs. There was nothing but the sound of the wind.

Where are those damn dogs? They are supposedly

such great trackers. So why aren't they closing in on me?

The wind gusted and swirled around Joanna, and that gave her the answer. The wind was blowing in from behind her. She was downwind, so the gusts were blowing her scent away from the dogs. That would give her time. As long as the direction of the wind didn't change.

Joanna gathered up all her strength and resolve. *Screw it!* If they were going to get her, make them work for it. And maybe, just maybe, if she could stay alive long enough she might find a way out of this mess.

Joanna knew that was wishful thinking, but she still forced herself to concentrate on survival. *Stay alive! Think!* Keep one step ahead of them. Remember, as long as you're alive, there's still a chance. *Stay alive! And think!* Devise a plan to outsmart them and their damn dogs.

Joanna heard the dogs barking in the distance. But they seemed far away and the wind was still swirling.

Make a plan, she told herself again, *and think it through. There's no room for mistakes now.*

First, do I run or hide?

Staying hidden would mean sure death, she quickly decided. It would be easier for the dogs to sniff out a sitting target. And if she remained in one place, she'd probably fall asleep and stay that way. And if the dogs or snakes didn't kill her, the exposure would. No. Better to keep moving and hide at opportune times when the dogs were thrown off her scent.

So run! But in what direction?

She didn't want to run back toward the Bio-Med plant and the dogs. That was the last thing she wanted to do. She had to move eastward, away from the plant. But which way was that?

Joanna rapidly glanced around, looking for something familiar that she might have passed on her way to the ravine. Everything was a blur in the darkness.

Her gaze went to the moon above and the stars around it. She picked out the Big Dipper and Little Dipper. Where was the North Star? Then she saw it shining brightly. It was in the handle of the Little Dipper. Joanna quickly oriented herself. This way north, this way south. This way east and away from Bio-Med and the dogs.

So now I know in what direction to run. But what do I run to? What am I looking for?

Look for hills and ravines and maybe caves to hide in. When daylight came she'd be an easy target to spot on flat terrain. And she'd be easier to track. Not only by the dogs but by the four-wheel-drive vehicles the guards would be sure to have. A cave would be a perfect hiding place, Joanna thought, but then she thought again. Wild animals used caves as their lairs. Not only coyotes, but wildcats, too. Big wildcats. Shit! She'd have to be careful.

The dogs barked again, louder now.

The wind was dying.

Joanna walked quickly away from the ravine, head down, watching for rocks and holes and snakes. The ground was rough and uneven, and with each step Joanna's boot rubbed up against her lacerated leg wound. The Kleenex fell off. Blood started flowing again. And the pain was worse.

Joanna plodded through the thick sand. Intermittently, she glanced up at the North Star and tried to keep her course due east. She seemed to be going uphill, the ground becoming more uneven. Her boot was rubbing hard against her leg wound, taking off scab and skin. Joanna could feel blood dripping down her leg and collecting in her boot. She pushed on, but the pain worsened to the point of being intolerable.

Reluctantly she stopped and sat on a small boulder. She carefully removed her boot and in the moonlight examined the leg wound. It was a jagged laceration at least two inches long with badly abraded edges. Blood was oozing out in a steady stream.

Joanna reached under her oxford cloth shirt and

took off her bra. She wound it around the laceration and then tied it tightly, making sure one of the cups was firmly pressed against the open cut. It's certain to get infected, Joanna thought miserably, wishing she had something to clean it with. Using her last Kleenex, she mopped up the blood from inside her boot and then discarded the tissue. With care, she eased her boot back on.

Joanna trudged through the desert sand, going down a slope then up another. The makeshift bra bandage helped some, but the pain was still bad enough to cause her to limp. She pressed on, wanting to put as much distance as possible between herself and her trackers. And her best chance to do it was now, before daylight came.

For some reason she could suddenly see farther and better. The desert floor was pitted and rocky, resembling the surface of Mars. In the distance were shadows that could be hills. Joanna couldn't be sure.

The makeshift bandage on her leg was slipping down. The top of her boot was again rubbing up against her leg wound. Joanna reached down to adjust the bandage. The bra cup was soaked through with blood.

The wind abruptly picked up and changed direction. It was now blowing into her face. A streak of fear went through Joanna as she realized what was happening. The wind would now carry her scent directly back to the tracking dogs. And they would have the perfect scent to follow. Joanna's blood.

Somewhere behind her, the dogs began to bark loudly and excitedly. They had picked up the trail and were closing in.

41

Jake awoke with a start. Sunlight was streaking through the windshield and directly into his eyes. He quickly blinked away his sleep and checked the dash-board clock. It was 7:20 A.M.

He shook his head to clear the cobwebs, thinking back to the shoot-out in the parking lot. The blond hitter and her accomplice had died at the scene. It had taken the police and the medical examiners over two hours to investigate the shooting incident. Then Jake had to go to police headquarters to complete a stack of paperwork. By the time everything was done, it was almost six o'clock. Jake had decided to return to Joanna's condominium, but never made it. He was driving through Brentwood when a sudden wave of fatigue flooded through his body. The fatigue was so intense he had to pull over to the curb or he would have fallen asleep behind the wheel. He had meant to doze for only a few minutes. Instead he had slept for an hour and a half. Jake turned on the ignition, curs-ing at himself for wasting valuable time.

He drove the final two miles to the condominium complex, thinking how lucky Joanna was that she'd stayed out late. Had she come home at her usual time, she would now be lying in a morgue somewhere, stone cold dead. And the hitter would have gone along her merry way. The goddamn hitter! Too bad she died before telling Jake things he wanted to know. Like why did she bring an accomplice with her? The hitter had always worked solo in the past. And it sure as hell doesn't require two people to kill a defenseless woman. Then there was Brennerman's threat to kill Joanna naturally. How do you put a couple of slugs into somebody and make it look like she died of natural causes? More and more questions, Jake thought miserably. And he didn't have an answer for any of them.

Jake turned into the driveway of the condominium complex. He parked in the visitors area, got out of his car, and stretched his back. The police investigators and medical examiners were gone, as was the yellow crime scene tape. Off to his right Jake saw the dried bloodstain on the pavement where the hitter had bled out. Again he wished she'd lived long enough to talk.

He walked on, glancing over at Joanna's parking space. Jake stopped in his tracks. Her space was still empty. He felt an awful hollowness in the pit of his stomach. Joanna never spent the night in the hospital.

Jake raced for the condominium complex. He jumped over a low hedge and sped by the mailboxes, almost knocking over a man walking his poodle. At the door to Joanna's apartment he rang the doorbell three times and waited. After thirty seconds Jake reached for the key Joanna had given him and turned the lock.

He entered slowly, listening for any sound but hearing nothing. The living room was neat and fresh smelling, the fireplace clean with no ashes or logs. Jake heard a noise and stopped, trying to locate its origin. The noise came again. It was coming from the upstairs neighbor. He moved into the bedroom. The bed was made and hadn't been slept in.

Jake hesitated, wondering if he should call Memorial Hospital. Maybe she had spent the night in her lab, or maybe she was in a car accident. Or maybe she had slept over at a friend's house. Shit! Better call Memorial, he decided.

Jake walked into Joanna's library. The drapes were opened, the computer turned off. He went to her desk and picked up the phone. He saw Joanna's handwriting on a legal pad. She had jotted down Nancy Tanaka's phone number and the directions to the technician's house.

Jake glanced over to Joanna's desk calendar. She was scheduled to meet with Nancy Tanaka at 6:30 last night.

Jake's throat went dry as he quickly put the pieces of the puzzle together. They were planning a break-in at Bio-Med. That had to be it. He hoped against hope that he was wrong or that they hadn't tried it yet. Nervously he fumbled for a cigarette and lit it. Then he dialed Nancy Tanaka's phone number.

An elderly woman answered. She was Nancy Tanaka's mother.

Jake introduced himself and told her he was looking for Dr. Joanna Blalock who was a friend of Nancy's.

"Oh, yes," Mrs. Tanaka said pleasantly. "She was here for a little while yesterday. Such a nice girl."

"Yeah," Jake said impatiently. "Do you know where they're at now?"

"In Nancy's lab at Bio-Med," Mrs. Tanaka told him. "They had to finish an experiment."

"And they haven't returned yet, huh?"

"No, not yet," Mrs. Tanaka replied, her voice now showing concern. "Is—is there something wrong?"

"I don't know," Jake said honestly. "Let me check it out."

"Please call me as soon as you know."

Jake hung up and ran for his car.

42

"I think we're too late, Jake," Farelli said somberly.

Jake nodded slowly, stunned by what he saw inside the Bio-Med compound. A California Highway Patrol car was blocking the entrance to the plant. Just inside the gate was another Highway Patrol car, and on the parking tarmac was a county sheriff's car, a medical examiner's car, and an ambulance with its rear doors opened.

Jake showed his shield to the Highway Patrol officer at the gate and drove through. The second highway patrolman waved him onto the parking lot. Jake took a deep breath, steeling himself against what he was about to face.

He got out of his car and saw Girish Gupta near the rear of the ambulance. The medical examiner was covering a corpse with a sheet.

"Want me to look first?" Farelli asked quietly.

"I can handle it," Jake said, and took another deep breath. He walked over slowly.

Gupta glanced up at the detective. "What a gruesome way to die," he said, shaking his head sadly. "Multiple rattlesnake bites."

Jake saw a black boot sticking out from under the sheet. It was the type Joanna wore. "Wh-who is she?"

Gupta pulled back the sheet. "A technician at Bio-Med."

Jake breathed a deep sigh of relief. He kept his expression neutral, but inside he was still shaking.

"So many bites," Gupta was saying. "I've never

seen or even read about anyone being bitten like this. Have you?''

Jake shrugged absently, his mind only on Joanna. Where was she? Was she still alive? "Was this the only body found?''

"Of course." Gupta stared at him strangely. "Do you expect there to be others?''

"Well, I—um—I," Jake stammered, thinking fast, "I saw all the cop cars and thought there might be multiple victims.''

"No, no. Just one accidental death." Gupta pointed at the corpse's neck and arms. "But look at all those bites. She must have received a huge dose of venom. And that would explain why she died so quickly.''

Jake took out his notepad and checked the time Joanna and Nancy had met the night before: 6:30. "How do you mean, she died so quickly?''

"Most snakebite victims don't die in hours," Gupta explained. "It usually takes days. But perhaps the massive dose of venom hastened the fatal process.''

Jake leaned over and studied the corpse of Nancy Tanaka. There were snake bites all over her upper arms and neck. The puncture marks were obvious despite the redness and swelling around them. "How the hell did she get bitten so many times on the upper arms and neck?''

"Good question," Gupta said, nodding. "Most snake bites are located on the foot or leg. But, as you can see, she was wearing boots.''

"Yeah, I see that," Jake seemed to agree. "But what I'm asking is this: How did those snakes get up to her neck? You don't figure they crawled up there, do you?''

Gupta considered the problem at length. "One possibility is that she tripped and fell getting into her car. Perhaps she landed in a nest of rattlesnakes.''

"Maybe," Jake said, not buying the scenario. He knelt down and examined Nancy's hands and elbows and knees, looking for bruises and abrasions. There weren't any.

"She was working late last night, you see," Gupta went on. "The warmth of her parked car must have attracted all the snakes. She must have tripped and fallen right into them. Perhaps she was stunned by the fall or struck her head."

"If she hit the pavement like that, where are the bruises to show it?"

Gupta gave the corpse a cursory glance. "I suspect I'll see them when she's examined more closely at autopsy."

And I suspect you won't, Jake wanted to say. People don't hit their heads when they trip on flat pavement. They land on their hands and knees. And if she did hit her head, where's the abrasion? Where's the blood? Something was off here.

Jake stepped over to Nancy's car and studied it briefly. Its doors were closed, its exterior covered with fine desert dirt. There was nothing inside. Jake turned away—then suddenly turned back and again studied the dusty exterior of the car. Desert sand was everywhere—on the car, on the pavement around the car, even on the sign that read PARKING LOT. But there was none on Nancy's corpse. He reached down and touched the cool body. "How long has she been dead?"

"Six hours or so," Gupta reported.

Jake checked his watch. "So she died around three a.m.?"

Gupta nodded. "That's correct."

"And who found the body?"

"The guards did when they changed shifts at seven."

Jake's eyes narrowed. Bullshit! Had Nancy Tanaka lain out here all night, her body would be covered with desert sand, like her car and the pavement around it. And the guards didn't find her body until seven? That was bullshit, too. Jake remembered the armed guards at Bio-Med from his earlier visit, and he remembered the dogs they used to patrol the grounds after midnight. Those dogs would have sniffed out the body pronto.

Unless the body wasn't there.

A sudden chill went through Jake as he recalled Lucy Rabb's confession, particularly the part where Eric Brennerman planned to kill Joanna in a natural way. The son of a bitch was using snakes.

Gupta saw the strange expression on Jake's face. "Is everything all right, Lieutenant?"

Jake waved away the question as more pieces fell into place. They killed Nancy Tanaka with rattlesnake bites. They caught her inside the plant and set the snakes loose on her. That must be it. They tied her down and let the snakes bite away. And since she was wearing thick jeans and boots, the snakes went for the exposed parts of her body, like the arms and neck. Then, after she died, they dumped her out on the parking lot to make it look like an accident. That would explain everything—the location of the snake bites, the absence of desert dust on the corpse, the failure of the dogs to find the body. Everything.

But where was Joanna? Jake asked himself again. Was she still alive? Finally he said to Gupta, "I think you've got everything pretty much in hand."

"A straightforward case," Gupta said, covering the corpse. "And a very tragic one."

"Where's Dr. Brennerman?" Jake asked.

"He is inside," Gupta answered. "But I must tell you that he is very shaken by this. Very shaken, indeed."

"I can imagine," Jake said flatly.

"He plans to give all employees the day off," Gupta added. "As a sign of respect for the girl. It's a nice gesture, don't you think?"

"Very nice," Jake agreed, envisioning Brennerman sitting in a gas chamber choking on cyanide.

Jake and Farelli walked away from the corpse and headed for the Bio-Med building. Jake put on dark glasses for protection against the sun's intense glare. The day was clear and bright and hot, the air barely moving.

Farelli pulled at his shirt collar with an index finger.

"It's a good thing they found her body early. In this heat she would have turned ripe real fast."

"Yeah," Jake said absently, still thinking about Joanna.

"You figure the girl really fell into a nest of rattlers?"

"No way!" Jake looked over his shoulder to make sure they were out of earshot. He continued in a low voice. "I think they caught her, tied her up, and let the snakes go at her."

"Shit." Farelli shivered. "How did you come up with that?"

"I'll tell you about it later," Jake said. "Now, we have to be real careful with Brennerman. All we've got on him is Lucy Rabb's confession, and he'll deny every word of it. We've got nothing solid to nail him with."

"And he's guilty as hell," Farelli muttered sourly.

"Tell me about it."

As they approached the steps to the building, Farelli asked, "You think the doc is still alive?"

"I don't know," Jake said hesitantly. "I really don't know."

"Well, the fact that we haven't found her body is a good sign, don't you think?"

"Maybe, maybe not." Jake removed his sunglasses and put them in his coat pocket. "They may have already killed her and are just waiting for the right moment to let the body turn up."

"Yeah," Farelli nodded in agreement. "They couldn't let two accidentally dead bodies show up at the same time. That'd be kind of suspicious."

Jake nodded back. "Brennerman is no dummy. He's not going to make stupid mistakes."

"How do you want to play him?"

"Soft and easy. If we push too hard, he might lawyer up. And that's the last thing we want him to do."

They entered the reception area and went down the corridor leading to the big laboratory. Everything was still and quiet. The only sound came from their footsteps on the tiled floor. Jake noticed that the overhead surveillance camera wasn't moving. He wondered if it was broken or just turned off. They came to the opened door of the main laboratory and walked in.

Eric Brennerman was standing by the giant fish tank. He had a black ribbon tied around the sleeve of his white lab coat.

"Can you believe that shit?" Farelli asked in a very low voice.

"The guy knows how to put on a show," Jake whispered.

"Fucking Hollywood," Farelli grumbled. "We're out in the middle of nowhere and we got fucking Hollywood."

Brennerman turned and waved them over. He had a very solemn look on his face.

"It's so tragic," Brennerman said, shaking his head sadly. "We've lost a wonderful person."

"A terrible way to die," Jake commented.

"The worst," Brennerman agreed. "It's awful. Just awful."

Jake asked, "The snakes are a big problem out here, huh?"

"The desert is full of them," Brennerman answered. "And of course, they're cold-blooded, so at night they look for a warm place to stay. Cars that have been recently parked are perfect for them."

"Have any of your other employees been bitten?"

Brennerman thought for a moment. "I don't think so. But we've had some close calls."

"But no actual bites."

"Not until now," Brennerman said, shaking his head again. "We warn our people about snakes all the time. And we discourage them from coming back at night for that reason. But Nancy would have none of that. If there was work to be done, she did it regardless of the time. She was a wonderful technician."

Yeah, Jake was thinking, *and a nosy one who knew too much. That's why you killed her.*

"A terrible way to die," Brennerman repeated softly. "A terrible accident that should never have happened."

Jake nodded sympathetically. "But you know, there are some unusual things about those bites."

"Oh?" Brennerman's eyes narrowed ever so slightly. "Such as what?"

Jake shrugged indifferently. "I don't know. The medical examiner said something didn't seem right and he'd check it out later at autopsy. Coroners are always looking for little things that other people miss. That's how they make their living."

"And they're very good at it, too," Brennerman said easily. "But our medical examiner is from India, I believe. I'm not sure how much he knows about rattlesnake bites. Probably not a great deal."

"But he knows a lot about snake bites in general," Farelli informed Brennerman. "They got snakes all over the place in India. As a matter of fact, there are more cobra bites there than anywhere else in the world."

Jake smiled inwardly, wondering where Farelli had gotten that information.

"I—ah—I wasn't aware of that," Brennerman mumbled unevenly.

Jake sensed the nervousness in Brennerman's voice. Not a lot, but some. Maybe Brennerman was becoming unnerved enough to start making mistakes. Jake decided to push a little harder. But before he could, Brennerman asked a question.

"Are you here because of Nancy's accidental death?"

"In a way," Jake replied. "Why?"

"I just thought it was a bit out of your territory."

"Well, we came out here for a couple of reasons," Jake said, quickly concocting a story to shake Brennerman up a little more. "We started out this morning to question Nancy Tanaka about the Mirren murder case. Some new developments have turned up. So we phoned her house and her mother told us Nancy was in her lab at Bio-Med. Then we got the call that Nancy was dead and we hustled out here."

Jake looked over to Farelli. "Too bad. Now we'll never get the information we needed from Nancy Tanaka."

Farelli thought for a moment and then said, "Maybe one of the other technicians will know."

"Perhaps I can help," Brennerman offered.

"Maybe you can."

Jake turned to the fish tank and tapped on the glass wall. The salmon ignored him. "It seems that Alex Mirren was conducting experiments on human fetuses."

"What!" Brennerman looked genuinely surprised.

"Yeah," Jake went on. "He was buying fetuses from an abortion clinic on a regular basis and obviously doing something with them out here."

"That's not possible," Brennerman said firmly. "I control everything that goes on at Bio-Med, and I would have known. I can guarantee you that never happened."

"Oh, it happened," Jake assured him. "And we have to find out if it's connected in any way to Mirren's murder."

"Well, if it occurred, I knew absolutely nothing about it."

"But we think Nancy Tanaka did," Jake said. "And she can't tell us about it now, can she?"

"Regrettably, no."

Jake felt like kicking himself. He'd played that card wrong and let Brennerman off the hook too easily. The scientist wasn't showing any signs of nerves. Jake decided to try another tack. "Nancy Tanaka's mother told us something else that's a little strange. She said Joanna Blalock was at their house last night and had come along with Nancy to the Bio-Med lab. Do you know anything about that?"

"I don't think Dr. Blalock could have gotten past the front gate," Brennerman said at once. "We have very tight security here, particularly at night. And, as you no doubt saw, there are no other cars in the parking lot."

Jake scratched his head, feigning puzzlement. "Maybe she snuck in in Nancy's car."

"Again, the guard would—" Brennerman stopped in midsentence, now thinking back. "You know, the guard at the gate reported that he thought he saw two women standing by Nancy's car in the parking lot last night. But when he looked again, he saw only one. He thought his eyes were playing tricks on him. The lighting in the lot isn't very good."

"What time was that?" Jake asked promptly.

"Right after they ar—" Brennerman realized his mistake before he completed his sentence. "I mean, right after *she* arrived. Somewhere around a quarter to nine."

Jake kept his expression even, but he had caught Brennerman's slip of the tongue. So Joanna had been here. But where was she now? And was she still alive? "Can we talk to this guard?"

"Sure," Brennerman said. "He's just outside. I'll call him in."

Farelli waited for Brennerman to walk across the laboratory to a wall phone. Then he moved in close to Jake. "He's going to rehearse that goddamn guard, if he hasn't done it already."

"Let him," Jake whispered back. "The guard can still tell us what we need to know."

"You figure they might have Joanna somewhere in the back of this building?"

"I doubt it. They're not stupid enough to keep a live witness here. Or a dead one, for that matter."

Farelli sighed wearily. "Things don't look so good for the doc."

"I know."

Brennerman hung up the phone and walked back to them. "The guard will be right in. But to be honest, I don't think he can add much to what I've already told you."

"He might remember some details for us," Jake said.

"If that was Joanna Blalock," Brennerman continued, "I hope she didn't wander around the grounds and get herself lost in the desert. It's very, very dangerous out there."

"Maybe she came into the lab with Nancy Tanaka," Jake suggested.

"I'm positive that didn't happen," Brennerman told him. "We looked at the surveillance film first thing this morning. It showed only Nancy Tanaka entering."

"But your surveillance camera is broken," Jake countered.

"The one in the corridor is," Brennerman countered back. "But we have a hidden camera in the reception area as well. That's the surveillance film we looked at."

The guard came through the door and glanced around.

Brennerman waved him over, pleased with the way things were going. The hidden camera had recorded Nancy Tanaka walking into the reception area by herself. It had later recorded Nancy and Joanna Blalock entering, but that segment of the film had been erased and appropriately doctored. There was absolutely no evidence to put Joanna inside the Bio-Med plant. And the detectives had been so useful in helping him place Joanna Blalock somewhere out in the desert. Now nobody would be terribly shocked when they found her body.

"Yes, sir," the guard said, coming to the military position of attention in front of Brennerman.

"The detectives have some questions for you regarding last night."

"Yes, sir," the guard said again, and turned to Jake.

"You remember Nancy Tanaka coming to work last night?" Jake asked.

"Yes, sir."

"Did you wave her through or search her car?"

"I searched it," the guard answered. "I looked in

the front seat and back. The girl was the only one in the car."

"Could somebody have been hiding on the floor in the back?"

The guard hesitated, thinking. "I don't think so. There wasn't much room back there."

"Did you search the trunk?"

"No, sir."

"I see," Jake said, wondering if that was where Jo-anna was hidden. "And then the car went in and over to the parking lot. Right?"

The guard nodded.

"What did you see next?"

"A minute or two later I glanced over at the parked car and thought I saw two women."

"But you couldn't be sure?"

"No, sir. When I looked again, I could see only one." The guard looked over at Brennerman, like someone seeking approval, then continued. "I saw Nancy walk into the building and that's all I saw."

"Could the other woman have run to the side or back of the building?" Jake asked.

"I don't think so. The dogs would have started raising hell."

"I thought the dogs weren't let out until midnight?"

"They aren't," the guard said. "The dogs were in their cages. But if anybody gets too close to the back of the plant, they bark like hell."

"What if somebody wandered out toward the desert?" Jake asked. "Would they get upset over that?"

"Probably not," the guard replied. "And they wouldn't go out after him, either. They're too damned smart to get themselves stuck in the desert somewhere."

"And the dogs were let out at midnight?"

The guard nodded. "Twelve o'clock sharp."

"And they didn't chase after anything, huh?"

"They were calm all night," the guard reported. "There wasn't anything out there."

Jake knew the guard was lying. According to the

medical examiner, Nancy Tanaka died at 3 A.M. and that meant her body would have lain out on the pavement most of the night. The dogs would have sniffed her out in a flash. But they didn't. Because she wasn't on the pavement most of the night. She was inside, where they killed her. "What time were the dogs taken back to their cages?"

"At dawn."

And that's when they dumped Nancy's body in the parking lot, Jake thought. And that's why the corpse wasn't covered with desert sand. It had been on the pavement for only an hour or so.

"Will there be anything else, sir?" the guard asked.

"No. That's fine. Thanks for your time."

Jake watched the guard leave, then turned to Brennerman. "I think we're done out here."

"I'm sorry we couldn't have been more helpful," Brennerman said sincerely. "And I'm really concerned about Joanna, if that was her. The desert around here can be so unforgiving."

Jake and Farelli walked through the laboratory and reception area, then out into bright sunlight. The day was hot now, very hot, with the air not moving at all. Both men started perspiring heavily under their suits. It felt like it was a hundred degrees. They headed for the parking lot.

"What do you think?" Farelli asked.

"They're lying their asses off," Jake said disgustedly. "And we can't prove a damn thing."

Farelli nodded. "We can't even prove the doc was out here."

"Oh, she was out here, all right."

"Not according to the surveillance film."

"Those damn tapes can be altered to show only what they want us to see."

Farelli rubbed his chin. "Maybe we should let the FBI take a look at that film."

Jake shook his head at the idea. "We've got to concentrate on finding Joanna, and those tapes won't help us do that."

"I think she's dead, Jake," Farelli said gloomily. "All we're going to find is a body. You may as well face up to that."

They walked onto the hot pavement of the parking lot. The heat of the asphalt was so strong it penetrated through the soles of their shoes. A highway patrolman was standing guard near Nancy's car. The ambulance had left.

Jake looked into the back seat of Nancy's Honda. It was small and cramped. The guard was right. Nobody could have hidden back there.

Jake went to the rear of the car and tried to open the trunk. It was locked. He turned to the Highway Patrol cop and asked, "Have you got something to open this trunk?"

The cop fetched a crowbar from his car and quickly pried the trunk lid open. A wave of heat came out of the enclosed space. Jake fanned the air with his hand and then leaned into the trunk. It appeared to be empty except for a deflated spare tire and a dirty towel. In the far corner Jake saw a woman's black purse. He reached for it and hurriedly opened it. The purse belonged to Joanna. "She was here," he said softly.

Jake backed away from the car and wiped the sweat from his forehead with an index finger. "She was here," he said again.

"And now they've probably got her body hidden away someplace," Farelli surmised.

Jake nodded sullenly. "They couldn't let her stay alive, not with what she knew."

"Two women murdered by that son of a bitch," Farelli growled. "And he's going to walk."

Jake asked himself, had they used rattlesnakes on Joanna? Probably, he had to admit. That way her death would look accidental and nobody could prove otherwise. There was just no solid evidence to nail the murdering bastards with. All they had was Lucy Rabb's confession, and all that would do was send her to jail for awhile. Yeah, she'd take the fall all right, and Eric Brennerman would walk. And Joanna would still be dead.

In the distance Jake heard the sound of trucks. He turned in the direction of the noise and scanned the flat desert terrain. At first he saw nothing, but then he spotted the desert sand being kicked up by the vehicles. Gradually they came into view. Two four-wheel-drive Jeeps were approaching.

"What the hell is that all about?" Farelli asked.

"I don't know," Jake answered, seeing the Jeeps more clearly. Uniformed guards were driving. Big rottweilers were in the back. The Bio-Med logo was painted on the sides of the vehicles. "I think they were searching for something."

"Yeah," Farelli said. "And from the looks of things, they didn't find it."

"Or maybe they didn't find *her*."

Farelli jerked his head around. "You think she's still out there? Alive?"

"Maybe," Jake said, trying not to get his hopes up. "But if she is, we'd better get to her before they do."

Farelli pointed at the county sheriff's car at the edge of the tarmac. "I'll bet that guy could form a posse real quick."

"I've got a better idea," Jake said, and reached for his cell phone.

43

The small cave Joanna was hiding in was going to be her tomb. She was trapped with no way out and she knew it. She also knew she was dying.

The heat in the cave was almost unbearable, and it was made worse by the fever Joanna had. She was on fire, burning up, her leg infected and worsening by the hour.

With care she peeled back the makeshift bandage on her leg and tried to examine the wound. The light was poor at the back of the cave, so she wriggled her way forward into the sunlight that was streaming in. Joanna waited for her eyes to adjust to the brightness and then inspected the wound. It was red and tender and swollen with yellow pus forming in its center. To make her situation even worse, there were red streaks extending up her thigh. The infection was spreading.

Joanna replaced the bandage and squirmed back to the rear of the cave. It was more of a hollow than a cave, extending back fifteen feet into the side of the hill. There was barely enough space for Joanna to sit up without striking her head. But it had saved her life. Without the cave, they would have caught her and she'd be dead.

The water bottle was empty, its contents long gone. She'd had to decide whether to drink the water or use it to clean her wound or divide it and do both. She ended up drinking the water, but it was only a hundred cc's, little more than a mouthful and not enough to survive. Without more water she'd be dead in a day.

Again she eyed the water bottle, her lips and throat

so dry she could barely swallow. She picked up the plastic bottle and tilted it into her mouth, hoping for a drop or two of water to trickle out. The bottle was stone dry. She tossed it aside.

Joanna thought she heard something outside. A scraping sound not far away. Was it footsteps? Rocks falling? Or maybe some desert creature? Quickly she reached for a pointed stick she'd found outside the cave and waited motionless, her ears pricked. If it was a guard, she was dead. If it was an animal, she might be able to fight it off. She waited inside the suffocating cave. Minutes passed. The sound didn't recur.

Joanna let the stick drop by her side, exhausted by the small amount of exertion. Dehydration was sapping all of her energy, and she knew it would get worse as the day went on. The blazing afternoon sun would raise the temperature another ten or fifteen degrees, and her fever was sure to increase as her infection spread. She would die of dehydration, the same way most people died who were lost in the desert. And eventually the dogs would find her body. Her decaying tissue would give off a powerful scent and attract them. But until then the dogs would continue to run in circles, chasing the trail of Joanna's blood.

She smiled weakly to herself, recalling how she had outwitted the guards and dogs the night before. Somehow in the darkness she had found the cave and lain down to catch her breath. Her head came to rest on a desert plant or bush of some sort. It had a dozen or more stems with fuzzy flowers at their ends. Joanna quickly ripped off a half-dozen stems and went back into the desert to a spot that was at least a hundred yards from the cave. Her wound had stopped bleeding, so she reopened it and soaked each flowered stem with blood. Then she carefully placed the bloodied stems in a circle with a circumference of approximately fifty yards. She hurried back to the cave, just ahead of the barking dogs. For hours the sharp-nosed rottweilers ran around in a giant circle chasing the scent of Joanna's blood. At dawn the barking and yelling had stopped.

But Joanna knew the guards would be back soon with fresh dogs that would again pick up the scent of her blood. And eventually they'd latch on to the smell of her infected wound. It would gradually fill up with pus and necrotic tissue, and that would give off a powerful odor. One way or another, Joanna thought miserably, the wound was going to kill her.

Joanna tried to think of ways to escape, but fever and dehydration had dulled her brain. Her thirst was so intense that all she could think of was water. She'd give anything for a glass of cool water. A picture of a frosted mug of beer flashed into her mind. So cold she could barely drink it. Jake was filling her mug with more beer. "I told you not to try it," he was telling her. "Why the hell didn't you listen to me?"

I should have listened. So stupid to try it. So stupid to fall right into a trap. Next time I'll listen. If there is a next time.

Jake and the frosty mug of beer disappeared from her mind's eye. Her thirst was so bad her tongue was sticking to the roof of her mouth. She tried to swallow but couldn't. Her thoughts went back to Jake, knowing she'd never see him again. Or her sister Kate. Or anyone else. It was over. She would die here.

Don't give up! Don't give up without trying!

Desperately she tried to focus her mind. But she was so tired and lethargic, and her eyelids felt so heavy. Maybe it would help if she slept for a while. Yes, she'd take a nap and get her strength back.

Don't be stupid. If I go to sleep and stay asleep, I'll just become more dehydrated and weaker yet. I won't even be able to move. It's now or never. But how do I escape? The first thing to do is leave the cave and find water. But where? Do I march farther out into the desert, or do I circle back to Bio-Med? Either choice is dangerous. And if I don't find water in the desert, I'm sure to die. The blazing afternoon sun would kill me in a matter of hours. I'd better wait for the cool of the evening. Yes, the evening would be better. If I become disoriented, I'll have the North Star to go by.

Joanna's fever suddenly spiked. She was burning up, on fire again. Perspiration began to pour off her and soak through her clothes. She quickly unbuttoned her shirt and frantically fanned herself with the opened edges. But her temperature kept climbing. She couldn't stand the heat any longer. On her hands and knees she crawled for the mouth of the cave and for the fresh air she hoped was just outside.

Then she heard it. The distinctive *put-put* sound of an approaching helicopter. She froze in place as the noise of the aircraft came nearer and nearer. Now it seemed to be directly overhead.

Slowly Joanna crawled backward to the rear of the cave and waited, hoping the sound of the helicopter would fade away. But it didn't. The noise increased and decreased in a steady fashion. It took Joanna a moment to realize the helicopter was circling over the area where she had planted the bloodied stems. They knew she had to be close by.

Joanna felt ill all over. She was so weak she could barely sit up. She had to lie down. Her eyelids were so heavy she couldn't keep them open. *Oh, God, please help me. Don't let me fall asleep. Don't let me die like this.*

But Joanna's eyelids kept closing. As she drifted off she said the prayer she'd said a thousand times before as a child—

> Now I lay me down to sleep
> I pray the Lord my soul to keep. . . .

44

The Los Angeles County police helicopter circled slowly above the desert, holding at an altitude of a thousand feet. Jake Sinclair carefully scanned the terrain below, searching with high-powered binoculars for any signs of life.

"Nothing," Jake shouted over to the pilot. "I don't see a damn thing."

"Don't just look for a person," the pilot shouted back. "Look for anything that moves."

Jake surveyed the desert again, but all he could see was sand and dunes and small hills. Off to the east he saw a ridge of low-lying mountains that marked the outer perimeter of the Bio-Med property. In front of the ridge was a large boulder with a shadow forming behind it. Everything was still. Even the sagebrush wasn't moving.

"Nothing," Jake reported, "Not a damn thing."

Gradually the helicopter turned to the west and headed into the sun. The ground beneath them was red and gold and orange. The bright colors blurred out all details.

Jake took the binoculars away from his eyes and asked, "Is there any way to narrow down the search area?"

"It might help if you gave me more information on the person we're looking for."

Jake hesitated, not wanting to talk about Joanna or the case they were involved in. For now, the fewer people who knew the better. Jake didn't want word of the Bio-Med mess or of Joanna's disappearance to reach the news media. "She's one of ours," Jake said carefully. "She was investigating a case, and now she's missing. We think she may be out here."

"A she, huh?"

"Yeah."

"Does she know the desert?"

"How do you mean?"

"I mean, does she know how to find water and shelter? Does she know how to protect herself against exposure?"

"No."

"Then we've got trouble."

Jake quickly rethought his answer. "She's not stupid. She knows enough to get the hell out of the sun."

"It's not just the sun," the pilot explained. "It's the high temperature and how you try to combat it. And the same goes for shelter. It's not simply finding shelter, it's finding the right kind of shelter."

"Give me an example," Jake said, totally out of his depth, just as Joanna would be.

"Let's say you go into a cave and it seems cool at first. So now you're out of the sun and you figure you got it made. Right?"

"Right."

"Wrong," the pilot went on. "If there's no crossventilation and if the sun can shine into the mouth of that cave, the temperature will jump up and turn that cave into an oven. Then you'll really start to sweat and get more and more dehydrated. And that's what kills most people out here. Dehydration."

The helicopter turned again onto a northeasterly course. Jake peered through the binoculars and saw hills and small mountains in the distance. "So, sometimes it might be better to stay under the ledge of a cliff rather than go inside a cave?"

"Sometimes," the pilot agreed. "But if the wind starts up, you've got to get the hell inside. It can actually blow you away."

The land below was flat and wide open. Jake saw tire tracks crisscrossing the desert floor. They were

probably made by Jeeps from Bio-Med, Jake thought.
But the vehicles were nowhere to be seen. No Jeeps. No
dogs. No search parties. And that bothered Jake.
Maybe they had already found Joanna's body and left
it out for the elements and desert creatures to work
on for a while. That would make her death seem more
natural, particularly with rattlesnake bites all over her.
Jake shuddered, thinking what Joanna's corpse would
look like.

He focused his binoculars back on the tire tracks,
trying to determine if there was any pattern to them.
In some places they were crisscrossing. In others they
formed half circles where the drivers had made U-
turns. To his left Jake saw a small ridge where the
tire tracks disappeared altogether. Then they started
again, going in a straight line.

"To the north," Jake shouted, pointing below. "Follow the tire tracks to the north."

The pilot guided the helicopter northward, descending to an altitude of five hundred feet.

Jake kept his binoculars fixed on the tire tracks.
They disappeared briefly into a cluster of mounds and
dunes before beginning again, straight ahead, on a
northeasterly course. Then the tracks stopped in the
middle of nowhere.

Jake motioned to the pilot. "I need to get a better
look at the tracks. Can we go down a little lower?"

The helicopter slowly descended to two hundred
feet and hovered over the tire tracks. Now Jake could
see animal tracks as well. He guessed they were made
by the rottweilers. But unlike the tire tracks, the animal trail was circular. The animals had run around in
a giant circle, approximately forty yards across.

"Let's take it down," Jake yelled over. "I want you
to land to the south of those tire tracks."

The helicopter slowly descended and touched down
near a cluster of dunes. Jake waited for the rotors to
come to a stop, then got out and hurried over to the
end of the tire marks. Then he moved ahead slowly,
watching each step until he picked up the animal trail.

"There," Jake said, pointing out the tracks to the pilot. "Those are dog tracks."

"Big dogs," the pilot commented.

"Real big," Jake agreed, again thinking it was probably the rottweilers. He followed the animal tracks as they gently curved around in a giant arc.

"They were circling something," the pilot surmised. "Maybe moving in on their prey."

Jake shook his head. "Attack dogs don't circle their prey. They come right at it."

Jake continued on slowly, following the dog tracks, his eyes glued to the ground. He kicked aside a small rock, then another, but saw nothing. Just ahead he spotted a long stem from a plant lying on the ground. But there were no plants or bushes nearby. As he reached down for it, he saw the bloodstains on the stem and the furry bud attached to it.

Jake walked on, faster, his eyes still riveted to the ground. He came upon another blood-soaked stem, but this one was sticking up in the desert soil. Jake broke into a run, his gaze never leaving the curving trail of animal tracks. Ahead of him was another bloody stem and then another and another.

"She's here!" Jake called out, stopping to catch his breath. "She's here!"

The pilot rushed over. "What have you got?"

"These," Jake said, and showed him the blood-soaked stems. "She planted these stems in a giant circle. The dogs must have spent half the night chasing their own tails. That's how Joanna got away."

The pilot's eyes narrowed. "Got away from what?"

"Some people who want her dead."

The pilot studied the stems briefly. "If that's her blood, she didn't get far."

"I know," Jake said somberly, thinking this much blood didn't come from a scratch. Joanna was bleeding and she was hurt. Her first instinct would have been to find cover, maybe to rest and somehow stop the bleeding. Jake glanced around the desolate area. There was no place to hide except in the low-lying hills to the north. Jake pointed at the foothills. "That's where she'd be."

The pilot rubbed the stubble on his chin. "Those mountains stretch for miles, and they're full of crevices and caves and canyons. If she's in there, she's going to be tough as hell to find."

"We've got to try and we've got to do it quick."

The pilot nodded. "Let's go back and organize a search party."

"We don't have time for that," Jake told him. "I want you to go back and get me a tracking dog. A bloodhound would be best."

The pilot looked at Jake oddly. "He'll just end up running in a circle, following the trail of blood."

"I know a way around that."

"Like how?"

"Like you landing upwind from the animal tracks when you return."

"I still think a search party would do better," the pilot advised.

"Just get the damn dog," Jake said tersely. "And get back as quick as you can."

The pilot reached in his back pocket for a plastic bottle of water and handed it to Jake. "Keep in the shade as much as you can."

Jake turned and headed for the foothills a hundred yards away. The sun was high in the sky and blazing down, the desert floor so hot Jake could feel the heat through the soles of his shoes. Again he thought about Joanna and how badly she must be hurt. All that bleeding had to make her weak. On top of that she was stuck out here where the temperature had to be a hundred and ten. It would take a miracle for her to survive.

Jake hurried on, scanning the ground for more blood, but finding none. Of course not, he thought to himself. She had to stop the bleeding until she got into the hills. That way the dogs would have no scent to follow except for the circle of blood-soaked stems. But was she smart enough to stay alive out here?

Jake came to the base of the foothills and stared up at the rugged terrain. There were no paths or trails, no easy way in.

Jake waited for the noise of the helicopter to fade in the distance. Then he cupped his hands together and yelled out for Joanna again and again at the top of his lungs. But the only reply he heard was the echoes of his own voice.

45

Eric Brennerman was pleased with the way Alex Mirren's office now looked. It was as if Mirren had never been there. His desk was bare and empty, his name no longer on the door. All plaques and pictures had been taken off the wall and packed away. They were to be sent to Mirren's daughter.

Brennerman carefully scanned the office once more, double-checking to make sure nothing of Alex Mirren or his work remained behind. The blackmailing little bastard, Brennerman thought, looking at the large file cabinet and its opened drawers. Every data book, every sheet of paper describing Mirren's experiments had been shredded and incinerated. Everything had been destroyed except for the method that detailed how to produce and extract fetal transforming factor. Brennerman had rewritten the research so it appeared that the work had been done in experimental animals. There was not even a trace of evidence to show that human fetuses had been used.

Brennerman's gaze went to the cardboard carton containing Mirren's framed pictures. The top one showed Mirren receiving the genetics award from Edmond and Lucy Rabb. There would only be Lucy to deal with, he thought, once Joanna Blalock's body was found. And Lucy Rabb would be easy to handle. Oh, she'd bitch and scream when she learned that she would no longer own controlling interest in Bio-Med. But the lawyers would show her the legal documents that allowed the surviving stockholders to buy the shares of any partner who died—at fair market value.

And although Bio-Med was profitable, its annual net income was only two million. Which meant Lucy's shares could be bought for about eight million dollars. The bank would be happy to lend Brennerman eight million, particularly with the Hoddings Family Trust agreeing to co-sign the note.

Lucy would raise hell about the transaction, but there wasn't anything she could do to stop it. The eight million dollars she received—tax-free, since it was part of her husband's estate—would soothe her some. And Brennerman planned on leaving her with a small percentage of ownership in Bio-Med. Say 5 percent or so. That would keep Lucy involved and keep her mouth shut. But for how long would she remain quiet? Brennerman sighed. That was one of Lucy Rabb's problems. She talked too much.

Brennerman reached for the phone and quickly dialed Lucy's number. He needed to meet with her and instruct her on what to say if the press approached her about Joanna Blalock. After all, Lucy owned most of Bio-Med, and Joanna's body would be found near the plant's perimeter.

On the fifth ring, Lucy's answering machine clicked on. Brennerman hung up immediately, cursing under his breath. He had phoned her twice yesterday and left messages, but she hadn't bothered to call back. That too was Lucy. Being coy like some goddamn high school sophomore. She'd wait another day, then call. She didn't want to seem too anxious, although she'd been sleeping with him on a regular basis. She was just being coy, Brennerman thought again. Good. Let her stay that way and play games. Let her keep believing that most men would die to get between her legs and that Brennerman was one of those men. He would string Lucy along until the day some time in the future when she too would die accidentally.

A uniformed guard ran into the office and said breathlessly, "Dr. Brennerman, I think they've found the woman's body."

"What do you mean, *you think*?" Brennerman asked sharply. "Either they have or they haven't."

The guard swallowed, trying to catch his breath. "Well, all hell is breaking loose in the parking lot. A Highway Patrol car and a cop car just pulled in, and an ambulance is coming up to the gate right now."

A bolt of fear ran through Brennerman. "An ambulance?"

"Yes, sir."

Brennerman hurriedly organized his thoughts. An ambulance was for live people. "You mentioned a body. Did you actually see a body?"

"No, sir," the guard replied. "I just guessed it's on the helicopter that's coming in from the desert."

She's got to be alive, Brennerman thought frantically. Somehow she survived in that damn desert. But how? "She's alive," he muttered under his breath.

"How do you figure that?"

"The ambulance, you idiot!"

The guard shook his head, unfazed by the insult. "They had an ambulance with the other dead woman, too. And cop cars and a coroner snooping all around. It all looks the same to me."

Brennerman suddenly brightened. "There's a medical examiner out there?"

"Yeah," the guard said, nodding. "That little foreign guy who speaks funny."

Brennerman smiled. "She's dead."

"Yes, sir," the guard affirmed. "Do you have any special instructions for the men?"

"Tell them to stay at their posts and say nothing."

Brennerman watched the guard leave, then tried Lucy's number again. And again there was no answer.

He didn't leave a message. He adjusted his tie and the black ribbon on his sleeve, then walked out of the office and through the laboratory. Everything was quiet. The workbenches were empty, all machines turned off. It was Friday and Brennerman had given the employees the day off. That would give them a long weekend to calm down and get rid of the jitters. It would also give Brennerman the time and privacy he needed to rethink his gene transfer research.

Brennerman stepped out into the bright sunlight. He quickly surveyed the paved parking lot. It was just as the guard had described. An ambulance with its rear doors opened was waiting. And lined up next to it was a Highway Patrol unit and two unmarked cars. In the distance Brennerman could hear the *put-put* of an approaching helicopter.

Brennerman put a solemn expression on his face and walked over to the medical examiner who was standing between the two unmarked cars. The two men exchanged nods.

"This nightmare never seems to end, does it?" Brennerman asked quietly.

"Heartbreaking," Gupta agreed. "Particularly when it happens to a wonderful person like Joanna Blalock."

The helicopter came into clear view. It drew closer and closer. Then it began circling as it prepared to land.

"Do you think Dr. Blalock suffered a great deal?" Brennerman shouted above the noise of the helicopter.

"From what I've heard, she did," Gupta yelled back. "It's very harsh out there, very harsh indeed."

"Did the animals get to her?"

"I don't think so, fortunately."

The helicopter started a slow descent.

Brennerman glanced around at the onlookers. All eyes were on the aircraft, all expressions somber. He straightened the black ribbon on his sleeve and said, "I suspect you'll find that Dr. Blalock died of natural causes."

Gupta's brow went up abruptly. "Died? She's not dead."

"Sh-she's not?"

"No," Gupta said quickly. "She's dehydrated and injured, but she's very much alive." He looked up at

Brennerman oddly. "Why did you think she was dead?"

Brennerman tried desperately to regain his composure. "Well, when I saw the medical examiner, I thought the worst."

Gupta nodded. "A very logical conclusion. But I'm not here to examine Dr. Blalock. I'm here for some information regarding Nancy Tanaka."

"Oh?" Brennerman watched the descending helicopter. It was still several hundred feet up, but it was kicking up clouds of desert sand. He wondered how badly Joanna was injured. Maybe her head was bashed in. Maybe she couldn't talk.

"You see, I had overlooked something at the scene," Gupta went on. "When I got Nancy's body back to the morgue, I went through her personal effects and I couldn't find her purse or keys. Now, that's strange, isn't it? I mean, we all envisioned her getting to her car late at night just before she was bitten. But there was no purse nor keys near the body. Which made me wonder if she was really trying to get into her car at all. Or was she hit over the head and robbed and then the snakes bit her? There are all sorts of possibilities. So I called Lieutenant Sinclair, who wasn't available. But Sergeant Farelli relayed my concerns and questions to him. I was told that there were some new and important developments, and that I was to report here immediately." Gupta looked puzzled. "I wonder what those developments are."

Brennerman strained to see through the dust-filled air. *Let her be badly hurt and unable to talk*, he prayed. *Or better yet, let her be comatose and dying. Let Mirren's and Bio-Med's secrets die with her.*

The helicopter touched down and the dust gradually settled.

Brennerman saw two figures walking away from the aircraft, but he couldn't make them out. They were like shadows. Then the air cleared.

Joanna Blalock was walking slowly toward the parking lot, leaning heavily on the big detective.

Brennerman turned to run, but there was another detective blocking his way.

"I—I've got to get back to my lab," Brennerman said.

Lou Farelli smiled thinly. He reached for a set of handcuffs and began to slowly twirl them around on his index finger.

Brennerman backed away, frantically thinking of possible escape routes. Abruptly he spun around. But that way out was now blocked. Joanna Blalock was limping toward him, her face filled with rage.

Epilogue

Jake and Joanna were driving south on the San Diego Freeway, heading for Long Beach. They were going to Mandrakis, a Greek restaurant that held fond memories for both of them.

"How long has it been since you've seen Dimitri?" Joanna asked, referring to Dimitri Mandrakis, a retired detective who owned the restaurant.

Jake thought for a moment. "It's been over a year since we've talked."

"Shame on you, Jake," Joanna said. "The guy treats you like a son and you don't even bother to call."

"I know, I know." Jake lit a cigarette with the dashboard lighter and cracked open a window. "It's strange how we tend to forget important things in life. We get busy at work, we get tied up, and we forget. Until it's too late." He puffed on his cigarette thoughtfully. "I wonder why the hell we do that."

"Because most of us arc self-centered, I guess." Joanna shifted around in her seat and carefully uncrossed and recrossed her legs. She winced briefly.

"Is your leg still hurting?" Jake asked.

"Some." Joanna pulled up her skirt and examined the two-inch scar above her knee. It was now a thin red line. "I think the deep tissues haven't healed completely yet."

Jake glanced over. "You can hardly see the scar."

"Plastic surgery can do amazing things," Joanna said, still staring at her knee and thinking for the hundredth time how lucky she'd been that Jake and a bloodhound had tracked her down in the desert. Otherwise she would have died. There was no way she could have lasted another day in that cave without water.

"And that little bit of redness will fade, too, huh?" Jake asked, breaking into her thoughts.

"With time," Joanna told him, and pulled down her skirt. "But I'll tell you something that won't fade with time. If I live to be a thousand, it'll never fade."

"What's that?"

"The memory of the bastard who did this to me," Joanna said. "Every time I look at this scar, I'm going to think of Eric Brennerman."

"Well, think of him being behind bars, because that's where he'll be for the rest of his life."

"He deserves the gas chamber," Joanna growled.

Jake grinned. "Are you turning conservative on me?"

"When it comes to Eric Brennerman, I am." Joanna took a deep breath and let her anger pass. "It's still hard for me to believe that a brilliant physician like Brennerman could murder all those people. Doesn't he have any conscience at all?"

Jake shrugged. "It's easier to do when you have somebody doing the killing for you."

"So it would seem." A picture of the blond hitter came into Joanna's mind. She thought back to the surveillance film that showed the blonde coldly putting a knife into Mervin Tuch's back. "Did you find out anything more about the hitter?"

"According to an informant, she was connected to some tough guys called The Westies." Jake told Joanna about the bar Club West and the New York–based gang that controlled it. "We think the bar was a front for their West Coast operations."

"Did you question them?"

"We couldn't," Jake replied. "They closed up shop and moved back east."

"Just like that."

"It seems their business died out," Jake said dryly.

They left the freeway and entered San Pedro, a small coastal town on the southern edge of Los

Angeles County. It was eight-thirty and a heavy mist was drifting in from the sea. The streets were deserted.

Joanna studied the neighborhood as they drove through. The area was lower class with mini marts, gas stations, and pizza parlors. Most of the stores had graffiti spray-painted on their doors.

They turned onto a narrow street and stopped in front of a small white building with a neon light that spelled *Mandrakis* in fancy script. The *M* was partially burned out.

"Do you think Dimitri will ever fix that sign?" Joanna asked.

"Naw," Jake replied, opening the door. "He thinks it gives the place character."

The crowded restaurant was larger than it looked from the outside. It had thirty small tables around a hardwood dance floor. At the far end was a bandstand. Musicians sat on the edge of the stage smoking cigarettes. The air was filled with exotic, spicy aromas.

A large, heavyset man with a protuberant abdomen and gray-black hair rushed over to greet them. He grabbed Jake in a bear hug, almost lifting him off the floor. "Where the hell have you been?"

"Busy," Jake said, gently pushing himself away.

"Too busy for an old friend, huh?" Dimitri Mandrakis shook his head in feigned disgust, then turned to Joanna. He bowed gracefully and kissed the back of her hand. "You are so young and beautiful. Why do you put up with this lout?"

"Because he's a hunk." Joanna grinned.

Dimitri looked into Joanna's eyes and smiled at her. "If I was twenty years younger, I'd sweep you off your feet."

"If you were twenty years younger, I'd let you."

"Ho! Ho! Ho!" Dimitri chuckled loudly. "I can see we're going to have a fine time tonight."

"If we ever sit down," Jake complained.

Dimitri snapped his fingers at a waiter across the room and yelled out commands in Greek, then led the way to a ringside table. A waiter hurried over uncorking a bottle of retsina, followed by another carrying a stack of white plates.

"Giassou," Dimitri said, raising his glass and toasting his guests. Then he leaned across to Jake. "I hear you worked the Bio-Med murder case."

"What else did you hear?" Jake asked.

"That they're going to let the grieving widow plead herself down to murder two."

Jake nodded, grumbling to himself. "She has five people whacked and she'll end up doing fifteen years. Maybe."

Dimitri's brow went up. "Why maybe?"

"Because Lucy Rabb is going to hire the same lawyers that got O. J. Simpson off."

"Shit," Dimitri grumbled softly. "They'll probably try to convince a jury that she was an unwilling coconspirator."

"You got it."

Dimitri lit a cigarette and inhaled deeply, thinking aloud. "All this happened because an old man saw himself getting older and wanted to feel young again. He wanted somebody to make the years disappear."

Joanna squinted an eye. "I'm not sure I follow you."

"Old men like Edmund Radd marry young women because they believe it will make them feel young again. Of course, it never works out like that. As time passes, they begin to rub on each other's nerves in a dozen different ways. She wants to stay up all night and party; he wants to sit in a comfortable chair at home and watch television. She wants to jump in the sack three times a day; he figures once a week is just about right. She demands more and more; he can deliver less and less. So eventually, the young girl ends up making the old man feel older and older and older."

"Sad," Joanna said.

"And deadly, too," Jake added. "An old man's money and a young woman's greed always spells trouble. In this case it caused five people to get whacked."

"Money and sex will do it every time." Dimitri refilled their wineglasses and turned to Jake. "Now tell me about the shootout in the parking lot. How did you know the hitter was going to be there?"

"I didn't," Jake admitted. "Joanna was late getting home from the hospital, and I was waiting for her in my car outside her condominium. If she had arrived home at her usual time, the hitters would have gotten to her."

Dimitri glanced over at Joanna. "Lucky girl."

"Very lucky girl," Joanna agreed.

Dimitri looked back at Jake. "Did they come at you straight on?"

"The goon accomplice did," Jake told him. "The blond hitter and I played cat and mouse for a while."

"I read where the goon's name was Santino. Right?"

Jake nodded. "He was a midlevel hood with a sheet a mile long."

"Was he from Las Vegas?"

"He used to be." Jake's eyes narrowed. "How did you know that?"

"I worked in Vegas when I first started on the job forty years ago," Dimitri explained. "I knew a hood named Scottie Santino who's now dead."

"Probably our guy's father," Jake said. "Was the old man a hitter, too?"

"Yeah. His specialty was making people disappear in the desert," Dimitri went on. "He'd put the victim in a grave and cover him with cement, then add sand back on top. Nice, huh?"

"I think the son followed in the father's footsteps," Jake said. "Here in Los Angeles, Scottie Santino ran a cement company."

Joanna shuddered as she realized what the hitters had in store for her. She was to be killed and then spend eternity encased in cement.

"You're a very lucky girl," Dimitri said again.

The door to the restaurant opened and a group of Greek sailors entered. They shouted greetings to the waiters and to some of the patrons. More tables were squeezed in to accommodate the new arrivals.

"Oh, yes," Dmitri said happily, pushing back his chair. "Some boys from the old country. I must welcome them."

Joanna watched Dimitri Mandrakis limp away, favoring the hip that had been torn apart by a thug's bullet. She thought how sad it must be when someone is forced to retire from a job they do so well and love so much. She moved closer to Jake. "Dimitri really misses being a detective. He misses it so badly."

"I know."

"That's why he's always so happy to see you," Joanna said softly. "You make him feel like he's back with the force again."

"I should come in more often," Jake said, nodding.

"Like once a month?"

"Like once a month."

"I've got your word on that, huh?"

"Sure do," Jake said. "But I'll need a promise from you in return."

"What?"

"That you won't try anything stupid again and get yourself killed."

Joanna smiled widely. "You got it."

Jake smiled back. "Do you know how the Greeks seal a promise?"

"How?"

Jake picked up a plate and threw it out onto the dance floor. It hit with a loud crack and broke into a hundred pieces.

The air was suddenly charged with electricity. The musicians started to play as the Greek sailors hurried onto the dance floor and formed a long line, their arms around each other's shoulders. Slowly, every so slowly, the beat picked up, becoming louder and louder. The sailors danced the dance of the Greeks, their feet flying and barely touching the floor. Someone yelled out *"Hoopa!"* and more plates flew through the air and shattered against the bandstand.

Joanna nestled her head against Jake's chest. "Damn, it's good to be alive."

"Tell me about it," Jake said, reaching for another plate.

Author's Note

The gene transfer therapy described in this novel is very real. Genes hooked onto viral vectors have been successfully administered to patients with a number of different disorders. Most notably, French researchers have used gene therapy to treat infants born with a life-threatening immune disorder. The immune defect in these babies was the same one that afflicted the well publicized "boy in the bubble." By contrast, the French infants treated with genes are alive and well and now have intact immune systems.

Gene transfer (the insertion of new, normal genes into a patient) offers real hope and even the promise of a cure for a long list of inherited diseases. These include disorders such as muscular dystrophy, cystic fibrosis, sickle cell anemia, and hemophilia, just to name a few. Other forms of gene therapy show equal promise. For example, manipulation of genes that control cell growth may well play an important role in the treatment of certain types of cancer. Even more fascinating, our ability to convert stem cells into heart and brain and nerve cells raises the distinct possibility that diseases of the heart, brain, and spinal cord will someday be treated with gene transfer and manipulation.

Because of the incredible potential of gene therapy, scientists are racing ahead, isolating genes and determining their functions so they can be used to treat diseases previously thought to be untreatable or incurable. Unfortunately, in some instances researchers have rushed ahead too fast and conducted risky experiments in human subjects with tragic outcomes. In one incident, an eighteen-year-old patient died after receiving gene therapy for liver disease at the University of Pennsylvania Institute of Gene Therapy. After his death, the FDA investigators determined that the institute had violated regulations in its conduct of the research and shut down the program. The FDA has also clamped down on several Boston gene therapy researchers. It now seems clear that these were not isolated incidences and that controversial experiments in gene therapy have taken place elsewhere as well.

The situation is so serious that the FDA has asked Congress to legislate new regulations and penalties for those involved in improper and risky gene research. These include a $250,000 fine for researchers conducting risky experiments and a $1,000,000 fine for the institutes where the research was performed. Rules will also be put in place to insure tighter monitoring and stricter regulation for all gene research in humans.

Only time will tell whether these rules and regulations and penalties will be strong enough to minimize the risks that are certain to be associated with gene therapy.

—Leonard Goldberg, M.D.

Karen Crandell hurried down the deserted corridor, her stomach growling loudly to remind her that she had skipped both lunch and dinner. She took the elevator to the main floor of the hospital and strode across the lobby, which was empty except for a young Hispanic couple on a couch near the information booth.

Karen went into a small cafeteria that was kept open for the staff on night call. She picked up a Diet Coke and a tuna sandwich, then returned across the lobby and down a wide corridor. With her back, she pushed through a set of double doors and entered a glass-enclosed bridge that connected the main floor of Memorial with the second floor of the Neuropsychiatric Institute.

At the far end of the bridge an armed guard jumped up from his chair and watched her approach. It took a moment before he recognized her and waved.

"Hi, Doc," the guard said cordially. "Late night, huh?"

"Aren't they all?" Karen asked, giving him a half smile.

"Don't forget, we lock these doors at midnight."

Karen nodded as she went by him, remembering a time when the doors were left open twenty-four hours a day. But that ended three years ago when a nurse was beaten and raped late at night by an assailant who had gained access to the institute through the glass-enclosed bridge. Now the only way into the institute after midnight was through the front entrance, where two guards were permanently stationed. Despite these precautions, a break-in had occurred last year. A nurse's purse and a long list of valuables belonging to patients had been stolen. The campus police never solved the crime, but went out of their way to tell everyone that it had to be an inside job. As if that would give the personnel some comfort.

She rode the elevator to the tenth floor where the Brain Research Institute was located. Stepping out of the elevator car, she heard loud conversation and laughter coming from the far end of the well-lighted corridor. For a moment she was uneasy, wondering if she had forgotten some departmental function. No, that wouldn't be it, she thought. Not this late at night, not at 9:48 P.M. Then she remembered that her colleagues met on Wednesday night to discuss their ongoing research projects. But they never included her. Never.

For the hundredth time she wondered why her colleagues had never really accepted her as part of the group. Part of the reason was gender related. But the main reason was her independence. From the beginning she demanded and got her own laboratory, and insisted on doing her own research projects. She would collaborate with the others, but only as their equal. And she refused to become involved in experiments that she knew were dead ends. This infuriated her superiors, who expected the junior faculty to work under them. Gradually she found herself alone and isolated in the institute, her research work separate from the others'. At times her colleagues barely acknowledged her existence. But that was okay. Her research was now going well and the best was yet to come. *Screw them,* she thought bitterly. *They can do their work and I'll do mine.*

Karen entered her small, darkened laboratory and decided not to turn on the lights. Her technician was gone but had left everything shipshape. The workbenches were clean and clear except for some neatly arranged racks of test tubes. Two small centrifuges were open and airing out.

A dim light shone through the glass door of an incubator in the far corner, casting eerie shadows on the wall.

Karen went into a crowded adjoining office and slumped down wearily into a swivel chair. She turned on a desk lamp, then opened her can of soda and sipped it. Reaching across her desk, she switched on a machine that resembled a television set. Its front was virtually all screen, with the control buttons and dials on the side. Karen pushed a button and the screen lit up instantly. The image looked like falling snowflakes. Then the sound came on loudly. It was all static. She carefully adjusted the dials, but the snowflakes stayed on the screen and the static only got louder.

Karen leaned back, discouraged by what she saw. Her latest research project was a big bust. Unlike the Streptokinase study, nothing was working here. Nothing. All that time and energy wasted, she thought miserably.

Karen's stomach began to growl. She glanced over at the unappetizing sandwich on her desk and tried to ignore her hunger pangs. But her stomach growled again, so she reached for the sandwich and slowly unwrapped it. She took a small bite and immediately put the sandwich down. The tuna was cold and tasteless. She decided to pick up fast food on the way home.

From across the office Karen heard a strange sound. The machine that resembled a television set was no longer emitting garbled static. Now it sounded like the roar of the ocean. And the picture had changed, too. There was still a snowflake pattern on the screen, but between the white dots Karen thought she saw figures.

She hurriedly pushed her swivel chair over to the machine and carefully adjusted the controls. A red light blinked. Karen pushed a button, and the light turned green. Abruptly the image sharpened, now clearer and more discernible. It was people! Karen thought excitedly.

She stared at the machine, not believing her eyes. It couldn't be this good. It just couldn't. She turned the sound up louder and now she could hear the words. The crowd was yelling "Hooray!" over and over again.

Oh, Lord! Was this really happening? Karen could only hope that it wasn't her imagination playing tricks on her.

Karen's jaw dropped as she suddenly realized what she was looking at. The people. The dress. The event.

"My God!" she blurted out. "I've done it."

Karen didn't see the intruder standing behind her in the shadows, watching her and the picture on the screen. Nor did she hear the swoosh of the blunt weapon that crushed her skull in. Karen slid down in the swivel chair, her bloodied head coming to rest on a chair arm.

The intruder fumbled with switches and knobs on the machine until he found the one that turned it off. He quickly extinguished the small lamp on the desk and then, using a pocket flashlight, began searching the drawers. There was nothing in them except for pens and stationery and other office supplies. He saw a handheld dictating machine atop the desk and took it. Next he went to the file cabinet in the corner, but its drawers were locked. He cursed under his breath and went back to the desk to look for keys. From down the hall he heard loud conversation, and it seemed to be coming closer and closer. The intruder crouched down in the darkness and waited. The sound of the conversation drew even closer, then became stationary. An elevator door opened and closed. The sounds disappeared.

The intruder searched the desk drawers for a key to the file cabinet, but couldn't find it. Then, using a nail file, he tried to pick the lock but was unsuccessful. Again he heard the sound of conversation in the corridor.

The intruder quickly reached down and reset the woman's wristwatch before smashing it with his weapon. As he leaned over to lift up the woman, he saw a word processor on a small table against the wall. He smiled and walked over to it. There was one more thing he wanted to do before he threw Karen Crandell to her death.

Her name was Elizabeth Ryan. She was twenty-eight years old with soft features, pale blue eyes, and perfectly contoured lips. Her hair had been shaved off, her skull surgically opened. She had died in the operating room the day before.

Dr. Dan Rubin, a neurosurgery intern, looked down at the corpse and remembered the first time he had seen her. She was so elegant and charming, with no outward signs of the brain tumor that would soon kill her. He studied her marble white skin, now cold as ice, and thought again how tragic it was when young people died. It seemed so damned unfair. But then, life wasn't fair. Never was, never would be. He had learned that the hard way.

Dan glanced around the brightly lighted autopsy room with its white tile walls and eight stainless steel tables lined up in rows of twos. He couldn't understand why anyone would choose to become a pathologist and be constantly surrounded by death and decay. His gaze went to the corpses on the tables and to the pathologists dissecting them. The work appeared so tedious and dull to Dan. It was the exact opposite of the excitement and drama seen daily in the operating room. And that's where Dan wanted to be now. The only reason he was here for the autopsy was a hard and fast rule lain down by Dr. Christopher Moran, the chief of neurosurgery at Memorial. Whenever one of Moran's patients died, a member of his surgical team had to be present at the autopsy to answer any questions and, most important, to learn the cause of death and report it immediately to Moran.

Dan looked at the wall clock. It was 10 A.M. If the autopsy moved along quickly, he might have time to scrub up for the rhizotomy that Dr. Moran was scheduled to do at noon.

Dan turned as a woman wearing a green scrub suit approached. She was young and petite, with long auburn hair, green eyes, and a flawless complexion except for scattered freckles across her nose and cheeks. Dan cleared his throat. "Are you Dr. Blalock?"

"No," Lori McKay said, smiling up at him. "I'm Dr. McKay, an associate of Dr. Blalock's."

"I'm Dan Rubin," he said, now realizing how foolish his question was. Joanna Blalock was director of forensic pathology at Memorial. She wouldn't be a twenty-something-year-old with freckles.

Lori glanced at the name tag pinned to Dan's scrub suit. "You're the surgery intern, huh?"

"Right," Dan answered, wondering what position this woman held in the department. Probably a postdoctoral fellow. She was too young to be on the staff. "Have you been working down here long?"

Lori's eyes narrowed. She hated it when people judged her

by her youthful appearance. "I'm an assistant professor; I've been on the faculty for four years. Is that long enough?"

"I guess so," Dan said, ignoring the sharpness in her voice.

"Well, now that we have that out of the way, let's look at your patient."

Lori slipped on a pair of latex gloves, carefully wiggling her fingers in. In her peripheral vision she continued to study the surgery intern. He was older than most of the house staff—at least in his mid-thirties—and handsome with a square jaw and wavy brown hair. And no wedding band on his ring finger. She brought her gaze back to the corpse, now examining the surgical window in the skull and the glistening brain beneath it. "As I understand it, she died just as the surgery was beginning."

Dan nodded. "We were mapping the brain to determine how much tissue around the tumor could be safely resected. We had just put in the final metallic slips."

Lori had seen the mapping procedure done on several occasions while she was in medical school. She shivered, thinking about how it was performed. With the patient awake and under local anesthesia, an electrical stimulator was applied to various areas adjacent to the tumor in order to determine what those particular parts of the brain did. Lori recalled a patient with a temporal lobe tumor who was reciting the names of his children. When an area near the superior aspect of the temporal lobe was stimulated, his speech became garbled and he could no longer remember names. This indicated that that particular area was important to speech and memory, and thus could not be surgically removed. The procedure had seemed so barbaric to Lori back then, but it was the only way to accurately construct a map that set the boundaries on what could and could not be resected. The procedure was considered safe with no real dangers. But like everything else in medicine, Lori thought, there were no guarantees.

"And she suddenly convulsed." Dan broke into her thoughts. "For no reason."

"Oh, there was a reason," Lori countered.

"I meant we weren't stimulating the brain when things went wrong," Dan corrected himself.

"Uh-huh," Lori said.

"Look," Dan said, a slight edge to his voice, "this was not really a surgical death."

"Any death that occurs in the OR is a surgical death," Lori shot back.

"You're not going to find a surgical cause to explain all this," Dan insisted.

"You never know, do you?" Lori asked mischievously.

Dan glanced up at the wall clock again. He tapped his foot on the floor impatiently, hating to waste time. Where the hell was Dr. Blalock? "Why are they insisting that a forensic pathologist do this case?"

"Because the patient's father and uncle are big-time lawyers and they don't think Elizabeth Ryan should have died on the table."

"Shit," Dan hissed under his breath, disliking lawyers in general and malpractice lawyers in particular. He considered them vultures. "There was no malpractice here."

"Nobody said there was."

But they'll look for it, Dan was thinking, and in the process try to crucify a wonderful surgeon. He looked up at the clock once more. "How long will this autopsy take?"

"Don't be in a rush," Lori advised, sensing his impatience. "Autopsies can teach you a lot."

"I know," Dan said, not meaning it. "It's just that I want to scrub up for a rhizotomy with Dr. Moran at noon."

"I don't think you'll make it."

Lori began circling the corpse, starting at the head and examining its exterior. There was nothing remarkable except for the window in the skull exposing glistening brain that was studded with silver clips. Lori moved down the abdomen and pubis, looking for abnormal features but finding none. She stopped at Elizabeth Ryan's legs and paid particular attention to the musculature of the thighs and calves. "Was she a runner?"

Dan shrugged. "I don't know. Why?"

"Because her legs are more muscular than her arms."

Dan glanced over at the corpse's legs and shrugged again. The muscles in her legs didn't have a damn thing to do with her dying.

The double doors leading into the autopsy room swung open and a strikingly attractive woman entered. She had soft, patrician features and sandy blond hair that was pulled back and held in place by a simple barrette.

Joanna Blalock waved to Lori, then turned to the intern. "You must be Dr. Rubin."

Dan snapped to attention, his shoulders back. "Yes, ma'am."

"Thank you for joining us," Joanna said, reaching for a pair of latex gloves. She glanced over at the X rays mounted on a nearby view box, then down at the corpse of Elizabeth Ryan. "Please give us a brief summary of the case, Dr. Rubin."

Dan cleared his throat audibly. "She was a twenty-eight-year-old woman who presented with severe, generalized headaches. She was seen by Dr. Karen Crandell and discovered to have a brain tumor. She was subsequently referred to Dr. Moran and at operation was found to have a highly malignant glioma. While we were mapping the brain, the patient suddenly convulsed. The bottom dropped out of her vital signs and we couldn't get her back."

"Was she seen by other consultants in the OR?"

"Two," Dan replied. "The cardiologist said the cause for her shock was non-cardiac. Then she was seen by Dr. Karen Crandell, who thought the patient had some type of encephalopathy."

Joanna nodded, returning her attention to the corpse. "I assume those metallic clips represent the resectable borders of the tumor."

"Correct," Dan answered.

Joanna began to slowly walk around the corpse, carefully examining its external features. The girl had been beautiful, Joanna thought, with a slender waist, flat abdomen, and lean, muscular legs. The calf muscles were particularly pronounced. Quickly Joanna went to the girl's feet and saw the calluses and bunions she expected to find. "Was she a professional dancer?"

"What?" Dan asked, caught off guard. "I don't know."

Joanna frowned. "Knowing a patient's occupation can sometimes be very helpful in making a diagnosis."

"Right." Dan nodded. He thought it was irrelevant, but wanted to stay on Joanna's good side. "Can I ask why you conclude that she was a dancer? Those muscles in her legs could be from any kind of exercise."

"True," Joanna said, "but you can see that her calf muscles are disproportionately large. That's because ballet dancers spend a lot of time on their tiptoes, which exercises the gastrocnemius muscle primarily, and this causes the calf to enlarge. And because of the special shoes they wear, they also have thick calluses under the first metatarsal heads and prominent bunions—just as this corpse has."

Lori groaned to herself. She had seen all the clues Joanna had, but hadn't been able to put them together. A ballerina, damn it, of all things. She reached for the patient's hospital chart and opened it to the front page. She quickly scanned Elizabeth Ryan's personal information, then nodded to Joanna. "Her profession is ballet dancer."

Dan stared at Joanna suspiciously, wondering if the forensic pathologist had prior knowledge of Elizabeth Ryan. Maybe she had watched her dance or had seen a picture of her somewhere.

Lori saw the look of disbelief on the intern's face. "I think we have a nonbeliever here, Joanna."

Joanna smiled at Dan. "You think I might have known about the patient before I started my examination?"

"I didn't say that," Dan said defensively.

"But you thought about it," Joanna said, her eyes now on the intern's muscular forearm.

Dan gestured with his hands, palms out. "I guess so."

"Well, let's see if we can convince you that we are for real down here," Joanna said, again studying the intern's forearm, then his face and brow. "May I tell you a few things about yourself, Dr. Rubin?"

Dan shrugged. "Of course."

"You joined the Marines when you were in college. Initially you were an enlisted man, but you were out of place and this may have caused you to be involved in a good number of fights. Eventually you saw the light and became an officer. I think you were in the Marines for at least eight years before you decided to return to college and apply for medical school."

Dan stared at Joanna, stunned by the accuracy of her information. She had summed up his entire adult life in one paragraph. "How do you know that?"

"Observation," Joanna said simply. "I knew you had been a Marine because of the faded tattoo on your forearm,

which reads *Semper fi*. That, of course, is the motto of the
Marines. In all likelihood you enlisted, because tattoos are
usually seen on enlisted men, not officers. You're reason-
ably bright and well spoken, and you wouldn't have ac-
quired those traits in the Marines. So it's safe to assume
you joined the Marines out of college."

"How can you be so sure I didn't join after college?"
Dan asked.

"Because with a college degree you would have gone
into the service as an officer," Joanna replied. "The scars
about your eyebrows tell us about the fights you've had,
and these probably occurred while you were an enlisted
man. I suspect your background was different from the
other enlisted men and this caused some of the fights."

"Jesus," Dan hissed softly, his eyes fixed on Joanna.
"How do you know I became an officer?"

"You have the bearings of an officer—your posture, your
presence, your speech. And again, your intelligence." Joanna pointed to the faded tattoo on Rubin's forearm. "I
would guess you attempted to have your tattoo removed
by laser after you returned to college, maybe when you
received the notice that you had been accepted to medical school."

"And what told you I had been in the Marines for at
least eight years?"

"Your age," Joanna said. "You're at least eight years
older than your fellow interns. So we need something to
fill that eight-year gap. It had to be your service in the
Marines."

"And you won most of your fights," Lori chimed in.

"How can you be so sure of that?" Dan asked.

"Because your nose is not bent and there's no evidence
of split lips," Lori explained. "Those are the signs of a man
who wins more than he loses."

Dan's eyes darted back and forth between the two
women. Nobody in the world knew that much about him.
Nobody. "I feel like running for my life."

"You'll have to forgive us, Dr. Rubin," Joanna said, smiling at the intern's amazement. "But I'm glad I took you
through this little exercise. You have to learn how to observe carefully and pay particular attention to anything

that's unusual. Every time you examine a patient, remember the ballerina's legs and the tattoo on your arm. Remember to observe. It'll make you a better surgeon."

"I'll keep that in mind," Dan said sincerely.

Joanna turned back to the corpse just as the doors to the autopsy room swung open.

"Dr. Blalock," a young secretary said breathlessly, "Dr. Murdock just called and wants you to come over to the Brain Research Institute stat. He said it was urgent."

"Did he say why?"

"No, ma'am."

Joanna turned to Lori and Dan, thinking about her tight schedule for most of the day. "We'll have to postpone this autopsy until four P.M. Is that convenient for you, Dr. Rubin?"

"No problem," Dan said, delighted he would now be able to scrub in on the rhizotomy.

Joanna stripped off her gloves and walked quickly toward the door, the secretary a step behind her. "Did Dr. Murdock give any clue why he needed me so urgently?"

"No, ma'am. But I think I know." The secretary stopped and stared at Joanna. "Didn't you hear what happened at the BRI this morning?"

"No," Joanna said impatiently. "What?"

"Dr. Karen Crandell committed suicide."